ANOTHER VIEW
THE END OF SUMMER

Also by Rosamunde Pilcher and available from Coronet:

The Shell Seekers
September
The Blue Bedroom
Flowers in the Rain
Wild Mountain Thyme
Sleeping Tiger
The Day of the Storm
The Empty House
The Rosamunde Pilcher Collection Volume I
The Rosamunde Pilcher Collection Volume II

About the author

Rosamunde Pilcher was encouraged to write from an early age and had her first story published in *Woman and Home* at the age of eighteen. During the Second World War, she worked first in the Foreign Office, and then in the Women's Royal Naval Service, serving in Portsmouth and Trincomalee, Ceylon, with the East India fleet. After the war she married and moved to Scotland. She and her husband live near Dundee. They have four children and eight grandchildren. Throughout this time Rosamunde Pilcher has been writing continuously, for magazines as well as thirteen novels.

Her two bestselling novels, *The Shell Seekers* and *September,* captured the world's imagination and became the best-loved novels of the decade. Her short story collections, *The Blue Bedroom* and *Flowers in the Rain,* have also been wonderfully popular.

Another View
The End of Summer

Rosamunde Pilcher

CORONET BOOKS
Hodder & Stoughton

First published as two separate volumes:

Anothet View © 1968 by Rosamunde Pilcher
First published in Great Britain in 1990
by Hodder & Stoughton
A division of Hodder Headline

The End of Summer Copyright © 1971 by Rosamunde Pilcher
First published in Great Britain in 1990
by Hodder & Stoughton
A division of Hodder Headline
A Coronet Paperback

This paperback omnibus edition, 2000

ISBN 0 340 79422 4

Printed and bound in Great Britain by
Clays Ltd, St Ives plc

Hodder & Stoughton
A division of Hodder Headline
338 Euston Road
London NW1 3BHA

ANOTHER VIEW

1

In Paris, in February, the sun was shining. At Le Bourget Airport, it gleamed coldly from an ice blue sky, and this was reflected, with much dazzle, from the runways, still wet after a night's rain. From inside, the day looked inviting, and they had been tempted out on to the terrace, only to discover that the bright sun held no real warmth and the gay breeze that blew the wind socks out at right angles had an edge to it like a knife. Defeated, they withdrew to the restaurant to wait for Emma's flight to be called, and sat now, at a small table, drinking black coffee and smoking Christopher's Gauloises cigarettes.

Unselfconscious, absorbed in each other, they nevertheless attracted a certain amount of attention. This was inevitable, for they made an arresting pair. Emma was tall and very dark. Her hair, worn back off her forehead and held in place by a tortoiseshell band, fell in a straight black tassel to below her shoulder-blades. Her face was not beautiful – it was too clearly boned and strongly built for beauty, with a straight nose, and a square and determined chin. But these features were redeemed and given much charm by large and unexpectedly grey-blue eyes, and a wide mouth, which, although it was quite capable of drooping disconsolately if she did not get her own way, could grin, from ear to ear, like a boy's, when she was happy. She was happy now. She wore, on this cold bright day, a bitter green trouser suit and a white polo-necked sweater that made her face look very brown, but her sophisticated appearance was off-set by the mass of luggage with which she was surrounded, and which appeared, to the casual passer-by, to have been salvaged from some disastrous act of God.

It was, in fact, the accumulation of six years of living abroad, but no one was to know this. Three suitcases, at enormous expense, had already been checked in. But there was still a canvas grip, a Prisunic paper carrier sprouting long French loaves, a basket bulging with books and records, a raincoat, a pair of ski-boots and an enormous straw hat.

Christopher surveyed it all, speculating, in a detached and unbothered fashion, as to how it was all going to be conveyed into the aeroplane.

"You could wear the hat and the ski-boots and the raincoat. That would make three less things to carry."

"I've already got a pair of shoes on, and the hat would blow off. And the raincoat's disgusting. I look like a displaced person in it. I can't think why I bothered to bring it at all."

"I'll tell you why. Because it will be raining in London."

"It may not be."

"It always is." He lit another Gauloise from the stub of the first. "Another good reason for staying in Paris with me."

"We've had this out a hundred times. And I'm going back to England."

He grinned without rancour. He had been teasing her. When he smiled, his yellow-flecked eyes slanted upwards at the corners, and this, combined with his lanky, idle body, gave him a curiously feline appearance. His clothes were colourful, casual, faintly Bohemian. Narrow cord trousers, battered chukka boots, a blue cotton shirt worn over a yellow sweater, and a suède jacket, very old and shiny about the elbows and the collar. He looked French, but in fact he was as English as Emma and even related to her in a tenuous way, for, years ago, when Emma was six and Christopher ten, her father, Ben Litton, had married Hester Ferris, Christopher's mother. The arrangement had lasted, with only the smallest degree of success, for eighteen months, before it finally fell apart, and now Emma remembered it as the only time in her life when she had ever known anything vaguely approaching an ordinary family life.

It was Hester who had insisted on buying the cottage at Porthkerris. Ben had owned a studio there for a number of years, since long before the war, but its conveniences were non-existent, and after one look at the squalor in which she was expected to live Hester went straight out and acquired two fisherman's cottages, which she proceeded, with taste and charm, to convert. Ben was disinterested in any such activity, so it became very much Hester's house, and it was she who insisted on a kitchen that would work, and a boiler that would heat water, and a big fireplace blazing with driftwood, a heart to their home, a focal point around which the children could gather.

Her intentions were splendid, her methods of carrying them out not so successful. She tried to make allowances for Ben. She had married a genius, and she knew his reputation and she was prepared to turn a blind eye to his love affairs, his disreputable companions and his attitude towards money. But in the end, as so often happens in quite ordinary marriages, she was defeated by the small things. By meals, forgotten and uneaten. By trivial bills left unpaid for months. By the fact that Ben preferred to drink in the local pub, rather than in a civilised fashion, at home, with her. She was defeated by his refusal to have a telephone, to own a car; by the stream of apparent derelicts whom he invited to sleep on her sofa; and finally by his total inability to show at any time any sort of affection.

She left him at last, taking Christopher with her, and sued almost immediately for a divorce. Ben was delighted to let her have it. He was delighted, too, to see the back of the small boy. The two of them had never got on. Ben was jealous of his male priority, he liked to be the only man of importance in his household, and Christopher, even at ten years old, was an individual who refused to be ignored. Despite all Hester's efforts, this antagonism endured. Even the boy's good looks, which Hester truly believed would charm Ben's painter's eye, had the very opposite effect, and when Hester tried to persuade Ben to do a portrait of him, he refused.

After their departure, life at Porthkerris slid easily back into its old seamy routine. Emma and Ben were cared for by a series of messy females, either models or student painters, who moved into and through and out of Ben Litton's life with the monotonous regularity of a well-ordered cinema queue. The only thing they had in common was an adulation of Ben, and a lofty disregard for housekeeping. They took as little notice of Emma as possible, but, in fact, she did not miss Hester as much as people thought she would. She had become weary – as Ben was – of being organised, and perpetually buttoned into clean clothes, but Christopher's going left a great void in her life which refused to be filled. For a little, she had mourned for him, tried to write him letters, but had not dared to ask Ben for his address. Once, in the desperation of loneliness, she ran away to find him. This entailed walking to the station and trying to buy a ticket to London, which seemed as good a place as any to look for him. But she had only one and ninepence in the world, and the stationmaster, who knew her, had taken her into his office which smelt of paraffin lamps and the black railway coal he burnt in his grate, and had given her a cup of tea out of an enamel pot, and walked her home. Ben was working, and had not noticed her absence. She never tried to look for Christopher again.

When Emma was thirteen, Ben was offered a teaching fellowship at the University of Texas for two years, which, without thought of Emma, he instantly accepted. There was a small hiatus while Emma's future was discussed. When taxed with the question of his daughter, he announced that he would simply take her to Texas with him, but someone – probably Marcus Bernstein – persuaded Ben that she would be better off away from him, and she was sent to a school in Switzerland. She stayed in Lausanne for three years – never returning to England, and then went to Florence to study Italian and Renaissance Art, for another year. At the end of this time, Ben was in Japan. When she suggested that she should join him, he replied by telegram. ONLY SPARE BED OCCUPIED BY CHARMING GEISHA GIRL WHY DONT YOU TRY LIVING IN PARIS.

Philosophically, for she was now seventeen and life was no longer surprising, Emma did as he suggested. She found herself a job with a family called Duprés who lived in a tall scholarly house in St Germain. The father was a professor of medicine, and the mother a teacher. Emma cared for their three well-behaved children, taught them English and Italian, and took them, in August, to the modest family villa at La Baule, and all the time waited patiently until Ben should return to live in England. He stayed in Japan for eighteen months, and when he did return it was by way of the United States, where he spent a month in New York. Marcus Bernstein flew out to meet him there, and it was typical that Emma learned the reason for this reunion, not from Ben himself, nor even from Leo, who was her usual source of information, but from a long and fully illustrated article in the French *Réalités*, which dealt with a newly built

Museum of Fine Arts in Queenstown, Virginia. This museum was a memorial created by his widow, to a rich Virginian called Kenneth Ryan, and the opening of the Art Section was to be a retrospective exhibition of the paintings of Ben Litton, ranging from his pre-war landscapes, right through to his latest abstractionisms.

Such an exhibition was an honour and a tribute, but inevitably suggested a painter to be revered, a Grand Old Man of the arts. Emma, studying one of the photographs of Ben, all angles and contrasts, dark-tanned skin and jutting chin and snowy hair, wondered how he felt about such veneration. He had been a rebel all his life against convention, and she could not imagine him tamely submitting to being a Grand Old anything.

"But what a man!" said Madame Duprés, when Emma showed her the photograph. "He is very attractive."

"Yes," said Emma, and sighed, because that had always been the trouble.

With Marcus, he returned to London in January, and went straight back to Porthkerris to paint. This was confirmed by a letter from Marcus. The day the letter arrived, Emma went to Madame Duprés and gave in her notice. They tried to coax, cajole, bribe her into changing her mind, but she was adamant. She had scarcely seen her father for six years. It was time they got to know each other again. She was going back to Porthkerris, to live with him.

In the end, because they had no option, they agreed to letting her go. Her flight was booked, and she started to pack, throwing out some of the accumulated possessions of six years, and cramming the rest into a variety of battered and much-travelled suitcases. But even these were sadly inadequate, and Emma was eventually driven to going out and buying herself a basket, a huge French marketing basket that would accommodate the number of awkwardly-shaped objects that refused to go into anything else.

It was a grey and cold afternoon, two days before she was due to fly home. Madame Duprés was at home, so Emma, explaining her errand, left the children with her, and went out alone. To her surprise, she found that it was raining, lightly, in a chill drizzle. The cobbled pavements of the narrow street shone with wet, and the tall bleached houses stood quiet and closed against the murk, like faces which give nothing away. From the river a tug hooted, and a solitary gull hung, high above, in the mist, screaming dismally. The illusion of Porthkerris was suddenly more real than the reality of Paris. The resolve to return, which had for so long been in the back of her mind, was crystallised now into the impression that she was already there.

This street would lead – not to the busy Rue St Germain, but out on to the harbour road, and it would be flood tide, the harbour full of grey sea and bobbing boats, and a heavy swell running out beyond the north pier, the Atlantic crested with white horses. And there would be familiar smells – fish from the market, and hot saffron buns from the baker's; and all the little summer shops would be shuttered and closed for the season. And back at the studio Ben would be working, hands mittened against the cold, the brilliance of his palette a scream of colour against the sweep of grey cloud that was framed by his towering north window.

She was going home. In two days, she would be there. The rain was wet on her face and all at once she felt that she could not wait, and this sense of happy urgency made her run, and she ran all the way to the little épicerie in the Rue St Germain, where she knew she would be able to buy the basket.

It was a tiny shop, fragrant with fresh bread and garlic-flavoured sausage meat, with onions strung like white beads from the ceiling, and jars of wine, which the local workmen bought by the litre. The baskets hung at the door, strung together and suspended by a single piece of rope. Emma did not dare untie it and choose herself a basket in case the whole lot fell to the pavement, so she went into the shop to find someone to do it for her. There was only the fat woman with the mole on her face, and she was busy with a customer, so Emma waited. The customer was a young man, fair haired, his raincoat streaked with damp. He was buying a long loaf and a pat of country butter. Emma eyed him and decided that, from the back at least, he looked attractive.

"Combien?" he said.

The fat woman did a sum with a stub of pencil. She told him. He felt in his pocket and paid, turned, smiled at Emma and made for the door.

And there he stopped. With his hand against the edge of the door, he swung slowly around, to take a second look. She saw the amber eyes, the slow, incredulous smile.

The face was the same, the familiar, boy's face on the unfamiliar man's body. With the illusion of Porthkerris so near and so strong, it seemed that he was simply an extension of that illusion, a figment of her own highly-stimulated imagination. This was not him. This could not be . . .

She heard herself say "Christo," and it was the most natural thing in the world to call him by the name that only she had ever used. He said, quietly, "I simply don't believe it," and then he dropped his parcels and held out his arms and Emma fell into them, pressed close against the shiny, wet front of his raincoat.

They had two days to spend together. Emma told Madame Duprés, "My brother is in Paris," and Madame, who was kind-hearted, and had, anyway, resigned herself to being without Emma, set Emma free to spend them with Christopher. They used up these two days in slowly walking the streets of the city;

hanging over the bridges to watch the barges slip away below them, bound for the south and the sun; sitting in the thin sunshine and drinking coffee at the small, round iron tables, and when it rained, taking refuge in Notre Dame or the Louvre, perched on the stairs beneath the Winged Victory and always talking. They had so much to ask and so much to tell. She learned that Christopher, after a number of false starts, had decided to become an actor. This was much against his mother's wishes – after eighteen months of Ben Litton she had had enough of artistic temperaments to last her for the rest of her life – but he had stuck to his guns and even managed to get a scholarship to RADA. He had worked for two years in a repertory theatre in Scotland, had moved, unsuccessfully, to London, done a little television work, and then had been diverted by an invitation from an acquaintance, whose mother owned a house in St Tropez.

"St Tropez in the winter?" Emma could not help asking.

"It was then or never. We'd never have been offered it in the summer."

"But wasn't it cold?"

"Freezing. Never stopping raining. And when the wind blew all the shutters rattled. It was like some ghastly film."

In January he had returned to London to see his agent, and had been offered a twelve-month contract with a small repertory company in the south of England. It was not the sort of work he wanted, but it was better than nothing, and he was running out of money, and it was not too far from London. The job, however, did not start until the beginning of March, and so he had returned to France, finished up in Paris, and finally met Emma. Now, it irked him that she was returning so soon to England, and did everything he could to make her change her mind, postpone her flight, stay in Paris with him. But Emma was adamant.

"You don't understand. This is something that I have to do."

"It's not even as though the old boy asked you to go. You're just going to get in his way, and interfere with all his amorous adventures."

"I never have before – interfered, I mean." She laughed at his stubborn expression. "Anyway, there's no point my staying, if you're coming back to England next month."

He made a face. "Wish I wasn't. That lousy little theatre at Brookford. I shall get lost in the jungle of fortnightly rep. Besides, I'm not due there for two weeks. Now if you would only stay in Paris . . ."

"No, Christo."

"We could rent a tiny attic. Think of all the fun we could have. Bread and cheese every night for supper and lots of rough red wine."

"No, Christo."

"Paris in the Spring . . . blue skies and blossom and all that rot?"

"It isn't spring yet. It's still winter."

"Were you always so unco-operative?"

But still she would not agree to staying, and in the end he admitted defeat. "Very well, if I can't persuade you to keep me company, I shall simply behave in a very well-bred and British way, and come and see you on to your plane."

"That would be perfect."

"It's very self-sacrificing of me. I hate saying goodbyes."

Emma agreed with this. Sometimes, it felt as if she had been saying goodbye to people all her life, and the sound of a train moving out of a station, gathering speed, was enough to reduce her to tears. "But this goodbye is different."

"How is it different?" he wanted to know.

"It isn't really goodbye. It's *au revoir*. A stepping stone between two hellos."

"My mother and your father are not going to approve."

"It doesn't matter if they approve or not," said Emma. "We've found each other again. For the moment, that's all that matters."

Above them, the loudspeakers gave a click, began to speak with a feminine voice.

"Ladies and gentlemen. Air France announce the departure of their flight Number 402 for London . . ."

"That's me," said Emma.

They stubbed out their cigarettes, stood up, began to gather in the baggage. Christopher took the canvas grip and the Prisunic paper carrier, and the great bulging basket. Emma slung the raincoat over her shoulder, carried her handbag, the ski-boots and the hat.

Christopher said, "I wish you'd wear the hat. It really would complete your ensemble."

"It would blow off. Not to say look funny."

They went downstairs, crossed the expanse of shining floor towards the barrier where a small queue of passengers was already forming.

"Emma, are you going down to Porthkerris today?"

"Yes, I'll get the first train I can."

"Have you got any money? Pounds, shillings and pence, I mean?"

She had not thought of this. "No. But it doesn't matter. I'll cash a cheque somewhere."

They joined the queue behind a British businessman who carried only his passport and a slim brief-case. Christopher leaned forward.

"Oh, sir, I wonder if you could help."

The man swung round, and found to his surprise Christopher's

11

face only inches from his own. Christopher was wearing his sincere expression. ''I am sorry, but we're in rather a predicament. My sister's returning to London, she's not been home for six years, and she has such a lot of hand luggage, and she's only just recovered from a serious operation . . .''

Emma remembered Ben saying that Christopher never told a small lie if he could get away with a bigger one. Looking at him as he came out with this outrageous fabrication, she decided that he had chosen his career wisely. He was a wonderful actor.

The businessman, thus approached, could make no excuse. ''Well, yes, I suppose . . .''

''It's more than kind of you . . .'' The canvas grip and the carrier with the bread went under one arm, the basket in the other along with the slim brief-case. Emma felt sorry for him.

''It's just till we get on to the plane . . . it is so kind of you, and you see my brother isn't coming with me . . .''

The queue moved forward, they had reached the barrier.

''Goodbye, darling Emma,'' said Christopher.

''Goodbye, Christo.'' They kissed. A brown hand whipped away her passport, riffled the pages, stamped it.

''Goodbye.''

They were divided by the barrier, by the formalities of the French government, by other travellers, surging forward.

''Goodbye.''

She would have liked him to wait and see her safely on to the plane, but even as she waved, flapping the sun hat, he had turned, and was walking away from her, the light shining on his hair, and his hands buried deep in the pockets of his leather coat.

2

In London, in February, it was raining. It had started to rain at seven o'clock in the morning, and it had rained without ceasing ever since. By half past eleven only a handful of people had visited the exhibition, and those enthusiasts, one suspected, had simply come in order to get out of the rain. They shed wet raincoats and dripping umbrellas, and stood around, bemoaning the weather before they had even bought themselves a catalogue.

At eleven-thirty, the man came in to buy a picture. He was an American, staying at the Hilton, and he asked to see Mr Bernstein. Peggy, the receptionist, took the card which he proffered, asked him politely if he would mind waiting for a moment, and then came through to the office to speak to Robert.

"Mr Morrow, there's an American outside by the name of . . ." she glanced at the card. "Lowell Cheeke. He was here a week ago, and Mr Bernstein showed him the Ben Litton of the deer, and thought he was going to buy it, but he went off without making up his mind. Said he wanted to mull it over."

"Have you told him Mr Bernstein's in Edinburgh?"

"Yes, but he can't wait. He's going back to the States the day after tomorrow."

"I'd better see him," said Robert.

He stood up, and while Peggy went to open the door and

13

invite the American in, did a swift spring-clean of his desk, squaring some letters, emptying the ash-tray into the wastepaper basket and shoving the basket under the desk with the toe of his shoe.

"Mr Cheeke," said Peggy, announcing the visitor like a well-trained parlourmaid.

Robert came around the desk to shake hands.

"How do you do, Mr Cheeke? I'm Robert Morrow, Mr Bernstein's partner. I am sorry, I'm afraid he's in Edinburgh today, but perhaps I could help you . . . ?"

Lowell Cheeke was a short, powerful-looking individual in a dacron raincoat and a narrow-brimmed hat. Both of these were very wet, indicating that Mr Cheeke had not arrived in a taxi. He began divesting himself, with Robert's help, from these sodden garments, and revealed an uncrushable navy blue terylene suit and a pin-striped nylon shirt. He wore rimless spectacles and behind them his eyes were cool and grey, and it was impossible to assess any sort of potential either financial or artistic.

"Thank you very much . . ." said Mr Cheeke. "What a terrible morning . . ."

"It doesn't look as though it's going to let up either . . . A cigarette, Mr Cheeke?"

"No, thank you, I no longer smoke." He coughed self-consciously. "My wife made me give it up."

They grinned at this female idiosyncrasy. The grin did not reach Mr Cheeke's eyes. He reached for a chair and settled himself into it, hitching a polished black shoe across his knee. He already looked very much at home.

"I was in here a week ago, Mr Morrow, and Mr Bernstein showed me a painting by Ben Litton – your receptionist probably told you."

"Yes, she did, the deer painting."

"I'd like to see it again if I may. I'm returning to the States the day after tomorrow, and I have to make up my mind."

"But of course . . . !"

The picture waited for Mr Cheeke's decision, resting, where Marcus had left it, against the wall of the office. Robert drew the padded easel into the centre of the room, turned it towards the light, and gently lifted the Ben Litton into position. It was a large picture, an oil of three deer in a forest. Light filtered through the barely-suggested branches, and the artist had used a quantity of white which gave the work an ethereal quality. But its most interesting feature was the fact that it had been painted, not on stretched canvas, but on jute, and the coarser weave of this textile had blurred the artist's brush, like the outlines of an action photograph taken at high speed.

The American swung his chair into position, and turned the cold beam of his spectacles on to the painting. Discreetly, Robert removed himself to the back of the room so as not to obtrude in any way upon Mr Cheeke's own assessment, and his own view of the painting was obscured by the round crew-cut head of his potential customer. Personally, he liked the picture. He was not a fan of Ben Litton's. He thought his work affected and not always easy to understand – a reflection, perhaps, of the artist's own personality – but this swift sylvan impression was a thing to be looked at and lived with and never tired of.

Mr Cheeke got out of his chair, moved up to the painting, examined it minutely, backed away once more, and finished up leaning against the edge of Robert's desk.

"Why do you suppose, Mr Morrow," he said, without turning round, "that Litton was inspired to paint it on burlap?"

The word burlap made Robert want to laugh. He longed to say irreverently, *Probably had an old sack lying around* but Mr Cheeke did not look as though he would appreciate irreverence.

Mr Cheeke was here to spend money – always a serious business. Robert decided then that he was buying the Litton as an investment, and he hoped it would pay him off.

He said, "I'm afraid I have no idea, Mr Cheeke, but it does give a most unusual quality to the work."

Mr Cheeke turned his head to send Robert a cold smile over his shoulder.

"You are not as well informed on such aspects as Mr Bernstein."

"No," said Robert. "I'm afraid I'm not."

Mr Cheeke relapsed once more into contemplation. The silence settled and lasted. Robert's own concentration had begun to wander. Small sounds intruded. The ticking of his own wristwatch. A murmur of voices from the other side of the door. The thunderous rumble, like distant surf, that was Piccadilly traffic.

The American sighed gustily. He began to feel in his pockets, one by one, searching for something. A handkerchief, perhaps. Some change for his taxi ride back to the Hilton. His attention had strayed. Robert had not convinced him that the Litton was worth buying. He was going to make some excuse and go away.

But Mr Cheeke was simply searching for his pen. When he turned round, Robert saw that he already held his cheque book in the other hand.

Their business finally completed, Mr Cheeke relaxed. He became quite human and even took off his glasses and stowed them away in a tooled leather case. He accepted the offer of a drink, and he and Robert sat for a little, with two glasses of sherry, and talked about Marcus Bernstein and Ben Litton, and the two or three paintings which Mr Cheeke had purchased on his last visit to London, with which to form, with his latest acquisition, the nucleus of a small private collection. Robert told him about the retrospective Ben Litton exhibition which was being held in

Queenstown, Virginia, in April, and Mr Cheeke made a note of it in his diary, and then they both stood up, and Robert helped Mr Cheeke into his raincoat, and gave him his hat, and they shook hands.

"I've enjoyed meeting you, Mr Morrow, and doing business with you."

"I hope we'll see you next time you come to London."

"Most certainly I shall pay you a visit . . ."

Robert held the door open and they moved out into the Gallery. Bernstein's were showing, that fortnight, a collection of bird and animal paintings by an obscure South American with an unpronounceable name, a man of humble origins, who had somehow, sometime, incredibly, taught himself to paint. Marcus had met him last year in New York, had been instantly impressed by his work, and invited him then and there to stage a London exhibition. Now, his brilliant pictures lined the straw-green walls of the Bernstein Gallery and on this gloomy morning seemed to fill the room with the verdancy and sunshine of a more salubrious climate. The critics had loved him. Since the exhibition opened ten days ago, the Gallery had never once been empty, and within twenty-four hours there was not a picture that had not been sold.

At this moment, however, there were only three people in the Gallery. One of them was Peggy, neat and unobtrusive behind her kidney-shaped desk, busy with the proofs of a new catalogue. Another was a black-hatted man, stooped as a crow, doing a slow round of inspection. The last was a girl, who sat, facing the office door, on the circular buttoned sofa in the middle of the room. She wore a bright green trouser suit and was surrounded by luggage, and appeared to have wandered into Bernstein's under the mistaken impression that it was the waiting-room of a railway station.

Robert, with considerable self-possession, managed to behave as if she was not there. Together he and Mr Cheeke moved
across the thick carpet towards the main door, Robert's head
bent to catch the last of Mr Cheeke's small talk. The glass doors
opened and swung shut behind them, and they were swallowed
into the gloom of the dismal morning.

Emma Litton said, "Is that Mr Morrow?"

Peggy looked up. "That's right."

Emma was not used to being ignored. The single swift glance
had made her feel uncomfortable. She wished that Marcus was
not in Edinburgh. She crossed her legs and then uncrossed them
again. From outside came the sound of the departing taxi. In a
moment, the glass door opened, once more, and Robert Morrow
came back into the Gallery. He did not make any comment,
simply put his hands in his pockets, and calmly regarded Emma
and her attendant chaos.

She decided that she had never, in her life, seen a man who
looked less like an art dealer. His was the sort of face that,
groggy and unshaven, is helped from a small sailboat at the end
of a single-handed circumnavigation; or, darkly goggled, looks
down from the peak of a previously unconquered mountain. But
here, in the precious and rarefied atmosphere of the Bernstein
galleries, he did not fit at all. He was very tall, wide-shouldered,
long-legged; all this emphasised – and yet made incongruous
– by his smoothly-tailored dark grey suit. In his youth his hair
might have been red, but the years had tamed it to a tawny brown,
and in contrast his grey eyes seemed pale as steel. He had high
cheek-bones and a long, stubborn jaw, and she was diverted
by the discovery that such a collection of features could be so
attractive, and then remembered that Ben always averred that
the character of a man lies, not in his eyes, where emotions are

18

fleeting and can always be masked, but in the physical shape of his mouth, and this man's mouth was wide, with a jutting lower lip, and looked now as though it was trying, hard, not to laugh.

The silence became uncomfortable. Emma tried a smile. She said "Hello!"

For enlightenment, Robert Morrow turned to Peggy. Peggy was amused. "This young lady wants to see Mr Bernstein."

He said, "I am sorry, he's in Edinburgh."

"Yes, I know, so I've been told. The thing is, I only wanted him to cash me a cheque." He looked more puzzled than ever. Emma decided it was time to explain. "I'm Emma Litton. Ben Litton's my father."

His puzzlement cleared. "But why on earth didn't you say so? I am sorry, I had no idea." He came forward. "How do you do . . ."

Emma stood up. The straw hat, which had been on her knee, floated to the carpet and lay there, adding to the confusion which she had already wrought to the elegantly designed room.

They shook hands. "I . . . there wasn't any reason why you should know who I was. And I'm terribly sorry about all this stuff, but you see I haven't been home for six years, so there's bound to be quite a lot."

"Yes, I can see that."

Emma was embarrassed. "If you can just cash me a cheque, I'll take it all out of your way again. I only want enough to get back to Porthkerris. You see, I forgot to get any sterling when I was in Paris, and I've run out of traveller's cheques."

He frowned. "But how did you get this far? From the airport, I mean?"

"Oh." She had already forgotten. "Oh, there was a kind man on the plane, he helped me to carry my stuff on, and off again at London, and he lent me a pound. I'll have to send it back. I've got his address here . . . somewhere." She felt vaguely in pockets, but could not find the man's card. "Well, anyway, I've got it somewhere." She smiled again, hoping to disarm him.

"And when are you going down to Porthkerris?"

"There's a train at twelve-thirty, I think."

He glanced at his wrist-watch. "You've missed that. When's the next?"

Emma looked blank. Peggy broke into the conversation in her usual polite and practical fashion. "I think there's one at two-thirty, Mr Morrow, but I can check."

"Yes, do that, Peggy. Would the two-thirty be all right for you?"

"Yes, of course. It doesn't matter what time I arrive."

"Is your father expecting you?"

"Well, I wrote him a letter and told him I was coming. But that doesn't mean he's *expecting* me . . ."

He smiled at this. "Yes. Well . . ." He glanced at his watch again. It was twelve-fifteen. Peggy was already on the telephone, inquiring about train times. His eyes returned to the turmoil of suitcases. In a feeble effort to improve the situation, Emma stooped and picked up her sun hat.

He said, "I think the best thing would be to get all this out of the way . . . we'll pile it up in the office, and then . . . Have you had anything to eat?"

"I had some coffee at Le Bourget."

"If you catch the two-thirty, there's time for me to give you lunch before you go."

"Oh, you don't have to bother."

"It's no bother. I have to eat anyway and you might as well eat with me. Come along now."

He picked up two of the suitcases, and led the way into the office. Emma gathered up as much as she could carry, and followed him. The deer painting was still on the stand, and she saw it at once and was diverted.

"That's one of Ben's."

"Yes, I just sold it . . ."

"To the little man in the raincoat? It's good, isn't it?" She continued to admire it, while Robert toted the remainder of her luggage. "Why did he paint it on sacking?"

"You'd better ask him when you see him tonight."

She turned and grinned at him over her shoulder. "Influenced, do you think, by the Japanese school?"

"I wish," said Robert, "I'd thought of saying that to Mr Cheeke. Now, are you ready for lunch?"

He took an enormous black umbrella out of a stand, and stood aside for Emma to go out through the door ahead of him, and they left Peggy to hold the fort, sitting in a gallery restored once more to its usual ordered calm, and they went out into the rain and walked together, beneath the black umbrella, shouldering their way through the lunch-hour jostle of Kent Street, London, W1.

He took her to Marcello's where he normally lunched if he was not expected to entertain some important expense-account customer. Marcello was an Italian who ran a small upstairs restaurant, two streets from Bernstein's, and a table was perpetually reserved for either Marcus or Robert, or both of them, on the odd occasion when they were able to lunch together. It was a modest table, in a quiet corner, but today when Robert and Emma came up the stairs, Marcello took one look at her, with her long tassel of black hair, and her green trouser suit, and suggested that they might prefer to sit in the window.

Robert was amused. "Would you like to sit in the window?" he asked Emma.

21

"Where do you usually sit?" He indicated the small corner table. "Well, why don't we just sit there?"

Marcello was charmed by her. He led the way to the smaller table, held Emma's chair for her, gave them each an enormous menu written in dubious purple ink and went to fetch two glasses of Tio Pepe while they decided what they were going to eat.

Robert said, "My stock with Marcello will have gone up. I don't think I've ever brought a girl here for lunch."

"Who do you usually bring?"

"Just myself. Or Marcus."

"How is Marcus?" . . . her voice was warm.

"He's well. He'll be sorry to have missed you I know."

"It's my fault. I should have written and told him I was coming. But as you've probably realised, we Littons aren't very good at letting anybody know about anything."

"But you knew Ben had gone back to Porthkerris."

"Yes. Marcus wrote and told me that. And I know all about the retrospective exhibition, because I read an article on it in *Réalités*." She smiled wryly. "Being the daughter of a famous father does have some compensations. Even if he never does anything except send telegrams, you can usually read up what is happening to him in some paper or other."

"When did you last see him?"

"Oh," she shrugged. "Two years ago. I was in Florence, and he stopped off on his way to Japan."

"I didn't know you went through Florence when you went to Japan."

"You do if you happen to have a daughter living there." She put her elbows on the table, and rested her chin in her hand. "I don't suppose you even knew Ben had a daughter."

"Yes, of course I did."

"Well, I didn't know about you. I mean, I didn't know Marcus

22

had a partner. He was still on his own when Ben went to Texas and I was bundled off to Switzerland.''

''It was about that time that I joined Bernstein's.''

''I . . . I never knew anyone who looked less like an art dealer. Than you, I mean.''

''Perhaps that's just because I'm not an art dealer.''

''But . . . you just sold that man Ben's painting.''

''No,'' he corrected her. ''I simply accepted the cheque. Marcus had already sold it to him a week ago, but even Mr Cheeke didn't realise that.''

''But you must know something about painting.''

''Now, I do. One couldn't work with Marcus for all these years and not have some of his boundless knowledge rub off. But I'm basically a business man, and that's why Marcus asked me to join him.''

''But Marcus is the most successful business man I know.''

''Exactly, and so successful that the whole venture of the Gallery grew too big for him to handle on his own.''

Emma continued to regard him, a slight frown between her thickly-marked brows.

''Any more questions?''

She was not disconcerted. ''Were you always a very close friend of Marcus?''

''What you really mean is, why did he take me into the firm? And the answer is that Marcus is not only my partner, but my brother-in-law as well. He married my older sister.''

''You mean Helen Bernstein is your sister?''

''You remember Helen?''

''But of course. And little David. How are they? You'll send them my love, won't you? You know I used to go and stay with them when Ben came up to London and there wasn't anyone to leave me with at Porthkerris. And when I went to Switzerland, it was Marcus and Helen who put me on to the plane, because Ben had already gone to Texas. Will you tell Helen I'm home, and that you gave me lunch?''

''Yes, of course I will.''

''Do they still have that little flat in the Brompton Road?''

''No, as a matter of fact, when my father died, they moved in with me. We all live in our old family house, in Kensington.''

''You mean you all live together?''

''Together and apart. Marcus and Helen and David live on the first two floors, and my father's old housekeeper lives in the basement, and I roost in the attics.''

''Aren't you married?''

Momentarily, he looked put out. ''Well, no, I'm not.''

''I was sure you'd be married. You have a very married look about you.''

''I don't quite know how to take that.''

''Oh, it wasn't meant in a derogatory fashion at all. It's really quite a compliment. I only wish Ben had that look about him. It would make life so much easier for all concerned. Especially me.''

''Don't you want to go back and live with him?''

''Yes, of course I do, more than anything. But I don't want it to be a failure. I was never very good at coping with Ben, and I don't suppose I'll be any better now.''

''Then why are you going?''

''Well . . .'' Under Robert Morrow's cool grey regard, it was difficult to be coherent. She picked up a fork and began to make patterns with it on the white damask cloth. ''I don't know. You only have one family. If people belong to each other, they should at least be able to live together. I want to have something to remember. When I'm old I want to be able to remember that once, even if it was only for a few weeks on end, my father

24

and I were making some sort of a life together. Does that sound crazy?''

''No, it doesn't sound crazy, but it sounds as if you might be disappointed.''

''I learned all about being disappointed when I was a little girl. It's a luxury I can well do without. Besides, I only plan to stay until it becomes painfully obvious that we cannot stand each other's company for another hour.''

''Or,'' said Robert gently, ''until he prefers some other person's company.''

Emma's head came up, her eyes a sudden furious blaze of blue. She was, in that instant, her father at his most unscrupulous, when there was no retort too cruel or too cutting to be made. But her anger provoked no reaction, and after a cold pause, she looked down again, and continued to draw patterns on the tablecloth, and only said, ''All right. Until then.''

The small tension was broken by the return of Marcello bringing their sherry and ready to take the order. Emma chose a dozen oysters and fried chicken; Robert, more conservatively, a consommé and a steak. Then, taking advantage of the interruption, he tactfully changed the subject.

''Tell me about Paris. How was it looking?''

''Wet. Wet and cold and sunny all at once. Does that convey anything to you?''

''Everything.''

''You know Paris?''

''I go over on business. I was there last month.''

''On business?''

''No, on my way back from Austria. I had three weeks' splendid ski-ing.''

''Where did you go?''

''Obergurgl.''

"So that's why you're so brown. That's one of the reasons you don't look like an art dealer."

"Perhaps, when my tan fades, I shall look more authentic and be able to command higher prices. How long did you spend in Paris?"

"Two years. I shall miss it. It's so beautiful, and doubly so now all the buildings have been cleaned. And somehow, at this time of the year, there's that special feeling in Paris. That the winter's nearly over and the sun's just a day or so away and it's going to be spring again . . ."

And buds unfolding, and the scream of gulls, swooping over the chopped brown waters of the Seine. And barges, strung like necklaces, slipping away beneath the bridges, and the smell of the Metro, and garlic, and Gauloises. And being with Christopher.

All at once it became important to talk about him, to speak his name, to reassure herself of his existence. She said, casually, "You never met Hester, did you? My stepmother? At least for eighteen months she was my stepmother."

"I know about her."

"And about Christopher? Her son? Do you know about Christopher? Because, quite by chance, Christopher and I met up again in Paris. Just two days ago. And he came, this very morning, and saw me off at Le Bourget."

"You mean . . . you just bumped into each other . . . ?"

"Yes, we really did . . . in a grocer's shop. It could only happen in Paris."

"What was he doing there?"

"Oh, filling in time. He'd been to St Tropez, but he comes back to England in March to join some repertory theatre or other."

"He's an actor?"

26

"Yes. Didn't I tell you that? There is just one thing . . . I'm not going to say anything to Ben. You see, Ben never liked Christopher, and I don't think Christopher lost any love over him. To be truthful, I expect they were a little jealous of each other. But there were other things as well, and Ben and Hester didn't exactly part company on the best of terms. I don't want to start off by having a row with Ben about Christopher, so I'm not going to say anything. At least not right away."

"I see."

Emma sighed. "You've got a very stuffy expression on your face. You obviously think I'm being underhand."

"I don't think anything of the sort. And when you've finished making patterns on the tablecloth, your oysters have arrived."

By the time they had finished lunch and drunk their coffee, and Robert had paid the bill, it was half past one. They got up from the table, and said goodbye to Marcello, and collected the big black umbrella and went downstairs. They walked back to Bernstein's, asked the doorman to get Emma a taxi.

"I'd come with you and put you on to the train, but Peggy has to go out and get herself some lunch."

"I'll be all right."

He took her into the office and unlocked the safe.

"Will twenty pounds be enough?"

She had already forgotten her reason for coming to the Gallery in the first place. "What? Oh, yes, of course . . ." She began to feel for her cheque book, but Robert stopped her.

"Don't bother. Your father has a sort of petty cash account with us. He's always running out of small change when he's in London. We'll put your twenty pounds down to that."

"Well, if you're sure . . ."

"Sure I'm sure. And, Emma, there is one other thing. The man who lent you the pound. Somewhere you have his address.

If you find it and give it to me now, I'll see he gets the pound back again.''

Emma was amused. Searching for the card, finding it at last, entangled with a French bus ticket and a book of matches, she began to laugh, and when Robert asked her what was so funny, she simply said, "How well you know my father!"

3

It stopped raining at tea-time. There was a subtle lifting of the atmosphere, a freshness in the air. An errant shaft of sunlight even found its way into the Gallery, and by five-thirty, when Robert locked up his office, and went out to join the rush hour torrent of home-going humanity, he found that a small breeze had got up and blown the clouds away, leaving the city to sparkle beneath a pale, pellucid blue sky.

It was somehow more than he could bear to plunge into the subterranean stuffiness of the tube, so he walked as far as Knightsbridge, and then got on a bus and rode the rest of the way home.

His house, in Milton Gardens, was separated from the busy artery of the Kensington High Street by a maze of small streets and squares, a pleasant neighbourhood of miniature, early-Victorian houses, cream-painted, and with bright front doors and small gardens that in summer bloomed with lilac and magnolia. The streets had wide pavements where nannies pushed prams and small, well-dressed children walked to their expensive schools and the local dogs were rigorously exercised. After this, Milton Gardens came as something of a let down. It was a terrace of large and shabby houses, and Number Twenty-three, which was Robert's – the centre house, and crowned with the main pediment of the terrace – quite often looked the shabbiest. It had a black front door, and two dried-up bay trees in tubs, and a brass letter-box that Helen always meant to polish, but quite often forgot. The household cars were parked at the pavement's edge – a big dark-green Alvis coupé which was Robert's, and a dusty red Mini which was Helen's. Marcus did not own a car because he had never found time to learn how to drive.

Robert went up the steps, feeling in his pocket for his latch-key, and let himself in. The hall was large and spacious, a surprisingly wide and shallow staircase curved up to the first floor. Beyond the staircase, the hall continued in a narrow passage, which led to a glassed door, and the garden. This beguiling vista of distant grass and sun-touched chestnut trees gave the immediate impression of being in the country, and was one of the most endearing aspects of the house.

The front door slammed shut behind him. From the kitchen, his sister Helen called his name.

"Robert."

"Hello!"

He chucked his hat on to the hall table, and went in through the door at the right of the hall. In the old days this room, facing out over the street, had been the family dining-room, but when Robert's father had died, and Marcus and Helen and David had moved in, Helen had converted it into a kitchen dining-room, with a scrubbed country table, and a pine dresser, crammed with patterned china and a counter, like a bar, behind which she could work. There were also a great many plants in pots, straggling geraniums, and herbs, and bowls of bulbs. Bunches of onions and marketing baskets hung from hooks, and there were recipe books, and racks of wooden spoons, and the cheerfulness of bright rugs and cushions.

Helen was behind her counter now, in a blue and white butcher's apron, peeling mushrooms. The air was filled with fragrant smells – of baking and lemons, and warm butter and the lightest suggestion of garlic. She was an exceptional cook.

She said, "Marcus called from Edinburgh. He's coming home tonight. Did you know?"

"What time?"

"There's a plane at a quarter past five. He was going to try and get a seat on that. It gets in to the terminal at half past seven."

Robert pulled a high stool up to the counter, and perched on it, like a man sitting at a bar.

"Does he want to be met at the airport?"

"No, he'll get the bus in. I thought one of us would go and pick him up. Are you in or out for dinner tonight?"

"It smells so good, I think I'm in."

She smiled. Facing each other across the counter, the family resemblance between them was very marked. Helen was a big woman, tall and heavy-boned, but when she smiled her face and her eyes lit up like a girl's. Her hair, like Robert's, was reddish, but softened by streaks of grey, and she wore it drawn tightly back into a knot, to reveal a small and unexpectedly neat pair of ears. She was proud of her pretty ears, and always wore ear-rings. She had a whole boxful of them in her dressing-table drawer, and if you didn't know what to give her for a present, you simply bought a pair of ear-rings. This evening they were green, some sort of semi-precious stone, set in a narrow rope of woven gold, and their colour brought out the green lights in her indeterminate, speckled eyes.

She was forty-two, six years older than Robert, and she had been married to Marcus Bernstein for ten years. Before that she had worked for him, as secretary, receptionist, book-keeper, and – on occasions when finances were shaky – as office cleaner as well, and it was as much due to her efforts and faith in Marcus that the Gallery had not merely survived the initial lean patches, but had grown to achieve its present international reputation.

Robert said, "Did Marcus tell you anything . . . about how he got on . . . ?"

"Not much, there wasn't time. But the old Lord of the Glens, whoever he is, has three Raeburns, a Constable and a Turner. So that should give you all something to think about."

"Does he want to sell them?"

"Apparently. He says that at the current price of whisky, he can no longer afford to keep them hanging on the wall. Anyway, we'll hear all about it when Marcus gets back. How about you . . . what have you been doing today . . . ?"

"Nothing much. An American called Lowell Cheeke came in and wrote a cheque for a Ben Litton . . ."

"That's fine . . ."

"And . . ." he watched his sister's face ". . . Emma Litton's home."

Helen had started to slice the mushrooms. Now, swiftly, she looked up and her hands were still.

"Emma. You mean Ben's Emma?"

"Flew back from Paris today. Came into the Gallery to collect enough money to get her back to Porthkerris."

"Did Marcus know she was coming back?"

"No, I don't think so. I don't think she wrote to anyone except her father."

"And of course Ben wouldn't say a word." Helen made an exasperated face. "Sometimes I could just strangle that man."

Robert was amused. "What would you have done if you'd known she was coming?"

"Well, met her at the airport. Given her lunch. Anything."

"If it's any comfort to you, I gave her lunch."

"Well, good for you." She sliced another mushroom, considering this. "What does she look like now?"

"Attractive, in a rather unusual way."

"Unusual," Helen repeated dryly. "Tell me she's unusual and you tell me nothing I don't already know."

Robert picked up a slice of raw mushroom and ate it, experimentally. "Do you know about her mother?"

"Of course I do." Helen rescued her mushrooms, whisking them out of his reach, and taking them to her cooker, where a pan simmered with warm butter. With another deft movement, she spilled the mushrooms into the butter, and there were faint sizzling sounds and a delicious smell. She stood there, moving the mushrooms around with a wooden spatula, her strong features profiled.

"Who was she?"

"Oh, a little art student, half Ben's age. She was very pretty."

"Was he married to her?"

"Yes, he did marry her. I think, in his way, he was very fond of her. But she was simply a child."

"Did she leave him?"

"No, she died, having Emma."

"And then, later on, he married someone called Hester."

Helen turned to look at him, her eyes narrowed. "How do you know about that?"

"Emma told me today at lunch."

"Well, I never did! Yes, Hester Ferris. That was years ago."

"But there was a boy. A son. Called Christopher?"

"Don't say he's turned up again."

"Why do you sound so alarmed?"

"You'd sound alarmed, too, if you'd lived through those eighteen months when Ben Litton was married to Hester . . ."

"Tell me."

33

"Oh, they were murder. For Marcus, for Ben . . . I suppose for Hester, and certainly for me. If Marcus wasn't being roped in to referee some sordid domestic fracas, then he was being showered with ridiculous little bills which Hester said Ben refused to pay. And then, you know how Ben has this phobia about telephones, and Hester put one into her house and Ben tore it out by the roots. And then Ben ran into some sort of mental block and couldn't do any work, and spent all his time in the local pub, and Hester would get hold of Marcus and say that Marcus must come because he was the only person who could do anything with him, and so on, and so on. Marcus aged, visibly, before my eyes. Can you believe that?"

"Yes. But I don't see what it has to do with the boy."

"The boy was one of the bones of contention. Ben couldn't bear him."

"Emma said he was jealous."

"She said that? She was always a perceptive child. I suppose in a way Ben was jealous of Christopher, but Christopher was a devil. He looked like a saint, but his mother spoiled him rotten." She drew her pan of mushrooms away from the heat, and came back to lean her elbows on the counter. "What did Emma say about Christopher?"

"Just that they'd met in Paris."

"What was he doing there?"

"I don't know. I suppose having a holiday. He's an actor. Did you know that?"

"No, but I can well believe it. Was she looking very starry-eyed about him?"

"I should say so, yes. Unless it was the thought of going back to live with her father."

"That's the last thing in the world for her to be starry-eyed about."

"I know that. But when I started to say as much, I near as dammit got my head bitten off."

"Yes, you would. They're as loyal as thieves to each other." She patted his hand. "Don't get involved, Robert; I couldn't bear the strain."

"I'm not involved, simply intrigued."

"Well, for your own peace of mind, take my advice and keep it that way. And while we're on the subject of involvements, Jane Marshall called at lunch-time, and she wants you to ring her up."

"What about, do you know?"

"She didn't say. Just said she'd be in any time after six o'clock. You won't forget, will you?"

"No, I won't forget. But don't you forget, either, that Jane is not an involvement."

"What you're jibbing at, I cannot imagine," said Helen, who had never, with her brother at any rate, bothered to mince words. "She is charming, attractive and efficient."

Robert made no comment on this, and exasperated by his silence, she went on, justifying herself. "You have everything in common, interests, friends, a way of life. Besides, a man of your age should be married. There's nothing so pathetic as an elderly bachelor."

She stopped. There was a pause. Robert said politely, "Have you finished?"

Helen sighed deeply. It was hopeless. She knew, had always known, that no words would provoke Robert into any action that he did not choose to make. He had never been talked into anything in his life. Her outburst had been a waste of breath and she already regretted it.

"Yes, of course I've finished. And I apologise. It's none of my business and I have no right to interfere. It's just that I like

35

Jane, and I want you to be happy. I don't know, Robert. I can't work out what it is you're looking for.''

"I don't know either," said Robert. He smiled at his sister, and ran a hand over his head and down the back of his neck, a familiar gesture made when he was either confused or tired. "But I think it has something to do with what exists between you and Marcus.''

"Well, I just hope you find it before you drop dead of old age.''

He left her to her cooking, collected his hat and the evening paper and a handful of letters, and went upstairs to his own flat. His sitting-room, which looked out over the big garden and the chestnut tree had once been the nursery. It was low-ceilinged, close-carpeted, lined with books, and furnished with as much of his father's stuff as he had been able to get up the staircase. He dropped his hat and the paper and the letters on a chair, and went to the antique bombé cupboard where he kept his drink, and poured himself a whisky and soda. Then he took a cigarette from the box on the coffee table, lit it, and, cradling his glass, went to sit at the desk, to lift the telephone receiver and dial Jane Marshall's number.

She took some time to answer. While he waited, he doodled on the blotting paper with a pencil, and glanced at his watch and decided that he would have a bath, and change before he went to pick Marcus up at the Cromwell Road terminal. And, as a peace offering to Helen, he would take a bottle of wine downstairs and they would have it with their dinner, the three of them, sitting round the scrubbed table in Helen's kitchen and, inevitably, talking shop. He discovered that he was very tired, and the prospect of such an evening was comforting.

The double burr stopped. A cold voice said, "Jane Marshall here.''

She always answered the telephone in this manner, and Robert still found it chilling, although he knew the reason for it. At twenty-six, Jane, with a broken marriage and a divorce behind her, had been forced to start earning her own living, and had ended up with a modest interior decorating business which she ran from her own house. Thus, a single telephone number had to do double duty, and she had long since decided it was prudent to treat an incoming call as potential business until it proved to be otherwise. She had explained this to Robert when he complained about her frigid manner.

"You don't understand. It might be a client ringing up. What's he going to think if I sound all sexy and treacle-voiced?"

"You don't need to sound sexy. Just friendly and pleasant. Why don't you try it? You'd be ripping out walls and running up curtains and loose covers before you knew where you were."

"That's what you think. More likely to be fending him off with a curved upholstery needle."

Now he said, "Jane . . . ?"

"Oh, Robert." Her voice was at once its normal self, warm and obviously pleased to hear him. "I am sorry, did Helen give you my message?"

"She asked me to call you."

"It's just that I wondered . . . Look, I've been given two tickets for the ballet on Friday. It's La Fille Mal Gardée and I thought you might like to come. Unless you're going away or something."

He looked down at his own hand, drawing boxes, in perfect perspective, on the blotting pad. He heard Helen's voice. *You have everything in common. Interests, friends, a way of life.*

"Robert?"

"Yes. Sorry. No, I'm not going away. I'd love to come."

"Shall we eat here first?"

37

"No, we'll go out. I'll book a table."

"I'm glad you can make it." He could tell that she was smiling. "Is Marcus back yet?"

"No, I'm just going to meet him."

"Send him and Helen my love."

"I will."

"See you Friday, then. Goodbye."

"Goodbye, Jane."

After he had replaced the receiver, he did not get up from his desk, but sat there, his chin in his hand, putting the final touches to the last box. When it was finished, he laid down the pencil and reached for his drink, and sat, looking at what he had drawn, and wondered why it should make him think of a long line of suitcases.

Marcus Bernstein came through the glass doors of the terminal building looking, as he always looked, like a refugee or a street musician. His overcoat sagged, his old-fashioned black hat had somehow got turned up in the front, his long, lined face was sallow with tiredness. He carried his bulging brief-case, but his grip had travelled from the airport in the luggage compartment of the bus, and when Robert found him, he was standing, patiently, by the circular conveyor-belt, awaiting its arrival.

He managed to look both humble and dejected, and the casual passer-by would have found it hard to believe that this modest and unassuming man was, in fact, a powerful influence in the art world on both sides of the Atlantic. An Austrian, he had left his native Vienna in 1937, and after the horrors of an alien's war, had burst upon the post-war art world like a bright flame. His obvious knowledge and perception quickly drew attention, and his backing of young artists showed an example which other dealers were quick to follow. But his real impact upon the lay public was made in 1949, when he opened his own gallery in Kent Street with an exhibition of abstracts by Ben Litton. Ben, already famous for his pre-war landscapes and portraits, had been moving for some time towards this new medium, and the 1949 exhibition was the beginning of a working friendship which rode all personal storms and quarrels. It also marked the end of Marcus's initial struggles, and the start of a long, slow haul to success.

"Marcus!"

He gave a small start, and turned and saw Robert coming towards him, and looked surprised, as though he had not expected to be met.

"Hello, Robert. This is very kind of you."

After thirty years in England, his accent was still strongly marked, but Robert no longer noticed it.

"I would have come to the airport, but we weren't sure if you'd get on the plane. Did you have a good flight?"

"It was snowing in Edinburgh."

"It's been raining here all day. Look, there's your bag." He whipped it off the conveyor-belt. "Come on, now . . ."

In the car, waiting for the lights in the Cromwell Road to change, he told Marcus about Mr Lowell Cheeke returning to Bernstein's to buy the Litton of the deer. Marcus acknowledged this with a grunt, giving the impression that he had known all along that the sale was simply a matter of time. The lights went from red to yellow to green and the car moved forward and Robert said, "And Emma Litton is home from Paris. She flew in this morning. Didn't have any sterling, so she came to the gallery to get you to cash her a cheque. I gave her lunch and twenty pounds and sent her on her way."

"On her way to where?"

"Porthkerris, and Ben."

"I suppose he is there."

"She seemed to think he would be. For the time being, at any rate."

"Poor child," said Marcus.

Robert made no answer to this, and they drove home in silence, each busy with his own thoughts. Back at Milton Gardens, Marcus got out of the car, and went up the steps, feeling for his latchkey, but before he could run it to earth, the door was opened by Helen, and Marcus, in his sagging coat and comic's hat, was silhouetted against the hall light.

She said, "Well, how lovely!" and because he was so much smaller than she, stooped to embrace him, and Robert, extracting Marcus's grip from the boot of the Alvis, tried to work out why it was that they never looked ridiculous.

It seemed to have been dark for a long time. But when the London express came to the junction where she had to change for Porthkerris, and Emma got out of the train, she found that it was not really dark at all. The sky was bright with stars, and the night blown through with a buffeting wind that smelt of the sea. When she had unloaded all her luggage, she stood waiting on the platform for the express to pull out, and above her the tattered leaves of a palm tree rattled incongruously in this restless wind.

The train moved on, and she saw the single porter on the opposite platform, occupied, in a leisurely fashion, with a barrow-load of parcels. When at last he noticed her, he set down the handles of his barrow, and called, across the lines, "Want some help, do you?"

"Yes please."

He jumped down on to the tracks and walked across to her side, and somehow gathered all her belongings into his two arms, and then Emma followed him back across the tracks, and he gave her a hand up on to the other platform.

"Where are you going?"

"Porthkerris."

"Taking the train?"

"Yes."

The smaller train waited on the single line branch track that ran round the coast to Porthkerris. Emma appeared to be the only passenger. She thanked the porter and tipped him and collapsed into a seat. Exhaustion consumed her. Never had a day seemed so long. After a little she was joined by a country woman in a brown hat like a pot. Perhaps she had been shopping, for she carried a bulging, checked leather bag. Minutes passed, the only sound the wind thudding at the closed windows of the train. At last, the engine gave a single whistle and they were off.

It was impossible not to feel excited as familiar landmarks loomed up through the darkness, and were recognised, and then fled past. There were only two small halts before Porthkerris and then, at last, the steep cutting which in spring was quilted in primroses, and then the tunnel, and then the sea was below them, dark as ink, the tide out, the wet sands like satin. Porthkerris was a nest of lights, the curve of the harbour seemed strung with a necklace, and the riding lights of fishing boats were reflected in a maze of shimmering black and gold water.

They had begun to lose speed. The platform slid alongside. The name PORTHKERRIS passed and fell behind. They finally stopped alongside a shiny tin advertisement for boot polish which had been there ever since Emma could remember. Her companion, who had spoken not a word the entire journey, now stood up, opened the door, and stepped sedately out, disappearing into the night. Emma stood in the open door, looking for a porter, but the only visible official was up at the other end of the train, unnecessarily shouting, "Porthkerris! Porthkerris!" She saw him stop to chat to the driver, pushing his cap back off his forehead, and standing with his hands on his hips.

There was an empty barrow by the boot polish advertisement, so she loaded her luggage on to this, and then abandoned it, carrying only a small overnight bag. She began to walk up the platform. In the stationmaster's office, the lights were on, they shone out in warm yellow patches, and a man sat on a bench, reading a newspaper. Emma walked by him, her footsteps ringing on the stone flags, but as she passed, he put down the newspaper and said her name.

Emma stopped, and slowly turned. He folded the newspaper and stood up, and the light seemed to turn his white hair into a halo.

"I thought you were never going to arrive."

"Hello, Ben," said Emma.

"Is the train late, or did I get the times all wrong?"

"I don't think we're late. Perhaps we were late starting from the junction. We seemed to wait there a long time. How did you know what train I'd be on?"

"I had a telegram from Bernstein's." *Robert Morrow*, thought Emma. *How kind*. Ben glanced at her bag. "You haven't much luggage."

"I have a barrow-load at the other end of the platform."

He turned to vaguely peer in the direction that Emma indicated. "Never mind. We'll fetch it some other time. Come on, let's get back."

"But someone might take it," Emma protested. "Or it might rain. We'd better tell the porter."

The porter had by now finished his social chat with the engine driver. Ben attracted his attention, told him about Emma's luggage. "Put it somewhere, would you, we'll collect it tomorrow." He gave him five shillings. The porter said, "Yes, Mr Litton, don't worry, I'll do that," and went off down the platform whistling, tucking the money in the pocket of his waistcoat.

"Well," said Ben again, "what are we waiting for? Come on, let's get moving."

There was no suggestion of a car or a taxi, they were simply going to walk home. They did this by way of a series of narrow short-cuts, steep flights of stone steps, tiny sloping alleys, always leading downhill, until finally they emerged on to the brightly lighted harbour road.

Emma, trudging beside her father, still carrying the overnight bag which he had not thought to carry for her, took a long sideways look at Ben. It was the first time she had seen him for nearly two years, and she thought that no man changed as little as he. He was no fatter, no thinner. His hair, which had been snow-white as long as Emma could remember, was neither thinning nor receding. His face, weathered by years of working in the sun, in the outdoors, by the sea, was darkly tanned and netted with fine lines which could never be described as anything so prosaic as wrinkles. From him, Emma had inherited her strong cheek-bones, and her square chin, but her pale eyes must have come from her mother, for Ben's were deep-set beneath craggy brows, and of so dark a brown that in certain lights they looked black.

Even his clothes did not seem to have changed. The sagging corduroy jacket, the narrowly cut trousers, the suède shoes of immense elegance and age – they could have belonged to no one else. Tonight his shirt was a faded orange wool, a paisley cotton handkerchief did duty as a necktie. He had never owned a waistcoat.

They came to his pub, the Sliding Tackle, and Emma half expected him to suggest that they should go in for a drink.

She did not want a drink, but she was ravenously hungry. She wondered if there was any food in the cottage. She wondered, in fact, if they were actually going to the cottage. It was quite within the bounds of possibility that Ben had been living in his studio, and would expect Emma to shake down there with him.

She said, tentatively, "I don't even know where we're heading for."

"The cottage, of course. Where did you imagine?"

"I didn't know." They were safely past the pub. "I thought perhaps you might have been living at the studio."

"No, I've been staying at the Sliding Tackle. This is the first time I've been to the cottage."

"Oh," said Emma, glumly.

He caught the inflexion in her voice and reassured her. "It's all right. When they knew at the Sliding Tackle that you were turning up there was a positive deputation of eager ladies all wanting to get the place ready for you. In the end Daniel's wife saw to it for me." Daniel was the barman. "She seemed to think that after all these years everything would be covered in blue mould, like Gorgonzola cheese."

"And was it?"

"No, of course it wasn't. A bit cobwebby, perhaps, but perfectly habitable."

"That was kind of her . . . I must thank her."

"Yes, she'd like that."

The cobbled road climbed steeply away from the harbour. Emma's tired legs ached. Suddenly, and with no word of explanation, Ben removed her bag from her grasp.

"What the hell have you got in this?"

"A toothbrush."

"It weighs like pig-iron. When did you leave Paris, Emma?"

"This morning." It seemed a lifetime ago.

"And how did Bernstein's know about you?"

"I had to go there to get some money. Some sterling. I was given twenty pounds out of your petty cash account. I hope you don't mind."

"I don't give a damn."

They passed his studio, shuttered and dark. "Have you started painting yet?" asked Emma.

"Of course I have. That's what I came back for."

"And the work you did in Japan?"

"I left it in America for the exhibition."

Now, the air was full of the sound of surf, of breakers rolling up on to the beach. The big beach. Their beach. And then the uneven roof of their cottage came into view, illuminated by the street lamp which stood by the blue gate. As they approached it, Ben felt in his jacket pocket for the key, and he went ahead of Emma, through the gate and down the steps, unlocking the door, and letting himself in, switching on the lights as he went, so that in a moment every window was blazing.

Emma followed more slowly. She saw at once the bright flicker of firelight and the almost inhuman cleanliness and order which Daniel's wife had somehow created out of neglect. Everything shone, was scrubbed and whitewashed and polished to within an inch of its life. Cushions had been plumped and placed with geometrical precision. There were no flowers, but the house was pervaded with a strong smell of carbolic.

Ben sniffed and made a face. "Like a bloody hospital," he said. He had put down Emma's bag, and now disappeared in the direction of the kitchen. Emma crossed the room and stood at the fireplace, warming her hands at the blaze. Cautiously, she was beginning to feel more hopeful. She had been afraid that there would be no welcome. But Ben had met her train and there was a fire in the fireplace. No human being could ask for much more.

Over the mantelshelf was the room's only picture, the painting that Ben had done of Emma when she was six years old. It was the first time in her life – and, it transpired, the last – that she had been the centre of his attention, and, for this reason alone she had borne uncomplaining the long hours of sitting, the boredom, the cramps, and his unleashed fury if she moved. For the picture, she had worn a wreath of marguerite daisies, and each day had brought the recurring pleasure of watching Ben's clever hands make a fresh wreath, and then the pride of having him place it on her head, solemnly, as though he were crowning a queen.

He came back into the room. "She's a good woman, that wife of Daniel's. I shall tell him so. I told her to stock up with a few supplies." Emma turned, and saw that he had found himself a bottle of Haig and a tumbler. "Get me a jug of water, would you, Emma?" A thought occurred to him. "And I suppose another glass, if you want a drink."

"I don't want a drink. But I'm hungry."

"I don't know if she laid in *those* sort of supplies."

"I'll look."

The kitchen, too, had been scoured and scrubbed and swept. She opened the fridge and found eggs and bacon and a bottle of milk, and there was bread in the bin. She took a jug off a hook on the dresser and filled it with cold water, and carried it back into the sitting-room. Ben was wandering about, fiddling with the lamps, trying to find something wrong. He had always hated this house.

She said, "Do you want me to cook you some scrambled eggs?"

"What? Oh, no, I don't want anything. You know, it's odd being back here. I keep feeling Hester's going to appear and tell us to start doing something we don't want to."

Emma thought of Christopher. She said, "Oh, poor Hester."

"Poor nothing. Interfering bitch."

She went back to the kitchen, found a saucepan, a bowl, some butter. From the living-room, she could hear the continued sounds of Ben's restlessness. He opened and shut doors, drew a curtain, kicked a log back on to the fire. Presently, he appeared in the kitchen doorway, a cigarette in one hand, his glass cradled in the other. He watched Emma, stirring eggs. He said, "You've grown up, haven't you?"

"I'm nineteen. Whether I've grown up or not, I really wouldn't know."

"It's odd, your not being a little girl any longer."

"You'll get used to it."

"Yes, I suppose so. How long are you going to stay?"

"Let's say I've made no plans for going away again."

"You mean, you want to live here?"

"For the time being."

"With me?"

Emma glanced at him, over her shoulder. "Would that be so painful?"

"I don't know," said Ben. "I've never tried it."

"That's why I came back. I thought perhaps it was time you did."

"You couldn't, by any chance, be reproaching me?"

"Why should I reproach you?"

"Because I abandoned you, and went off to teach in Texas. Because I never came to see you in Switzerland. Because I wouldn't let you come to Japan."

"If I really minded about those things, I shouldn't have wanted to come back."

"And supposing I decide to go away again?"

"Are you going to go?"

"No." He looked down at his drink. "Not for the moment.

47

At the moment I'm tired. I've come back for a bit of peace." He looked up again. "But I shan't stay here for ever."

"I shan't stay here for ever, either," said Emma. She put the toast on a plate, the egg on the toast, opened a drawer to find a knife and fork.

Ben watched all this with some agitation. "You aren't going to be an efficient little housewife, are you? Another Hester? If so, I shall throw you out."

"I couldn't be efficient if I tried. If it's any comfort to you, I miss trains, burn food, lose money, drop things. I had a sun hat, this morning, in Paris, but by the time I'd got to Porthkerris, it had gone. How could anyone lose a sun hat in this country, in February?"

But he was still not convinced. "Won't you want to be driving around in a car all the time?"

"I don't know how to drive a car."

"And television and telephones and all that rubbish?"

"They've never figured largely in my life."

He laughed then, and Emma wondered if there was something wrong in thinking your own father so attractive.

He said, "You know, I wasn't sure how well this was going to work. But under such favourable circumstances, I can only say I'm glad you came back. Welcome home."

And he raised his glass to Emma and finished his drink, and then went back to the sitting-room to retrieve the bottle and pour himself the other half.

4

The bar of the Sliding Tackle was small and snug, blackly panelled, very old. It boasted only one tiny window, which looked out over the harbour, so that a visitor's first impression, as he came in from the glaring outside light, was one of utter darkness. Later, when his eyes became accustomed to the gloom, other peculiarities became evident, the most prominent being that there were not two parallel lines in the place, for over the centuries the little pub had settled into its foundations, like a deep sleeper in a comfortable bed, and various irregularities, like optical illusions, were apt to make potential customers feel intoxicated before they had even downed their first drink. The flagged floor sank in one direction, displaying a sinister gap between stone and wainscoting. The blackened beam, which formed the framework of the bar itself, sloped in another. And the whitewashed ceiling had such a lethal tilt to it that the landlord had been driven to put up notices saying "Watch That Beam" and "Mind Your Head".

Over the years the Sliding Tackle had remained, stubbornly, itself. Set in the old and unfashionable part of Porthkerris, slap on the harbour, with no space for chi-chi terraces or tea gardens, it had managed to resist the spate of summer tourism which engulfed the rest of the town. It had its regulars, who came to drink, and talk in comfortable, undemanding grunts, and play shove-ha'penny. It had a dart board and a small blackened grate where, winter and summer, a fire always burned. It had Daniel, the barman, and Fred, turnip-faced and squint-eyed, who was employed in the summer cleaning trash from the beaches and hiring out deckchairs, and spent the rest of the year blissfully drinking his takings.

And it had Ben Litton.

"It's a matter of priorities," said Marcus, as he and Robert set forth in the Alvis to run Ben Litton to earth. It was so fine that Robert had put the hood down, and so Marcus wore, with his habitual black overcoat, a tweed cap like a mushroom that looked as though it had been bought for some other person. "Priorities and timing. At mid-day on a Sunday, the first place to look is the Sliding Tackle. And if he isn't there, which I very much doubt, we'll go on to the studio, and then try the cottage."

"Or maybe, on such a wonderful morning, just out and about?"

"I don't think so. This is his drinking time, and as far as that is concerned, he has always been a creature of habit."

Still only March, it was indeed a freak day of unbelievable beauty. The sky was cloudless. The sea, driven obliquely into the curve of the bay by a buffeting north-west wind, lay streaked before them in every shade of blue, from deep indigo to palest turquoise. From the top of the hill, the view stretched to infinity, distant headlands merging into a haze that suggested the full heat of midsummer. And below, down the twisting road, the town dropped steeply, a jumble of narrow cobbled lanes, and whitewashed houses, and bleached, crooked roofs, clustered around the harbour.

Each year, during the three months of summer, Porthkerris

became a small hell on earth. Its inadequate streets were jammed with cars, its pavements overflowed with underdressed humanity, its shops spilled over with postcards, sun hats, sand-shoes, shrimping-nets, surfboards and inflatable plastic cushions. On the big beach the tents and the bathing huts went up, and the cafés opened, their terraces crammed with round iron tables, speared by umbrellas. Orange banners flapped in the wind, advertising Raspberry Sticks, and Frozen Chocolate-Coated Clusters and other horrors, and if these were not sustenance enough, there were Cornish splits for sale, and pasties, filled with soggy grey potato.

And around Whitsun, the amusement arcade opened up, with pin-ball machines and juke boxes blaring, and perhaps another cluster of ramshackle but picturesque houses would go down before the bulldozers, to clear the space for yet another car park, and the residents, and the people who loved the town, and the artists, would be horrified witnesses to this rape and say, *It's worse than ever. It is ruined. We can stay no longer.* But each autumn, once the last train had borne away the last peeling-nosed invader, Porthkerris settled back, miraculously, in its normal tempo. The shops put up their shutters. The tents came down, and the beaches were washed clean by the winter storms. The only flags which flew were lines of washing, flapping from house to house, like pastel-coloured bunting, or propped high over the greenswards where the fishermen spread their nets to dry.

And it was then that the old magic reasserted itself, and it became easy to understand why a man like Ben Litton should return time and time again, like a homing pigeon, for refreshment, and the security of familiar things, to be caught up once more in the painter's obsession with colour and light.

The Sliding Tackle was at the far end of the harbour road. Robert drew up outside its crooked porch and killed the engine.

It was very warm and quiet. The tide was out, the harbour full of clean sand and seaweed and screaming gulls. Some children, coaxed out by the sunshine, played with buckets and spades, watched over by a couple of knitting grannies in pinafores and hairnets, and a scrawny black cat sat on the cobbles and washed its ears.

Marcus got out of the car. "I'll go and see if he's inside. You wait here."

Robert took a cigarette from the packet on the dashboard and lit it, and watched the cat. Above his head the inn sign creaked in the wind, and a gull came and sat on it and eyed Robert with malevolence, screaming defiance. Two men came down the road, walking with the slow righteous gait of a restful Methodist Sunday. They wore navy blue guernseys and white cloth caps.

" 'Morning," they said as they passed.

"Lovely day," said Robert.

"Yes. Lovely."

After a little, Marcus appeared once more. "All right, I've found him."

"What about Emma?"

"He says she's back at the studio. Whitewashing."

"Want me to go and get her?"

"If you would. It's . . ." he glanced at his watch, "twelve-fifteen. Suppose you're back here at one. I said we'd lunch at one-thirty."

"Right. I'll walk. It's not worth taking the car."

"Can you remember the way?"

"Of course." He had been before, twice, to Porthkerris, chasing up Ben Litton for some reason or other when Marcus had not been available to do it for himself. Ben's phobia about telephones and cars and all forms of communication, presented,

from time to time, the most hideous complications, and Marcus
had long since accepted the fact that it was quicker to make the
journey from London to Cornwall and beard the lion in his den
than to wait for an answer to the most impassioned of reply-paid
telegrams.

He got out of the car and slammed the door shut. "Do you
want me to tell her what it's all about, or shall I leave that
pleasant task to you?"

Marcus grinned. "You tell her."

Robert pulled off his narrow tweed cap and dropped it on to
the driving seat. He said, amiably, "You bastard."

He had had a letter from Emma, a week or two after she passed
through London.

Dear Robert,

*If I call Marcus Marcus, I can't possibly call you Mr
Morrow, can I? No, of course I can't, not possibly. I should
have written at once to thank you so very much for the lunch
and for letting me have the money, and for letting Ben know
that I was on the train. He actually came to meet me at
the station. Everything is going wonderfully well, so far we
haven't had a row, and Ben is working like a fiend on four
canvases at once.*

*I didn't lose any of my luggage except the sun hat, which
I'm sure someone stole.*

My love to Marcus. And you.
Emma.

Now, he made his way through the baffling maze of narrow
streets and tightly-packed houses that led to the north shore of
the town. Here, there was another beach, a bleak and unprotected
bay only esteemed for the long surfing rollers which poured in,

53

straight from the Atlantic. Ben Litton's studio faced out over this beach. Once, long ago, it had been a net store and its only access was a cobbled ramp which sloped down from the street to a double, black-tarred door. There was a printed sign with his name, and an immense iron knocker, and Robert took hold of this and banged it, and called "Emma."

There was no reply. He opened the door, and it was immediately almost torn from his hand by a gust of wind which poured, like a torrent of water, through the open window on the far side of the studio. Once the door had slammed shut again behind him, the draught subsided. The studio was empty and bitterly cold. There was no sign of Emma, but a step ladder and whitewash brush and bucket bore witness to her recent occupation. She had finished the whole of one wall, but when he went to touch it with his hand, he found that it was still cold and damp.

From the middle of this wall protruded an ugly old-fashioned stove, empty now and unlit, and beside it a gas ring, a battered kettle, and an upturned orange box containing blue and white striped mugs and a jar of sugar lumps. On the opposite side of the room stood Ben's work table, littered with drawings and papers, tubes of paint, and hundreds of pencils and brushes all contained on sheets of corrugated cardboard. The wall above this table was dark and dirty with age, and smeared with the scrapings of countless palette knives, that had built up, over the years, into a crustaceous shell of colour. At the top of the desk was a narrow level shelf, and on this ranged a selection of *objets trouvés* which at some time or another had caught Ben's eye. A stone from the shore, a fossilised starfish. A blue jug of dried grasses. A postcard reproduction of a Picasso; a piece of bleached driftwood, carved by sea and wind to abstract sculpture. There were photographs, a fan of curling snapshots, arranged in an old silver menu-holder; an invitation to a private view that had taken place six years ago, and, finally, a heavy, old-fashioned pair of binoculars.

At floor level, the walls were stacked with leaning canvases, and in the middle of the room the current work stood, easeled and shrouded with a faded pink cloth. Turned towards the empty stove was a sagging sofa, draped in what looked like the remains of an Arabic rug. There was also an old kitchen table, with its legs cut short, and on this a tin of cigarettes, and an overflowing ash-tray, a pile of *Studios*, and a green glass bowl, full of painted china eggs.

The north wall was all glass, squared off by narrow wooden partitions and designed so that its lower portions would slide aside. Along the foot of this was a long seat, piled with cushions, and from beneath this protruded further ill-assorted flotsam. The spars of a boat, a stack of surfboards, and a crate of empty bottles, and, in the middle, beneath the open window, two iron hooks had been screwed into the floor, and on to those were looped the spliced ends of a rope ladder. This disappeared out of the window, and Robert, going to investigate, saw that it dropped straight down to the sand, twenty feet below.

The beach appeared to be empty. The ebb tide had left it a sweep of hard clean sand, divided from the sky by a narrow line of frothing white breakers. Further inshore, there was a stratum of rock, crusted with shellfish and seaweed, and over this the seagulls hovered, occasionally pouncing to fight and scream over some prize. Robert sat on the window-seat, and lit himself a cigarette. When he looked up again, a figure had appeared on the horizon, right on the edge of the sea. It wore a long white gown, like an Arab's, and as it walked back towards the studio, appeared to be wrestling with some large and unidentifiable red package.

He remembered the binoculars on Ben's table and went to

fetch them. Focused, the figure sprang into relief, and revealed itself as Emma Litton, long hair blowing, dressed in a huge white towelling robe and lugging, with some difficulty, for the wind kept catching it broadside and jerking it out of her grasp, a scarlet surfboard.

"You surely haven't been swimming?"

Emma, struggling with the surfboard, had not seen him at the window. Now, with a hand on the rope ladder, she nearly jumped out of her skin at the sound of his voice. She looked up, trailing the surfboard in the sand, her wet black hair ripped to ribbons by the wind.

"Yes, I have, and what a fright you gave me. How long have you been there?"

"About ten minutes. How are you going to get the surfboard up the ladder?"

"I was wondering that, but now you've turned up all my problems are solved. There's a rope under the seat. If you chuck one end down, I'll tie it on, and you can pull it up for me."

This was duly accomplished. Robert hauled the board through the open window, and hard on its heels came Emma herself, her face and hands and feet crusted with dry sand, and her black lashes spiked like starfish.

She knelt on the window-seat, and laughed at him. "Now, wasn't that the luckiest thing! What would I have done? I could hardly get it over the beach, let alone up the ladder."

Beneath the sand, her face looked blue with cold. He said, "Come along in, and get the window shut . . . that wind's freezing. How could you bear to go and swim? You'll die of pneumonia."

"No I won't." She stepped down on to the floor, and watched him furl the ladder in and slide the window shut. It did not fit properly and there was still a draught like the edge of a knife. "Anyway, I'm used to it. We always used to swim in April when we were children."

"This isn't April. It's March. It's winter. What would your father say?"

"Oh, he wouldn't say anything. And it's such an utterly gorgeous day and I was sick of whitewashing . . . have you seen my lovely clean wall? The only thing is, it makes the rest of the studio look like a slum. Besides, I wasn't swimming, I was surfing, and the breakers kept me warm." And then, without any noticeable change of expression, "Have you come to see Ben? He's down at the Sliding Tackle."

"Yes, I know."

"How do you know?"

"Because I left Marcus there with him."

"Marcus." She raised her strongly-marked eyebrows, considering this. "Has Marcus come too? My goodness, it must be important business!"

She shivered slightly.

Robert said, "Do get some clothes on."

"Oh, I'm all right." She went to take a cigarette from the table, and lit it, and then collapsed on to the old sofa, flat on her back, with her feet propped on the arm.

"Did you get my letter?"

"Yes, I did." With Emma taking up all the sofa, there was nowhere to sit but on the table, so he eased the pile of magazines on to the floor, and sat there. "I was sorry about your sun hat."

Emma laughed. "But glad about Ben?"

"Of course."

"It's amazing how well it's working. Unbelievable. And he really likes having me around."

"I never imagined for a moment that he wouldn't."

"Oh, don't start being gallant. You know you did. At lunch that day, you were all quizzical eyebrows and scepticism. But you see, it really is the perfect arrangement. Ben doesn't have to pay me to keep house for him, or be bothered with tedious details like days off and insurance stamps, nor does he have to become emotionally involved. He never knew that life could be so simple."

"Have you heard from Christopher?"

Emma turned her head sideways to look at him. "How do you know about Christopher?"

"You told me yourself. At Marcello's. Remember?"

"So I did. No, I haven't heard. But he'll be at Brookford by now, in the thick of rehearsals. He won't have had time to write. Anyway, there's been such a lot to do here, getting the cottage organised and cooking and things. Don't believe people when they say that artists never eat. Ben's inner man is quite insatiable."

"Have you told him you met up with Christopher again?"

"Good heavens, no! And spoil the even tenor of our life? I haven't even mentioned his name. You know, you look much nicer in those tweedy sort of clothes than you do in the London kind. I thought when I first saw you that you weren't the type to spend his days buttoned up in a charcoal grey suit. When did you get down here?"

"We drove yesterday afternoon. We spent last night at The Castle."

Emma made a face. "In with all the potted palms and the cashmere cardigans. Ugh!"

"It's very comfortable."

"The central heating gives me hay fever. I can't even breathe."

She stubbed her half-smoked cigarette out in the overflowing ash-tray, and swung her feet off the sofa, and stood up and walked away from him, towards the window, untying the sash of the robe as she went. She took a pile of clothes from beneath a cushion, and with her back to him, started to dress. She said, "Why did you and Marcus come together?"

"Marcus doesn't drive."

"There are trains. And that wasn't what I meant."

"No, I know." He picked up one of the painted china eggs and began to play with it as an Arab handles a string of worry beads. "We've come to try and persuade Ben to go back to the United States."

There was a sudden great squall of wind. It broke over the glass window of the studio like a wave, poured, roaring over the roof above them, with the thunder of a passing train. A cluster of gulls rose screaming from the rocks, were flung across the sky. And then, as suddenly, it was over.

Emma said, "Why does he have to go back?"

"This retrospective exhibition."

She dropped the white towelling robe, and stood silhouetted, in jeans, pulling a navy blue sweater over her head.

"But I thought he and Marcus fixed all that when they were in New York in January."

"We thought so too. But you see, this exhibition is being sponsored by a private individual."

"I know," said Emma, turning, and flipping her dark hair free of the turtle-neck of the sweater. "I read all about it in *Réalités*. Mrs Kenneth Ryan. The widow of the wealthy man whose memorial is the Queenstown Museum of Fine Arts. You see how well informed I am. I hope you're impressed."

"And Mrs Kenneth Ryan wants a private view."

"Then why didn't she say so?"

"Because she wasn't in New York. She was sunning it in

Nassau or the Bahamas or Palm Beach or somewhere. They never met her. They only saw the curator of the museum.''

"And now Mrs Ryan wants Ben Litton to go back, so that she can throw a nice little champagne party and show him off, like a trophy, to all her influential friends. It makes me sick.''

"She's done more than decide, Emma. She's come to persuade him.''

"You mean come to England?''

"I mean come to England, come to Bernstein's, come to Porthkerris. She drove down with Marcus and me yesterday and at this very moment, is sitting in the bar of The Castle Hotel, drinking very cold Martinis and waiting for us all to go and have lunch with her.''

"Well, I for one am not going.''

"You have to. We're all expected." He glanced at his wrist-watch. "And we're running late. Do hurry up.''

"Does Ben know about the private view?''

"He will by now. Marcus will have told him.''

She picked up a brown sailcloth smock off the floor and pulled it on over her sweater. As her head came through the neck, she said, "Ben may not want to go.''

"You mean you don't want him to go?''

"I mean that he's settled down here again. He's not prowling, he's not restless, he's not even drinking very much. He's working like a young man, and what he's doing is fresh and new and better than ever. Ben is sixty, you know. Looking at him, it's hard to believe, but he's nearly sixty. Isn't it possible that all this hopping about all over the world may no longer stimulate him, but simply wear him out?'' She came back to the sofa to sit down, facing Robert, her earnest face on a level with his own. "Please. If he doesn't want to go, don't try to persuade him.''

Robert still held the china egg. He looked at it intently as though its convolutions of blue and green would miraculously provide the answer to every problem. Then, with care, he laid it back in the glass dish, along with its fellows.

He said, "You talk as though this were something important, as though he were returning to the States to teach again, as though he weren't going to come back for years. But it isn't. It's simply a party. He needn't be away for more than a few days." She opened her mouth with a fresh protest, but he talked her down. "And you mustn't forget that this exhibition is a great tribute to Ben. A lot of money's been ploughed into it, and a great deal of organisation, and perhaps the least he can do . . ."

Furiously, Emma interrupted. "The least he can do is go and parade up and down like a pet monkey for some fat old American. And what makes it so awful is that he likes that sort of thing. That's what I hate, that he likes it."

"So he likes it. So, if he wants to, he'll go."

She was silenced. She sat, eyes downcast, her mouth sulky as a child's. Robert finished his cigarette and stubbed it out, and stood up and said, more gently, "Now, do come on or we're going to be late. Have you got a coat?"

"No."

"Some shoes then, you must have some shoes."

She felt under the sofa and produced a pair of thong sandals, and stood up, thrusting her bare feet into them. Her feet were still covered in sand, and the sailcloth smock spotted in whitewash.

She said, "I can't go to The Castle, for lunch, looking like this."

"Nonsense." He tried to sound bracing. "You'll give the residents something to talk about. Brighten their dull lives no end."

"Isn't there time to go back to the cottage? I haven't even got a comb."

"There'll be a comb at the hotel."

"But . . ."

"There simply isn't time. We're late already. Now come along . . ."

They went together, out of the studio and up the ramp, and into the sunlit street, and began to walk back towards the harbour. After the chill of the studio the air felt warm, and the brightness of the sea was reflected from the whitewashed walls of houses, and assailed the eye like the glare of snow.

5

Emma did not want to go into the Sliding Tackle.

"I'll wait here. You go and prise them out."

"All right."

He went across the cobbles, and she noticed how he had to duck his tall head to get in under the porch. The door of the pub swung shut behind him. She wandered over to his car and inspected it with interest, because it belonged to him, and should therefore provide further clues to his character, as a shelf of book-titles will do, or the pictures that a man hangs on his walls. But, apart from the fact that it was dark-green, had fog lights and wire wheels and a couple of car-club badges, the Alvis gave little away. Inside on the driving-seat was a tweed cap; cigarettes in the dashboard cupboard, a book of maps. On the back seat, neatly folded, a thick, expensive-looking tartan rug. She decided that he was either trusting, or careless, but also lucky, for the rug had not been stolen.

A gust of wind blew in from the sea and Emma shivered. After the swim and the session in the draughty studio, she still was very cold. Her hands had gone numb, quite colourless, the fingernails tinged with blue. But the metal of the car was warm, and, for comfort, she leaned against it, spreadeagled across the bonnet, with her hands splayed like starfish.

The pub door opened and Robert Morrow emerged once more, ducking cautiously. He was alone.

"Aren't they there?"

"No. We're late, and they got fed up with waiting, so they got a lift back to the hotel." He opened the driving-seat door, picked up his cap and pulled it on, jerked down over his nose, to add yet another sharp angle to his formidable profile. "Come on . . ." And he leaned over and opened the other door, and Emma unpeeled herself from the bonnet, and slid in beside him.

They left the harbour behind and below them, roared up through the town, up the steep narrow streets, up between terraces of prim houses, and the signs which said Bed and Breakfast, and front gardens where sad palm trees tossed their heads in the alien wind. They came out on to the main road, still climbing, turned into the drive of The Castle Hotel; climbed on, between banks of hydrangeas, and landward-leaning elm trees, and at last came out at the very top of the hill, into an open space of tennis courts, and lawns, and a miniature golf course. The hotel had once been a country house, and prided itself on its authentic atmosphere. A white post and chain fence kept cars away from the gravel sweep in front of the hotel, and here, in deckchairs, sat a handful of hardy residents, scarved, gloved and swaddled in rugs, like the passengers of some trans-Atlantic liner. They read books or newspapers, but when the Alvis roared up the drive and drew up with a massive scrunch of gravel, these were lowered, and in some cases, spectacles were removed, and Robert and Emma's progress observed and noted as though they were visitors from another planet.

Robert said, "We're probably the first exciting thing to happen since the manager fell into the swimming-pool."

Once inside the revolving doors, the heat of the place struck like a newly-opened oven. Emma professed to despise such comfort, but today it was blissfully welcome.

She said, "I expect they'll be in the bar. You go, I'll be there in a moment. I must try and get rid of some of this sand."

In the Ladies', she washed her hands and her face, and rubbed the sand off her feet on to the back of her jeans, like a schoolboy trying to polish his shoes. There was a pretentious set of brushes and combs on a beruffled dressing-table, and she used the comb on the snarls of her hair, breaking half the teeth, but reducing the tangled mass into some sort of order. As she turned back for the door, she caught sight of herself in the long mirror. No make-up, faded jeans, whitewash stains. She pulled off the offending smock, and then was infuriated with herself for minding about anything so trivial as her own personal appearance, and pulled it on again. They would think she was a beatnik art student. A model. Ben Litton's mistress. Let them. As Robert Morrow had so rightly said, it would give them something to talk about.

But as she emerged from the Ladies' and went down the long, carpeted hall, she was grateful to see that Robert Morrow had not abandoned her and gone to join the others, as she had told him to, but was waiting for her by the porter's desk, reading a Sunday paper which had been left on a chair. When he saw her coming, he folded the paper and tossed it down again, and gave her a grin of encouragement.

"You've done splendidly," he said.

"I've ruined the hotel comb. Ever so nice it was, too, one of a matching set. You didn't need to wait. I've been before and I know the way . . ."

"Come along, then."

It was a quarter to two, and the busy Sunday lunch-time session was over. Only a few serious drinkers still sat at the bar, cradling their gin and tonics and beginning to look a bit red in the face. Ben Litton, Marcus Bernstein and Mrs Kenneth Ryan were over on the other side of the room, grouped in the bay formed by a huge picture window. Mrs Ryan was on the window-seat, against a backdrop like a travel agent's poster — a shout of blue sea, a sweep of sky, and the green undulations of the miniature golf course. The two men, Ben in his French workman's *bleus*, and Marcus in his dark suit, were talking, turned slightly towards her, so that it was Mrs Ryan who first saw Emma and Robert.

"Well, look who's here . . ." she said.

They turned. Ben remained sitting, but Marcus stood up and came to greet Emma, his arms outstretched, his pleasure at seeing her both genuine and demonstrative and very un-British. He could on occasion be almost embarrassingly Austrian.

"Emma, my darling child. Here you are at last." He put his hands to her shoulders and kissed her, formally, on both cheeks. "What a pleasure to see you again, after this very long time. How long is it? Five years? Six years? What a lot we have to talk about. Come along, and meet Mrs Ryan." He took her hand to lead her over. ". . . But your hand is like a block of ice. What have you been doing?"

"Nothing," said Emma, catching Robert's eyes, and daring him to say more.

"And your bare feet . . . how can you stand it? Mrs Ryan, this is Ben's daughter, Emma, but don't shake hands with her, or you will die of shock."

"I can think of worse ways to die," said Mrs Ryan, and held out her hand. "How do you do?"

They shook hands. "I must say, you are very cold."

On an insane impulse, Emma said, "I was swimming. That's why we're late. And why I'm so untidy. There wasn't time to go back to change."

"Oh, but you don't look untidy, you look charming. Sit down
. . . we have time for another drink, don't we? The dining-room
isn't going to shut down on us or anything like that. Robert,
would you be a darling, and order another round for us. What
would you like, Emma?"

"I . . . I don't really want anything." Ben gave a small cough.
"Well . . . a glass of sherry."

"And we're all drinking martinis, Robert. If you want one
too?" Emma lowered herself carefully on to the chair that
Marcus had vacated, aware of her father watching her from the
other side of the table.

"I simply don't believe," said Mrs Ryan, "that you really
have been swimming."

"Not really. I just went in and out again. There were huge
waves."

"But won't you get the most terrible chill? It can't be good
for you." She turned to Ben. "You don't approve, surely, of
swimming when it's as cold as this? Haven't you got any
influence on your daughter?"

Her voice was gay and teasing. Ben made some reply, and she
went on, telling him that he should be ashamed of himself . . .
that she could see he was an outrageous father . . .

Emma did not listen. She was far too busy looking. For Mrs
Ryan was not old and fat, but young and beautiful and very
attractive, and from the top of her smoothly-coiffed golden
blonde head to the tips of her shining crocodile pumps there
was no single detail that did not give active pleasure. Her eyes
were enormous and blue as violets, her mouth full and sweet-
tempered, and when she smiled, as she did now, revealed two
perfect rows of even, white, American teeth. She wore a most
becoming suit of rose-pink tweed, the collar and cuffs edged
with starched white pique. Diamonds sparkled from her ears,

her lapel, her neatly-manicured hands. There was nothing vulgar about her, nothing brash. Even her scent was flower-like.

". . . The fact that she has been away from you for six years is all the more reason for you to take care of her now."

"I don't take care of her . . . she takes care of me . . ."

"Now there is a real man talking . . ." Her soft, southern voice made the words sound like a caress.

Emma's eyes moved round to her father. His attitude was a characteristic one, legs crossed, right elbow resting on his knee, his chin supported by his thumb, a cigarette between his fingers, its smoke rising before his eyes. The eyes were dark as black coffee, deeply shadowed, and they watched Mrs Ryan as though she were a fascinating new specimen, caught between the glass plates of a laboratory slide.

"Emma, your drink."

It was Marcus. She dragged her eyes from Ben and Mrs Ryan and turned to him in relief.

"Oh, thank you . . ."

He sat beside her. "Robert has told you about the private view?"

"Yes, he told me."

"Are you angry with us?"

"No." And this was true. You could not be angry with such an honest man who came so instantly to the point.

"But you don't want him to go?"

"Did Robert say that?"

"No, he didn't say. But I know you very well. And I know how long you've waited to be with Ben. But it's only for a little while."

"Yes." She looked down at her drink. "He really is going, then?"

"Yes, he really is going. But not until the end of the month."

"I see."

Marcus said, gently, ". . . if you wanted to go with him . . ."

"No. No, I don't want to go to America."

"Do you mind being alone?"

"No. It doesn't bother me. And, as you say, it won't be for long."

"You could come to London, and stay with Helen and myself. You could have David's room."

"Where would David sleep?"

"It is so sad, he is away at boarding school. It broke my heart, but I am now an Englishman and my son was torn from me at eight years old. Come and stay, Emma. In London, there is a lot to see. The Tate Gallery has been re-hung, and it is a masterpiece . . ."

Despite herself Emma began to smile.

"What are you laughing about, you horrible child?"

"I'm laughing at your shamelessness. You take my father away with one hand, and offer me the Tate Gallery with the other. And," she added, dropping her voice, "nobody bothered to tell me that Mrs Kenneth Ryan was the Beauty Queen of Southern Virginia."

"We didn't know," said Marcus. "We had never seen her. She flew to England on an impulse, she walked into the Bernstein Galleries the day before yesterday and said she wanted to see Ben Litton, and that was the first time I had ever set eyes on her."

"Well, she's certainly worth setting eyes on."

"Yes," said Marcus. He looked across at Mrs Ryan with his sad, hound's eyes. He looked at Ben. He looked back into his Martini, and touched the sliver of lemon peel with his forefinger. "Yes," he said again.

Their arrival, late, in the dining-room caused something of a stir. The best table had been reserved for them, the round one in the window, and it was necessary to cross the length of the floor to get there. Mrs Ryan led the way, aware of adulation from every eye in the room, and apparently unconcerned. She was quite used to it. Behind her came Marcus, shabby, but oddly distinguished and obviously interesting. Then Robert and Emma, and finally Ben. Ben fell behind to stub out his cigarette and made what amounted to a star entrance, stopping for a moment in the doorway to speak to the head waiter, so that by the time he did move forward into the room, he was the sole centre of attraction.

Ben Litton . . . There's Ben Litton, the whispers went up, as he walked between the tables, magnificent in his blue French overalls, the red and white scarf knotted at his throat, his white hair thick as a young man's, a quiff like a comma falling across his forehead.

Ben Litton . . . you know, the painter.

It was exciting. Everybody knew that Ben Litton had a studio in Porthkerris, but if you were determined to actually see him, you had to make your way down to the town, and find a fisherman's pub called the Sliding Tackle, and there sit, in the stuffy gloom, making a glass of warm beer last as long as possible, and wait for him to come. It was rather like a strange form of bird-watching.

But today, Ben Litton had abandoned his usual haunts, and was here, at The Castle Hotel, about to eat Sunday lunch, like any other ordinary human being. The mountain had come to Mahomet. An elderly lady stared openly at him through her lorgnette, and a visiting Texan was heard mourning the fact that he had left his flash camera in the bedroom.

Emma caught Robert Morrow's eye, and just managed to suppress a snort of laughter.

Ben reached the table at last, settled himself in the place of honour at Mrs Ryan's right, picked up a menu, and suggested, simply by raising a finger, that the wine waiter should be fetched. Gradually, the excitement in the dining-room died down, but it was obvious that for the rest of the meal they would be the object of all attention.

Emma said to Robert, "I know I shouldn't approve – I should be ashamed of such blatant exhibitionism, but somehow, he gets away with it every time."

"Well, at least it's made you laugh, and you've stopped looking all pinched and nervous."

"You might have told me Mrs Ryan was young and beautiful."

"She's certainly beautiful. But I don't think she's as young as she appears. Well-preserved more like it."

"That's the sort of bitchy remark a woman would make."

"I'm sorry. It was meant with the best will in the world."

"You still should have told me."

"You never asked."

"No, but I made some remark about fat old Americans, and even then you didn't put me right."

"Perhaps I didn't realise that it was so important to you."

"A beautiful woman and Ben Litton, and you didn't realise it was important? It's more than that; it's lethal. One thing, you and Marcus won't have to do any persuading. Ben is going to America. One sweep of those lashes, and he was already mid-Atlantic."

"I don't think you're being entirely fair. The longest lashes in the world wouldn't sweep him into anything he didn't want to do."

"No, but he could never resist a challenge."

Her voice was cold.

Robert said, "Emma."

She turned to look at him. "What?"

"Your resentment is showing." He measured between his forefinger and thumb. "Just the very smallest amount."

"Yes... well..." She decided to change the subject. "When do you go back to London?"

"This very afternoon." He glanced at his watch. "We're running late, as it is. We'll need to leave, as soon as I can coax Little Miss Millions away."

But Mrs Ryan was not to be hurried. The luncheon wore on through four courses, through wine and brandy and coffee, served in the now-empty dining-room, because she did not want to move from their table. At last, taking advantage of a pause in the conversation, Robert cleared his throat, and said, "Marcus, I am sorry to interrupt, but I really think we should make a start, we've got a three hundred mile drive."

Mrs Ryan seemed astonished. "But whatever time is it?"

"Nearly four o'clock."

She laughed. "Already! It's like being in Spain. I once went to a lunch party in Spain, and we didn't get up from the table until half past seven in the evening. Why does time have to go so fast when you're really enjoying yourself?"

"Cause and effect," said Ben.

Across the table, she smiled at Robert. "You don't want to leave right away, do you?"

"Well... as soon as possible."

"But I wanted to see the studio. I can't come all the way across the Atlantic, and all the way down to Porthkerris and not see Ben's studio. Couldn't we drop in just for a moment, on the way back to London?"

This light-hearted suggestion was received in silence. Robert and Marcus both looked momentarily confused; Robert, because he did not want to put off any more time, and Marcus, because he knew that of all things, Ben hated to have his studio inspected. Emma also experienced a sinking of the heart. The studio was in chaos – not Ben's chaos which was of no account, but her own chaos. She thought of the step ladder, and the whitewash bucket, the wet towelling coat, and the bathing-suit which she had left abandoned on the floor, the brimming ash-trays, and the sagging sofa, and the sand everywhere. She looked at Ben, praying for him to refuse. They all looked at Ben, waiting like puppets, to see which way he would jerk the strings.

But for once he did not let them down.

"My dear Mrs Ryan, despite the pleasure it would give me to show you my studio, I think I should point out that it is not on the way to London."

They all looked at her, to see how she would take this. But she merely pouted, and they laughed in relief, and Mrs Ryan laughed too, with good grace.

"All right, I know when I'm beaten." She began to collect her bag and gloves. "But there is just one thing. You've all been so sweet to me, and I don't want to feel like a stranger any longer. My name's Melissa. Do you-all think you could manage to call me that?"

And later, when the men were loading the car, she got Emma to herself.

"You've been specially sweet," she said. "Marcus told me that you'd come back from Paris to be with your father, and here I am, taking him away from you again."

Emma, who knew that she had not been specially sweet, felt guilty. "The exhibition has to come first . . ."

"I'll take good care of him," Melissa Ryan promised.

Yes, thought Emma, *I'm sure you will*. And yet, despite herself, she liked the American woman. And there was something

73

about the set of her chin and the clarity of her violet-blue eyes that made Emma wonder if perhaps, this time, Ben would not enjoy his usual walkover. And if things did not go his way from the very beginning he was apt to become discouraged. She smiled at Mrs Ryan. She said, "I don't suppose it'll be long before he's home again." And she picked up the honey-coloured mink which lay across the back of a chair and helped Mrs Ryan into it. They went out of the hotel together. It was colder now. The warmth of the sun had left the sky and a chill, like frost, swept up from the sea. Robert had put up the hood of the Alvis, and Melissa, wrapped in the mink, went to say goodbye to Ben.

"But it isn't goodbye," he told her, holding her hand, and gazing darkly down at her. "It's au revoir."

"Of course. And if you let me know when your flight arrives at Kennedy Airport, I'll arrange to have you met."

Marcus said, "I will do that. Ben has never in living memory let anybody know anything, least of all his time of arrival. Goodbye, Emma, my darling child, and don't forget that I have invited you to stay with us for as long as you like when Ben is in America."

"Bless you, Marcus. You never know. I might come."

They kissed. He got into the back of the car, and Melissa Ryan into the front, her elegant legs wrapped in Robert's car rug. Ben shut the door, then stooped to continue his conversation with her through the open window.

"Emma." It was Robert.

She turned. "Oh, goodbye, Robert."

To her surprise he took off his cap and bent to kiss her. "You'll be all right?"

She was touched. "Yes, of course."

"If you want anything, give me a ring, at Bernstein's."

"What could I want?"

"I don't know. Just a thought. Goodbye, Emma."

They stood, she and Ben, watching until the car had disappeared down the tunnel of trees. After it had gone, neither of them spoke, and then Ben cleared his throat, and said, portentously, as though he were giving a lecture, "What an interesting head that young man has. The narrow skull and the strong facial bones. I should like to see him with a beard. He would make a good saint – or perhaps, a sinner. Do you like him, Emma?"

She shrugged. "I suppose so. I scarcely know him."

He turned to move off, and caught sight of the small gathering of hotel guests, who, setting off for walks, or coming in from golf, or aimlessly snatching at the smallest straw of entertainment, had stayed to witness Melissa's departure. As Ben fixed them with his dark eyes, they became discomfited, turned away and moved on as though they had been caught doing something shameful.

He shook his head in amazement. "I think," he said, "I have had enough of being stared at as though I were a two-headed chimpanzee. Come along, we'll go home."

6

Ben Litton left for America at the end of March, travelling from Porthkerris to London via British Railways and from London to New York on a BOAC Boeing. At the last moment Marcus Bernstein decided to go with him, and the evening papers carried photographs of their departure, Ben with his white hair a coxcomb in the breeze, and Marcus almost obliterated by his black hat. Both looked faintly self-conscious.

It was from Marcus that Emma received the airmail bundle of American newspapers, carrying in their columns the comments of every worthwhile art critic in the country. They were unanimous in their praise of the whole concept of the Queenstown Museum of Fine Arts, acclaiming it as a perfect example of architecture, lighting, and immaculate display. And the Ben Litton exhibition was on no account to be missed. Never again would the artist's work be available to the public in its entirety, and the two or three pre-war portraits, lent by private individuals, were alone worth a visit, if only to see how a single man could be painter, psychiatrist and absolving priest at one and the same time.

"Ben Litton uses his brush as a surgeon's scalpel, first laying bare the hidden sickness, then treating it with the utmost compassion."

The word compassion was used again for his war-time drawings, the shelter groups, the fire-fighters, and a handful of sketches salvaged from the time of the Allied advance in Italy. And of his post-war work they said, "Other painters abstract from nature. Litton abstracts from imagination, and an imagination so lively that it is difficult to believe that these vital paintings were not turned out by a man of half his age."

Emma read these and allowed herself to feel proud. The private view took place on the 3rd of April, and by the tenth there was still no word of Ben's return, but she filled in the days with time-consuming household chores, and eventually moved back to the studio to finish the whitewashing. This took little mental concentration, and her mind wandered aimlessly into the future, indulging in the sort of day dreams that, a month ago, she would never have allowed herself. But now, she truly felt that things had changed. When she had gone to the station to put Ben on to the London train, he had kissed her goodbye – absentmindedly to be sure, as though he had forgotten for the moment who she was, but still, he had kissed her and that surely marked a milestone. And when he did eventually tear himself away from the adulation of the American public and returned to Porthkerris, she saw herself meeting the train, cool and composed, the perfect social secretary. And, maybe the next time he took off for some far-flung, but obviously colourful, corner of the globe, he would take Emma with him, and she would book flights, and see that he caught connections, and keep Marcus informed as to his movements.

And then, a day or two later, there was a letter from Marcus, postmarked London. She opened it hopefully, thinking that it would tell her that Ben was coming back, but, in fact, it was simply to say that Marcus had returned to London alone, and Ben had stayed in Queenstown.

ANOTHER VIEW

The Ryan Memorial Museum is fascinating, and if I had been able, I should have stayed as well. It embraces all forms of art, has a small theatre and concert hall and a collection of Russian jewellery which has to be seen to be believed. Queenstown itself is charming, full of red brick Georgian houses, set in green lawns and veiled in flowering dogwood . . . they all look as though they have been there since the days of William and Mary, but in fact, I saw one in the process of being built, the mature lawn being laid in turves, and the dogwoods planted, fully grown. What it is to have a warm and temperate climate, to be sure.

Redlands (the Ryan homestead) is a great white house with a pillared "porch" where Ben sits in a long chair and gets brought mint juleps by a coloured butler called Henry. Henry comes to work each day in a lilac Chevrolet, and hopes, in the not-too-distant future, to become a lawyer. He is a bright young man and should achieve his ambition. There are also a couple of tennis courts – a paddock (corral) full of spirited horses, and the inevitable swimming-pool. Ben, as you can imagine, neither rides nor plays tennis, but spends long hours, when he isn't adding a little local colour to the retrospective exhibition, floating around the pool on a rubber mattress. I am sorry that he has stayed away from you for so long, but honestly believe that he needs this rest. He has been working hard for the last few years, and a little harmless relaxation will do him no harm. If you are lonely, our invitation still stands. Come and stay with us. We should so love to have you.

Always your loving Marcus.

The whitewashing was finished, the studio floor scrubbed. Ben's drawings had been stacked and stowed in numbered folios. His pens and brushes graded and various tubes of solidified oil paint, used once, and then abandoned, had been discreetly shovelled into the dustbin.

There was nothing left to do.

He had been gone two weeks when the postcard came from Christopher. Emma was in the kitchen of the cottage, making coffee and squeezing orange juice, still wrapped in her dressing-gown and with her hair tied back in a pony tail, when the postman, who was a cheeky young man in an open-necked shirt, put his head round the door and said, "Well, and how are you this morning, my handsome?"

"Splendid, thank you," said Emma, who had been putting up with this camaraderie ever since she returned from Paris.

He flapped a bundle of letters at her. "All for your old man. But . . . here . . . is a postcard for you." He inspected the picture before Emma snatched it from him. "So vulgar those things are; I don't know how decent folks can buy them."

"No, you wouldn't," said Emma rudely, scarcely glancing at the bulging lady in the bikini before turning the card over to see who it was from. The postmark was Brookford.

Emma darling, when are you coming to see me? I can't come and see you, because we're up to the ears in rehearsals for Dead on Time. *Phone number Brookford 678, best about ten in the morning before we start work. Producer nice chap, stage manager bloody, all girls have spots, and not as pretty as you. Love Love Love Christo.*

The nearest phone box was a mile away, so Emma went down the street to the ramshackle grocer's where she bought cigarettes and tins of food and soap flakes, and used the telephone there.

It was an old-fashioned one, in two separate bits, and with a hook that you jiggled to get the operator. She sat on a beer crate and waited while the call was put through and a grey and white cat, fat as a cushion, came and lay exhaustedly across her knee.

The phone was answered at last by a cross-sounding female.

"Brookfield Theatre."

"Can I speak to Christopher Ferris?"

"I don't know if he's in yet."

"Could you go and look?"

"Oh, I suppose so. Who shall I say it is?"

"Say Emma."

The cross female departed. Various voices could be heard, chattering. A man in the distance shouted, "*Here I said, you clot, not there.*" And then there were footsteps and a voice, and it was Christo.

"Emma."

"You are there. They didn't know if you were in."

"Yes, of course I'm in . . . we're rehearsing in five minutes . . . Did you get my postcard?"

"This morning."

"Did Ben read it?" (He obviously hoped that he had.)

"Ben isn't here. He's in America. I thought you'd know."

"How should I know?"

"It's been in all the papers."

"Actors don't read papers and if they do it's always the *Stage*. But if the old boy's in America, why didn't you let me know and come and stay with me?"

"For a hundred reasons."

"Name two."

"Well, he only meant to go for a week at the most; and I didn't know where you were."

"I told you. Brookford."

"I don't even know where Brookford is."

"Thirty-five minutes from London, trains run every half hour.

Look, do come. Come and stay. I've been moved into a sinister basement flat. It smells of dry rot and old cats, but it's ever so cosy.''

"Christo, I can't. I must be here. Ben'll be home any day now, and . . .''

"Did you tell him about meeting me again?''

"No, I didn't.''

"Why not?''

"The subject never came up.''

"You mean you were scared?''

"I was nothing of the sort. It was simply – irrelevant . . .''

"Nobody's ever called me irrelevant and got away with it. Oh, do come, ducky. My little basement nest needs the touch of a woman's hand. You know, scrubbing and all that jazz.''

"I can't come till Ben's home. Then I'll try.''

"It'll be too late by then. I'll have got it clean. Please. I'll get you a free ticket for the show. Or two tickets and you can bring a friend. Or three tickets and you can bring them all.''

His voice dissolved into amusement. He had always laughed at his own jokes.

"Oh, very funny,'' said Emma, but she was laughing too.

"You're just playing hard to get. You wouldn't stay with me in Paris, and you won't come and keep house in the wilds of Surrey. What have I got to do to win your heart?''

"You won it years ago and you've had it ever since. Truthfully, I'm longing to see you. But I can't come. I simply can't come till Ben gets back.''

Christo said a rude word.

The telephone went pip-pip-pip.

"That's it, then,'' said Christo. "Let me know when you make up your mind. Goodbye.''

"Goodbye, Christo.'' But he had already hung up. Smiling

foolishly, going back over every word he had said, she put the receiver back on to the hook. The cat on her knee purred momentously, and Emma realised it was about to produce a family at any moment. An old man came into the shop to buy two ounces of plug, and when he had gone Emma picked up the cat and placed her gently on the floor, and felt in her pocket for loose change to pay for the call.

"When are the kittens due?" she asked.

The old woman behind the counter was called Gertie, and wore, indoors and out, an enormous brown beret pulled down over her eyebrows.

"Only time can tell, my dear." She put Emma's money into her till, which was an old tin box, and gave her her change. "Only time can tell."

"Thank you for letting me use your phone."

"It's a pleasure," said Gertie, who always listened, shamelessly, and relayed every word she heard.

In March it had been like midsummer. Now, in May, it was cold as November, and pouring with rain. He had never imagined Porthkerris in the rain; had always pictured it painted in the bright blues of summer, gay with the white wings of gulls and yachts, everything dazzling in a glaring sunlight. But now squalls, borne in on a cutting east wind, were flung against the windows of the hotel, sounding like fistfuls of pebbles. The gusts rattled the casements and then whined away beneath doors, down chimneys, blowing curtains, chilly and inescapable.

It was a Saturday, and Robert, flat on his bed, had been asleep. He looked at his watch and saw that it was five to three, so he reached for a cigarette, and lit it, and lay, watching the leaden sky race across the window, and waiting for the telephone to ring.

It did, at precisely three o'clock. He lifted the receiver.

"Three o'clock, sir," said the hall porter.

"Thank you very much."

"Sure you're awake, sir?"

"Yes. I'm awake."

He finished the cigarette, and stubbed it out, and got up, pulling on his white towel robe and heading for the bathroom for a hot shower. He hated sleeping in the afternoon, hated waking with the feeling that his teeth were itching, and that he was on the verge of a splitting headache, but after driving all through the night from London it had been impossible to stay awake. He had had an early lunch, and left word with the porter to call him. But the wind, blown up while he slept, had wakened him first.

He dressed, put on a clean shirt, tied his tie, picked up the jacket of his suit, and then changed his mind, and pulled on a polo-necked sweater instead. He combed his hair, slid his belongings from the top of the dressing-table into his trouser pockets, took a raincoat from the back of the door and went downstairs.

The lounge was thick with the silence of mid-afternoon. Elderly residents snoozed, snoring lightly in dry heated air. Frustrated golfers watched the rain, rattling loose change in the pockets of their tweed knickerbockers, wondering if the weather was going to let up, if there would be time for nine holes before it got dark.

The hall porter took Robert's key and hung it up.

"Going out now, sir?"

"Yes, and perhaps you can help me. I want to get to the Society of Artists Gallery. I believe it's an old chapel, converted. Have you any idea where it is?"

"That's down the old part of the town. Know your way round, do you?"

"I know the Sliding Tackle," said Robert, and the hall porter grinned. He liked a man who used pubs as landmarks.

"Well . . . say you're going to the Sliding Tackle, but turn up the street before you get there. Up, away from the harbour. Narrow little road, very steep, and there's a square at the head of it. Gallery's on the other side of the square. You can't miss it. Got great posters up outside . . . not that any living soul can make head nor tail of them . . ."

"Well, we'll have to see. Thank you very much."

"You're welcome." The porter swung the revolving door, and Robert was ejected into the bitter cold. Rain hammered at his unprotected head, he hunched himself into his raincoat, and picked his way across the gravel, trying to avoid the worst of the puddles. Inside, his car smelt damp and musty, an alien smell over the usual one of leather and cigarettes. He switched on the engine and the heater began to hum. A leaf was stuck in the blade of the windscreen wiper, but when he turned it on, the leaf was dislodged and torn from the wet glass by the wind.

He drove down to the town, and it was all deserted, abandoned, the inhabitants in a state of siege from the weather. Only a drenched policeman stood at point duty at the foot of the hill, and an old lady fought with an umbrella. The narrow streets acted as chimneys for the wind, which funnelled up them, cold and ferocious as a torrent of water, and when he came out on to the harbour road, he saw that the tide was full, and the harbour itself grey and choppy, fleeced with white-capped waves.

He found the street the porter had described. It climbed away from the harbour between crowded cottages, the cobbles wet and shining like the scales of a newly-caught fish. It crested the hill, and opened out into a picturesque square, and he saw the old chapel, a solid, gloomy building, quite at odds with the poster at its door.

PORTHKERRIS SOCIETY OF ARTISTS
SPRING EXHIBITION
Admission 5/-

Beneath this was a strange motif in purple – the suggestion of a staring eye, a six-fingered hand. Robert decided that he could see the hall porter's point of view.

He parked the car, and went up the streaming steps, and through the door, and was immediately assailed by the smell of a paraffin stove. He saw that the old chapel had been whitewashed, the walls soared to high private windows, and liberally hung with every sort and size of painting.

Just inside the door, her knees covered with a rug, sat a lady in a felt hat. On one side of her was a wooden table, with catalogues and a bowl for money, on the other was the paraffin heater, at which she was trying to warm a pair of purple-knuckled hands.

"Oh, close the door, close the door," she implored as Robert blew in on a gust of wind. He leaned against the door, shutting it, and feeling in his trouser pocket for two half-crowns. "What a freezing day," she went on, "and this is meant to be summer. You're my first visitor this afternoon. You are a visitor, aren't you? I haven't seen your face around the place."

"No, I haven't been here before."

"We've got a most interesting collection, you'll have a catalogue, of course. Another half-crown, please. But I think you'll agree, well worth it."

"Thank you," said Robert, feebly.

He took the catalogue, decorated with the same purple hand-and-eye motif as the poster outside, and opened it casually, running his eye down the list of artists for the name he wanted. ". . . er . . . any particular artist?" The woman at the desk managed to sound diffident, but she had an inquisitive gleam in her eye.

"No . . . not really."

"Just generally interested, I expect. Are you staying in Porthkerris?"

"Yes . . ." he began to move away from her. "For the moment I am."

He took it slowly, pacing down the long room, feigning interest in every picture. He had found the name, Pat Farnaby. Number 24. The Journey, by Pat Farnaby. He stayed a long time at number 23, then moved on again.

The colour pounced at him. There was a sensation of great height, a dizzying sensation, like vertigo. And yet with it, a sense of elation, as though he were above the clouds, caught, suspended, between the blue and the white.

You must go, Marcus had said. *I want you to form an opinion of your own. You can't remain the man who keeps the books for the rest of your life. Besides, I'd like to see your reaction.*

And this was it. This pure, high note of simple colour.

After a little, he went back to the persistent lady. He was aware that all the time she had been watching him. Now, he thought, she was bright-eyed as a greedy robin, waiting for a bread crumb.

"Is that Pat Farnaby's only exhibit?"

"I'm afraid so. It was all we could persuade him to let us have."

"He lives around here, doesn't he?"

"Oh, yes. Out at Gollan."

"Gollan?"

"That's about six miles away, out on the moor road. It's a farm."

"You mean he's a farmer?"

"Oh, no." She laughed. *Merrily*, thought Robert, as though

87

she were following the directions in an old-fashioned play. "He lives in the loft over the barn. Here," she drew a scrap of paper towards her, wrote an address. "If you want to see him, I'm sure you'll find him here."

He took the paper. "Thank you very much." He started for the door.

"But don't you want to look at the rest of our exhibition?"

"Another time, perhaps."

"It's so *interesting*." She sounded as though her heart would break if he did not look at some more pictures.

"Yes, I'm sure. But another time." It was at this moment that he thought of Emma Litton. His hand on the doorknob, he turned back. "By the way, if I wanted to find Ben Litton's house . . . is it near here? The house, I mean, not the studio?"

"Well, of course, it's just round the corner. About a hundred yards down the road. It's got a blue gate. You can't miss it. But you do know that Mr Litton's not at home?"

"Yes, I know."

"He's in America."

"Yes, I know that, too."

It was still streaming with rain. He got back into the car, and started the engine, and nosed it forward down a street as narrow as a burrow. At the blue gate he left it, parked, completely filling the road, and went through the gate, and down a flight of steps which led to a flagged courtyard where tubs stood, filled with drowned-looking plants, and a painted wooden seat disintegrating slowly in the damp. The house itself was long and low, single-storied, but the uneven roofs and ill-matched chimney pots indicated that it had once been two small cottages, or even three. The front door was painted blue to match the gate, and had a copper dolphin as a knocker.

Robert knocked. From above a stream of water poured down upon him from a faulty gutter. He stepped back and looked up to see where it came from, and as he did so, the door was opened.

He said, "Good afternoon. Your gutter's leaking."

"Where on *earth* have you sprung from?"

"London. You should get it mended or it'll rust away."

"Have you come all the way from London to tell me that?"

"No, of course I haven't. Can I come in?"

"Of course . . ." She stood back, holding the door open for him. "But you are the most disconcerting man. You keep just turning up, with no notice at all."

"How can we give you notice if you aren't on the telephone? And there wasn't time to write a letter."

"Is it about Ben?"

Robert went into the house, ducking his head beneath the lintel of the door, unbuttoning his wet raincoat.

"No. Should it be?"

"I thought he might be home."

"As far as I know he's still basking in that balmy Virginia sunshine."

"Well, then?"

He turned to face her. It occurred to him then that in an odd way she was unpredictable as the weather itself. Each time he met up with her, she seemed a different person. Today she wore a dress in red and orange stripes, and long black stockings. Her hair had been caught back on the nape of her neck with a tortoise-shell slide, and her fringe had grown. It was too long, it would get into her eyes, give her a squint. As he watched her, she pushed it back, off her face, with the heel of her hand. It was a gesture both defensive and disarming and it made her seem very young.

He took the scrap of paper out of his pocket and handed it across to her. Emma read it aloud.

89

"Pat Farnaby, Gollan Home Farm." She looked up at him. "But where did you get this?"

"From the female at the Art Gallery."

"Pat Farnaby?"

"Marcus is interested."

"Why didn't he come himself?"

"He wanted a second opinion. Mine."

"Have you formed one?"

"It's difficult to say after seeing only a single painting. I thought I might be able to see some more."

Emma said warningly, "He's a very odd young man."

"I should expect him to be. Do you know where Gollan is?"

"Of course. It belongs to Mr and Mrs Stevens. We used to go out in summer for picnics on the cliffs. But I haven't been since I got back this time."

"Will you come with me now? Show me the way?"

"How do we get there?"

"The car's outside. I drove down from London last night."

"You must be exhausted."

"No, I've had a sleep."

"Where are you staying?"

"At the hotel. Can you come? Now?"

"Of course."

"You'll need a coat."

Emma smiled at him. "If you can spare thirty seconds, I'll get one."

When she had gone, her footsteps clattering away down an uncarpeted passage, Robert lit a cigarette and stood, looking about him, intrigued not only by the oddly-shaped little house, but also because it represented the unfamiliar, domestic side of Ben Litton's stormy personality.

The blue front door had led them straight into the living-room, low ceilinged and darkly beamed. There was a huge window with a view of the sea, its deep sill crowded with indoor plants – geraniums and ivy and a Victorian jug full of pink roses. The floor was flagged with slate and scattered with bright rugs, and there were books and magazines everywhere, and a great deal of blue and white Spanish pottery. In a granite hearth, flush with the floor, a log fire smouldered, flanked by baskets of weathered driftwood, and over this hung the only picture in the room.

His professional eye had noticed this as soon as he came into the house, but now Robert went over to inspect it more closely. It was a large oil of a child on a donkey. She wore a red dress, carried a bunch of white daisies, wore a garland of them on her dark head. The donkey stood knee-deep in the lush grass of summer, and, far beyond, the sea and the sky were suffused by a haze of fine weather. The child's dangling feet were bare, her eyes pale in the brown bloom of her face.

Emma Litton, by her father. Robert wondered when it had been painted.

The wind rose, with a sudden witch's shriek, and flung a torrent of rain at the window. It was an eerie sound and he realised that this could be a lonely place to live, and wondered what Emma found to do on such a day. When she came back, carrying her coat and a pair of gumboots, which she proceeded to pull on, he asked her about this.

"Oh, I clean the house, and I cook things and I go and shop. It all takes quite a long time."

"And this afternoon? What were you doing this afternoon when I knocked on the door?"

Emma tugged at the gumboot. "I was ironing."

"And what about evenings? What do you do in the evenings?"

"I usually go out. I go for walks and things. I watch the gulls

91

and the cormorants. I look at the sunset, pick up driftwood for the fire.''

''Alone? Haven't you got any friends?''

''Oh, yes, but the children who lived here when I was little have all grown up and gone away.''

It sounded bleak. On an impulse, Robert said, ''You could come back to London with me. Helen would love to have you.''

''Yes, I know she would, but it's hardly worth it, is it? After all, Ben'll be back any day now. It's only a matter of days.''

She began to pull on her coat. It was navy blue and, with her black stockings and gumboots, made her look like a schoolgirl.

''Have you had any word from Ben?'' Robert asked.

''From Ben? You must be joking.''

''I'm beginning to wish we'd never suggested he went back to America.''

''Why?''

''Because it doesn't seem fair on you.''

''Oh, heavens, I'm all right.'' She smiled. ''Shall we go?''

The Stevens's farm lay in a grey stretch of moor that swept down to the cliffs. Grey, lichened, sunk like a boulder into the land, it might have been simply another larger outcrop of granite. The lane which led down from the road wound deep between tall stone hedges, crowned with hawthorn and brambles. The car bumped and jolted down the track, crossed a small bridge, came to the first cottages, a flock of white geese, and finally the farmyard, shrill with the voice of a screaming cockerel.

Robert stopped the car and switched off the engine. The wind was dying, the rain seemed to have congealed into a sea-mist, thick as smoke. There were various farm sounds; cows lowing, hens clucking, the distant churning of a tractor.

''Now,'' said Robert, ''how do I find this man?''

''He lives in the loft of that barn . . . you go up the stone steps to his door.'' The stone steps were already occupied by a number of wet hens, pecking for scraps of grain, and a bored-looking tabby cat. Below them, in the mud of the yard, a huge sow was rootling about. There was a strong smell of manure. Robert sighed. ''The things I am expected to do, and all in the name of Art.'' He opened the door of the car and began to get out. ''Do you want to come?''

''I think I'd be more use out of the way.''

''I'll try not to be too long.''

She watched him pick his way across the sodden farmyard, toe the pig aside, cautiously climb the steps. He knocked on the door, and then, when there was no reply, opened it and stepped inside. The door shut behind him. Almost at once another door opened, in the farmhouse this time, and the farmer's wife emerged, in boots and a raincoat to her ankles, and a black sou'wester. She carried a stout stick and came down the garden path, peering through the rain to see who was in the big green car.

Emma rolled down the window. ''Hello, Mrs Stevens. It's me.''

''Who?''

''Emma Litton.''

Mrs Stevens broke into a cackle of delighted astonishment, slapped her side, put her hand over her heart. ''Emma! Well, what a surprise you gave me. I haven't seen you since goodness knows how long. What are you doing here?''

''I came out with a man who wants to see Pat Farnaby. He's up there now.''

''Is your father home yet?''

''No, he's still in America.''

''On your own, are you?''

''That's right. How's Ernie?'' Ernie was Mr Stevens.

''He's lovely, but had to go into town today to see the dentist

about his plate. Agony, it gives him, he can scarcely bear
to keep it in his mouth. That's why I'm getting the cows in
for him . . .''

On an impulse Emma said, ''I'll come with you . . .''

''Too wet for you.''

''I've got boots . . . besides, I'd like the walk.'' She liked Mrs
Stevens, too, a woman who remained unquenchably cheerful
under all circumstances. They climbed a stile and started out
over the sodden fields. ''You've been abroad, haven't you?''
said Mrs Stevens. ''Yes, I thought you had. I never knew you
were home. Pity your Daddy had to go off like this. Still, can't
be helped, I suppose, him being the sort of man he is . . .''

The interview with Pat Farnaby was a difficult one, to say the
least of it. He was an intense young man, very pale and under-
nourished, with a shock of carroty hair and a beard to match.
His eyes were green and suspicious as a hungry cat's, and he
appeared to be very dirty. His abode was also dirty, but this
Robert had expected and, accordingly, ignored.

What he had not expected, though, was such antagonism.
Pat Farnaby did not like strangers walking in, uninvited and
unannounced, when he was working. Robert apologised and
explained that he had come on business, whereupon the young
man simply asked Robert what he was trying to sell.

Beating down his irritation, Robert tried another tack. With
some ceremony, he produced Marcus Bernstein's card. ''Mr
Bernstein asked me to come and see you, perhaps to look at your
work, find out what your plans are . . .''

''I haven't any plans,'' said the artist. ''I never make plans.''
He treated the card as though it were contaminated and must
not be touched, so that Robert was forced to put it down on the
corner of a littered table.

"I saw your picture at the Gallery in Porthkerris, but it is only one picture."

"So what?"

Robert cleared his throat. Marcus was infinitely better at dealing with this sort of thing, and Marcus never lost his temper. It took time to cultivate such patience, Robert knew. His own was slipping away, like greasy rope between his fingers. He took a firm grip of it.

"I'd like to see some more of your work."

Pat Farnaby's pale eyes narrowed. "How did you find me?" he asked, sounding like a cornered criminal.

"They gave me your address at the Gallery. Emma Litton came with me to show me the way. Perhaps you know Emma."

"I've seen her around."

They seemed to be getting nowhere. In the silence that followed Robert let his eyes travel over the unsavoury studio. There were only the most sordid signs of human habitation; a bed like a disintegrating nest, a dirty frying pan, some nasty socks soaking in a bucket, an opened tin of beans, the jagged edge of the lid sticking up. But there were also many canvasses, stacked, scattered, propped on chairs, against walls. A potential treasure trove. Anxious beyond belief to inspect them, he dragged his eyes back to meet the cold unwinking stare of the artist.

He said at last, gently, "Mr Farnaby, I haven't all the time in the world."

Put to the test, Pat Farnaby's resistance cracked. He seemed, all at once, unsure of himself. Arrogance and rudeness were his only defences against the whims of a more sophisticated world. He scratched his head, frowned, made a face of resignation, and at last went to lift a random canvas and turn it to face the light.

"There's this," he said uncertainly, and backed away from it to stand by Robert. As he did so, Robert took a new packet of cigarettes from his pocket and handed them across to the young man. In the silence that followed, Pat Farnaby cautiously slit the cellophane wrapper, took out a cigarette and lit it, and then, with the stealthy movements of a man who does not wish to be observed, slid the packet into his own trouser pocket.

An hour later Robert returned to the car. Emma, waiting for him, saw him come down the steps of the barn, pick his way across the farmyard. She leaned across to open the door for him, and as he got in beside her, asked, "How did you get on?"

"I think all right." He sounded cautious, but excited.

"Did he show you his work?"

"Most of it."

"And it's good?"

"I think so. We may be on the verge of something enormously important, but it's all in such an appalling mess that it's hard to be sure. Nothing's framed, there's no sequence or order . . ."

"I was right, wasn't I? He's a real oddball?"

"Crazy," said Robert. He grinned at her. "But a genius."

He turned the car in the yard and headed back up the lane towards the road. He was whistling tunelessly through his teeth and Emma sensed, beneath his excitement, the satisfaction of a job well done.

She said, "You'll want to speak to Marcus now."

"I said I'd telephone right away." He eased his cuff from the face of his watch, checked on the time. "A quarter past six. He said he'd wait in the Gallery till seven and then go home."

"If you like, you can drop me at the crossroads and I'll walk home."

96

"Now, why should I do that?"

"I haven't got a telephone, and you'll want to hurry back to the hotel."

He smiled. "It's not as urgent as all that. And if it hadn't been for you, I'd probably still be looking for Pat Farnaby. The least I can do is to take you home."

They were on the moor now, high above the sea. The wind had eased off considerably, veering round to the west, and ahead the sky seemed to be opening and breaking up, and there were unexpected scraps of blue, growing larger every moment, and watery fingers of sunlight. Emma said, "It's going to be a lovely evening," and as she spoke was conscious that she did not want Robert to go back to the hotel and leave her to spend it on her own. He had blown, unexpectedly, into the gloomy day, given it shape and purpose, filled with companionship of a shared venture, and now she did not want it to end.

She said, "When are you going back to London?"

"Tomorrow morning. Sunday. Back in the Gallery Monday morning. It's been a full weekend."

So there was only this evening. She imagined him telephoning Marcus from the phone by his bed. Then he would have a bath, perhaps a drink, go down for dinner. On Saturday evenings The Castle Hotel held little dinner dances; there was a band in white mess jackets and a patch of floor cleared for dancing. Deeply influenced by Ben, Emma had been brought up to regard such functions as unbearably genteel and boring, but tonight she felt that it would be fun to let Ben's rigid opinions go to the devil. She yearned for the starched white table-cloths, the last year's hit tunes, the ritual of the wine list, the souped-up glamour of pink-shaded lights.

Beside her Robert spoke unexpectedly, interrupting her train of thought.

"When did your father paint the picture of you on the donkey?"

"Why did you suddenly ask that?"

"I was thinking about it. It's enchanting. You look so solemn and important."

"That's the way I felt, solemn and important. I was six, and it was the only painting he ever did of me. The donkey was called Mokey. He used to carry us up and down to the beach along with all the picnic baskets and things."

"Have you always lived in the cottage?"

"Not always. Just since Ben married Hester. Before that we used to stay anywhere – in boarding-houses, or with friends. Sometimes we just camped in the studio. It was rather fun. But Harriet said she had no intention of living like a gipsy, so she bought the cottages and converted them."

"She did a good job."

"Yes, she was clever. But Ben has never thought of that house as home. His home is his studio and when he's in Porthkerris, he spends as little time as possible in the cottage. I think its associations with Hester slightly get him down. He's always expecting her to walk in and tell him that he's late for something, or that he's tracking mud on to the floor, or he's putting paint on the sofa cushions . . ."

"The creative instinct seems to thrive in disorder."

Emma laughed. "Do you suppose, that when you and Marcus have made Pat Farnaby rich and famous, he will still want to roost with Mrs Stevens's chickens?"

"That remains to be seen. But if he does come to London, there's no doubt that somebody will have to scrub him down and comb the dust of ages out of that scrofulous beard. Still . . ." He stretched luxuriously, arching his back against the leather seat. "It'll be worth it."

They had crested the hill and were now running down the long road that led to Porthkerris. The sea, in the calm evening light, had turned the translucent blue of butterfly wings; the tide was out, and the great bay an arc of newly-washed sand. The rain had left everything sparkling and fresh, and as the moors and the fields fell behind them, and they drove down through the narrow streets, Emma saw windows flung open to the fresh evening air, and caught, from tiny stamp-sized gardens, the heady smells of roses and lilac.

And there were other smells, too. Saturday evening smells, of fish frying and cheap scent. And there were people strolling the pavements in their best clothes, a smattering of early summer visitors, and boys and girls, hand in hand, headed for the cinema and the little cafés that lined the harbour road.

Stopped at the crossroads by the point-duty policeman, Robert observed them.

"What does young love do in Porthkerris on Saturday night, Emma?"

"It depends on the weather."

The policeman waved them on.

"What are we going to do?" asked Robert.

"We?"

"Yes. You and I. Do you want to be taken out for dinner?"

For a mad moment Emma wondered if she had been yearning aloud. "Well . . . I . . . you don't have to feel you have to . . ."

"I don't feel I have to. I want to. I'd like to. Where shall we go? My hotel? Or would you hate that?"

"No . . . of course . . . I wouldn't hate it . . ."

"Perhaps you've got some amusing little Italian place you like better."

"There aren't any amusing little Italian places in Porthkerris."

"No, I was afraid there wouldn't be. So it'll have to be the palm court and the central heating."

"There's a band too," said Emma, feeling she should warn him. "On Saturday nights. And people dance."

"You make it sound indecent."

"I thought perhaps you disliked that sort of thing. Ben does."

"I don't dislike it at all. Like most things, it can be quite fun if you do it with the right person."

"I never thought of it that way."

Robert laughed and looked again at his watch. "Half past six. I'll take you home, then go back to the hotel and change, and speak to Marcus, and then come back for you. Would half past seven be time enough?"

"I'll give you a drink," said Emma. "There's a bottle of Uncle Remus's Genuine Ole Rye Whisky that Ben was given ten years ago, and it's still not been opened. I've always longed to see what was inside."

But Robert was unenthusiastic. "Perhaps I'd better just make a martini."

At the hotel he collected his key, and three messages with it.

"When did these come?"

"The times are noted, sir. Three forty-five, five o'clock, half past five. A Mr Bernstein, telephoning from London. He says to call him the moment you come in."

"I was going to do that anyway, but thanks."

Frowning a little, for such impatience was foreign to Marcus, Robert went upstairs to his room. The copious telephone calls were disturbing. He wondered if Marcus had heard rumours that some other Gallery was after the young artist. Or perhaps he had had second thoughts about Farnaby's work, and wanted to cancel the whole thing.

In his room, the curtains had been drawn, the bed turned down, the fire turned on. He sat on the bed, and picked up the receiver and gave the number of the Gallery. He took the three telephone messages out of his pocket and put them in a neat row on top of the bedside table. *Mr Bernstein would like you to call him. Mr Bernstein called, will ring later. Mr Bernstein . . .*

"Kent 3778. Bernstein Galleries."

"Marcus . . ."

"Robert, thank God I've got you at last. Did you get my message?"

"Three of them. But I said I would call you about Farnaby."

"This isn't about Farnaby. This is much more important. This is about Ben Litton."

There was a dress, seen in Paris, wildly expensive, coveted, and finally bought. It was black, sleeveless, very plain. "But when will you wear such a dress?" Madame Duprés had asked, and Emma, basking in the luxury of possession, had replied, "Oh, some time. Some special time."

There had never been such an occasion until tonight. Now, with her hair coiled high and pearl earstuds set in her ears. Emma drew the black dress carefully over her head, zipped it up and fastened the tiny belt, and her reflection in the mirror reassured her that all those thousands of francs had been well spent.

When Robert came, she was in the kitchen, struggling with a trayful of ice-cubes for the martinis that he had promised to make. She heard his car, the slam of the door, the gate open and shut and his footsteps as he ran down the steps, and in a panic, she tumbled the ice into a glass dish and went to let him in, and found that the sullen day had turned into a clear and perfect night, jewel-blue and scattered with stars.

In surprise, she said, "What a beautiful night."

"Amazing, isn't it? After all that wind and rain Porthkerris is looking like Positano." He came into the house and Emma closed the door behind him. "There's even a moon rising over the sea to complete the illusion. All we need now is a guitar and a tenor singing 'Santa Lucia'."

"Perhaps we'll find one."

He had changed into a dark grey suit, a starched shirt with an impeccable collar and a gleam of white cuff, linked with gold, showing at his wrist. His tawny hair was once more tamed and smoothly brushed, and he brought with him the crisp, lemony smell of aftershave.

"Do you still want to make a martini? I've got everything ready, I was just trying to get the ice . . ." She went back to the kitchen, raising her voice to talk through the open door. "The gin and the martini are on the table and a lemon. Oh, and you'll need a knife to cut the lemon with."

She opened a drawer and found one, pointed and very sharp, and she carried the knife and the bowl of ice back into the living-room. "What a pity Ben isn't here. He adores martinis, only he can never remember the right proportions and he always drowns them with lemon . . ."

Robert made no reply to this. It occurred then to Emma that he had made no effort to make himself at home. He had done nothing about their drinks, he had not even lit himself a cigarette, and this in itself was unusual, for he was normally the most relaxed and composed of men. But now there was a definite constraint about him, and with a sinking heart, Emma wondered if he was already regretting the evening they were to spend together.

She went to put the lemon down beside the empty glasses, told herself she was imagining things, turned to swiftly smile at him. "Now, what else do you need?"

"Not another thing," said Robert, and put his hands into his trouser pockets. *Not the gesture of a man who is about to make a martini.* In the fire a burning log settled and broke, sending up a shower of sparks.

Perhaps it was the telephone call that had upset him. "Did you speak to Marcus?"

"Yes, I did. As a matter of fact, he'd been trying to get me on the telephone most of the afternoon."

"And of course you were out. Was he pleased when you told him about Pat Farnaby?"

"He wasn't calling about Farnaby."

"He wasn't?" Suddenly she was afraid. "Is it bad news?"

"No, of course not, but you may not be very pleased. It's about your father. You see, he called Marcus this morning, from the States. He wanted Marcus to tell you that yesterday, in Queenstown, he and Melissa Ryan were married."

Emma realised that she was still holding the knife, that it was very sharp and that she might cut herself with it, so she set it down, very carefully alongside the lemon . . .

Married. The word conjured up a hysterical image of a wedding; of Ben with a white flower in the button-hole of his sagging corduroy jacket; of Melissa Ryan in her pink wool suit, misted in white veiling and paper confetti; of demented church bells jangling their message out across the verdant Virginia countryside that Emma had never seen. It was like a nightmare.

She realised that Robert Morrow was still talking, his voice even and calm. ". . . Marcus feels that in some obscure way, he is to blame. Because he thought the private view was a good idea, and because he was with them in Queenstown – he saw them together all the time, and he never had the faintest inkling that this was going to happen."

Emma remembered Marcus's description of the beautiful

house, saw Ben caged by Melissa's money, a pacing tiger with all his creative impulses smothered by luxury; and she realised that she had underestimated Melissa Ryan in imagining that Ben would be put off by having to fight for what he wanted. She had not appreciated how much he would want it.

Suddenly, she was angry. "He should never have gone back to America. There was no need. He simply wanted to be left alone and to get on with his painting."

"Emma, nobody made him go."

"It isn't as though the marriage will last. Ben's never stayed faithful to a woman longer than six months, and I can't see Melissa Ryan standing for that."

Robert said mildly, "Perhaps this time it will work, and it will last."

"But you saw them together that day they met. They couldn't keep their eyes off each other. If she had been old and ugly, nothing would have dragged him away from Porthkerris."

"But she wasn't old and ugly. She's very beautiful, and highly intelligent and very rich. And if it hadn't been Melissa Ryan, very soon it would have been somebody else, and what is more . . ." he went on, swiftly, before Emma could interrupt, ". . . you know as well as I do that that is true."

She said bitterly, "But at least we would have had more than a month together."

Hopelessly, Robert shook his head. "Oh, Emma, let him go."

His tone infuriated her. "He's my father. What's wrong in wanting to be with him?"

"He's not a father, any more than he's a husband or a lover or a friend. He's an artist. As that dedicated maniac we went to see this afternoon is an artist. They have no time for our values or standards. Everything, and everybody else, has to take second place."

"*Second* place? I wouldn't mind taking second place, or third, or fourth. But I've always come at the bottom of a long list of priorities. His painting, his love affairs, his perpetual shunting about all over the world; even Marcus, and you. You're all more important to Ben than ever I was."

"Then leave him alone. Think about something else for a change. Chuck all this, leave it behind. Get yourself a job."

"I've done all those things. I've been doing them for the past two years."

"Then come back to London with me tomorrow and stay with Marcus and Helen. It'll get you away from Porthkerris, give you time to get used to the idea of Ben being married again, decide what you want to do next."

"Perhaps I've already decided."

It was there, in the back of her mind. Like watching the revolving stage from the darkened auditorium of a theatre. One set moves out of sight and as it does the new scenery comes slowly on to the stage. A different set. Another room, perhaps. Another view from another window. "But I don't want to come to London."

"And this evening?"

Emma frowned. She had forgotten. "This evening?"

"We're having dinner together."

She felt that she could not bear it. "I really would rather not . . ."

"It'll do you good . . ."

"No it won't. And I've got a headache . . ." It was an excuse, made-up, and it was with astonishment that she realised it was true. A pain that felt like the start of a migraine, with her eyeballs dragged by wires into the back of her head; the thought of food, chicken in gravy, ice-cream, was nauseous. "I couldn't come. I couldn't."

Robert said gently, "It isn't the end of the world," and the old, comforting cliché was somehow more than Emma could take. To her horror, she began to cry. She covered her face with her hands pressing her fingertips into her thudding scalp, trying to stop, knowing that crying would make it worse, that she would be blinded with pain, that she would be sick . . .

She heard him say her name, and in two strides he had covered the space between them, and he put his arms around her, cradling her, letting her cry all over the immaculate grey lapels of his good suit. And Emma did not try to move away, but stayed still, tightly clenched against her own grief, rigid and unresponsive and hating him for what he had done to her.

7

Jane Marshall, her hand curved round a half full tumbler of Scotch-on-the-rocks, said, ". . . so what happened then?"

"Nothing happened. She didn't want to come out to dinner, and she looked as though she was going to have a bilious attack, so I put her to bed, and gave her a hot drink and an aspirin, and then I went back to the hotel and had dinner on my own. Then, the next morning, the Sunday, I went down to the cottage to say goodbye before I drove back to London. She was up and about, rather pale, but she seemed to be all right."

"Did you try again to make her come back with you?"

"Yes, I did, but she was adamant. So we said goodbye, and I left her. And since then there has been no word."

"But you can surely find out where she is?"

"There is no way of finding out. There's no telephone, never has been. Marcus wrote, of course, but Emma seems to have inherited Ben's built-in aversion to answering letters. There hasn't been another word."

"But this is crazy. In this day and age . . . there must be someone who can tell you . . ."

"There's no one. No one Emma ever talked to. There was no daily woman, coming in to clean, she did it all herself. That was the big reason for going back to Porthkerris in the first place, so that she could keep house for Ben. Of course, after two weeks of frigid silence, Marcus could stand it no longer, and put through a telephone call to the landlord of the Sliding Tackle, which was the pub Ben used to frequent, but Ben had been gone for six weeks, anyway, and Emma never went near the place.''

''Then you'll have to go down to Porthkerris and ask around.''

''Marcus isn't prepared to do that.''

''Why not?''

''For reasons. Emma isn't a child. She's been hurt, and Marcus respects the fact that if she wants to be left alone, he has no right to interfere. He's asked her to come to London and live with Helen and himself . . . anyway until she's found her feet again. He can scarcely do more. And there's another reason, too.''

''I know,'' said Jane. ''It's Helen, isn't it?''

''Yes, it is,'' said Robert, hating to admit it. ''Helen has always resented the hold Ben has over Marcus. There have been times when she would gladly have seen Ben at the bottom of the ocean. But she's accepted it because she had to, because wet-nursing Ben's career is part of Marcus's job, and without Marcus to keep him, more or less on the rails, God knows what would have happened to Ben Litton.''

''And now she doesn't want him to start killing himself over Emma.''

''Precisely.''

Jane rocked her glass, letting the ice clink against its side. She said, ''And you?''

He looked up. ''What about me?''

''Do you feel involved?''

''Why do you ask that?''

''You sound involved.''

"I scarcely know the girl."

"But you're worried about her."

He considered this. "Yes," he said at last. "Yes, I suppose I am. God knows why."

His glass was empty. Jane laid down her own drink, and got up to take his glass and pour him another whisky. From behind him, busy with ice, she said, "Why don't *you* go down to Porthkerris and find out?"

"Because she isn't there."

"She isn't . . . ? You know? But you never told me that."

"After the abortive telephone call to the Sliding Tackle, Marcus got the wind up. He rang the local police, and they found out a few facts and called us back. Cottage closed up, studio closed up, Post Office told to keep all mail until further notice." He reached up to take the fresh drink that Jane handed him over the back of the sofa. "Thanks."

"And her father . . . ? Does he know?"

"Yes, Marcus wrote and told him. But you can't expect Ben to get unduly excited. After all, he's still in the throes of what is virtually a honeymoon, and Emma's been sculling round Europe on her own since she was fourteen. Don't forget, that this is not a normal father-daughter relationship."

Jane sighed. "It most certainly isn't."

Robert grinned at her. She was a comfortingly down-to-earth person and it was for this reason that, on an impulse, he had dropped in this evening for a drink on his way home from work. Usually, the double life he led with Marcus Bernstein, working with him at the Gallery, as well as living in the same house, offered no strain at all. But just now, things were difficult. Robert had come back from a business trip to Paris, to find Marcus on edge, and unable to concentrate for very long on anything but the problem of Emma Litton. After discussing it with him, Robert realised that Marcus blamed himself for what had happened, and refused to be talked out of his guilt. Helen, on the other hand, was unsympathetic, and determined that he should not get himself more deeply involved in the whole sorry business, and for the moment the tensions had got on top of them, and split the ménage at Milton Gardens from top to bottom.

The situation was not improved by the weather. After a cool spring, London had suddenly been caught up in the throes of a veritable heatwave. The early mornings broke in a pearl-like mist which gradually dissolved into day after day of baking sun. Girls went to work in sleeveless dresses, men shed their jackets and sat at their desks in shirt-sleeves. The parks at lunch-time were filled with recumbent picnickers; shops and restaurants sprouted striped awnings, windows were flung open to the smallest breeze, and in the streets, parked cars frizzled and pavements glared, and melted tar stuck to the soles of shoes.

The heat, like some monstrous epidemic, had invaded even the quiet, pond-green recesses of the Bernstein Gallery. All day long there had been an endless stream of visitors and prospective clients, for the trans-Atlantic tourist season had started, and this was apt to be their busiest time. And at the end of it all, Robert, driving home, had found himself longing for a new face, a cool drink, and some conversation that had nothing to do with Artists, be they Renaissance, Impressionist or Pop.

Jane Marshall sprang immediately to mind.

Her little house was in a narrow mews between Sloane Square and Pimlico Road. As he turned the car into the street, and eased down over the cobbles, he gave a double toot on the horn, and she appeared at the open upstairs window, her hands on the sill, her fair hair falling over her face as she leaned out to see who it was.

"Robert! I thought you were still in Paris."

"I was till two days ago. Have you got such a thing as a long, cool, alcoholic drink for an exhausted working man?"

"Of course I have. Hold on. I'll come down and let you in."

Her tiny house had always charmed him. Originally a coachman's cottage, it had a steep, narrow staircase, which led straight up to the first floor. Here there was an open hall-way, a sitting-room, and a kitchen, and upstairs again, in the slope-roofed loft, her bedroom and bathroom. As such it was inadequate enough, but since she had started her interior decorating business, it had become a joke. The sitting-room she had turned into a workroom, but still the bales of fabric, the fringing and the cushions, and the small bits of bric-à-brac she so cleverly picked up, overflowed into every available corner of space, rendering it all as gay and colourful as a patchwork quilt.

She was delighted to see him. She had spent the morning with a tiresome woman who wanted her entire house in St John's Wood done up in cream, which she called "Redecorating in Magnolia." And then there had been a session with a young and rising actress who demanded something startling for her new flat.

"She sat here for hours, showing me pictures of the sort of thing she had in mind. I tried to tell her she should get a bulldozer in, not an interior decorator, but she wouldn't listen. These people never do. Whisky?"

"That," said Robert, collapsing on the sofa in front of the open window, "is the nicest thing anybody has said to me all day."

She poured two drinks, made sure he was supplied with cigarettes and an ash-tray, and then settled herself composedly down to face him. She was a very pretty girl. Her blonde hair was straight and thick, cut in a curve to her chin. Her eyes were green, her nose tip-tilted, her mouth sweet, but implacable. Her broken marriage had left certain scars upon her character and she was not always the most tolerant of people, but there was a directness about her that he found as refreshing as a drink of cold water, and she always looked delicious.

Now he said, "I came here with the express purpose of not talking shop. How did we get on to the subject of Ben Litton anyway?"

"I brought it up. I was intrigued. Every time I saw Helen, she kept dropping maddening hints and then refusing to say more. She feels strongly about this, doesn't she?"

"Only because, in his day, Ben Litton has run poor Marcus ragged."

"Does she know Emma?"

"She hasn't seen her since she went to Switzerland six years ago."

"It's difficult," said Jane, "to be fair about people if you don't know them very well."

"It's sometimes difficult to be fair even if you do. And now . . ." He leaned forward to stub out his cigarette. "Let's drop the subject and make a tacit agreement not to mention it again. Are you doing anything this evening?"

"Not a thing."

"Then why don't we go and find somewhere with a roof garden or a terrace, and have a quiet dinner together?"

"I'd like that," said Jane.

"I'll call Helen and tell her I'm not coming back . . ."

"In that case . . ." She stood up. "I shall go and have a shower and change. I shan't be long."

"There isn't any hurry."

"Make yourself at home . . . get yourself another drink. There are cigarettes here, and an evening paper somewhere if you care to look for it . . ."

112

She went up the stairs. He heard her moving about, high heels tapping on the polished floor. She sang under her breath, slightly out of tune. He put down his glass and went into her living-room, and ran her telephone to earth at last, beneath a bundle of flowered chintzes, and called Helen to say he would not be home for dinner. Then he went back to pour the third drink of the evening, and loosened his tie, and flopped once more on the sofa.

The whisky had revived him slightly, and beneath its clean cold bite, his tiredness had changed from end-of-the-day fatigue to a pleasant lassitude. The paper protruded from beneath a cushion, and he pulled it out, and then saw that it was not the *Evening Standard*, but the *Stage*.

"Jane."

"Hello!"

"I didn't know you took the *Stage*."

"I don't."

"Well it's here."

"Is it?" She didn't sound particularly interested. "Dinah Burnett must have left it behind. You know she's the actress who needs the bulldozer."

He opened it aimlessly. "Wanted One All Round Girl Dancer. Why does she have to be all round? Why can't she be all square?"

"Search me."

He turned to the Repertory page. They were doing Shakespeare at Birmingham, a restoration revival at Manchester, and at Brookford, staging the première of a new play . . .

Brookford.

The name leapt at him from the page like a bullet. Brookford. He sat up, slapped the paper into shape, and read the whole item.

*

113

Brookford Rep's summer season opens this week with the world première of *Daisies on the Grass*, a comedy in three acts by local writer Phyllis Jason. This light but well-knit play stars actress Charmian Vaughan in the lead role of Stella. Other parts are supplementary, but John Rigger, Sophie Lambart and Christopher Ferris all help to bring the mirthful suspense to its climax, and Sara Rutherford is charmingly natural as the bride. Tommy Childers' production is fast and furious, and the set, by scenic artist Brian Dare, evoked a spontaneous applause from the enthusiastic first-night audience.

Christopher Ferris.

He laid the paper carefully down, and reached for a cigarette, and lit it. Christopher Ferris. He had forgotten Christopher.

But now, out of a jumble of memories, he heard Emma's voice again, that first day, when he had given her lunch at Marcello's.

Did you know about Christopher? Quite by chance Christopher and I met up again in Paris. And he came this very morning and saw me off at Le Bourget.

And he remembered – facing her across the table – being suddenly wise, and knowing the reason for her smile and the bloom of her skin and the brightness of her eyes.

And later, in the draughty studio at Porthkerris, the subject of Christopher had, fleetingly, come up again, sandwiched between other more important items of discussion. *He'll be at Brookford by now*, Emma had said. *In the thick of rehearsals*.

He stood up and went to the foot of the stairs.

"Jane."

"Hello!"

"How nearly ready are you?"

"I'm just doing my face."

"Where's Brookford?"

"In Surrey."

"How long will it take us to get there?"

"Brookford? Oh, about forty-five, fifty minutes."

He glanced at his watch. "If we leave right away, or as near as we can . . . we shouldn't be too late."

Jane appeared at the head of the stairs, with a mirror in one hand and an eyeliner brush in the other.

"Late for what?"

"We're going to the theatre."

"I thought we were going out for dinner."

"Later, perhaps we will. But first we're going to Brookford, to see a well-knit comedy called *Daisies on the Grass* . . ."

"Have you gone out of your mind?"

". . . by local writer Phyllis Jason."

"You have gone out of your mind."

"I'll explain on the way down. Be a darling and hurry."

As they roared down the M4 Jane said, "You mean that nobody knows about this young man except you."

"Emma didn't tell Ben, because he'd never liked Christopher anyway – Helen says he was jealous of the boy."

"And Emma didn't tell Marcus Bernstein."

"I don't think so."

"But she told you."

"Yes, she told me. She told me that very first day. And why the devil I didn't think of him before I cannot imagine."

"Is she in love with him?"

"I wouldn't know. She's certainly very fond of him."

"Do you think we'll find her at Brookford?"

"If we don't, then I'll bet even money that Christopher Ferris will know where she is." Jane did not reply. After a little, he added, his eyes still fixed on the speeding road, "I'm sorry about this. I promised the subject wasn't to be raised again, and here I am whisking you off to the wilds of darkest Surrey.''

''Why,'' asked Jane, ''are you so anxious to find Emma?''

''Because of Marcus. I should like to set Marcus's mind at rest.''

''I see.''

''Because if Marcus's mind is at rest, then Helen will relax and life will be a great deal more comfortable for all of us.''

''Well, that's fair enough . . . Look, I think we should turn off here.''

The Brookford Repertory Theatre took some finding. They cruised up and down the High Street, then asked directions from a tired-looking policeman in shirt-sleeves. He sent them a half a mile from the centre of town, and, off a back street, up a cul-de-sac, they found the large brick edifice, looking more like a mission hall than anything else, but for the word THEATRE written above the door in neon letters, deadened by the hot evening light.

Outside, by the pavement, were parked a couple of cars, and alongside them, with their feet in the gutter, sat two small girls playing with a broken perambulator.

There were posters.

WORLD PREMIERE
DAISIES ON THE GRASS
by PHYLLIS JASON
A comedy in Three Acts
Produced by
TOMMY CHILDERS

Jane stood, taking in this inauspicious façade. ''So much for the living theatre.''

Robert put his hand under her elbow. ''Come along now.''

They went up a flight of stone steps, and into a small foyer, with a cigarette kiosk on one side, and a box office on the other. In the box office a girl sat knitting.

"I'm afraid the show's started," she said, as Robert and Jane appeared on the other side of the glass.

"Yes, we thought it would have. But we'll have a couple of tickets anyway."

"What price?"

"Oh . . . well – stalls."

"That's fifteen shillings. But you'll have to wait till the second act."

"Is there anywhere we could get a drink?"

"The bar's upstairs."

"Thank you very much." He took the tickets and his change. "I expect you know all the people who work here."

"Well, yes . . ."

"Christopher Ferris . . ."

"Oh, is he a friend of yours?"

"Well, a friend of a friend. The thing is, I wondered if he has his sister here . . . at least, she's his step-sister. Emma Litton."

"Emma's working here."

"She's *working* here. In the theatre?"

"That's right. As ASM – Assistant Stage Manager. Our last girl suddenly went off ill with an appendix, and Emma said she'd come and help out. Of course," her voice became professional ". . . Mr Childers usually likes someone in the job who's had a bit of stage training, you know, RADA, or a bit of experience somewhere, so that they double up in small parts. But as she was here, and didn't have anything to do, he let her have the job. Just until the regular girl's better."

"I see. Do you think we'd be able to see her?"

"Well, after the show, yes. But Mr Childers won't have anyone back stage until it's over."

"That's all right. We can wait. Thank you very much."

"Not at all. It's a pleasure."

They went upstairs to a second, larger foyer with a bar in the corner, and sat there, drinking lager and talking to the barman until a light spatter of applause announced the end of the first act. The lights went up, the doors opened, and a small stream of people emerged for refreshment. Jane and Robert waited until the first curtain bell, and then went into the auditorium themselves, buying a couple of programmes on their way, and being shown to their seats by an eager young girl in a nylon overall. Attendance that night was certainly sparse, and Jane and Robert were the only two people sitting in the third row. Jane looked about her with a professional eye.

"I think it was once a mission hall," she decided. "Nobody would have built anything so ugly as a theatre. But I must say, they have done it up quite imaginatively, and the lighting and the colours are good. What a shame they don't get better audiences . . ."

The curtain at last went up on the second act. "The lounge hall of Mrs Edbury's house in Gloucestershire" said the programme note, and there it was, complete with french windows, staircase, settee, table with drinks, table with telephone, low table with magazines (for leading lady to pick up and idly flick through in moments when she did not know what to do with her hands?) and three doors.

"Draughty house," murmured Jane.

"It's better when they shut the french windows."

But the french windows had to be open, for in bounced the *ingénue* (*Sara Rutherford is charmingly natural as the bride*), flung herself on the settee and burst into tears. Jane's profile was alert with delighted disbelief. Robert settled more deeply into his seat.

It was a terrible play. Even if they had seen the first act, and so been able to unravel the tangled skein of the plot, it would still have been a terrible play. It bristled with clichés, with stock characters (there was even a comic charlady), with contrived exits and entrances, and with telephone calls. There were eight of these in the course of the second act alone.

When the curtain came down, Robert said, "Let's go and have another drink. I could do with a double brandy after that."

"I'm not going to move," said Jane. "I'm not going to break the spell. I haven't seen a play like this since I was seven. And the set makes me positively nostalgic. But there's one thing, Robert, that sticks out like a sore thumb."

"What's that?"

"Christopher Ferris is very, very good . . ."

He was, too. When he had shambled on stage, as the vague young university student who was eventually to win the heroine from her stockbroker fiancé, *Daisies on the Grass* showed its first, faint spark of life. His lines were not better than anyone else's, but his timing was impeccable, and he managed to make them funny or sad, or wryly charming. For the part he wore corduroys, a sagging sweater and horn-rimmed spectacles, but even these could not disguise his elegance and his good looks and the natural long-legged grace with which he moved.

". . . and he's not merely very good, he's very attractive," Jane went on. "I can see why his step-sister was so pleased to bump into him again in Paris. I wouldn't mind bumping into him myself."

The third act had the same set, but now it was night. Blue moonlight shone through the open window, and down the stairs

119

came the little bride, carrying a suitcase, tiptoeing, all ready to run away or elope or whatever it was she'd spent the last hour in deciding to do. Robert couldn't remember. He was waiting for Christopher to come back on stage. When he did, Robert simply watched him the entire time, detachedly, absorbed and full of admiration. By now, he had the audience, small as it was, in the palm of his hand. As Robert watched, so they watched. Christopher scratched the back of his head and they laughed. He took off his spectacles to kiss the girl, and they laughed again. He put them back on to say goodbye for ever, and there was silence, and then people began to blow their noses. And when it was all over, and the cast lined up for the curtain call, the applause was long, and real, and it was all for Christopher.

"What do we do now?" asked Jane.

"It's not closing time for another ten minutes. Let's go and find a drink."

They went back to the bar. The barman said, "Well, how did you enjoy the show, sir?"

"Well, I don't know . . . I . . ."

Jane was braver. "We thought it was terrible," she said, but quite politely. "And I've fallen in love with Christopher Ferris."

The barman grinned. "Quite something, isn't he? Pity you had to come tonight, when the audience was so thin on the ground as it were. Mr Childers did hope, Miss Jason being local and all that jazz, that this play would bring them in. But you can't fight a heatwave."

"Do you usually have good houses?" Jane wanted to know.

"They go up and down. Now, last show we did was *Present Laughter* . . . that fairly filled the place up."

"It's a good play," said Robert.

"What part did Christopher Ferris have?" asked Jane.

"Now, let me see. Oh, I know, he was the young playwright.

You know, the one that bounces round on the chairs and eats biscuits. Ronald Maule he's called in the play. Oh, very funny, Christopher Ferris was in that part. Brought the house down, he did . . ." Wiping away at his tumblers, he glanced up at the clock. "I'm afraid I'll have to ask you to drink up, sir . . . closing time . . ."

"Yes, of course. By the way, how do we get back stage? We want to see Emma Litton."

"You can just go down the auditorium, sir, go through the door at the right of the stage. But watch out for Mr Collins the Stage Manager. He doesn't exactly relish visitors."

"Thanks," said Robert. "And good night."

They went back into the theatre. The curtains had been drawn back, and the stage was revealed once more, but without footlights the set looked less inspiring than ever. On stage a young boy was struggling with the sofa, trying to heave it to one side, and someone, somewhere, had left a door open, so that the whole theatre was swept with a stuffy draught of used-up air. The programme girl was going round, slapping up the empty seats and collecting empty chocolate boxes and cigarette cartons in a trash can.

"There is nothing," said Jane, "so depressing as an empty theatre."

They started to walk down towards the stage. As they approached, Robert realised that it was not a boy who struggled, single-handed with the heavy sofa, but a girl, dressed in an old blue sweater and jeans.

When he was close enough, he said, "I wonder if you can help me . . . ?"

She turned to look at him, and Robert, with the shock of sheer disbelief, found himself face to face with Emma Litton.

8

After a second's gaping silence, Emma stopped trying to move the sofa, and straightened up. He thought that she seemed much taller and thinner, the cold stage light was not flattering, her wrists hung like sticks from her rolled-up sleeves. But the worst thing was her hair. She had cut off her hair, and now her head seemed small and vulnerable, furred like the pelt of an animal.

There was the animal feel of watchfulness about her, too. A scarey look as though she waited for him to make the first move, to say the first word, before she knew which way to jump. He slid his hands into his pockets, in a deliberate attempt to both look and feel casual, and he said, "Hello, Emma."

She gave the ghost of a smile. She said, "This sofa feels as though it's been stuffed with lead and lost its castors in the process."

"Isn't there anyone who can help you?" He came forward to the edge of his side of the stage, so that he was looking up at her. "It looks very heavy."

"Yes, there'll be someone in a moment." She did not seem to know what to do with her hands. She rubbed them on the seat of her jeans as though they were dirty, and then folded her arms. It was a curiously defensive movement, and made her shoulder-bones jut forward beneath the thin cotton of her shirt. "What are you doing here?"

"We came down to see *Daisies on the Grass* . . . We drove down from town. This is Jane Marshall. Jane, this is Emma."

They smiled, nodded at each other, murmured how do you do? Emma turned back to Robert. "Did . . . did you know I was here?"

"No, but I knew Christopher was, and I thought you might be."

"I've been working for a couple of weeks. It gives me something to do."

Robert made no comment on this, and, perhaps disconcerted by his silence, Emma suddenly sat down on the sofa that she was meant to be shifting. Her hands hung listlessly between her knees. After a little, she said, "Did Marcus send you?"

"No. We just came to call. Make sure you're all right . . ."

"I'm all right."

"What time are you finished here . . . ?"

"I'll be about half an hour. I have to clear the stage for rehearsal tomorrow morning. Why?"

"I thought we might have all gone to some hotel or other, for a sandwich and a drink. Jane and I haven't had any dinner . . ."

"Oh, how kind!" She did not sound enthusiastic. "Well . . . the thing is . . . that I usually leave something in the oven at the flat . . . a casserole or something. Johnny and Chris never eat anything otherwise. We'll have to go back or it'll burn."

"Johnny?"

"Johnny Rigger. He was the fiancé. You know, the other man. He lives with Christo . . . and me."

"I see."

There was another silence. Emma, discomfited, struggled with her more hospitable instincts. "I would ask you to come back, if you'd like to, but there's nothing but a few cans of beer . . .''

"We like beer," said Robert promptly.

"And the flat's in a dreadful mess. There never seems to be time to clean it properly. Not now that I'm working, I mean."

"We don't mind. How do we get there?"

"Well . . . have you got a car?"

"Yes. It's outside."

"Yes . . . well. If you go out and wait, Christo and I will join you later. If that's all right. And then we can show you where it is."

"Splendid. How about Johnny?"

"Oh, he'll be along later."

"We'll wait for you."

He took his hands out of his pockets and turned, and he and Jane walked back up the slight slope of the auditorium. As they reached the double doors, and Robert held one half open for Jane to go through, all hell seemed to break loose on stage.

"Where the devil is that Litton girl?" Robert was in time to see Emma scramble off the sofa as though someone had set off a firework, and try once more to move the cumbersome thing. A small man with a black beard shot on stage, looking like the worst-tempered sort of pirate. "Look, ducky, I asked you to move the bloody sofa, not to go to sleep on it. God, I'll be thankful to see that other girl back and you safely out of this place . . ." One either had to go and knock him down, or withdraw. For Emma's sake Robert withdrew.

The door swung shut behind him, but as they crossed the foyer, the voice could still be heard ". . . She's a moron, we all know, but no one could be as crassly stupid as you . . ."

"Charming," said Jane, as they went down the stairs. Robert

did not reply, because, until the white-hot blaze of anger with which he had been suddenly consumed, died down, he was not capable of saying anything. ''That must be Mr Collins, the stage manager. Not a very nice man to work for.''

They reached the street door, and went down the steps and crossed the pavement and got into the car. It was dark now, a soft, bloomy dusk had descended upon the town, but the heat of the day still lingered, held by the narrow confines of the street, by sunbaked stone and paving. Above them the Theatre sign shone brightly, but as they got into the car, someone from inside the building turned it off. The evening's entertainment was over. Robert reached for his cigarettes, gave Jane one and lit it, and then took one for himself. After a moment he felt a little calmer.

He said, ''She's cut off all her hair.''

''Has she? What was it like before?''

''Long and silky and dark.''

''She doesn't want us to go tonight. You know that, don't you?''

''Yes, I know that. But we must. We don't need to stay long.''

''And I hate beer.''

''I'm sorry. Perhaps someone will make you some coffee.''

''. . . It isn't even as though it's a job that requires any sort of brain. The most idiotic creature straight out of RADA could do it more competently than you.''

Collins was letting fly, unloading the day's tensions and frustrations in a flood of invective that was directed solely at Emma. He hated her. It had something to do with Christopher; with the fact that her father was both successful and famous. At first, she had tried sticking up for herself, but now she knew better than to try and stem this venomous flood. With Collins,

126

you couldn't win. She simply listened, got on with her work, tried not to let him see how deeply he could upset her.

"... you got this job because I have to have someone to help me ... God help me. You didn't get it because Chris shoved his oar in, and you didn't get it because some fool is willing to pay twenty thousand for a Ben Litton of red spots on a blue background. I've got more sense than that, as by now you have no doubt found out. So don't start thinking you can loll around entertaining your toffee-nosed friends ... and the next time they condescend to visit our humble little show, tell them to bloody well wait till we've finished, will you? Now come on, get that sofa out of the bloody way ..."

It was nearly eleven before at last he let her go, and then she found Christo waiting for her in Tommy Childers' office. The door was open and she heard them talking, and she knocked and put her head in and said, "I'm ready now. I'm sorry I was so long."

Christo stood up. "That's all right." He stubbed out his cigarette. "Good night, Tommy."

" 'Night, Chris."

"Thanks for everything."

"That's OK, old chap ..."

They went downstairs towards the stage door. He put his arm around her as they went. Their warm bodies touched, it was too hot for such contact, but she found it comforting. Outside, in the little alley that led down to the street, he stopped by the dustbins to light another cigarette.

He said, "You were long enough. Collins playing up?"

"He was furious because Robert Morrow's here."

"Robert Morrow?"

"He's in Bernstein's, with Marcus. He's Marcus's brother-in-

127

law. I told you. He came down to see the show . . . He's brought a girl with him."

Christo stood looking down at her. "To see the show or to see you?"

"I think to see us both."

"He can't try to take you back. Say you're under age or anything?"

"Of course not."

"Then that's all right."

"Yes, I suppose it is. But, you see, like a fool, I asked them back to the flat. At least, I didn't mean to ask them, but somehow I did, and they're coming. They're waiting for us now, in the car. Oh, Christo, I am sorry."

He laughed. "*I* don't mind."

"They won't stay long."

"I don't mind if they stay all night. Don't look so tragic." He took her in his arms, and kissed her cheek. She thought that if only the evening, the day, the endless day, could end right here and now, she would be well content. She was afraid of Robert. She was too tired to fence with him, to answer questions, to try and evade those watchful grey eyes. She was too tired to compete with his friend, who was blonde and pretty and almost indecently cool-looking in her sleeveless navy-blue dress. She was too tired to tidy the flat for them, to shovel clothes and scripts and empty glasses out of sight, to open beer cans, and make coffee, and get Christo's dinner out of the oven.

Christo rubbed his chin against her cheek. "What's wrong?" he asked gently.

"Nothing." He did not like her to say she was tired. He was never tired. He did not know what the word meant.

He said, in her ear, "It's been a good day, hasn't it?"

"Yes, of course." She drew away from him. "A good day."

*With their arms entwined, they went down the alley towards
the street. Robert heard their voices, and got out of the car to
meet them. They came towards him, in and out of the patches of
light flung by the street lamps. They walked like lovers, Emma
trailing a sweater, Christo with a bulky script under one arm and
a cigarette between his fingers. When they reached the car, they
stopped. "Hello," said Christopher, smiling.*

"Christo, this is Robert Morrow, and Miss Marshall . . ."

*"Mrs Marshall," Jane corrected sweetly, leaning over the
back of the front seat. "Hello, Christopher."*

*"Sorry we've been so long," said Christo " . . . Emma's only
just told me you were here. And she was having her nightly set-to
with Collins, so we've all been fairly occupied. I believe you're
coming back to have a can of beer, or something. I'm afraid
we've got nothing stronger."*

"That's OK," said Robert. "If you can tell us the way . . ."

"Of course."

*The flat was in the basement of a row of daunting Victorian
houses that had once seen better days. They were much gabled,
and decorated with fancy brick work and stained windows, but
the street itself was dismal, and the curtains of bow-windowed
front rooms sagged sadly and were not always very clean. Worn
stone steps led down to an area where there were dustbins and
one or two dead geraniums in pots, and, as they descended, there
was a scream of fury from a frustrated cat, and a black, rat-like
form shot up the stairs between their legs. Jane let out a small
scream of fright.*

"It's all right," said Emma. "It's only a cat."

*Christo opened the door, and went ahead, turning on cold
overhead lights, for the flat was a furnished one, and not
supplied with lamps. Johnny had started making a couple out*

of Chianti bottles but had got no further than buying adaptors and a pair of fancy shades. The rooms of the flat had been sketchily converted, and it was still sadly obvious that their original intentions had been kitchens, larders, and wash-houses. An old range had been torn from the wall, and the resultant void filled with shelves, which no one had ever bothered to paint, and which acted as a catch-all for books, shoes, scripts, cigarettes, letters and a pile of old magazines. There was a divan which had been covered with an orange curtain and piled with thinly-filled cushions, but remained stubbornly a bed. There were one or two rickety kitchen chairs and a folding table, and the flagged floor was sparsely covered by an elderly carpet which had long since lost all colour and most of its pile. The walls had been whitewashed, but there were oozing damp stains like maps, and the corners of a bull-fighting poster, stuck to the bricks, was already beginning to curl. There was the smell of mice and dry rot, and, even on this hot summer evening, the very airlessness was clammy, like the inside of a cave.

Christo dropped his script on a table and went to open the window which was protected with iron bars, like a prison.

"Let's have some air. We have to keep the place shut up because of the cats, they get in anywhere. What would you like to drink? . . . There is beer, if Johnny hasn't drunk it all . . . or perhaps you'd like coffee. Have we got any coffee, Emma . . . ?"

"There's some instant coffee. I don't get the other sort, because there's nothing to make it in. Do sit down . . . sit on the bed. Sit anywhere. There are some cigarettes . . ." She found them, a box of fifty, handed them round, searched for an ash-tray while Robert lit them. There was no ash-tray, so she went down the flagged passage to the kitchen for a couple of saucers. The sink was full of dirty dishes, and for a moment she could not think when they had used them, when she had last been here, from what back-log of history they dated. Pinned down, remembered, the morning seemed three weeks away. No day had ever lasted for longer. And now, it was past eleven o'clock at night, and still it was not over. Still, the boys had to be given their supper, the kettle boiled for coffee, the can-opener found.

She found two clean saucers and took them back to the others. Christo had put on a record. He could do nothing, not even talk, without perpetual background music. It was Ella Fitzgerald and Cole Porter.

Every time we say good-bye
I die a little.

They were talking about *Daisies on the Grass*. "... if you can breathe life into a script like that," Jane was saying to Christopher, "... I'm sure you're going to go far." She was laughing. Emma put down the ash-tray, and Jane looked up. "Thank you ... is there anything I can do?"

"No, nothing. I'll just go and get some glasses. Would you like beer, or would you rather have coffee?"

"Would coffee be too much trouble?"

"No, not at all ... I'd like coffee too ..."

Back in the kitchen, she closed the door, so that they would not hear her clattering dishes, and tied on an apron, and put a kettle on to boil. When she lit the gas, it always backfired and frightened her out of her wits. She found a tray and cups and saucers, the tin of coffee, sugar, the cans of beer in a box beneath the sink. There were black beetles on the floor and Johnny had not emptied the trash can. She picked it up to take it out to the dustbin, but as she did so the door behind her opened, and she turned to face Robert Morrow.

He looked at the bucket. "Where are you taking that?"

131

"Nowhere," said Emma, furious at being caught. She turned to sling it back under the sink again, but he caught her arm and took it from her, looking with distaste at the mixture of old tea-leaves and of opened tins, and wet paperbags.

"Where does this go?"

Defeated, Emma told him. "In the dustbin. By the door. Where we came in."

He bore it off, down the passage, looking ridiculous, and Emma went back to the sink, and wished that he had not come. He didn't belong in Brookford; at the theatre; here, in the flat. She didn't want him to be sorry for her. For after all, there was nothing to be sorry about. She was happy, wasn't she? She was with Christo, and that was all that mattered, and how they managed their affairs had nothing whatever to do with Robert.

She prayed that he and his immaculate friend would be gone by the time Johnny Rigger returned.

When he came back with the empty bucket, she was clattering dishes, trying to give the impression that she was being busy. She half-turned over her shoulder and said coolly, "Thank you. I shan't be a moment," hoping that he would take the hint and leave her alone.

But it was no good. He shut the door, put the trash can down on the floor, and taking Emma by the shoulders, turned her round to face him. He wore an unrumpled and cool-looking suit, a blue shirt, and a dark tie, and Emma had the dish-mop in one hand and a plate in the other, and had to make herself look up and meet those probing grey eyes.

She said, "I wish you hadn't come. Why did you come?"

"Marcus has been worried about you." He took the dish-mop and the plate from her and leaned over to tip them back into the cluttered sink. "Perhaps you should have let him know where you were."

"Well, now you can tell him, can't you? And, Robert, I've got a lot to do, and there's just not room for two people in this kitchen . . ."

"Isn't there?" He was smiling. He settled himself on the edge of the table, and now his face was on a level with hers. He said, "You know, this evening, when I first saw you in the theatre I didn't know it was you. Why did you cut your hair?"

He could be very disarming. Emma put up a hand to stroke the stubbly nape of her neck. "When I started working at the theatre, it was such a nuisance. It got in the way, and then it was so hot, and it was always being splashed with paint when I was doing scenery. And there's nowhere here to wash it, and even if I did wash it, it took hours to dry." She hated talking about her hair. She missed it; missed its weight and familiarity and the soothing therapy of brushing it each night. "So one of the girls in the theatre cut it off for me." It had lain on the Green Room carpet like skeins of brown silk and Emma had felt like a murderer.

"Do you like working in the theatre?"

She thought of Collins. "Not much."

"Do you have to . . . ?"

"No, of course not. But Christo's there all day, you see, and there's nothing much to do here, on my own. Brookford's terribly dull. I didn't know such dull places even existed. So when this other girl went ill with appendicitis, Christo fixed it for me to go and help out."

"What will you do when she comes back?"

"I don't know. I haven't thought."

Behind her, the kettle boiled over. Emma turned swiftly to put out the gas, and lift the kettle on to the tray, but Robert said, "Not just yet."

She frowned. "I was going to make coffee."

"Coffee can wait. Let's get everything sorted out first."

Emma's face closed up. "There's nothing to sort out."

"Yes, of course there is. And I want to be able to tell Marcus what happened. For instance, how did you get hold of Christopher?"

"I rang him up – early that Sunday morning. I went to the call box and rang him up. They were having a dress rehearsal, so he was at the theatre. You see, he'd already asked me to come to Brookford and be with him, but I couldn't, because of Ben."

"You'd already spoken to him that morning, when I came to say goodbye?"

"Yes."

"And you never told me?"

"No, I didn't tell you. I wanted to start something quite new, a whole new life, without anybody knowing."

"I see. So you rang Christopher . . ."

"Yes, and that night he borrowed Johnny Rigger's car, and he came down to Porthkerris and brought me back here. We closed up the cottage together, and we left the key of the studio at the Sliding Tackle."

"The landlord didn't know where you were."

"I didn't tell him where I was going."

"Marcus phoned him."

"Marcus shouldn't have. Marcus isn't responsible for me any more. I'm not a little girl now."

"What Marcus feels is not simply responsibility, Emma, but a real fondness and you should realise that. Have you heard from Ben?"

"Yes, I had a letter on that Monday morning, before I left Porthkerris. And one from Melissa, too . . . asking me to go out and visit them."

134

"And did you write back?"

Emma shook her head. "No." She was ashamed of this, and swiftly looked down, to fiddle with a jagged thumbnail.

"Why not?"

She shrugged. "I don't know. I suppose I thought I'd be in the way."

"I should have thought that even being in the way was preferable to this . . ." His gesture embraced the littered kitchen, the whole seedy flat.

It was not the most fortunate of remarks. "What's wrong with it?"

"It's not just this place, it's that crumby theatre, the lunatic with a beard who was yelling at you to move the sofa . . ."

"Well, you told me to get a job."

"Not this kind of a job. You have a good brain, you speak three languages, and you appear to be moderately intelligent. What sort of a job is it pushing furniture around a third class re . . . ?"

"My real job is being with Christo!"

After this outburst, there was a terrible silence. A car passed in the street outside. Christopher's voice came up the stone passage, backed by the soft-playing record. A cat started yowling.

Robert spoke at last. "Do you want me to tell your father that?"

Emma blazed once more into the attack. "I supposed that's why you came. Spying for Ben."

"I simply came to find out where you were and how you were."

"Be sure to give him all the ghoulish details. It doesn't matter to us, and he won't take any notice, anyway."

"Emma . . ."

135

"Don't forget, he is no ordinary, run-of-the-mill parent, as you are only too fond of telling me."

"*Emma, will you listen . . . !*"

The last word was scarcely out of his mouth, when the door behind him burst open and a slurred and cheerful voice broke in. "Well, what a nice little chat you two are having!"

Robert wheeled. In the open doorway stood the young man who had played the part of the stuffy stockbroker in *Daisies on the Grass*. Only now he was stuffy no longer, but quite simply very drunk, and to steady himself hung on to the top of the doorway, like a monkey swinging on a trapeze. His legs, buckling slightly, did nothing to dispel this impression.

"Hello, darling," he said to Emma. He let go of the door and weaved into the tiny kitchen, rendering it unbearably crowded. With the palms of his hands flat on the table, he leaned forward to kiss Emma. The kiss was loud and smacking, but did not come within six inches of her face.

"We've got callers," he observed. "And a bloody great car parked outside. It adds great tone to the neighbourhood." His legs buckled again, and for a second his weight was supported solely by his arms. He smiled expansively at Robert. "What's your name?"

"He's called Robert Morrow," said Emma shortly, "and I'll make you some coffee."

"I don't want coffee. I do not want coffee." He raised his fist to the words, and once more his legs let him down. This time Robert caught him, and hauled him upright.

"Thanks, old boy. Very civil of you. Emma, how about a little sustenance? Feed the inner man; you know the routine. I do hope you've asked this nice chap Robert to stay for dinner. There's also a toothsome blonde in the other room, chatting Christopher up to no mean tune. Know anything about her?"

136

Nobody bothered to answer him. Emma turned back to the cooker, took the lid off the kettle and put it on again. Johnny Rigger stared at her back and then at Robert, apparently waiting for life, with all its confusions, to be explained to him.

Robert could not trust himself to speak. He yearned to pick up this shambling drunk by the scruff of his neck and chuck him somewhere; preferably in the dustbin, where he had just dumped the unsavoury contents of the trash can. Then he would come back to deal with Emma in the same way, flinging her into the back of his car, driving her to London, to Porthkerris, to Paris – anywhere, away from this terrible basement, from the theatre, from the depressing suburban town.

He stared at her stubborn back view, willing her to turn round and face up to him. But she did not move, and her thin neck, and her shorn head, and the droop of her shoulders, all of which, he knew, should touch on his sympathy, did nothing but infuriate him.

He said, at last, formally, "This is simply a waste of everybody's time. I think Jane and I should go."

Emma accepted this in silence, but Johnny was full of protests. "Oh, you must stay, old chap. Stay and have something to eat . . ."

But Robert had pushed past him and was already halfway down the flagged passage. He found the other two deep in conversation, and quite unaware of any sort of drama. Christopher was saying, "Yes, it's a wonderful play. And what a part! You can build on to it, yet never overload it, never interfere in any way with production . . ."

(And he remembered bitterly the old crack about actors. "Now, let's talk about *you*, my friend. What did *you* think of my performance?")

"I trust you're not discussing *Daisies on the Grass.*"

Christopher looked round. "Good God, no! *Present Laughter*. What's Emma doing?"

"Your friend has just arrived back."

"Johnny? Yes, we just saw him tottering by."

"He's drunk."

"He quite often is. We fill him up with black coffee and shovel him into his bed. He's right as rain in the morning. Most unfair, really."

"Is there any particular reason why he should have to be here with you and Emma?"

Christopher raised his eyebrows. "Every reason." His voice was cool. "It's his flat. He got here first. I was second. Emma made a very cosy third."

There was a pause in the conversation. Jane, sensing the worst sort of conflict, broke tactfully in.

"Robert, it is getting late . . ." She picked up her bag and her gloves, and got up off the divan. ". . . Perhaps we should be going."

"But you haven't had your coffee. Or beer, or anything. What is Emma doing?"

"Doing her best to prop up Mr Rigger," Robert told him. "I suggest you go and help her. His legs don't seem to be at their most reliable."

Christopher, shrugging, acknowledged this. He uncurled his length from the low chair in which he had been sitting, and stood up. "Well, if you really feel you have to go . . ."

"I think we should. Thank you for . . ."

The words died out. There was nothing to thank him for. Christopher looked amused and Jane once again came to Robert's rescue.

". . . thank you for your wonderful performance this evening. We won't forget it." She held out her hand. "Goodbye."

"Goodbye. And goodbye, Robert."

"Goodbye, Christopher." And then he had to make himself say it. "Look after Emma."

They drove with unlawful speed back to London. On the motorway the needle of the speedometer crept up and up. Eighty, ninety, a hundred . . .

Jane said, "You're going to get into trouble."

"I already am," said Robert shortly.

"Did you have a row with Emma?"

"Yes."

"I thought you were looking a little fraught. What was it about?"

"Snooping. And moralising. And interfering. And trying to make a basically intelligent girl see the smallest glimmer of sense. She looked awful, too. She looked ill."

"She'll be all right."

"Last time I saw her, she was brown as a gipsy, with hair to her waist and a sort of bloom about her, like a delicious ripe fruit." He remembered the pleasure of kissing her goodbye. "Why do people have to do such dreadful things to themselves?"

"I don't know," said Jane. "Perhaps because of Christopher."

"How did you get on with him? I mean, apart from falling in love with him."

She ignored this. "He is clever. He is single-minded. He is ambitious. I think he will go far. But alone."

"You mean, without Emma."

"I'd say that."

Even at one in the morning London was alive with lights and traffic. They turned down into Sloane Street, circled Sloane Square, took the narrow road that led to Jane's mews. Outside her little house, he killed the engine of the Alvis, and it was very quiet. Street lamps shone on to the cobbles, on to the gleaming bonnet of the car, on to Jane's blonde and shining head. Robert was suddenly very tired. He began to reach for a cigarette, but Jane was there first. She put the cigarette into his mouth and lit it for him. In that instant her eyes became large and mysteriously shadowed, and there was a small and beguiling shadow, like a smudge, below the curve of her lower lip.

She snapped out the lighter. He said, "It's been a bloody awful evening. And I'm sorry."

"It always makes a change. It was interesting."

He pulled off his cap and dropped it on to the back seat. "Do you suppose," he said, "that they're living together?"

"Darling, I wouldn't know."

"But she's in love with him."

"I would say so."

For a little they were silent. Then Robert stretched, flexing himself after the long drive. He said, "We never got any dinner, did we? I don't know about you, but I'm hungry."

"If you want, I'll cook you scrambled eggs. And pour you a big cold Scotch-on-the-rocks."

"You're twisting my arm . . ."

They laughed, quietly. Night time laughter, he thought. Pillow laughter. He put his left hand up and around her neck, slid his fingers up into her hair, and leaned forward to kiss her mouth. She tasted sweet and fresh and cool. Her lips parted, and he threw his cigarette away, and pulled her tightly and closely into his arms.

After a little, he took his mouth from hers. "What are we waiting for, Jane?"

"One thing."

He smiled. "What's that?"

"Me. I don't want to start something that isn't ever going to be finished. I don't want to be hurt again. Even for you, Robert, and God knows how fond I am of you."

He said, "I won't hurt you," and meant it, and kissed the shadow under her mouth.

"And please," she said, "no more Littons."

He kissed her eyes, and the end of her short nose. "It's a promise. No more Littons."

He let her go then, and they got out of the car, and closed the doors as quietly as they had laughed together. And Jane found her key, and Robert took it from her and opened the door, and they went in, and Jane turned on the light, and started up the narrow stairs, and Robert closed the door, gently, behind them.

9

One of the delights of the big old house in Milton Gardens was living there in the summer. At the end of a warm and stuffy June day, and after the frustrations of a snail's-pace, petrol-laden journey back down the Kensington High Street, it was a positive physical pleasure to come in through the front door and slam it with happy finality behind you. The house always felt cool. It smelt of flowers and wax-polish, and in June the chestnut trees were out and so thick with leaves and pink and white blossom that the surrounding terraces of houses were shrouded from sight, sounds of all traffic were muffled, and only the occasional aeroplane, passing overhead, broke the evening calm.

Today was a classic example of this particular relief. There was thunder about, and since morning the temperature had steadily risen as the storm clouds gathered. Beneath this doom-like atmosphere, the city sweltered. By now the parks were dusty and the trampled grass turning brown, and the air about as refreshing as a draught of used bath-water. But here, at home, Helen had the sprinklers working on the lawn, and a gust of sweet, damp air swept through the open door at the end of the hall, and greeted Robert as he came indoors.

He dropped his hat on the hall chair, picked up his letters, called ''Helen?''

She wasn't in the kitchen. He went down the hall and out of the door and down the steps to the terrace and found her there, with a tea-tray and a book – unread – and a basket of mending. She wore a sleeveless cotton dress and a faded pair of espadrilles, and the sun had brought freckles out, big as paint spots, across her nose.

He came across the grass towards her, shedding the jacket of his suit.

She said, "You have caught me, doing nothing."

"And very nice too." He slung the jacket over the back of a painted wrought-iron chair, and collapsed beside her. "What a day! Anything left in that teapot?"

"No, but I can make you some more."

"Why don't I?" said Robert automatically, but without notable enthusiasm.

She did not reply to this hypothetical question, simply got up and took the teapot indoors. There was a plate of biscuits, and he took one and began to eat it, pulling his tie loose with the other hand. Beneath the sprinklers the lawn lay thick and green. It needed cutting again. He leaned back and shut his eyes.

It was now six weeks since he had been to Brookford to find Emma Litton, and in all that time there had been no word from her. After some discussion with Marcus and Helen he had written to Ben, telling him that Emma was staying with Christopher Ferris, whom she had re-met in Paris. That she was working in the Repertory Theatre in Brookford. That she was well. He could not, in truth, say more. Surprisingly, Ben had acknowledged this, not directly, to Robert, but as a scribbled footnote to a letter to Marcus. The purpose of the letter itself was purely business, typewritten on the impressive engraved paper of the Ryan Memorial Museum of Fine Arts. The retrospective Litton Exhibition was now over. In every way it had been a resounding success. Now, the new exhibition – a posthumous collection of drawings of a Puerto Rican genius who had lately died in dismal circumstances in a Greenwich Village garret, was well under way, and he and Melissa were taking the opportunity of a trip to Mexico. He intended to start painting again. He did not know when he would be returning to London. He remained, always, Marcus's Ben. And then, under the signature, and in Ben's own indecipherable scrawl:

> Had a letter from R. Morrow. Please thank him. Emma always fond of Christopher. Only hope his manners have improved.

Marcus showed this to Robert. "I don't know what you expected," he said, dryly, "but this is what you have got."

So it was over. For the first time Robert found himself in whole-hearted agreement with his sister Helen. The Littons were brilliant, unpredictable and charming. But they refused to conform to any pre-set behaviour pattern and they would not help themselves. So they were impossible.

To his surprise, he found that Emma was easy to forget. He could put her out of his mind as ruthlessly as an old trunkful of junk, relegated to the darkest recesses of some distant, dusty attic. And his life immediately became so full that the void left by her going was, almost at once, filled by more worthwhile pursuits.

At the Gallery, they were furiously busy. His days were a round of prospective clients, foreign visitors, and eager young artists carrying folios which bulged with their unsalubrious paintings. Would Bernstein mount an exhibition for them? Would Bernstein back this flame of new talent? The answer was usually, No, Bernstein's would not, but Marcus was a kindly man, and it was a house rule that no young man was returned to Glasgow or Bristol or Newcastle, or wherever it was he lived, without a good meal in his stomach, and the price of his return fare in the pocket of genuinely work-stained jeans.

Robert found that his vitality leapt to meet these demands, and, running at full speed, his energy could not – or would not – slow down. He could not bear to find himself doing nothing, and deliberately filled his leisure time with extraneous diversions, and a surprising number of them were involved with Jane Marshall.

The fact that their working hours did not always coincide put him off not at all. Sometimes he would call in for a drink at her little house, on the way home from the Gallery, and find her still in an apron, sewing braid on to yards of curtain, or working out the intricacies of a scalloped pelmet on graph paper. Sometimes she was out of town, and then he would fill the evening with furious physical labour, digging the garden or mowing the lawn.

One weekend he and Jane went down to Bosham, where Jane's brother had a small cottage, and kept a catamaran moored out on the choppy waters of the Hard. They sailed all Sunday and there was a stiff breeze and a bright, burning sun, and at the end of the day, sleepy with all the fresh air, they sat in the village pub and drank draught bitter and played shove ha'penny, and drove back to London very late, with the roof of the Alvis down, and wind blowing scraps of cloud across the face of the stars.

Once more Helen started saying, "I think you should marry her."

Robert ignored the nudging suspicion that he was behaving badly, and only said, "Perhaps I will."

"But when? What are you waiting for?"

He did not answer because he did not know. He only knew that this was not the time to plan; or assess; or to start to analyse the feelings that he had for Jane.

Now, he was disturbed, by Helen, returning with his tea-tray. She set it down, and the iron table grated on the pavings as she pulled it towards him. She said, "Marcus phoned at lunch-time."

Marcus had had to return to Scotland. The whisky-loving Scottish baronet, who had been so anxious to part with his art treasures, was being balked by his son, who would presumably inherit the heirlooms and did not want them sold out of hand. Or, if they were to be sold, he wanted three times as much for them as his thirsty father was prepared to ask. After a great deal of expensive telephoning, Marcus had reluctantly decided that another visit must be paid north of the border. Business must always come before personal comforts and preferences, and if, to lay his hands on those pictures, he had to sleep in damp beds and icy rooms and eat appallingly-cooked food, then he was ready to do so.

"How is he getting on?"

"He was reserved. No doubt speaking from some soaring baronial hall, with the old Laird listening from one end of the room, and the young Laird listening from the other."

"Has he got the pictures?"

"No, but he will. If not all, then some of them . . ." She went away from him, across the grass, to move the sprinkler. "The Raeburn he is determined on," she said, over her shoulder. "He'll go to any price."

Robert poured his tea, and began to read the evening paper. When Helen came back, he handed it to her open at a middle page.

"What's this?" she asked.

"That girl. Dinah Burnett . . ."

"Who is she?"

"You should know her face by now. She's a young actress with an efficient publicity agent. Every time you open a paper or a magazine, there's a picture of her perched on a piano, or cuddling a kitten or something equally obnoxious."

Helen made a comic face at the thrusting, sexy photograph, and read the caption aloud.

Dinah Burnett, the red-head who made such an impact on the TV series *Detective*, is in rehearsal now for the new Amos Monihan play *The Glass Door*, her first serious stake in legitimate theatre. "I'm scared," she told our special reporter. "But so very proud to have been chosen for this wonderful play." Miss Burnett is twenty-two and comes from Barnsley.

"I didn't know there was a new Amos Monihan play on the stocks. Who's producing?"

"Mayo Thomas."

"Then she must be good. Extraordinary, what talent can lurk behind really very stupid faces. But why did you suddenly show this to me?"

"No reason, really. Just that Jane's doing up a flat for her. At first it was going to be a pretty modest affair, but as soon as she got this part, she reckoned she'd moved in with the big-time spenders; you know, mirror bathrooms and white mink bedcovers."

"Very nice," said Helen. She tossed the paper back into his lap but he was too hot and lazy to catch it, so it slipped from his knee and fell to the ground. After a little, Helen began, in a desultory fashion, to gather the tea things together. She picked up the tray and started indoors.

"How about dinner?" she asked. "You going to Jane's or are you staying here?"

"I'm going to Jane's."

"That's fine. I'll eat a piece of cheese. It's too hot to cook, anyway."

When she had gone, he lit a cigarette and sat, listening to the pigeons, and watching the shadows lengthen over the grass. The cool and the quiet were like a benediction. The cigarette finished, he got up and went back into the house, and upstairs to his own flat, where he showered and shaved, and changed into jeans and a cool shirt. As he was pouring the first drink of the evening, the telephone rang. He filled the tumbler halfway up with soda, and went to his desk to answer it. It was Jane.

"Robert?"

"Yes."

"Darling, it's me. Look I just wanted to warn you, don't get here till about eight . . ."

"Why, are you entertaining a lover?"

"Wish I were. No, it's Dinah Burnett, she's had a new idea for her bathroom, God rot her soul, and she wants to come along after rehearsals and talk about it."

"For a girl who is so proud about being in the blasted play, her mind does harp on material things, doesn't it?"

"So you've been reading the evening paper. That blurb makes me ill."

"I can't think why she didn't bother to mention that she was doing up a flat, and had chosen well-known interior decorator, twenty-seven-year-old Jane Marshall, 34, 26, 36, to help her. Were you expecting to be taken out for dinner, because I'm not dressed accordingly."

"Of course not, it's much too hot. I've got some cold chicken; I thought I'd make a salad."

"And I shall subscribe a frosty bottle of wine."

"Delicious."

"Till eight, then."

"Yes, eight." He was on the point of putting down the receiver when she said again, "Don't come before," and then rang off. Mildly puzzled, he put down the receiver and then decided that he must have imagined a certain urgency in her voice. He went to find ice for his drink.

Deliberately, he was a little late, but even so, when he drew up outside Jane's house, there was a small blue Fiat still parked by her door. He gave his double toot on the horn and got out of the car, carrying the bottle of wine, and almost at once the front door opened and Jane stood there, in a faded pair of pink cotton trousers and a sleeveless top. Her hair fell across her cheek and she looked, for Jane, mildly distraught, making flapping gestures with her hand, and pointing upstairs.

He was amused. He came to kiss her. "What is it?"

She took the bottle of wine from him. "She's still here. She won't go. She won't stop talking. And now you've come, nothing's going to shift her."

"We'll say we're going out, and that we're late already."

"I suppose it's worth a try." They had been talking in whispers. Now she said in clear and social tones, "I wasn't sure if it was you or not. Come along up."

He followed her up the narrow, steep stairs. "Dinah, this is Robert Morrow . . ." Casually she introduced them, before going into the kitchen with the wine. He heard the big fridge door open and shut as she put it away.

Dinah Burnett sat on Jane's big sofa by the open window, with her legs curled up beneath her, looking as though she was expecting a photographer, or an interviewer, or a prospective lover. She was a beautiful girl, ripe and colourful, and it occurred to Robert that no photograph could do her full justice. She had auburn hair and pale green eyes, and skin like an apricot, and was built on proportions that are normally described as "lavish". She wore a short shift dress in a green to match her eyes, and it might have been designed to display as much as possible of her smooth, well-rounded arms and endless legs. Her feet were thrust into wooden sandals, her wrists jangled with gold bracelets and in her ears, gleaming through the profusion of hair, were enormous gold hoop ear-rings. Her teeth were white and even, and her black lashes long and black as soot, and it was hard to believe that she had started life in Barnsley.

"How do you do," said Robert. They shook hands. "I've just been reading all about you in the evening paper."

"Wasn't it a dreadful photograph?" She still had an endearing trace of a Yorkshire accent. "I look like a broken-down barmaid. But still, I suppose it's better than nothing."

She smiled at him, all her feminine charm rising to the bait of a new and attractive man, and Robert, flattered and warmed by her friendliness, settled himself at the other end of the sofa. She went on, "I shouldn't really be here at all, but Jane's doing up this new flat for me, and today I found this American magazine with a fabulous bathroom and I just had to bring it along, after rehearsals, and show it to her."

"How's the play going?"

"Oh, it's most exciting."

"What's it about?"

"Well, it's . . ."

At this juncture Jane reappeared from the kitchen and briskly interrupted. "How about a drink? Dinah, Robert and I are actually going out, but there's just time for a drink before you go.''

"Oh, that's sweet of you. If you're sure. I'd love a glass of beer.''

"How about you, Robert?''

"Sounds very nice, let me get it . . .''

"No, that's all right. I'm up.'' She snapped the top off a beer bottle, and poured a glass expertly, with no head to it. "Dinah, Robert's an art dealer, he works in Bernstein's in Kent Street.''

"Oh, are you really?'' said Miss Burnett, looking wide-eyed and interested, but not very much wiser. "Do you sell pictures and stuff. . . ?''

"Well, yes . . .''

Jane brought Dinah's beer across, pulled up a small table and set the glass down.

"Robert is a very high-powered man,'' she said. "He's always dashing off to Paris or Rome, to pull off enormous deals, aren't you, Robert?'' She went back to her drink tray. "Dinah, you should get him to look out for a picture for the new flat. You need something modern over that fireplace and you never know, it might be an investment. Something to sell when they run out of good parts for you.''

"Don't talk about running out. I've only just started. Besides, wouldn't it be very expensive?''

"Not as expensive as that American bathroom.''

Dinah smiled engagingly. "But, I always feel a bathroom's terribly important.''

Jane had poured two more drinks, now she brought them over, and handed one to Robert. Then settled herself in the chair opposite the sofa, and faced them both across the low table.

"Well, it's your flat, ducky,'' she said.

Her voice was a little acid. Robert said quickly, "You still haven't told me about the new play . . . *The Glass Door*. When are you opening?''

"Wednesday. This Wednesday as ever is. At the Regent Theatre.''

"We must try and get seats, Jane.''

"Yes, of course,'' said Jane.

"The thought of a first night makes me sick with nerves. You see, it's my first shot at the living theatre, as it were, and if it wasn't for Mayo being such a fabulous producer I'd have dropped out weeks ago . . .''

"You still haven't told us what it's about.''

"Well, it's . . . oh, I don't know. It's about this young man, from an ordinary, working-class family. And he writes a book and it's a best seller, and he becomes a sort of celebrity – you know, on television and such. And then he gets mixed up with the film people, and all the time, he's getting richer, and nastier, and he's drinking and having affairs, and generally living it up. And then, of course, in the end, the whole racket falls round his ears like a pack of cards and he finishes up, right where he started, in his mother's house, in the kitchen, with his old typewriter and a blank sheet of paper. It sounds corny, I know, but it's moving and real and the dialogue is out of this world.''

"Do you think it's going to go?''

"I don't see how it can fail. But then I'm prejudiced.''

"What part do you play?''

"Oh, I'm just one of the many girls. But I'm different, because I get pregnant.''

"Charming,'' murmured Jane.

"But it isn't sordid, not a bit,'' Dinah assured her. "When I first read the script I didn't know whether to laugh or cry. Real life, I suppose.''

"Yes." Jane finished her drink, and put down the empty glass and looked at her watch. She said, pointedly, "Robert, I'm going up to change. We mustn't be late. We'll keep everybody waiting." She stood up. "You'll excuse me, Dinah, won't you?"

"Of course I will, and thank you for being so sweet about the bathroom. I'll ring you up and let you know what I've decided."

"Yes, you do that."

When she had gone upstairs, Dinah smiled once more, confidingly, at Robert. "I hope I'm not keeping you. I will go when I've finished my drink, but I live in such a dump just now, it's depressing. And it's so hot, isn't it? I wish it would thunder. It would be so much cooler if only it would thunder."

"It will this evening, I'm sure. Tell me, how did you get this part?"

"Well, Amos Monihan, you know, he wrote the play – he'd seen me on TV in *Detective*, and he rang Mayo Thomas and said he thought I'd be right for the part. So I had an audition. That's all really."

"And who plays the lead? The young man. The writer?"

"This is the gamble. The backers wanted a big name, somebody famous. But Mayo had found this new boy – he'd seen him in some provincial rep, and somehow, he convinced the man with the money to give him a try."

"So you have an unknown in the lead?"

"That's about it," said Dinah. "But, believe me, he's good."

She finished her drink. Upstairs Jane was moving about in her bedroom, going to and fro, opening and shutting drawers. Robert got up to retrieve the empty glass. "Would you like the other half?"

"No, really, I won't. I mustn't keep you any longer . . ."

She stood up, pulling down her dress, and tossing her long hair away from her neck. She called up the stair. "I'm off. Goodbye, Jane!"

"Oh, goodbye." Jane sounded more friendly now that her visitor was actually on her way out.

Dinah started downstairs, and Robert followed her, intending to politely see her off the premises. Over her bright head, he leaned forward to unsnib the latch of Jane's front door. Outside, the mews slumbered in the hot airless evening.

He said, "I'll keep my fingers crossed for Wednesday."

"Bless you."

They went out into the street. He opened the door of the Fiat for her. He said, "What's he called, this young actor?"

Dinah slid into the driving-seat, revealing more leg than was good for anybody's blood pressure.

She said, "Christopher Ferris."

He thought, *So that's why Jane didn't want me to meet you.*

"Christopher Ferris? I know him."

"Do you? How funny."

"At least . . . I knew his sister."

"I don't know anything about his family."

"He's never mentioned her? Emma?"

"Never a word. But then, chaps don't usually talk about their sisters, do they?"

She laughed, and slammed the car door shut, but the window was down, and Robert leaned his elbow on it, like a salesman with a foot in the door.

He said, "I'd like to wish him luck."

"I'll give him a message for you tomorrow."

"Could I ring him up?"

"Well, I suppose you could, but calls aren't exactly welcome when we're working." And then she had a bright idea. "Tell you what, I've got his home number somewhere. I had to ring up for Mayo, once, and leave a message.''

She picked her bag off the other seat, and started to delve. She brought out a script, a purse, a scarf, a bottle of sun oil, a diary. She leafed through the diary. ''Here it is, Flaxman 8881. Do you want me to write it down for you?''

''No. I'll remember.''

''He might be there now . . . I don't know what he does in his spare time.'' She smiled again. ''Fancy you knowing him. It's a small world, isn't it?''

''Yes. It's a small world.''

She started up her engine. ''Well, it's been fun meeting you. Cheerio.''

He stood back. ''Goodbye.''

The little car roared away down the mews, and he watched it go. At the junction at the end of the narrow street it paused for a moment, then shot away, turned left and was gone, the sound of its engine swallowed into the anonymous grumble that was London traffic.

He went back into the house, closed the door, went upstairs. There was no sound from the bedroom.

''Jane.''

She began immediately to move about, as though occupied.

''Jane.''

''What is it?''

''Come here.''

''But I'm not . . .''

''Come down here.''

After a moment, she appeared at the head of the stairs, wrapped in a thin dressing-gown. ''What is it?''

''It's Christopher Ferris,'' said Robert.

She stared down at him, her expression closed and suddenly implacable.

"What about him?"

"You knew he was in this play. That he's been in London all this time."

She came down the stairs towards him. When her face was on a level with his, she said coolly, "Yes, I knew."

"But you never told me. Why not?"

"Perhaps because I don't believe in stirring up muddy ponds. Besides, you promised. No more Littons."

"This has nothing to do with that promise."

"Then what are you getting so hot and bothered about? Look, Robert, I think I feel about this business much the same way as your sister Helen. Bernstein's act, in a professional capacity, for Ben Litton, and after that, their commitments to the family should end. I know about Emma and the sort of life she's led and I'm sorry for her. I went to Brookford with you, and I saw that creepy little theatre and that dreadful flat. But she is adult, and, as you said yourself, highly intelligent . . . What if Christopher is in London? That doesn't mean Emma has been abandoned. It's a part of his job, and she'll accept it as such, I'm sure."

"That still doesn't explain why you never told me."

"Perhaps because I knew all along that you'd start running round in circles like a demented sheepdog. Imagining the worst, nagged by responsibility, simply because the wretched girl is Ben Litton's daughter. Robert, you *saw* her. She doesn't want to be helped. And if you try, you'll just be interfering . . ."

He said slowly, "I don't know if you're trying to convince me, or yourself."

"You fool, I'm trying to make you see the truth."

"The truth is that, as far as we know, Emma Litton is alone, living in a damp basement with a paralytic drunk."

"Isn't that what she chose to do?"

She flung the question at him, and then, before he could reply, pushed past him and went to the trolley and began fiddling about with empty glasses and beer-bottle tops in a feeble pretence at tidying up. He watched, with a great sadness, her back view, the smooth bell of hair, the tiny waist, the small, capable hands. She was unrelenting.

He said gently, "Dinah Burnett gave me Christopher's number. Perhaps it would be better if I rang him from here."

"Do whatever you like." She carried the glasses through to the kitchen. Robert picked up her phone and dialled the remembered number. Jane came back to collect up the empty bottles.

"Hello." It was Christopher.

"Christopher, this is Robert Morrow speaking. You remember, I came down to Brookford . . ."

"To see Emma. Yes, of course. How splendid! How did you know where to find me?"

"Dinah Burnett gave me your number. She also told me about *The Glass Door*. Congratulations."

"You can save them till we see what the critics have to say."

"Still, it's a great effort. Look, I was wondering about Emma."

Christopher's voice turned cautious. "Yes?"

Jane had come back from the kitchen and now stood by the window, her arms folded, looking down into the street.

"Where is she?"

"In Brookford."

"In the flat. With your friend?"

"My friend? Oh, Johnny Rigger? No, he left. He came to rehearsals drunk one morning and the producer slung him out. Emma's on her own."

Carefully controlling his temper, Robert said, "You never thought of ringing up Marcus Bernstein or myself and telling us this?"

"Well, I would have, but before I left Brookford, Emma made me promise not to. So, you see, I couldn't." While Robert, in seething silence, tried to accept this excuse, Christopher went on, sounding suddenly much younger and not so sure of himself. "I tell you what I did do, though. I felt a bit of a heel leaving her like that . . . so I wrote to Ben."

"You wrote to *who*?"

"Her father."

"But what the hell could he do? He's in America . . . he's in Mexico . . ."

"I didn't know he was in Mexico, but I wrote to him care of Bernstein's, and put please forward on the envelope. You see, I felt *someone* should know what had happened."

"And Emma? Is she still working in the theatre?"

"She was when I left. You see, there was really no point her coming up to London with me. I rehearse dawn to dusk as it is, and we'd never have seen each other. Besides, if *The Glass Door* folds up after a week, then I'll need my old Brookford job back again. Tommy Childers is very kindly keeping it open for me. So we decided it would be better if Emma stayed down there."

"And if *The Glass Door* runs for two years?"

"I don't know what would happen then. But right now, I'll be honest with you, things are a bit tricky. This house I'm living in – it belongs to my mother. I'm living with my mother. You can see, what with things being the way they are, it is a bit tricky."

"Yes," said Robert. "Yes, I can see . . . as you say, it's tricky."

*

159

He put down the receiver. Jane, not turning from the window, said, "What's so tricky?"

"He's living with Hester, his mother. And she's obviously refusing to let a Litton darken her door. Silly old bitch. And the drunk flatmate has had the sack, so Emma's on her own. And, to ease his conscience, Christopher has written to Ben Litton to tell him what has happened. And I should like to tie the lot of them together with one great big millstone, and consign them all to a bottomless lake."

"I knew this would happen," said Jane. She turned, then, to face him, her arms still rigidly folded, and he saw that she was not only angry, but deeply upset. "It could be good, this thing between us . . . you know that, don't you, as well as I do. And that's why I didn't tell you about Christopher, because I knew, that if you knew, it would be the end of everything."

He wished he could say *It doesn't have to be the end*, but it was impossible.

"In a way, Robert, all this time, you did keep your promise. You never mentioned Emma. But she was never out of the back of your mind."

Now that it was said, and out in the open, he saw that this was true. He said, hopelessly, "Only because in some extraordinary way, I am involved with her."

"If you are involved with her, it's because you want to be. And it's not good enough, Robert. Not for me. I won't settle for second best. I'd rather go without. I hoped I'd made that clear. With me, it has to be all or nothing at all. I can't go through it all again."

He understood. But could only say that he was sorry.

"I think . . . perhaps, you'd better go."

Her arms were still folded, a barrier against him. There was no way to say goodbye. He could not kiss her. He could not lightly say, "It's been fun" in the best traditions of drawing-room comedy. And he could never forgive her for trying to keep him from Emma.

He said, "I'll go now."

"Yes, do that." But as he started downstairs, she remembered something. "You left the wine."

"Forget about the wine," said Robert.

10

The song was over. The lights were dimmed. Charmian as Oberon moved forward for her final speech. The taped Mendelssohn music – for the meagre proportions of the Brookford Rep did not allow space for an orchestra – stole out across the dark cave of the auditorium and evoked for Emma, sitting at the prompt desk – all the distilled magic of a summer night.

Now until the break of day
Through this house each fairy stray . . .

It was the end of the first week of *A Midsummer Night's Dream*. The financial fiasco of *Daisies on the Grass* had driven the management to a production of Shakespeare which, although it entailed double the work for everybody, ensured an Arts Council grant and full houses, composed mostly of school children and students.

By now Emma was no longer working for Collins, the stage manager. There was a new ASM, a young girl fresh from drama school, dedicated, tough and seemingly immune to Collins' barbed tongue. She was on-stage now, in the grey velvet tunic and silvered wings of Cobweb, the fairy, for the huge cast of *The*

Dream demanded that every member of the company should be called in and given a part.

Because of this, Tommy Childers had asked Emma to come back and lend a hand with the back-stage activities. During the past fortnight she had coped with a number of jobs; helping in the wardrobe, working in the scenery store; typing scripts, and all the time nipping out for sandwiches and cigarettes, and making endless pots of tea.

Tonight, she had been given the job of prompter, and had spent the evening with her eyes glued to the prompt copy, terrified of losing her place, of missing a cue, of letting somebody down. But now, as the play drew to its close, and, knowing the rest of it by heart, she allowed her concentration to relax a little, and indulged in the luxury of watching the stage.

Charmian wore a crown of emerald leaves, a silver tabard and silver tights on her long, slim legs. The audience, caught by the old magic of the words, stayed breathless, spellbound.

Trip away; make no stay;
Meet me all by break of day.

To eke out the cramped wing space on either side of the stage, Tommy Childers had had built a ramp which led down from the stage and into the centre aisle of the auditorium. Now Oberon and Titania, hand-in-hand, and followed by a retinue of fairies, made their exit down this ramp, running, with the draperies flying like exuberant wings, off the lighted stage, and down into the darkness; swift and quiet; up the aisle and out of the double doors at the back with such an airy suddenness that they were gone almost without a sound, without a trace.

And then it was left to Sara Rutherford, playing Puck, as

a tilt-eared teenager, with the stage to herself and a single spotlight.

If we shadows have offended,
Think but this, and all is mended.

She had a little pipe. When she got to "So good night unto you all," she played on it the single thread of notes that was the theme of the Mendelssohn music.

Then, triumphant, "Give me your hands, if we be friends, and Robin shall restore amends." And darkness, and curtain, and applause.

All over. Emma let out a sigh of relief that nothing had gone wrong, shut the prompt copy and sat back in her chair. The cast were surging back on stage for the first curtain call. As he went past her, the boy who played Nick Bottom leant over to whisper,

"Tommy asked me to tell you – there's some chap waiting to see you. He's been sitting in the Green Room for half an hour, but Tommy's put him in his office. Thought it might be a bit more private for you. Better go and see what it's all about."

"To see me? But who is it?"

But Bottom was already on stage. The curtain swept up, there was a fresh burst of applause, and smiles and bows and curtsies . . .

Emma's first thought was that it was Christo. But if it was Christo, why hadn't he said? She went down the wooden steps and along the cat-walk that led to the landing at the head of the stage door stairs. Ahead, down a short passage, the Green Room door stood ajar, showing a glimpse of sagging velvet sofa, the old playbills framed on the walls. Tommy Childers's office led off this passage. The door was shut.

Behind her, the applause died down, and then rose again for the second curtain call.

She opened the door.

It was a tiny room, scarcely bigger than a cupboard; scarcely big enough to contain the desk, and a couple of chairs and a filing cabinet. He sat behind the desk, in Tommy's chair, behind Tommy's personal and private chaos of scripts and letters and programme proofs and production notes. The wall behind him was thumb-tacked with stage photographs. Someone had made him a cup of tea, but he had not deigned to drink it, and it stood before him, horribly cold, untouched. He wore pearly-grey trousers, a russet corduroy jacket, a dark blue cotton shirt and a chrome yellow tie, loosely tied, so that his top button showed. He was browner than ever, and he looked about ten years younger, and almost indecently attractive.

He was smoking an American king-size cigarette, and an ash-tray full of butts was indicative of the length of time he had been waiting for Emma. When she came through the door, he turned his head to look at her, resting his elbow on the desk, his chin on his thumb. His eyes, through the veil of cigarette smoke, remained dark and shadowed and quite unreadable.

He said, sounding mildly irritated, "What have you been doing?" and Emma was too stunned to do anything but tell him.

"Prompting."

"Well, come along in and shut the door."

She did as she was told. The applause from the auditorium was closed away. She found that her heart was thudding, but whether this was due to shock, or pleasure, or a certain apprehension it was impossible to know. She said at last, feebly, "I thought you were in America."

"I was, this morning. Flew back today. And yesterday . . . at least I suppose it was yesterday, these International date lines

166

and clocks being changed complicate life to an alarming degree
. . . I was in Mexico. Yes; yesterday. Acapulco.''

Emma felt for a chair, lowered herself gently on to it before
her legs gave way.

"Acapulco?"

"Do you know that the aeroplanes that fly to Acapulco are
all painted different colours? And as you go south, the air
hostesses do a sort of uniform strip tease. Fascinating." He
continued to survey her. "Emma, there's something different
about you. That's it, you've cut your hair. What a good idea!
Turn around and let me see the back." She did so, swivelling her
head cautiously, and watching him out of the corner of her eye.
"Much better. Never knew you had such a good shape to your
head. Have a cigarette."

He pushed the packet across the desk. Emma took one, and he
lit it for her, leaning forward, cupping the flame with his familiar
and beautiful hands. As he shook out the match he said, casually,
"A great many letters have been winging their way across the
Atlantic. None of them written by you."

It was a rebuke. "No. I know."

"Difficult to understand. Not that I minded in particular –
though I must say, as it was about the first letter I'd ever written
you, it would have been pleasant to get a reply. But with Melissa
it was different. She wanted you to come out to the States, and
be with us, if only for a short visit. You've always been rather
good about these things. What happened?"

"I don't know. I suppose I was . . . disappointed because you
didn't come home. And the idea of your being married took a
bit of time to get used to. And then, by the time I got round to
accepting it . . . it had become too late to answer your letters. And
every day that passed made it worse; made it more impossible.
I never knew that if you did something you weren't particularly

167

proud of . . . it became progressively more difficult to undo it again.'' He did not comment on this. Simply continued to smoke, to watch her. ''You said a great many letters. Who else did you hear from?''

''Well, I heard from Marcus, of course. That was business. And then a rather stilted, formal affair from Robert Morrow. Saying that he'd been here to see some play or other, and had had a drink with you and Christopher. I couldn't gather, however, whether he had come specifically to see the play or to see you.''

''Yes. Well . . .''

''As soon as we realised that you were still alive and apparently occupied and with no intention of visiting us, Melissa and I set off in our coloured aeroplane for Mexico where we stayed with a mad old film star who lives in a house full of parakeets. Then, yesterday, we flew back to Queenstown, and what should I find waiting for me but yet another letter.''

''From Robert?''

''No. From Christopher.''

She could not help it. ''From *Christopher*?''

''He must be an exceptionally talented young man. A London production, so soon, with so little experience. Of course, I always knew that he'd make a flagrant success of his life. Either that or end up in prison . . .''

But even this provocation could not divert her. ''You mean *Christopher*? Wrote to *you*?''

''Said in that tone of voice, it sounds insulting.''

''But why?''

''One can only imagine that he felt mildly responsible.''

''But . . .'' An idea was forming. A suspicion so wonderful that, if it was not true, then it must be scotched immediately. ''But you didn't come home because of that letter? You came home to paint. To go back to Porthkerris and paint again?''

"Well, of course, taking the long view, I have. Mexico was inspiring. They have an extraordinary pink that keeps recurring in their buildings, and their pictures, and their very clothes . . ."

"Perhaps you'd had enough of Queenstown, and America," she persisted. "You've never been much good at staying in any one place for more than a couple of months. And, of course, you'll have to see Marcus. And start thinking about a new exhibition."

He stared at her blankly. "Why this catalogue of motives?"

"Well, there has to be some reason."

"I've just told you. I came to see you."

She did not want the cigarette he had given her. She leaned forward and stubbed it out, and then clasped her hands in her lap, the palms pressed tight together, the fingers interlaced. Misinterpreting her silence, Ben looked aggrieved. "I don't think, Emma, that you quite understand the situation. I literally flew in from Mexico, read Christopher's letter, kissed Melissa goodbye and flew out again. Didn't even have time to change my shirt. I then subjected myself to another twelve hours of flying, the tedium broken only by a series of uneatable meals, all of which tasted like plastic. Do you think I endure such tortures simply to talk to Marcus Bernstein about another exhibition?"

"But Ben . . ."

He was, however, well away, and in no mood to be interrupted.

"And, once arrived, do I go to Claridges, where Melissa has thoughtfully cabled in advance and reserved me a room? Do I indulge in a bath, or a drink, or a decent meal? No. I climb into the slowest taxi-cab this side of the Atlantic, and drive, through unspeakable rain, to Brookford" (he said the word as though it were something distasteful), "where, after interminable incorrect directions, I eventually run the repertory theatre to earth.

169

The taxi is at this moment outside, ticking up a monumental fare. And if you don't believe me, you can go and look.''

''I believe you,'' said Emma, quickly.

''And then, when you do deign to appear, all you can talk about is Marcus Bernstein and some hypothetical exhibition. Do you know something? You're an ungrateful brat. A typical example of the modern generation. You don't deserve to have a father.''

She said, ''But I've been alone before. For years I've been alone. In Switzerland and Florence and Paris. You never came to see me then.''

''You didn't need me then,'' said Ben flatly. ''And I knew what you were doing, and who you were with. This time, when I read that letter from Christopher, I knew the first, faint stirrings of concern. Perhaps because Christopher, of all people, would never have written if he hadn't been concerned himself. Why didn't you tell me you'd met him in Paris?''

''I thought you wouldn't be pleased.''

''It depends on what sort of a person he's turned into. Has he changed very much from the small boy who lived with us at Porthkerris?''

''He looks the same . . . but he's tall . . . he's a man now. Single-minded and ambitious and, perhaps, a little self-centred. And with all the charm in the world.'' Talking about him, to Ben, was like having a weight lifted from her shoulders. Emma smiled. She said, ''And I adore him.''

Ben, accepting this, returned the smile. ''You sound like Melissa, talking about Ben Litton. It seems that young Christopher and I have, after all, much in common. It's ironic that we should have wasted so many years in detesting each other. Perhaps I should make his acquaintance again. This time, we might get on a little better.''

"Yes, I think you might."

"Melissa is joining me in a week or two. Coming down to Porthkerris."

"Living at the cottage?" said Emma, unbelieving.

Ben was amused. "Melissa? At the cottage? You must be joking. A suite has already been reserved at The Castle Hotel. I shall lead the life of a goldfish in a bowl, but perhaps, as I get older, the sybaritic existence is beginning to reveal its charms."

"But didn't she mind? Your coming home like that? Kissing her and leaving her without even taking time to change your shirt?"

"Emma, Melissa is a clever woman. She doesn't try to pin a man down or to possess him. She knows that the best way to hold on to someone you love is to . . . very gently . . . let him go. Women take a long time to learn this. Hester never did. How about you?"

"I'm learning," said Emma.

"The extraordinary thing is, I believe you are."

By now, darkness had fallen. This had happened, unheeded, while they talked, the dusk deepening imperceptibly until Ben's face, across the tiny distance that separated them, was simply a blur, his hair a wing of white. There was a lamp on the desk, but neither of them reached out to turn it on. The twilight enclosed them, the shut door kept the rest of the world out. They were the Littons; a family; together.

As they talked, the backstage shell of the theatre had rung with routine sounds. The last curtain call. Voices; Collins swearing at some unfortunate electrician. Hurrying feet, running upstairs to the dressing-rooms, anxious to be away, to be free of costumes and make-up, to catch buses, to go home, to cook food and wash stockings and, perhaps, to make love. Footsteps passed to and fro, in and out of the Green Room, *Darling, have you got a cigarette? Where's Delia? Has anybody seen Delia? There wasn't a phone call for me, was there?*

The sounds thinned out, as in twos and threes they left the theatre. Down the stone stairs, out of the banging door, into the narrow alley. A car started up. Somewhere a man started to whistle.

Behind Emma the door was abruptly opened, and the soft darkness split with an oblong of yellow light.

"Sorry to interrupt you . . ." It was Tommy Childers . . . "Wouldn't you like some illumination?" He snapped on the switch, and Ben and Emma were transfixed, blinking, like a couple of sleepy owls. "I just wanted something off my desk, before I go home."

Emma stood up, pulling her chair out of the way.

"Tommy, did you know this was my father?"

"I wasn't sure," said Tommy, smiling at Ben. "I thought you were in America."

"Everybody thought I was in America. Even my wife did until I said goodbye to her. I hope we haven't inconvenienced you, sitting here for so long in your office."

"Not at all. The only thing is the night-watchman's getting a bit edgy about the stage door. I'll tell him you'll shut it, Emma."

"Yes, of course."

"Well . . . Good night, Mr Litton . . ."

Ben heaved himself to his feet. "I had thought of taking Emma to London with me tonight. You wouldn't have any objections to that?"

"None at all," said Tommy. "She's been working like a slave for the past two weeks. Do her good to have a few days off."

Emma said, "I don't know why you ask Tommy, when you haven't even asked me."

"I don't ask you things," Ben said. "I tell you."

Tommy laughed. He said, "In that case, I expect you'll be going to the first night."

Ben remained vague. "First night?"

Dryly, Emma enlightened him. "He means Christopher's private view. On Wednesday."

"So soon? I shall probably be back in Porthkerris by then. We shall have to see."

"You should try and make it," said Tommy. They shook hands. "It's been splendid meeting you. And Emma . . . I'll see you sometime . . ."

"Maybe next week if *The Glass Door* folds up . . ."

"It won't," said Tommy. "If what Chris did to *Daisies on the Grass* is anything to go by, it'll run as long as *The Mousetrap*. Don't forget to shut the door."

He went away, downstairs; they heard his footsteps fade down the alley below the window, out into the street. Emma sighed. She said, "I think we should go. The night-watchman gets traumas if he thinks the place isn't properly locked up. And that taxi driver of yours will either give up hope of ever seeing you again, or else die of old age."

But Ben had once more settled himself into Tommy's chair. "In a moment," he said. "There's just one more thing." He tapped a fresh cigarette from the American packet. "I wanted to ask you about Robert Morrow."

He had the most disconcertingly calm voice. It never changed or varied its inflections so that you were continuously being taken unawares. Every nerve in Emma's body leapt in warning, but she only said, casually enough, "What about him?"

"I always had a . . . strong feeling about that young man."

173

She tried being flippant. "You mean, apart from admiring the shape of his head."

He ignored this. "I asked you once if you liked him, and you said, 'I suppose so. I scarcely know him.'"

"What of it?"

"Do you know him any better now?"

"Well, yes, I suppose I do."

"When he came to Brookford that time, he wasn't simply visiting the theatre, was he? He came to see you."

"He came to find me. That isn't quite the same thing."

"But he took the trouble to find you. I wonder why."

"Perhaps he was prompted by the famous Bernstein sense of responsibility."

"Stop fencing."

"What do you want me to say?"

"I want you to tell me the truth. And to be honest with yourself."

"What makes you think I haven't?"

"Because a light has gone out of your eyes. Because I left you at Porthkerris, blooming and brown as a gipsy. Because of the way you sit, the way you talk, the way you look." He lit the cigarette then, broke the match, and dropped it meticulously into the ash-tray. "Perhaps you forget I've been watching people, dissecting their personalities, painting them, for more years than you've been alive. And it's not Christopher who's made you unhappy. You've as good as told me that yourself."

"Perhaps it was you."

"Rubbish? A father? Angry, maybe. Hurt and resentful. Never heart-broken. Tell me about Robert Morrow. What went wrong?"

The little room was suddenly unbearably stuffy. Emma got up and went to the window, and opened it wide, leaning her elbow on the sill, and breathing in great draughts of cool, rain-washed air.

She said, "I suppose I never bothered to understand what sort of a person he really was."

"I don't understand."

"Well . . . meeting him, for the first time, the way I did. That started everything off on the wrong foot. I never thought of him as a person with a private life, and a private existence, and likes and dislikes . . . and lovers. He was just part of Bernstein's, as Marcus is part of Bernstein's. Simply there to look after us. To arrange exhibitions, and cash cheques and reserve hotel accommodation, and make sure that life, for the Littons, at least, runs on oiled wheels." She turned to frown at her father, puzzled by her own revelation. "How *could* I have been so moronic?"

"You probably inherited it from me. What put an end to this happy illusion?"

"Oh, I don't know. Things. He came down to Porthkerris to look at Pat Farnaby's pictures, and he asked me to go out to Gollan with him, because he didn't know the way. And it was raining, and very stormy, and he had a big thick sweater on, and we laughed about things. I don't know, but it was nice. And we were going to have dinner together, but he . . . well . . . anyway, I had a headache, so I didn't go after all. And then I came to Brookford to be with Christo, and I didn't think about Robert Morrow any more until that evening when he came to the theatre. I was clearing the stage, and suddenly he spoke, just behind me, and I turned round and he was there. And he had this girl with him. She's called Jane Marshall, and she's an interior decorator, or something very talented. She's pretty, and successful, and they seemed so much a couple. Do you know what I mean? Contained and self-sufficient and . . . together. And I felt as

175

though someone had slammed a door in my face and left me out in the cold.''

She turned from the window then, and came back to the desk and sat on it, with her back to her father, and picked up a rubber band and began to play with it, snapping it like a catapult through her fingers.

''And they came back to the flat, for a beer or a coffee or something, and everything was hideous, and Robert and I had a horrible row, and he just walked out without saying goodbye and took Jane Marshall with him. And drove back to London, and, one imagines . . .'' she tried desperately to keep her voice light, ''. . . lived happily ever after. Anyway, I haven't seen him since.''

''Is that why you wouldn't let Christopher tell him that you were on your own?''

''Yes.''

''Is he in love with this girl?''

''Christo thought he was. Christo thought she was gorgeous. He said that if Robert didn't marry her, he ought to have his head examined.''

''And what was the row about?''

Emma could scarcely remember. In retrospect, it jarred as painfully as a gramophone record, played backwards, at full pitch. An exchange of shouted words, meaningless, hurtful, regretted.

''Oh, everything. You. And not answering your letter. And Christo. I think he imagines Christo and I are madly in love, but by the time we'd got round to that I was so angry I didn't bother to disillusion him.''

''Perhaps that was a mistake.''

''Yes, perhaps it was.''

''Do you want to stay here, at Brookford?''

"There's nowhere else to go."

"There's Porthkerris."

Emma turned to smile down at him. "With you? At the cottage?"

"Why not?"

"A thousand reasons. Running home to Daddy never solved anything. Besides, you can't run away from the inside of your own head."

He was on his way at last, and the self-delusion and the restlessness of the past six weeks were over. The Alvis – like a home-bound hunter – streamed west, out over the Hammersmith fly-over and on to the M4. Robert settled her permanently in the fast outer lane, and kept her speedometer prudently, carefully down to seventy, for the frustration, at this stage, of being stopped by a police patrol would be almost more than he could bear. As he approached Heathrow Airport, the first rumble of thunder broke the heavy, quiet air, and he stopped in at the first lay-by and put up the hood. He was only just in time. As he moved out into the road again, the sullen evening erupted like a volcano. The wind, with staggering abruptness, swept up from the west, bearing towering black thunderheads before it, and when the rain came it was a positive explosion of water, sheets of it, like a monsoon downpour, against which the windscreen-wipers could scarcely compete. In seconds, the surface of the road was awash, reflecting the livid streaks of forked lightning which split the sky.

It occurred to him that perhaps it would be wise to stop, and wait until the worst of the storm was over, but by now his sense of relief at doing what he had for weeks been subconsciously wanting to do, was stronger than any ideas of caution. So he went on, and the huge cambered curve of the motorway pouted up towards him, and roared beneath his wheels, and was flung away in a wave of water; already a thing of the past; rejected and forgotten, along with his own feeble uncertainties.

He found the theatre closed. By the light of the street lamp, he was able to read the posters. A MIDSUMMER NIGHT'S DREAM. Unlit, deserted, the place looked gloomy as the mission hall it had once been. The door was barred and bolted; all the windows dark.

He got out of the car. It was cooler now, and he reached into the back seat and took out a sweater that had been lying there since the Bosham weekend, and pulled it on over his shirt. He slammed the door shut, and then saw the solitary taxi, waiting at the pavement's edge, the driver slumped over his wheel. He might have been dead.

"Is there anyone in there?"

"Must be, Guv-nor. I'm waiting for a fare."

Robert walked down the pavement, as far as the narrow lane, down which, so long ago, Emma and Christopher had come, walking like lovers, with their arms about each other. On this side of the sombre building a first-floor window blazed with uncurtained light. He went down the shadowed alley, tripped over a dustbin, found an open door. Inside, a flight of stone stairs led upwards, illuminated palely from a light which burned on the first-floor landing. He was assailed by the stale theatre smell of grease-paint, oil-paint, musty velvet. From above came the murmur of voices and he went upstairs, towards it, and found the short passage, and the door marked PRODUCER'S OFFICE, ajar, and edged with bright light.

He pushed the door open and the voices ceased abruptly, and he found himself on the threshold of a tiny, crowded office, looking down into the astonished faces of Ben and Emma Litton.

Emma sat on the desk, with her back to her father, facing

Robert. She wore a short dress, cut simply as an overall, and her long legs were bare and brown. The room was so small that as he stood there in the doorway, he was only an arm's length from her. If he wanted he could reach out and touch her. He thought that she had never looked so beautiful.

His relief and pleasure at seeing Emma was so great that the unexpectedness of Ben Litton's appearance became insignificant. Ben himself was equally unsurprised. He simply raised his dark eyebrows and said:

"Well, bless my soul, see who's turned up now."

Robert put his hands in his pockets, and said, "I thought . . ."

Ben held up a hand. "I know. You thought I was in America. Well, I'm not; I'm in Brookford. And the sooner I get out of the place and back to London, the better."

"But when did you . . . ?"

But Ben was stubbing out his cigarette, standing up, ruthlessly interrupting. "You didn't by any chance notice a taxi-cab at the front of the theatre, did you?"

"Yes, I did. The driver looked as though he had become fossilised to the wheel."

"Poor fellow. I must go and put his mind at rest."

"I've got my car," said Robert. "If you like I'll drive you back to London."

"Even better. I can pay the man off." Emma had not moved. Now, Ben edged his way around the desk, and Robert stood aside to let him out of the door.

"By the way, Robert, Emma's coming too. Will you have room for her?"

"But of course." In the doorway, they eyed each other. Then Ben gave a satisfied nod. "Splendid," he said. "I'll wait outside for you both."

*

"Did you know he was coming?"

Emma shook her head.

"Did it have anything to do with the letter Christopher wrote to him?"

Emma nodded.

"He flew back, today, from the States, to make sure you were all right?"

Emma nodded again, her eyes shining. "He'd been in Mexico with Melissa. But he came straight here. Even Marcus doesn't know he's in the country. He didn't even go to London. He took a taxi from the airport to Brookford. And he wasn't angry about Christopher, and he says if I want I can go back to Porthkerris with him."

"And are you?"

"Oh, Robert, I can't go on, all my life, making the same mistakes. And it was Hester's mistake, too. We both wanted Ben to conform to our ideas of a nice reliable husband, and a kind domestic father. And it was as realistic as trying to cage a panther. And when you come to think of it, how dull caged panthers are! Besides, Ben isn't my problem any longer. He's Melissa's."

Robert said, "So what price now, coming at the bottom of a long list of priorities?"

Emma made a face at him. "You know, Ben once said that you had a noble head, and that you should grow a beard and then he would paint you. But if I tried to paint you it would be with a great big balloon coming out of your mouth with I TOLD YOU SO written on it."

"I never said that to anyone in the whole of my life. And I certainly didn't come all the way down here tonight to say it."

"What did you come to say?"

"That if I'd known you were on your own, I'd have been here

weeks ago. That if I can get two seats for Christo's first night, I want you to come with me. That I'm sorry about shouting at you, that last time I was here.''

''I shouted too.''

''I hate having rows with you, but in some extraordinary way, being away from you is a thousand times worse. I kept telling myself that it was simply something that was over, and best forgotten. But all the time you were never out of the back of my mind. Jane knew. She told me this evening, she'd known all along.''

''Jane . . . ?''

''I'm ashamed to say I've been running Jane round in demented circles trying to keep myself from squaring up to the horrible truth.''

''But it was because of Jane that I made Christopher promise not to ring you up. I thought . . .''

''And it was because of Christopher that I didn't come back to Brookford.''

''You thought we were having an affair, didn't you?''

''Wasn't that what I was meant to think?''

''But you silly man, Christopher's my brother.''

Robert took her head between his hands, and put his thumbs beneath her chin and turned her face up to his. Just before he kissed her, he said, ''And how the hell was I supposed to know that?''

When they got back to the car, there was no sign of Ben, but he had left a message for them, tucked between the windscreen-wiper and the wind-shield. ''Like a parking ticket,'' said Emma.

It was an unconventional letter, written on a sheet of cartridge paper torn from Ben's sketch book, and headed by two thumbnail sketches – two profiles turned to face each other.

There was no mistaking her own determined chin and Robert's formidable nose!

"It's us. It's for both of us. Read it aloud."

Robert did so. *"The cabby seemed morose at the thought of returning to London on his own, so I decided to accompany him. I shall be at Claridges, but would prefer not to be disturbed before noon tomorrow."*

"But if I'm not to go to Claridges before noon, where am I meant to go?"

"You're meant to come home with me. To Milton Gardens."

"But I haven't any things. I haven't even got a toothbrush."

"I will buy you a toothbrush," said Robert, and kissed her, and then went on reading the letter. *"By then I should have caught up on my sleep and had time to cool the champagne, and will be ready to celebrate anything you may have to tell me."*

"The wily old brute! He knew, all along."

"My love, and God bless you both. Ben."

After a little while, Emma said, "Is that all?"

"Not quite." He handed her the letter and Emma saw, beneath Ben's signature, a third little drawing. A wing of white hair, a brown face, a pair of dark and cruelly observant eyes.

"Self-portrait," said Robert. "Ben Litton by Ben Litton. It must be unique. One day, we might sell it for thousands of pounds."

My love and God bless you both.

"I shan't ever want to sell it," said Emma.

"Nor I. Come on, my darling, it's time to go home."

THE END OF SUMMER

For Di and John

All summer long the weather had been heavy and clouded, the warmth of the sun blanketed by sea fogs which had continually rolled in from the Pacific. But by September, as so often happens in California, the fogs retreated, far out into the ocean, where they lay along the edge of the horizon, sullen as a long bruise.

Inland, beyond the coastal range, farmlands, heavy with crops, with bursting fruit, and corn and artichokes, and orange pumpkins, simmered in the sunshine. Small wooden townships dozed, skewered by the heat, grey and dusty as specimen moths. The plains, rich and fertile, stretched east to the foothills of the Sierra Nevada, and through it all arrowed the great freeway of the Camino Real, north to San Francisco, and south to Los Angeles, crammed and glittering with the hot steel of a million cars.

Through the summer months, the beach had been deserted, for Reef Point was the end of the line and seldom patronised by the casual day-tripper. For one thing, the road was unsurfaced, unsafe, and uninviting. For another, the little resort of La Carmella, with its charming tree-shaded streets, exclusive country club and spotless motels, lay just over the point, and anyone with sense and a few dollars to spare, stayed put right there. Only if you were adventurous, or broke, or surfing mad, did you risk the last mile and come slipping and scrambling over the dirt track that led down to this great, empty, storm-washed bay.

But now, with the fine hot weather and the clean rolling breakers pouring up on to the beach, the place flowered with people. Cars of all sorts came tumbling down the hill, to park in the shade beneath the cedars, and disgorge picnickers, campers, surfers and whole families of hippies, newly wearied of San Francisco, and heading south for New Mexico and the sun, like so many migrating birds. And the weekends brought the university students up from Santa Barbara in their old convertibles and their flower-stickered Volkswagens, all packed with girls and crates of canned beer, and hung about with the big brightly-coloured Malibu surf boards. They set up little camps all over the beach and the air was full of their voices and laughter, and the smell of sun oil.

And so, after weeks and months of being virtually on our own, we were surrounded by people and every sort of activity. My father was hard at work, trying to write a script to a deadline, and in an impossible frame of mind. Unnoticed by him, I moved out on to the beach, taking sustenance with me (hamburgers and Coca-Cola), a book to read, a large bath-towel for comfort and Rusty for company.

Rusty was a dog. My dog. A brown woolly thing of indeterminate breed, but great intelligence. When we first moved to the cabin, back in the spring, we hadn't got a dog, and Rusty, spying us, had decided to remedy this. Accordingly he hung around. I chased him off, shooed him away, Father threw old boots at him, still he returned, unrepentant and bearing no malice at all, to sit a yard or two from the back porch, smiling and thumping away with his tail. One hot morning, taking pity on him, I gave him a bowl of cool water to drink. He lapped it clean, then sat down and smiled and started thumping again. The next day, I gave him an old ham bone, which he took politely, removed, buried, and was back again in five minutes. Smiling. Thump, thump, went the tail.

My father came out of the house and threw a boot at him, but without much enthusiasm. It was simply a half-hearted show of force. Rusty knew this and moved in a little nearer.

I said to my father, "Who do you suppose he belongs to?"

"God knows."

"He seems to think he belongs to us."

"You're wrong," said my father. "He thinks we belong to him."

"He's not fierce or anything and he doesn't smell."

He looked up from the magazine he was trying to read. "Are you trying to say you want to keep the bloody thing?"

"It's just that I don't see . . . I don't see how we're going to get rid of him."

"Short of shooting him."

"Oh don't."

"He'll have fleas. Bring fleas into the house."

"I'll buy him a flea collar." Father watched me over his spectacles. I could see he was beginning to laugh. I said, "Please. Why not? He'll be company for me while you're away."

Father said, "All right," so I put on some shoes, then and there, and whistled up the dog, and walked over the hill into La Carmella where there is a very fancy vet's, and there I waited in a little room filled with pampered poodles and Siamese cats, and their various owners, and at last I was let in, and the vet looked at Rusty and pronounced him fit, and gave him an injection, and told me where I could buy a flea collar. So I paid the vet and went out and bought the flea collar, and we walked home again. We came into the house, and Father was still reading his magazine, and the dog came politely in, and after standing around a little, waiting to be asked to sit down, he sat, on the old rug in front of the empty fireplace.

My father said, "What's his name?" and I said, "Rusty," because I'd once had a dog-nightdress-case called Rusty and it was the first name that came into my head.

There was no question of his fitting into the family, because it seemed that he had always belonged. Wherever I went, Rusty came too. He loved the beach, and was forever digging up splendid treasures and bringing them home for us to admire. Old bits of flotsam, plastic detergent bottles, long dangling strips of seaweed. And sometimes things that he had obviously not dug up. A new sneaker, a bright bath-towel, and once a punctured beach-ball, which my father had to replace once I had run its small and weeping owner to earth. He liked to swim too, and always insisted on accompanying me, although I could swim much faster and farther than he could, and he was always tagging behind. You'd have thought he'd have got discouraged, but he never did.

We had been swimming that day, a Sunday. Father, the deadline met, had driven down to Los Angeles to deliver the script in person, and Rusty and I had kept each other company, in and out of the sea all afternoon, gathering shells, playing with an old stick of driftwood. But now it was getting cooler and I had put some clothes on again, and we sat, side by side, the setting sun gold and blinding in our eyes, watching the surfers.

4

They had been at it all day, but it seemed that they would never tire. Kneeling on their boards, they paddled out to sea, through the breakers to the smooth green water beyond. There they waited, patient, perched on the skyline like so many cormorants, waiting for the swell to gather, to form and finally break. They chose a wave, stood as the water curved up and crested and showed white at its edge, and as it curled over and thundered in, so the surfers came too, riding across the wave, a poem of balance, arrogant with the confidence of youth; riding the wave until it swept up on to the sand, and then stepping casually off, and gathering up the board, and back into the sea again, for the surfer's creed is that there is always a bigger and a better comber, just around the corner, and now the sun was setting and it would soon be dark, and there was not a moment to be lost.

One boy in particular had caught my eye. He was blond, crew cut, very brown, his skinny knee-length shorts the same bright blue as his surf board. He was a wonderful surfer, with a style and a dash that made all the others look clumsy amateurs. But now, as I watched, he seemed to decide to call it a day, for he rode in on a final wave, beached himself neatly, stepped off the board, and with a final long look at the rose-washed evening sea, turned and picked up the surf board and began to walk in up the sand.

I looked away. He came close beside me, and then went on a few yards to where a pile of neatly folded clothes had been waiting. He dropped the surf board and picked up a faded college sweatshirt from the top of the pile. I glanced his way again, and as his face came out of the opening at the top of the sweatshirt, he looked straight at me. Firmly, I met his eye.

He seemed amused. He said, "Hi."

"Hello."

He settled the sweatshirt down over his hips. He said, "Want a cigarette?"

"All right."

He stooped and took a packet of Luckys and a lighter out of a pocket and came over the sand to where I was sitting. He flipped a cigarette up for me and took one himself and lit them both, and then let himself down beside me, stretching full length and leaning back on his elbows. His legs and his neck and his hair were all lightly dusted with sand, and he had blue eyes and that clean, well-scrubbed look still to be seen on the campuses of American universities.

He said, "You've been sitting there all afternoon. When you weren't swimming."

"I know."

"Why didn't you join us?"

"I haven't got a surf board."

"You could get one."

"No money."

"Then borrow one."

"There's no one I know to borrow one from."

The young man frowned. "You're British, aren't you?"

"Yes."

"You visiting?"

"No, I live here."

"In Reef Point?"

"Yes." I jerked my head, indicating the line of faded clapboard cabins visible just over the curve of the sand dunes.

"How d'you come to live here?"

"We rented the cabin."

"Who's we?"

"My father and I."

"How long have you been here?"

"Since spring."

"But you're not staying over the winter."

It was a statement of fact more than a question. Nobody stayed in Reef Point over the winter. The houses weren't built to withstand the storms, the access road became impassable, the telephone lines blew down, the electricity failed.

"I think so. Unless we decide to move on."

He frowned. "Are you hippies, or something?"

Knowing how I looked at the time, I kindly did not blame him for asking this question.

"No. But my father writes film scripts and stuff for TV. But he hates Los Angeles so much he refuses to live there, so . . . we rented this cabin."

He seemed intrigued. "And what do you do?"

I took up a handful of sand, let it run away, coarse and grey through my fingers.

"Nothing much. Buy food and empty the garbage can and try to keep the sand swept out of the house."

"Is that your dog?"

"Yes."

"What's his name?"

"Rusty."

"Rusty. Hey, Rusty, fella!" Rusty acknowledged his advances with a nod that would have done credit to Royalty and then continued to gaze out to sea. To make up for his lack of manners I said, "Are you from Santa Barbara?"

7

"Uh-huh." But the young man did not want to talk about himself. "How long have you lived in the States? You still have a terribly terribly British accent."

I smiled politely at a joke heard many times before. "Since I was fourteen. Seven years."

"In California?"

"All over. New York. Chicago. San Francisco."

"Is your father American?"

"No. He just likes it here. He came in the first place because he wrote a novel, and it was bought by a film company and he came to Hollywood to write the script."

"No kidding? Have I heard of him? What's his name?"

"Rufus Marsh."

"You mean, *Tall as the Morning*?" I nodded. "Boy, I read that cover to cover, when I was still in high school. I got all my sex education out of that book." He looked at me with new interest, and I thought that this was how it always was. They were friendly and quite kind, but never interested until I mentioned *Tall as the Morning*. I suppose it had something to do with the way I look, because my eyes are pale as sixpences, and my lashes are quite colourless, and my face doesn't go brown but gets splashed and splattered with hundreds of enormous freckles. Besides that, I am too tall for a girl, and the bones in my face all show. "He must be quite a guy."

A new expression had come into his face, puzzled, and crossed with questions that he was obviously going to be too polite to ask.

If you are Rufus Marsh's daughter, how come you're sitting on this god-forsaken beach in the backwoods of California wearing patched jeans and a man's shirt that should have been

relegated to the ragbag decades ago, and you haven't even got
enough dollars raked together to buy yourself a surf board?

He said, following with laughable predictability the line of
my own reflections, "What kind of a man is he, anyway? I
mean, apart from being a father."

"I don't know." I could never describe him, even to myself.
I took another handful of sand, trickled it into a miniature
mountain, stubbed my cigarette out on its apex, forming a little
crater, a tiny volcano, with a cigarette stub as its smoking core.
A man who must always be on the move. A man who makes
friends easily and loses them the next day. A quarrelsome,
argumentative man, talented to the point of genius, but utterly
baffled by the small problems of day-to-day living. A man who
can charm and infuriate. A paradox of a man.

I said again, "I don't know," and turned to look at the boy
beside me. He was nice. "I'd ask you home for a beer, and
then you could meet him and see for yourself. But he's in Los
Angeles just now, won't be home until tomorrow morning."

He considered this, scratching thoughtfully at the back of his
head and dislodging a small storm of sand.

"Tell you what," he said, "I'm coming back next weekend
if the weather holds."

I smiled. "Are you?"

"I'll look out for you."

"All right."

"I'll bring a spare board. You can surf."

I said, "You don't need to bribe me."

He pretended to be offended. "Whaddya mean, bribe?"

"I'll take you up to meet him next weekend. He likes new
faces around the place."

9

"I wasn't bribing. Honest."

I relented. Besides, I wanted to surf. I said, "I know."

He grinned and stubbed out the cigarette. The sun, sinking towards the edge of the sea, was taking shape and colour – an orange pumpkin of a sun. He sat up, screwing his eyes against its glare, yawned slightly and stretched. He said, "I must go," and stood up and then hesitated for a moment, standing over me. His shadow seemed to stretch for ever. "Goodbye then."

" 'Bye."

"Next Sunday."

"OK."

"That's a date. Don't forget."

"I won't."

He turned and moved off, stopping to collect the rest of his gear, and turning to sketch a final salute before walking away, the length of the beach, to where the old sand-buried cedars marked the track that led up to the road.

I watched him go, and realised that I didn't even know his name. And, worse, he hadn't bothered to ask mine. I was simply Rufus Marsh's daughter. But still, next Sunday, if the weather held, he would maybe be back. If the weather held. That was always something to look forward to.

2

It was because of Sam Carter that we were living at Reef Point.
Sam was my father's agent in Los Angeles, and it was in sheer
desperation that he eventually offered to find somewhere cheap
for us to live, because Los Angeles and my father were so
acutely antipathetic that not one sellable word was he able to
write while we lived there, and Sam was in danger of losing
both valuable clients and money.

"There's this place at Reef Point," Sam had said. "It's a
one-horse set-up, but real peaceful . . . end of the world type
peace," he added, conjuring up visions of a sort of Gauguin
paradise.

And so we had taken a lease on the cabin, and packed all our
worldly possessions, which were sadly small, into Father's old
beat-up Dodge, and driven here, leaving the smog and ratrace
of Los Angeles behind us, and excited as children by the first
smell of the sea.

And at first, it had been exciting. After the city it was magic
to wake to nothing but the sound of sea birds and the endless
thunder of the surf. It was good, in the early mornings, to walk
out on to sand, to watch the sun rise over the hills, to hang out a

11

line of washing, and watch it billow and fill with the sea wind, white as new sails.

Our housekeeping was necessarily simple – I have never been much of a housekeeper anyway, and at Reef Point there was only one small shop – a drugstore, but back in Scotland my grandmother would have called it a Jenny a' Thing, for it sold everything from gun licences to house frocks, from frozen foods to packets of Kleenex. It was run by Bill and Myrtle, in a half-hearted, time-consuming sort of way, for they always seemed to be clean out of fresh vegetables, fruit, chickens and eggs, which were the sort of things I wanted to buy. However, over the summer we became quite fond of tinned chilli con carne and frozen pizza pie, and all the various species of ice-cream that Myrtle obviously adored, for she was enormously fat, her great hips and thighs bulging in blue jeans, and her ham-like arms fully exposed by the girlish sleeveless blouses she chose to wear with them.

But now, after six months of Reef Point, I was getting restless. This fine Indian summer weather would last – how long? Another month, perhaps. And then the storms would start in earnest, the darkness fall earlier, the rains would come and the mud and the wind. The cabin had no sort of central heating, only the enormous fireplace in the draughty living-room, which burned driftwood at a terrifying pace. I thought of homely buckets of coal with longing, but there was no coal. Every time I came up off the beach, I lugged a spar or branch of driftwood with me, like some pioneer woman, and added it to the pile by the back porch. It was assuming vast dimensions, but I knew that once we started needing fires, it would take no time to get through the lot.

THE END OF SUMMER

The cabin lay just back off the beach, a small rise of sand dune its only shelter from the sea winds. It was built of wood, faded to a silvery grey, and stood up on piers, so that a couple of steps led up to the front and back porches. Inside, there was a big living-room, with picture windows facing over the ocean; a tiny, narrow kitchen; a bathroom – with no bath, but a shower – and two bedrooms, one large "master" bedroom where my father slept, and a smaller one, with a bunk, perhaps intended for a small child or an unimportant elderly relative, which was mine. It was furnished in the faintly depressing manner of summer cabins, in that all the furniture had obviously been thrown out of other, and larger, houses. Father's bed was a vast brass monstrosity, missing knobs, and with a set of springs that squeaked every time he turned over. And in my room hung an ornate gilt mirror which looked as though it had started life in a Victorian bordello, and gave me back a reflection of a drowned woman covered with black spots.

The sitting-room was not much better – the old armchairs sagged, their worn patches disguised with crocheted Afghans, the hearthrug had a hole in it, and the other chairs were stuffed horsehair with the horsehair fighting a winning battle to get out. There was only one table, and Father had taken over one end of this as a desk, so that we were forced to take our meals, cramped and with elbows jammed in, at the other end. The best thing in the house was the window seat, which took up the whole width of the room, was padded with foam and warm rugs and cushions, and was inviting as an old nursery sofa, if you wanted to curl up and read, or watch the sunset, or simply think.

But it was a lonely place. At night the wind nudged and

whined through the gaps around the window, and the rooms were filled with strange rustlings and creakings, for all the world like a ship at sea. When my father was there, none of this mattered, but when I was left alone, my imagination, inspired by the tales of everyday violence, culled from the columns of the local newspapers, really got to work. The cabin itself was a fragile thing, none of the locks on the doors or windows would have deterred a determined intruder, and now, with the summer over, and the occupants of the other cabins packed up and returned to their various homes, it was completely isolated. Even Myrtle and Bill were a good quarter of a mile away, and the telephone was a party line, and not always very efficient. One way and another, the possibilities didn't bear thinking about.

I never spoke to my father about these fears – he had, after all, a job of work to do, but he was essentially a perceptive man, and I am sure knew that I was capable of working myself up into a state of jitters, and this was one of the reasons that he let me keep Rusty.

That evening, after the day on the crowded beach, the cheerful sunshine, and my encounter with the young student from Santa Barbara, the cabin seemed doubly deserted.

The sun had slid down over the edge of the sea, an evening breeze was stirring, and soon it would be dark, so, for company, I lit a fire, recklessly piling on the driftwood; and, for comfort, took a hot shower, washed my hair, and then, wrapped in a towel, went into my room for a pair of clean jeans and an old white sweater which had belonged to my father until I mistakenly shrank it.

Underneath the bordello mirror was a varnished chest of

drawers which had to do duty as a dressing-table. On it, for lack of anywhere else, I had put my photographs. There were a lot of them and they took up a lot of space, and most of the time I didn't even look at them very much, but this evening was different, and as I combed the snarls out of my long wet hair I studied them, one by one, as though they belonged to a person I scarcely knew, were of places that I had never seen.

There was my mother, a formal portrait, framed in silver. Mother with her shoulders bare and diamonds in her ears, and her hair newly done by Elizabeth Arden. I loved the picture, but it was not as I remembered her. This was better, an enlarged snapshot on a picnic, wearing her tartan skirt, and sitting waist deep in heather, and laughing as though something ridiculous were about to happen. And then there was the collection – more of a montage – with which I had filled both sides of a big leather folding frame. Elvie – the old white house, set against a fold of larch and pine, the hill rising behind it, the glimmer of the loch at the end of the lawn, the jetty, and the baulky old dinghy we had used when we fished for trout. And my grandmother, at the open french windows, the inevitable pair of secateurs ready in her hand. And a coloured postcard of Elvie Loch that I had bought in the Thrumbo post office. And another picnic, with my parents together, our old car in the background, and a fat liver-and-white spaniel sitting at my mother's feet.

And there were the photographs of my cousin Sinclair. Dozens of them. Sinclair with his first trout, Sinclair dressed in his kilt, headed for some outing or other. Sinclair in a white shirt, captain of his prep school cricket team. Sinclair skiing; at the wheel of his car; wearing a paper top hat at some New Year's Eve party and looking a little drunk. (In this photograph he had his arm around a pretty, dark girl, but I had arranged the pictures so that she didn't show.)

Sinclair was the child of my mother's brother, Aylwyn. Aylwyn had married – far too young, everybody said – a girl called Silvia. The family disapproval of his choice unhappily proved well-founded, for, as soon as she had borne her young husband a baby son, she upped and left the pair of them, and went off to live with a man who sold real estate in the Balearic Islands. After the initial shock had worn off, everybody agreed that it was the best thing that could have happened, specially for Sinclair, who was handed over to his grandmother, and brought up at Elvie under the happiest of circumstances. He had always seemed, to me, to have the best of everything.

His father, my Uncle Aylwyn, I had no recollection of at all. When I was very small, he had gone to Canada, presumably returning every now and then to visit his mother and his child, but never at Elvie when we were there. My only concern with him was the possibility of his sending me a Red Indian headdress. Over the years, I must have made the suggestion a hundred times, but nothing ever came of it.

And so Sinclair was, virtually, my grandmother's child. And I could not remember a time when I hadn't been more or less in love with him. Six years older than I, he had been the mentor of my childhood, enormously wise and endlessly brave. He had taught me to tie a hook on a line, to swing upside-down on his trapeze, to bowl a cricket ball. Together we had swum and sledged, lit illegal bonfires, built a tree house, and played pirates in the leaky old boat.

When I first came to America, I wrote to him regularly, but

eventually became discouraged by his lack of response. Soon our correspondence dwindled to Christmas cards, or a scribbled note on a birthday, and it was from my grandmother that I got news of him, and from her too that I had received the photograph of the New Year party.

After my mother died, as if Sinclair on her hands was not enough, she had offered to give me a home as well.

"Rufus, why not leave the child with me?" This was just after the funeral, back at Elvie, with grief put away and the future to be discussed in her usual practical fashion. I was not meant to be listening, but I was there, on the stairs, and their voices came clearly from beyond the closed library door.

"Because one child on your hands is more than sufficient."

"But I would love to have Jane . . . and she would be company for me as well."

"Isn't that a little selfish?"

"I don't think so. And, Rufus, it is her life you should think about now, her future . . ."

My father said a single very rude word. I was horrified, not at the word, but because he had said it to her. I wondered if he was a little drunk . . .

Ignoring this, in her usual ladylike fashion, my grandmother went on, but her voice was buttoned down, the way it always got when she began to be angry.

"You've just told me that you're going to America to write the film script of your book. You can't drag a fourteen-year-old all the way to Hollywood."

"Why not?"

"What about her schooling?"

"There are schools in America."

17

"It would be so easy for me to have her here. Just until you've settled, found yourself a place to live."

My father pushed back his chair with a scrape. I heard his feet, pacing the floor.

"And then," he said, "I send for her and you put her on the next plane?"

"Of course."

"It won't work, you know."

"Why shouldn't it work?"

"Because if I leave Jane here with you for any length of time, Elvie would become her home and she'd never want to leave it again. You know she'd rather be at Elvie than anywhere else in the world."

"Then for her sake . . ."

"For her sake, I'm taking her with me."

There was a long silence. Then my grandmother spoke again. "That isn't the only reason is it, Rufus?"

He hesitated, as though he wished not to offend her. "No," he said at last.

"With all considerations, I still think you're making a mistake."

"If I am, it's my own. Just as she's my own child and I'm holding on to her."

I had heard enough. I sprang up and ran helter-skelter up the dark staircase. In my room, face down across my bed, I burst into miserable tears, because I was leaving Elvie, because I would never see Sinclair again, and because the two people I loved most in all the world had been fighting over me.

I wrote, of course, and my grandmother replied, and Elvie with all its sounds and smells was contained in her letters. And then, after a year or two had passed, "Why don't you come back to Scotland?" she wrote. "Just for a little holiday, a month or so. We all miss you dreadfully and there is such a lot for you to see. I made a new rose border in the walled garden, and Sinclair will be up for August . . . he has a little flat in Earls Court, and gave me lunch last time I was up in town. If there is any difficulty about the fare you know you only have to say, and I shall get Mr Bembridge at the travel agent's to send you your return ticket. Talk it over with your father."

The thought of Elvie, in August, with Sinclair, was almost irresistible, but I could not talk it over with my father, because I had overheard that angry discussion in the library and I did not think that he would let me go.

Besides, it seemed that there was never the time nor the opportunity to make the journey home. It was as though we had become nomads – we arrived in a place, we settled, and then it was time to go somewhere else. Sometimes we were rich, more often broke. My father, without my mother's restraining hand, spent money like water. We lived in Hollywood mansions, in motels, in Fifth Avenue apartments, in crummy lodging houses. As the years went by, it seemed as if we had spent our whole lives travelling America, and that we should never settle down anywhere again, and the memory of Elvie faded and became unreal, as though the waters of Elvie Loch had risen and engulfed the whole place, and I had to remind myself forcibly that it was still there, peopled by living beings who were part of me, and whom I loved, and not drowned and lost for ever, blurred and dimly seen through the deep waters of some terrible natural disaster.

At my ankles, Rusty whined. Startled, I looked down and

for a moment, so far away had I been, I couldn't think who he was or what he was doing. And then, like a home-movie that has stuck in the middle, there was a click in the machinery, and everyday life moved on again, and I realised that my hair was nearly dry, that Rusty was hungry and wanted his dinner, and what was more, so did I. So I laid down my comb, and pushed Elvie out of my mind, and went to throw more wood on the fire, and then inspect the icebox for something that we could eat.

It was nearly nine o'clock when I heard the car come down the hill, over the track that led from La Carmella. I heard it because it came, as all cars necessarily do, in bottom gear, and because I was alone, and all my perceptions were subconsciously sharpened to catch the smallest unfamiliar sound.

I was reading a book, and in the act of turning over a page, but I froze still and pricked my ears. Rusty sensed this, and sat up immediately, very quiet, as though he did not wish to disturb anything. Together, we listened. A log slid down in the fire, the surf distantly boomed. The car came on down the hill.

I thought . . . *Myrtle and Bill. They've been to a movie, in La Carmella*. But the car didn't stop at the drugstore. It came on, still grinding along in low gear, passed the cedars where the picnickers parked their cars, on along the lonely road that could lead only to me.

My father? But he wasn't due back until tomorrow night. The young man I had met today, returning for a glass of beer? A vagrant? An escaped convict? A sex maniac . . . ?

I sprang up, dropping my book on the hearthrug, and fled to check the snibs on the doors. They were both locked. But the cabin had no curtains, anyone could look in and see me, and

20

I wouldn't be able to see them. In a frenzy of fear, I dashed
to turn off all the lights, but the fire still burned bright, and
filled the living-room with flickering light . . . it played up the
walls and over the furniture, giving the old chairs a brooding,
pouncing look.

The approaching headlights probed the darkness outside.
Now, I could see the car coming, gently, bumping over the dried
ruts of the road. It passed the last empty cabin next to ours, and
coasted gently to a halt right alongside our back porch. And it
wasn't my father.

I whispered Rusty to my side, for the comfort of holding
his flea collar and feeling the warmth of his furry brown coat.
Growls and mutters went on in the back of his throat but he
didn't bark. Together we heard the engine of the car being killed,
then the door opened and slammed shut. Silence for a moment.
Then steps came softly over the sandy ground that lay between
the back porch and the road, and the next instant there was a
knocking at the door.

I let out a sort of gasp and it was too much for Rusty who tore
from my grip and ran, barking his head off, to get at whatever
waited outside.

"Rusty!" I went after him, but he went on and on barking.
"Rusty, don't do it . . . Rusty!"

I caught him by the flea collar and dragged him back from
the door, but he went on barking, and it occurred to me that he
sounded so large and so fierce that this was possibly the best
thing that could have happened.

I pulled myself together, gave him a shake which finally
silenced him, and then straightened up. My shadow, thrown by
the firelight, danced against the locked door.

I swallowed, took a deep breath and said in a voice as firm and clear as I could make it:

"Who is it?"

A man spoke. "I'm sorry to disturb you, but I'm looking for Mr Marsh's house."

A friend of Father's? Or just a trick to get in? I hesitated.

He spoke again.

"Is this where Rufus Marsh lives?"

"Yes it is."

"Is he at home?"

Another trick?

"Why?" I said.

"Well, I was told I might find him here." I was still trying to decide what to do when he added, in quite a different voice, "Is that Jane?"

There is nothing more disarming than having a stranger know your name. Besides, there was something about his voice . . . even blurred as it was through the tightly closed door . . . something . . .

I said, "Yes."

"Is your father there?"

"No, he's in Los Angeles. Who are you?"

"Well, my name's David Stewart . . . I . . . look, it's rather difficult to talk through the door . . ."

But, before the word was out of his mouth, I had undone the snib, lifted the latch and opened it for him. And I did that apparently crazy thing because of the way he had said his own name. Stewart. Americans invariably find it difficult to pronounce . . . Stoowart, they call it. But he had said Stewart the way my grandmother said it, so he wasn't an American, he

22

came from home. And, with a name like that, he probably came from Scotland.

I suppose I had imagined that I should immediately recognise him, but in fact I had never seen him before in my life. He stood before me, with the headlights of his car still bright behind him, and only firelight to show me his face. He wore horn-rimmed spectacles and he was tall . . . taller than I was. We stared at each other, he startled by my swift change of policy, and I suddenly engulfed by a great wave of pure fury. Nothing makes me so angry as being frightened, and I had been scared half crazy.

"What do you want to come sneaking up like that for, in the middle of the night . . ." Even to myself my voice sounded shrill and not entirely in control.

He answered, reasonably enough, "It's only nine o'clock, and I didn't mean to sneak up."

"You could have phoned and let me know you were coming."

"I couldn't find any number in the book." He had made no move to come in. Rusty was still glowering away in the background. "And I had no idea you'd be on your own or I'd have waited."

My rage was subsiding, and I felt a little ashamed of my outburst. "Well . . . now you're here, you'd better come in." I backed off and reached for the switch. The room sprang into cold, bright, electric light.

But he still hesitated. "Don't you want any credentials . . . you know, credit card? passport?"

I looked at him sharply, thought I detected a gleam of amusement behind the glasses, wondered what he found so damn funny. "If you'd lived out here as long as I have, you wouldn't open the door to any creepy prowler either."

"Well, before the creepy prowler comes in, perhaps he'd better go and turn off the car lights. I left them on so that I could see my way."

Without waiting for the snappy answer which I would have loved to be able to deliver, he went back outside. I left the door open and went back to the fire and put on another log, and found that my hands were shaking and my heart thumping like a drum. I straightened the hearthrug, kicked Rusty's bone under the chair and was lighting myself a cigarette when he came back into the cabin, shutting the back porch door behind him.

I turned to face him. He was dark, with the pale skin and black hair that a good many Highlanders possess, thin and rather scholarly looking in an angular and uncoordinated way. He wore a smooth tweed suit, worn slightly at elbows and knees and buttonholes, a brown-and-white checked shirt, and a dark green tie, and he looked as though he might be a schoolmaster or a professor of some obscure science. There was no guessing at his age. He could have been anything between thirty and fifty.

He said, "How do you feel now?"

"I'm all right," but my hand was still shaking and he saw it.

"It wouldn't do you any harm to have a little drink."

"I don't know if there's anything in the house."

"Where could we look?"

"Under the window seat?"

He went over and opened the cupboard, groped around a bit, and came out with fluff all over the sleeve of his coat and a quarter of a bottle of Haig in his hand.

"The very thing. Now all we need is a glass."

I went into the kitchen and came back with two and a jug of water, and the ice-tray out of the refrigerator, and watched while he poured the drinks. They looked suspiciously dark. I said, "I don't like whisky, much."

"Think of it as medicine." He handed it to me.

"I don't want to get plastered."

"On that, you won't."

It made sense. The whisky tasted smoky and was marvellously warming. Comforted by it, embarrassed at having been such a ninny, I smiled tentatively at him.

He grinned back. "Why don't we sit down?"

So we sat, me on the hearthrug, and he on the edge of Father's big chair, his hands loose between his knees, and the drink on the floor between his feet. He said, "Out of interest, what made you suddenly open the door?"

"It was the way you said your name. Stewart. You come from Scotland, don't you?"

"Yes."

"Whereabouts?"

"Caple Bridge."

"But that's near Elvie."

"I know. You see, I'm with Ramsay McKenzie and King ..."

"My grandmother's lawyers."

"That's right."

"But I don't remember you."

"I didn't join the firm until five years ago."

There was a coldness around my heart, but I made myself ask: "There's nothing ... wrong?"

"Nothing wrong." His voice was very reassuring.

"Then why have you come?"

"It's a question," said David Stewart, "of a number of unanswered letters."

25

3

After a little I said, "I don't understand."

"Four, to be exact. Three from Mrs Bailey herself and one from me, written on her behalf."

"Written who to?" It was not a time to worry about my grammar.

"Your father."

"When?"

"During the course of the last two months."

"Did you send the letters here? I mean, we move around so much."

"You had written to your grandmother yourself, giving her this address."

This was true. I always let her know when we moved. I threw my half-smoked cigarette into the fire, and tried to get used to this extraordinary situation. My father, for all his faults, was a most un-secret man . . . if anything, he erred in the opposite direction, loudly fuming and complaining for days on end if anything annoyed or disturbed him. But I had heard nothing about any letters.

He prompted me. "You haven't seen any letters?"

"No. But that's not surprising because Father always collects the mail himself, every day, from the drugstore."

"Perhaps he never opened them?"

But this, too, was out of character. Father always opened letters. He didn't necessarily read them, but there was always the happy possibility that the envelope might contain a cheque.

I said, "No, he wouldn't do that." I swallowed the nervous lump in my throat and pushed my hair back off my face. "What were they about? Or perhaps you don't know."

"Yes, of course I know." He could sound very dry, and it wasn't difficult to imagine him ensconced behind an old-fashioned desk, clearing his throat along with his emotions, and dealing crisply with all the incomprehensible pitfalls of wills, affidavits, sales, leases and orders to view. "It's just that your grandmother wants you to come back to Scotland . . . pay a visit . . ."

I said, "I know she does – she's always talking about it in her letters."

He raised an eyebrow. "Don't you want to come?"

"Yes . . . of course I do . . ."

I thought of Father, remembered that long-ago overheard conversation. "I don't know . . . I mean, I can't just make up my mind like that . . ."

"Is there any reason why you shouldn't come?"

"Well, of course there is . . . my father . . ."

"You mean, there's no one to keep house for him?"

"No I don't mean that at all." He waited for me to enlarge on this statement, perhaps to tell him what I did mean. I didn't want to meet his eye, and turned away from him to stare into the fire. I had an uncomfortable suspicion that my face wore an expression which could be described as sheepish.

He said, "You know, there was never any bad feeling about the fact that your father brought you over to America . . ."

"She wanted me to stay at Elvie."

"You know that, then?"

"Yes, I heard them quarrelling. They never quarrelled usually. I think they got on very well. But there was a terrible row over me."

"But that was seven years ago. Now, surely, between us, we can make some arrangements."

I made the most obvious excuse. "But it's so expensive . . ."

"Mrs Bailey, of course, will stand you the fare." (I imagined, ruefully, Father's reaction to this.) "You don't need to be away for more than a month." He said again, "Don't you want to come?"

His manner disarmed me. "Yes, of course I do . . ."

"Then why this lack of enthusiasm?"

"I don't want to upset my father. And he obviously doesn't want me to come, or he'd have answered those letters you spoke about."

"Yes, the letters. I wonder where they would be."

I indicated the table behind him, the pile of manuscript and reference books, old files, envelopes and regrettably unpaid bills. "Over there, I suppose."

"I wonder why he never told you about them."

I said nothing, but thought that I knew. In a way, he resented Elvie and the fact that it meant so much to me. He was, perhaps, a little jealous of my mother's family. He was afraid of losing me.

I said, "I've no idea."

"Well, when are you expecting him back from Los Angeles?"

I said, "I don't think you should see him. It would only make him miserable, because even if he agreed to my going, I couldn't leave him alone, here."

"But surely we could arrange something . . ."

"No, we couldn't. He has to have someone to look after him. He's the most impractical person in the world . . . he'd never buy any food, or gas for the car, and if I left him, I'd just be worried sick about him all the time."

"Jane . . . you do have to think about yourself . . ."

"Some other time I'll come. Tell my grandmother some other time."

In silence he considered this. He finished his drink, and then set down the empty glass. "Well, let's leave it like this. I'm driving back to Los Angeles tomorrow morning, about eleven. I have a seat booked for you on the plane to New York, Tuesday morning. There's no reason on earth why you shouldn't sleep on this, and if you change your mind . . ."

"I won't."

He ignored this. "If you change your mind, there's nothing to stop you coming with me." He stood up, looming over me. "And I still think that you should."

I don't like being loomed over, so I stood up too.

"You seemed very sure that I would come with you."

"I hoped that you would."

"You think I'm just making excuses, don't you?"

"Not entirely."

"I feel very guilty that you've travelled so far for nothing."

"I was in New York, on business. And I've enjoyed meeting

30

you, and only sorry that I missed your father." He held out
his hand. "Goodbye, Jane." After a second's hesitation, I put
mine into it. Americans aren't much good at shaking hands
and one gets out of the habit. "And I'll send your love to your
grandmother."

"Yes, and Sinclair."

"Sinclair?"

"You see him, don't you? When he comes to Elvie?"

"Yes. Yes, of course I do. And I'll certainly give him
your love."

I said, "Tell him to write," and then bent to make a fuss
of Rusty, because my eyes were filled with tears, and I didn't
want David Stewart to see.

When he had gone, I went back into the cabin, and over to
the table where my father kept all his papers. After a little I
found, one by one, the four unanswered letters, all opened, and
obviously read. I didn't read them. My finer instincts prevailed
– and anyway I already knew what they contained – so I simply
replaced them, buried as before.

I went to kneel on the window seat, to open the window and
hang out. It was very dark, the ocean inky, the air cold, but
my terrors had evaporated. I thought of Elvie, and longed to be
there. I thought of geese flying the winter skies, and the smell
of peat burning in the fireplace in the hall. I thought of the
loch, brilliant blue and calm as a mirror, or grey and lashed into
white waves by northern gales. I wanted to be there, suddenly,
so badly that it was a physical ache.

And I was angry with my father. I didn't want to leave him,
but surely he could have discussed the matter with me, given
me the chance to make my own decision. I was twenty-one, no

longer a child, and resented what I considered an unbearably selfish and old-fashioned attitude.

Just wait till he gets back, I promised myself. Wait till I face him with those letters. I'll just tell him . . . I'll . . .

But my anger was short-lived. I could never stay angry for long. Cooled by the night air, perhaps, it simmered away and died, and I was left, feeling strangely flat. Nothing, after all, had changed. I would stay with him because I loved him, because he wanted me, because he needed me. There was no possible alternative. And I would not confront him with the letters, because to be found out would embarrass and demean him, and it was important, if we were to have any sort of a future together, that he should always be bigger and stronger and wiser than I was.

I was engaged in scrubbing the kitchen floor the next morning, when I heard the unmistakable grinding of the old Dodge as it came over the hill and down the track to Reef Point. I hastily swiped at the last square foot or so of cracked brown linoleum, then got up off my knees, wrang out the floor cloth, emptied the dirty water down the drain, and went out through the back porch door to meet my father, wiping my hands on the old striped apron as I went.

It was a gorgeous day: the sun hot, the sky blue and scudding with bright white clouds, the sparkling morning filled with wind and the crash of high-tide rollers pouring up on to the beach. I had already done a line of washing and now it strained and flapped at the rope, and I ducked beneath this and went out on to the road as the car came bumping and lurching over the ruts towards me.

I saw at once that my father was not alone. Because of

the fine weather, he had put the hood down, and beside him, unmistakable head of red hair a-blow in the breeze, sat Linda Lansing. When she saw me she hung over the side of the car to wave, and her white poodle, sitting on her knee, hung out too, and went into a paroxysm of barking as though I had no right to be there.

Rusty, who had been out on the beach having a good game with an old bit of basket, heard the poodle, and came at once to my rescue, galloping around the corner of the cabin in full cry, snarling and barking, and making little dashes at the Dodge with his teeth bared, unable to wait for the happy moment when he could sink them into the poodle's neck. My father swore, Linda screamed and hugged the poodle, the poodle yapped, and I had to take Rusty by his flea collar and haul him indoors and order him to shut up and behave, before there was the slightest chance of any sort of human conversation.

I left Rusty sulking and went back out again. My father was out of the car. "Hello, cutie." He came around to give me a hug and a kiss. It was like being hugged by a gorilla and his beard scraped my cheek. "Everything all right?"

"Yes, fine," I turned from his embrace. "Hi, Linda."

"Hi, honey."

"Sorry about the dog." I went to open the door for her. She wore full make-up, false eyelashes, a pale blue jump suit and gold ballet slippers. The poodle had a pink collar, studded with rhinestones.

"That's OK. Mitzi's highly-strung I guess. Something to do with being so highly-bred." She put up her face, lips bunched, to receive my kiss. I gave her one and the poodle started yapping again.

"For God's sake," said my father, "keep that bloody dog quiet," whereupon Linda tipped it unceremoniously out of the car and climbed out after it.

Linda Lansing was an actress. Twenty years or so ago she had turned up in Hollywood as a starlet, which meant a prodigious personal publicity campaign followed by a string of undistinguished movies, in which she usually played some sort of a gipsy or peasant girl, wearing an off-the-shoulder drawstring blouse, dark red lips and brooding expression, very sulky. But, inevitably, this type of movie, along with her style of acting, went out of fashion, and Linda went with them. Astutely, for she was never stupid, she swiftly married. "My husband comes before my career," read the captions beneath their wedding photographs, and for some time she disappeared from the Hollywood scene altogether. But lately, having divorced her third husband, and not yet having buttonholed the fourth, she had started to appear again, in small parts and on television. To a young generation of viewers, she was a new face, and, with clever direction, revealed an entirely unsuspected flair for comedy.

We had met her at one of those dreary Sunday brunch pool parties which were so much part of the Los Angeles scene. My father had latched on to her at once, as being the only woman in the place worth talking to. I like her as well. She has a vulgar sense of humour, a deep plummy voice and a surprising ability to laugh at herself.

My father is attractive to women, but has always handled his liaisons with an admirable discretion. I knew that he had embarked on an affair with Linda, but I had hardly expected that he would bring her back to Reef Point with him.

I decided to play it very cool. "Well, this is a surprise. What are you doing in this neck of the woods?"

"Oh, you know how it is, honey, when your father starts twisting your arm. And just smell that sea air." She took a great lungful, coughed slightly, and turned back to the car to extricate her handbag. It was then that I saw the lavish luggage piled on the back seat. Three cases, a wardrobe-bag, a beauty box, a mink coat in a plastic bag, and Mitzi's dog basket, complete with pink rubber bone. I gaped at its quantity, but before I could say anything, my father had elbowed me out of the way and already lifted out two of the cases.

"Well, don't stand there with your mouth open," he said. "Bring something in."

And with that he headed for the cabin. Linda, after one look at my expression, tactfully decided that Mitzi needed a run on the beach and disappeared. I started after my father, and then thought better of it, went back for the dog basket, and started off again.

I found him in the living-room, having put the two suitcases down in the middle of the floor, thrown his long-peaked cap on to a chair, and unloaded some bundles of old letters and papers out of his pocket on to the table. The room, which I had only just cleaned and tidied, became immediately disordered, impermanent, frantic. My father could do this to any place simply by walking into it. Now, he went over to the window to lean out and check on the view, and get a good lungful of sea air. Over his massive shoulder I could see the distant figure of Linda, skittering about with the poodle at the sea's edge. Rusty, still sulking on the window seat, did not even thump his tail.

My father turned, reaching in his shirt pocket for his cigarettes. He appeared delighted with himself. "Well," he said, "aren't you going to ask how everything went?'' He lit the cigarette, and then looked up, and frowned, flicking the lighted match out of the window behind him. ''What are you standing holding the dog basket for? Put the bloody thing down.''

I didn't. I said, ''What's going on?''

''What do you mean?''

I realised that all this hearty good cheer was part of a big bluster.

''You know very well what I mean. Linda.''

''What about Linda? You like her, don't you?''

''Of course I like her, but that's hardly the point. What's she doing here?''

''I've asked her to stay.''

''With all that luggage? How long for, for heaven's sake?''

''Well . . .'' he gestured vaguely with his hand. ''For as long as she wants.''

''Isn't she working?''

''Oh, she's chucked all that.'' He went prowling off to the kitchen in search of a can of beer. I heard the refrigerator opening and shutting. ''She gets just about as sick of L.A. as we did. So I thought why not?'' He appeared again at the kitchen door with the open beer can in his hand. ''The suggestion was hardly out of my mouth, when she found someone to rent her house, along with the maid, and she was packed and ready.'' He frowned again. ''Jane, have you conceived some sort of an affection for that dog basket?''

I continued to ignore him. ''For how long?'' I insisted grimly.

''Well, as long as we do. I don't know. For the winter maybe.''

I said, ''There isn't room.''

''Of course there's room. And whose house is this anyway?''

He drained the beer can, tossed it neatly across the kitchen into the trash can, and went out to bring in the next load of luggage. This time he carried the cases into his bedroom. I put down Mitzi's dog basket and followed him. What with the bed and the suitcases and the two of us, there wasn't much room.

I said, "Where's she going to sleep?"

"Well, where do you think she's going to sleep?" He sat on the monstrous bed, and the springs complained bitterly. "Right here."

I could think of nothing to say. I simply stared at him. This had never, ever happened before. I wondered if he had gone out of his mind.

Something in my face must have got through to him then, for he suddenly looked contrite and took my hands.

"Janey, don't look like that. You're not a kid any more, I don't have to pretend to you. You like Linda, I wouldn't have brought her back if I didn't know you liked her. And she'll be company for you, I won't have to leave you alone so much. Oh, come on, take that dismal face off and go and make a pot of coffee."

I pulled my hands free. I said, "I haven't got time."

"What do you mean?"

"I . . . I have to go and pack."

I went out of his room, and into my own, and I pulled my suitcase out from under the bed, and put it on the bed and opened it, and started to pack, like people do in films, opening drawers one by one and emptying them into the suitcase.

From the open door behind me my father spoke.

"What do you think you're doing?" I turned to look at him, my hands full of shirts and belts and scarves and handkerchiefs. I said, "I'm going."

"Where?"

"Back to Scotland."

He took a single step into the room, and jerked me round to face him. I went on quickly, not letting him say a word. "You had four letters," I told him. "Three from my grandmother and one from the solicitors. You opened them and you read them and you never told me, because you didn't want me to go back. You didn't even discuss them with me."

His grip on my arm never loosened, but I thought his face lost a little of its colour.

"How did you know about those letters?"

I told him about David Stewart. "He told me everything," I finished. "Not that I needed to be told," I added recklessly, "because I knew it all anyway."

"And just what exactly did you know?"

"That you never wanted me to stay at Elvie after Mother died. That you wouldn't ever want me to go back." He watched me, puzzled. "I was *listening*," I shouted at him, as though he had suddenly gone deaf. "I was in the hall, listening, and I heard everything that you and my grandmother said to each other."

"And you never said a word?"

"What good would it have done?"

He sat carefully on the edge of my bed, so as not to disturb my packing. "Did you want to be left behind?"

His obtuseness infuriated me. "No, of course I didn't, I've loved being with you, I wouldn't have had it any other way, but that was all seven years ago, and now I'm an adult, and you had no right to hide away those letters and not say anything to me."

"Do you want to go back so badly?"

"Yes, I do. I love Elvie, you know how much it means to

me.'' I picked up a hairbrush, my photographs, jammed them down the sides of the case. ''I . . . I wasn't going to say anything about the letters. I thought it would make you miserable, and I couldn't go anyway, because you hadn't anyone to look after you. But now, it's different.''

''All right, so it's different, and you're going. I'm not going to stop you. But how are you going to get there?''

''David Stewart's leaving La Carmella at eleven. If I hurry I can catch him. He has a seat booked for me on the New York plane tomorrow morning.''

''And when are you coming back?''

''Oh, I don't know. Some time I suppose.'' I pushed in a book, Anne Morrow Lindbergh's *Gift from the Sea*, which I can never be without, and my Simon and Garfunkel LP. I shut down the lid of the case, and everything bulged out and it wouldn't close, so I opened it again, and flattened things frantically, and still it wouldn't work, and in the end it was my father who did it for me, by sheer brute force, holding down the lid of the case, and forcing the locks to snib.

Over the closed suitcase, I met his eye. I said, ''I wouldn't be going if Linda hadn't come . . .'' My voice trailed away. I took my raincoat from the hook on the back of the door, and put it on over my shirt and jeans.

My father said, ''You're still wearing your apron.''

It was the sort of thing that once we would have laughed at. Now, in deathly silence I reached round and untied it, and tore it off, and dropped it across the bed.

I said, ''If I take the car, and leave it at the motel, could you or Linda pick it up?''

''Sure,'' said my father . . . and then, ''Wait . . .'' and he disappeared into his room again, only to return with a fistful of money, five-dollar bills, ten-dollar, one-dollar, all dirty and ragged as a bundle of old newspapers. "Here," he said, and shoved them into the pocket of my raincoat, "you'd better take this. You might need it."

I said, "But you . . ." but at that moment Linda and Mitzi chose to return from the beach, Mitzi shedding sand all over the floor, and Linda delighted with her short commune with nature.

"Oh, those waves, I've never seen anything like them. They must be ten feet high." She noticed then, my suitcase, my raincoat, my presumably miserable face. "Jane, what are you doing?"

"I'm going away."

"Where, for heaven's sakes?"

"To Scotland."

"I hope not because of me."

"Partly. But only because it means that there's someone to look after Father."

She looked a little disconcerted, as though looking after Father had been the last thing she expected to do, but she gamely covered up and made the best of it. "Well, that's fun for you. When're you going?"

"Today. Now. I'm taking the Dodge over to La Carmella . . ." I had already started to back away, because the situation was becoming more than I could bear. My father picked up my case and came after me. "And I hope you have a good winter. And that there aren't too many storms. And there are eggs and canned tuna fish in the icebox . . ."

I went backwards down the porch steps, was out of the house, turned, and ducked under the line of washing (would Linda have the sense to bring it in?), and I got in behind the wheel of the car and my father heaved the suitcase in on to the back seat.

"Jane – " but I was incapable of saying goodbye. I was actually moving, on my way, when I remembered Rusty. By then it was too late. He had heard me, heard the car door, heard the engine start up, and he was out of the house and after me like a shot, barking indignantly, racing alongside me, his ears flat against his head, and in imminent danger of almost certain death.

It was the last straw. I stopped the car. My father with a great bellow of "Rusty!" came after the dog. Rusty stood on his back legs and scratched and scrabbled with his claws on the car door, and I leaned over and tried to push him off and said, "Oh, Rusty, don't. Get down. I can't take you. I can't take you with me."

Father, actually running, had caught up with us. He swept Rusty up into his arms and stood looking down at me. Rusty's eyes were hurt and reproachful, but my father had an expression on his face which I had never seen before and did not wholly understand. But I knew in that moment I didn't want to say goodbye to either of them, and I burst into tears.

"You will look after Rusty, won't you?" I bawled, my mouth going square. "Shut him up so that he can't follow the car. And don't let him get run over. And he only likes Red Heart dog food, not the other kind. And don't leave him alone on the beach, someone might steal him." I groped for a handkerchief. As usual I hadn't got one, and as usual, my father took one out of his pocket, and silently handed it to me. I blew my nose, and then I put up my arms, and pulled him down so that I could kiss him, and Rusty too, and I said goodbye and Father said, "Goodbye, my Pooch," which he hasn't called me since I was six, and bawling harder than ever, and hardly able to see a thing, I never looked back, but I knew that they stood there, and that they watched until I was over the ridge and out of sight.

It was a quarter to eleven when I walked into the reception office of the motel and the man behind the desk looked at my blurred and tear-stained face without interest, as though weeping females came in and out all day long.

I said, "Has Mr David Stewart left yet?"

"No, he's still around. Got a phone bill to settle up."

"What number's his room?"

He glanced at a board. "Thirty-two." His eyes ran over my raincoat, my jeans, my stained sneakers, and his hand reached for the phone. "You want to see him?"

"Yes, please."

"I'll call him . . . tell him you're coming. What's your name?"

"Jane Marsh."

He ducked his head in the direction of the door, sending me on my way. "Number thirty-two," he said.

I set off blindly, down a covered path which led alongside a large, very blue swimming-pool. Two women lay in long chairs and their children swam and screamed and fought over a rubber ring. Before I had got halfway, David Stewart was coming to meet me. When I saw him I started to run, and much to the interest of the two women, and also to my own surprise, I ran straight into his arms, and he caught me and gave me a reassuring sort of hug, and then held me off and said, "What's wrong?"

"Nothing's wrong." But I had started to cry again. "I'm coming with you."

"Why?"

"I've changed my mind, that's all."

"Why?"

I hadn't meant to tell him, but it all started spilling out. "Father's got a friend, and she's come from Los Angeles . . . and she's . . . she said . . ."

He took a look at the two goggling women, said, "Come along," and led me back to the privacy of his room, pushed me inside, and shut the door behind us.

"Now," he said.

I blew my nose and made a real effort to pull myself together.

"It's just that he has someone to look after him. So I can come with you."

"Did you tell him about the letters?"

"Yes."

"And doesn't he mind your coming?"

"No. He said OK."

David was quiet. I looked at him and saw that he had turned his head, was now regarding me thoughtfully from the corner of his right eye. I found out later that this was a habit picked up over the years on account of his bad eyesight and the fact that he had to wear glasses, but at the moment it was both disconcerting and uncomfortable; like being nailed to the wall.

I said miserably, "Don't you want me to come with you?"

"It's not that. It's just that I don't know you well enough to know if you're telling the truth."

I was too unhappy to be offended. "I never lie," I said, and then amended this. "And when I do I go all shifty and blush. And Father did say it was all right." And to prove this I put my hand in my raincoat pocket and pulled out the dirty bundle of dollars. Some of the bills fell, like old leaves, to the carpet. "He gave me some money to spend."

David stooped and picked them up and handed them back to me. "I still think, Jane, I should make a point of seeing him before we fly off. We could . . ."

"I couldn't say goodbye again."

His face lost its severity. He touched my arm. "Stay here then. I won't be more than fifteen minutes."

"You promise?"

"I promise."

He went, and I wandered around the room he had occupied, and read a bit of a newspaper, and looked out of the open door, and then went into the bathroom and washed my face and my hands, and combed my hair and found a rubber band and fastened it back. I went out and sat by the pool and waited for him, and when he returned and had loaded our luggage, I got into the car beside him, and we drove out and on to the highway and south to Los Angeles. We stayed the night in a motel near the airport, and the next day we flew to New York, and the next night, to London, and it was not until we were halfway out over the Atlantic that I remembered the young boy who had been coming, next Sunday, to take me surfing.

4

I had lived for most of my life in London, but returning was like coming to a city I had never seen before, so changed was it. The airport buildings, the approach roads, the skyline, the great towering blocks of flats, the mass of traffic . . . all this had happened in the last seven years. In the taxi I sat wedged in a corner with my case at my feet, and it was foggy so that the street lights still burned, and damply cold in a way that I had forgotten.

I had not slept in the plane and was dizzy with fatigue; nauseated by unlikely meals presented to me at what was, according to my watch, which I had kept at California time, two o'clock in the morning. My body, my head, my eyes ached with travelling, my teeth felt gritty, and my clothes as though I had been wearing them for ever.

There were billboards, flyovers, rows of houses, and London enclosed us. The taxi turned off at some traffic lights, nosed its way down a quiet crescent, lined with parked cars, and stopped in front of a terrace of tall, early Victorian houses.

I watched them dully and wondered what I was meant to do now. David leaned across me and opened the door and said, "This is where we get out."

"Uh?" I looked at him and wondered how any man, who had shared the – to me – soul-destroying experience of flying, non-stop, halfway round the world, could continue to look clean, relaxed and in charge of the situation. But I fell obediently out of the taxi and stood on the pavement, blinking like an owl and yawning, while he paid the driver off, collected our suitcases, and led the way down a flight of basement steps. The railings which enclosed them were shiny black, the little paved area was clean and swept, and there was a wooden tub full of geraniums . . . a little sooty, but still bright and gay. He took out a key, the yellow door swung inwards, and I followed him blindly into the flat.

It was white-painted, smelled of country houses, the floor was scattered with Persian rugs, there were chintz covers on the sofa and armchairs, small, old, polished pieces of furniture, a Venetian mirror over the fireplace. I saw books and a pile of magazines, a glass-fronted cabinet filled with Dresden, small patches of hand-worked tapestry . . . and, beyond the windows on the far side of the room, a miniature sunken patio garden, with a plane tree, ringed by a wooden seat, and a small statue set into the recess of the faded brick wall.

I stood, yawning. He went to open a window, and I said, "Is this your flat?"

"No, it's my mother's, but I use it when I come to London."

I looked around vaguely. "Where is your mother?" It sounded as though I expected her to be hiding under the sofa, but he didn't smile.

"She's in the South of France, on holiday. Come on now, take off your coat, and get comfortable. I'll go and make a cup of tea."

He disappeared through a door. I heard the sound of a tap turned on, a kettle being filled. A cup of tea. The very words were comforting and homely. A cup of tea. I thought of elocution lessons. How Now Brown Cow How Would You Like A Cup Of Tea. I fumbled with the buttons of my raincoat, and eventually got them undone, pulled the coat off and draped it across what looked like a Chippendale chair. I let myself down on to the sofa. It had leaf-green velvet cushions and I took one and pulled it into position and put my head down, but I think I was asleep before I actually had time to get my feet up off the floor. I certainly don't remember doing this.

When I awoke, the light had changed. A long beam of sunshine, dancing with dust, lay like a spotlight across my line of vision. I moved, and knuckled the sleep from my eyes, and looked again, and there was a rug over me, warm and light.

In the fireplace, a fire flickered. I looked at it for some time before I realised that it was an electric one with sham logs and coal and flames. It seemed, at that moment, infinitely cosy. I turned my head slightly and saw David, deep in an armchair, awash in papers and briefcases. He was wearing different clothes – a blue shirt, a cream-coloured sweater with a V-neck. I wondered in a detached sort of way if he was one of those people who never needed to sleep. He had heard my stirrings and was watching me.

I said, "What day is it?"

He was amused. "Wednesday."

"Where are we?"

"London."

"No, I mean whereabouts?"

"Kensington."

47

I said, "We used to live in Melbury Road. Is that far?"

"No. Quite near."

After a little, "What time is it?"

"Nearly five."

"When do we go to Scotland?"

"Tonight. We've got sleepers booked on the Royal High-lander."

With an enormous effort I sat up, and yawned and tried to wipe sleep out of my system and hair out of my face. I said, "I suppose I couldn't possibly have a bath?"

"Of course you can," he said.

So I had a bath, boiling water that wouldn't lather properly and handfuls of his mother's bath salts which he kindly said I could use. When I had bathed I got my suitcase, and found some clean clothes and put them on, and jammed all the dirty ones back in the case, and somehow got the case shut again, and went back into the sitting-room, and found that he had made tea, and that there was hot buttered toast and a plate of chocolate biscuits – the proper kind, not chocolate flavoured cookies which you get in America, but plain biscuits covered with real chocolate.

I said, "Are these your mother's?"

"No. I went out and bought them while you were asleep. There's a little shop around the corner, very handy when you run out of things."

"Has your mother lived here always?"

"Not at all, only a year or so. She used to have a house in Hampshire, but it got too big for her and the garden was a worry . . . it's not easy to get help. So she sold it, and kept a few of her favourite things and moved here."

So that explained the country house atmosphere. I looked out at the little patio and said, "And she has got a garden."

"Yes, a small one. But she can manage that herself."

I took another piece of toast and tried to imagine my grandmother in such a situation. But it was not possible. Grandmother would never be defeated by the size of her house or the amount she had to do, or the difficulties of getting and keeping cooks and gardeners. Indeed, Mrs Lumley had been with her ever since I could remember, standing on her swollen legs at the kitchen table, and rolling out pastry. And Will, the gardener, had a little cottage and an allotment of his own, where he grew potatoes and carrots and enormous mop-headed chrysanthemums.

"So you didn't ever live in this flat?"

"No, but I stay with her when I come to London."

"Is that often?"

"Fairly."

"Do you ever see Sinclair?"

"Yes."

"What does he do?"

"He works for an advertising agency. I would have thought you knew that."

It occurred to me that I could ring him up. After all, he lived in London, it would take only moments to look up his number. I thought of doing this, and then decided against it. I was not entirely sure of Sinclair's reaction, and did not wish David Stewart to witness my possible discomfiture.

I said, "Has he got a girlfriend?"

"Heaps, I should think."

"No, you know what I mean. Anyone very special."

"Jane, I really wouldn't know."

I licked hot butter, thoughtfully, from the ends of my fingers.

I said, "Do you suppose he'll come up to Elvie when I'm there?"

"Bound to."

"And his father? Is Uncle Aylwyn still in Canada?"

David Stewart pushed his glasses up his nose with a long, brown finger. He said, "Aylwyn Bailey died, about three months ago."

I stared. "Now I never knew *that*. Oh, poor Granny. Was she very upset?"

"Yes, she was . . ."

"And the funeral and everything . . ."

"In Canada. He'd been ill for some time. He never managed to get home."

"So Sinclair never saw him again."

"No."

I digested this information, and felt sad. I thought of my own father, infuriating as he was, and knew that not for anything would I have missed a single moment of the time we had spent together, and I felt sadder than ever for Sinclair. And then I remembered that in the old days it had been I who envied him, for, while I merely spent holidays at Elvie, it was Sinclair's home. And as for missing a father's companionship, the place had always been teeming with men, for as well as Will the gardener – whom we loved – there was Gibson the keeper, a dour man but wise in all respects; and Gibson's two sons, Hamish and George, who were about Sinclair's age and included him in all their pursuits, both legal and otherwise. And so he had been taught to shoot and cast a fly, play cricket and climb trees, and one way and another had a good deal more time and attention lavished on him than most boys of his age. No, all things considered, Sinclair had missed very little.

We caught the Royal Highlander at Euston, and it seemed that I spent half the night getting out of bed to look out of the window and gloat over the fact that the train was tearing northwards, and nothing, save a disastrous act of God, could stop it. In Edinburgh I was wakened by a female voice, sounding like Maggie Smith being Miss Jean Brodie, saying "Edinburgh Waverley. This is Edinburgh Waverley," and I knew that I was in Scotland, and I got up and put my raincoat on over my nightdress and sat on the cover of the washbasin and watched as the lights of Edinburgh slid away, and waited for the bridge, when the train, suddenly making an entirely different sound, plunged out and over the Forth, and the river lay miles below us, a gleam of dark water, touched with the riding lights of miniature craft.

I got back into bed, and dozed until we reached Relkirk, when I got up again, and opened the window, and the air poured in, cold and edged with the smell of peat and pine. We were on the edge of the Highlands. It was only a quarter past five, but I dressed and spent the last part of the journey with my cheek pressed against the dark, rain-spattered glass. To begin with I could see little, but by the time we had ground our way over the pass, and started in on the long run down the gentle gradient that finally leads to Thrumbo, the day was beginning to lighten. There was no sign of the sun, simply an imperceptible fading from darkness. Clouds were thick, grey and soft over the tops of the hills, but as we ran down into the valley, they thinned and shredded away to nothing and the great wide sweep of the glen lay before us, golden brown and tranquil in the early morning light.

51

There was a thump on my door and the attendant looked in.

"The gentleman's wanting to know if you're awake. We'll be in to Thrumbo in ten minutes or so. Will I take your case?"

He removed it, and the door shut behind him and I turned back to the window, because now the countryside was becoming closely familiar and I didn't want to miss a thing. I had walked on that bit of road, ridden a Highland pony in that field, had been taken to tea in that white cottage. And then there was the bridge which marked the boundaries of the village, and the filling station, and the refined hotel that was always filled with elderly residents, and where you could never buy a drink.

The door opened again, and David Stewart stood there, filling the doorway.

"Good morning."

"Hi."

"How did you sleep?"

"OK."

Now the train was slowing, braking. We moved past the signal box, under the bridge. I slid off the top of the washbasin, and followed him out into the corridor, and over his shoulder watched the sign saying Thrumbo sail triumphantly past, and then the train stopped and we were there.

He had left his car in a garage, so he abandoned me to wait in the station yard while he went to fetch it. I sat there on my suitcase, in the deserted, slowly waking village, and watched as lights came on, one by one, and chimneys smoked, and a man came wobbling down the street on a bicycle. And then I heard, far above me, a honking and a chattering and it became louder and passed clear overhead but I couldn't see the formations of wild geese, because they were flying above the cloud.

THE END OF SUMMER

*

Elvie Loch lay about two miles beyond the village of Thrumbo, a wild expanse of water looped to the north by the main road to Inverness and enclosed, on the opposite shore, by the great bastions of the Cairngorms. Elvie itself was very nearly an island, shaped like a mushroom and joined to the mainland by its stalk, a narrow spit of land that was no more than a causeway between reed-filled marshes, nesting-place for hundreds of birds.

For many years the land had belonged to the church, and indeed there were still the ruins of a little chapel, roofless now and deserted, although the small graveyard surrounding it was still kept neat and tidy, the yews tightly clipped, the grass mown smooth as velvet, and, in spring, gay with the tossing heads of wild daffodils.

The house where my grandmother lived had been the manse for this little church. Over the years, however, it had outstripped its original modest bounds, as wings were added and extra rooms to accommodate, one supposed, large Victorian families. From the back, from the approach road, it appeared tall and forbidding, the windows to the north being small and sparse in order to conserve warmth in the bitter winters, and the front door was snug and unimpressive, and usually tightly closed. This fortress-like impression was enhanced by the two high garden walls, which, like arms, reached from the house to east and west, and against which even my grandmother had been unable to coax a climber to grow.

But, from the other side, the aspect of Elvie was entirely different. The old white house, protected and enclosed and facing due south, blinked and drowsed in the sunlight. Windows and doors stood open to the fresh air, and the garden sloped down to a shallow ha-ha, dividing it from a narrow field where a neighbouring farmer grazed his cattle. The field dipped to the water's edge, and the lap of small waves on shingle, and the gentle lowing and munching of cattle were so constant a part of Elvie that after a little you stopped hearing them. It was only when you'd been away, and returned, that you became aware of them all over again.

David Stewart's car was a surprise, a dark blue TR4, and unexpectedly racy for such a solid-seeming citizen. We packed in our cases, and headed out of Thrumbo, and I sat forward on my seat and churned with excitement. Familiar landmarks appeared, and flew away behind us. The garage, the sweet shop, and the McGregors' farm, and then we were out in open country. The road swept up through fields of golden stubble, the hedges were spattered scarlet with the hips of wild roses, and there had been frost already, for trees were touched with the gold and red of the first autumn colours.

And then we swung around the last corner and the loch stretched away to our right, grey in the grey morning, and the mountains on the far side were lost in cloud. And, not half a mile away, stood Elvie itself, the house hidden by trees and the roofless church looking romantically desolate. Excitement made me speechless and, with a rare understanding, David Stewart offered no sort of comment. We had come a long way together, so far indeed that it was hard to comprehend, but it was in silence that we finally turned off by the roadside cottage, and the car wound down through the high hedges, over the causeway between the marshes, and up under the copper beeches, to come to a halt at the front door.

THE END OF SUMMER

I was out of the car in an instant, running across the gravel, but my grandmother was quicker than I. The door opened and she appeared, and we met, our arms tight around each other, and she kept saying my name, and she smelled of the scented sachets she keeps with her clothes, and I told myself that nothing had changed.

5

A reunion after so many years is always confusion. We said things like, "Oh, you're really here . . ." and "I never thought I'd make it . . ." and "Did you have a good journey . . ." and "Everything's just the same," and we held each other off, and laughed at our idiocies, and hugged again.

Next the dogs added to the turmoil, boiling out of the house, barking around our feet, demanding attention. They were liver-and-white spaniels, new to me, and yet familiar too, because there had always been liver-and-white spaniels at Elvie, and these were no doubt descended from the ones I remembered. And no sooner had I started to greet the dogs than we were joined by Mrs Lumley, who had heard the din and was unable to resist the temptation to be in on the homecoming. She was fatter than ever in her green overall, and she appeared out of the house smiling from ear to ear, to be kissed, to tell me I'd grown awful tall and that I'd got more freckles than ever and that she was making a really big breakfast.

Behind me David was quietly unloading my suitcase, and now my grandmother went to greet him.

"David, you must be tired out." Rather to my surprise she gave him a kiss. "Thank you for bringing her safely back."

"You got my wire."

"Of course I did. I've been up since seven. You'll come in and have breakfast with us, won't you? We're expecting you."

But he excused himself, saying that his housekeeper would be expecting him, that he must get home and change and then get to the office.

"Well, then, come back for dinner tonight. Yes, I insist. About half past seven. We want to hear all about everything."

He allowed himself to be persuaded, and we looked at each other, smiling. It occurred to me, with some surprise, that I had only met him four days ago, and yet now, when it was time to say goodbye, I felt that I was leaving an old friend, someone I had known all my life. He had been given a difficult job to do, and he had done it tactfully and with good humour, and as far as I knew, had offended nobody.

"Oh, David . . ."

He hastily forestalled my garbled thanks.

"I'll see you this evening, Jane," and he backed away, and got into his car, and slammed the door, and we watched him turn and drive away, under the beeches, down the road and so around the corner and out of sight.

"Such a nice man," said my grandmother thoughtfully. "Don't you think so?"

"Yes," I said, "sweet," and dived to prevent Mrs Lumley picking up my case, and carried it into the house myself, and Grandmother and the dogs came behind me, and the door was shut and David Stewart was, for the moment, forgotten.

I was assailed by the smell of peat smoke from the hall fire,

THE END OF SUMMER

the smell of roses from the big bowl of pink blooms on the chest
by the clock. One of the dogs was panting for attention, tail
wagging and all excitement, and I stopped to scratch his ears and
was just going to tell them about Rusty, when my grandmother
said, "I've got a surprise for you, Jane," and I straightened
and looked up and saw a man coming down the stairs towards
me, silhouetted against the light of the staircase window. For
an instant I was dazzled by this light, and then he said, "Hello
Jane," and I realised that it was my cousin Sinclair.

I could only gape, while Grandmother and Mrs Lumley stood,
delighted by the success of the surprise they had planned. He
had reached my side, and taken my shoulders between his hands
and stooped to kiss me before I found breath to say weakly,
"But I thought you were in London."

"Well I'm not. I'm here."

"But how . . . ? Why . . . ?"

"I've got a few days' leave."

For me? Had he taken them so that he could be at Elvie
for my return? The possibility was both flattering and exciting,
but before I could say anything more, my grandmother started
organising us.

"Well, there's no point in our standing around here . . .
Sinclair, perhaps you'd carry Jane's case up to her room, and
then when you've washed your hands, dear, you'd better come
down and have some breakfast. You'll be tired out after that
journey."

"I'm not tired." And indeed I wasn't. I felt vital and wide
awake and ready for anything. Sinclair picked up my case, and
went upstairs two at a time, and I followed his long legs as
though I had wings on my heels.

59

My bedroom, looking out over the garden and the loch, was inhumanly neat and polished but otherwise unchanged. Still, the white-painted bed stood, pushed in the bay of the window which was where I always preferred to sleep. And there was a pin cushion on the dressing-table and lavender bags in the wardrobe and the blue rug, covering the worn patch of carpet.

While I shed my coat and washed my hands, Sinclair went and dumped himself on my bed, sadly creasing the starched white cover, and watched me. In the seven years that had passed he had changed, of course, but the differences I saw in him were almost too subtle to be pin-pointed. He was thinner, certainly, there were fine lines round his mouth and at the corners of his eyes, but that was all. He was very good looking, with dark brows and lashes and deep blue eyes, which slanted tantalisingly up at the corners. His nose was straight and his mouth curved and full, with a lower lip which, when he was young, could look very sulky. His hair was thick and straight, and he wore it long, tapered down the back of his neck on to his collar, and used as I was to the hair fashions of Reef Point, either crew cut (surfers) or shoulder length (hippies), I thought the effect was very attractive. He wore that morning a blue shirt with a cotton handkerchief knotted in the open neck and a pair of washed-out cord trousers hitched round his waist with a belt of plaited wool.

I said, fishing for confirmation of what I hoped was true, "Are you really on leave?"

"Of course," he said shortly, confirming nothing.

I resigned myself to never knowing. "You're with an advertising firm?"

"Yes. Strutt and Seward. P.A. to the Managing Director."

"Is that a good job?"

"It includes an expense account."

"You mean boozy lunches with prospective clients."

"It doesn't have to be a boozy lunch. If the prospective client is pretty, it's just as likely to be an intimate candle-lit supper."

A twinge of jealousy had to be firmly battened down. I was at the dressing-table now, combing out the long heavy tassel of my hair, and he said, without any change of expression, "I'd forgotten how long it was. You used to wear it in plaits. It's like silk."

"Every now and then I swear I'm going to get it cut off, but I never get round to it." I finished my hair and laid down the comb and went to join him on the bed, kneeling to open the window and hang out.

"Delicious smell," I told him. "All damp and autumny."

"Doesn't California smell damp and autumny?"

"Most of the time it smells of petrol." I thought of Reef Point. "When it isn't smelling of gum trees and the Pacific."

"And how is life with the Redskins?"

I shot him a sharp look, daring him to start being offensive, and he relented. "Honestly Jane, I was terrified you'd come back chewing gum and slung with cameras, and say 'Gee, Sin' every time you addressed a remark in my direction."

"You're out of date, brother," I told him.

"Protesting, then, you know, with a picket saying, 'Make Love Not War'." He said this in a fake American accent which I found as tedious as being kidded in California about my terribly terribly British voice.

I told him so and added, "I promise you that when I start protesting, you will be the first to know."

He acknowledged this with a wicked gleam. "How's your father?"

"He's grown a beard and he looks like Hemingway."

"I can imagine." A pair of mallards flew down out of the sky, came in to land on the water, with that little scud of white foam, just as they touched down. We watched them and then Sinclair yawned and stretched and gave me a brotherly slap and said it was time for breakfast, so we got up off the bed and closed the window again and went downstairs.

I found that I was ravenous. There was bacon, and eggs and Cooper's marmalade and hot floury rolls which I remembered were called baps, and while I ate, Sinclair and my grandmother talked, in a desultory fashion – breakfast chat concerning news in the local paper, the result of a flower show, a letter that my grandmother had received from an elderly cousin who had gone to live in a place called Mortar.

"What the hell's he gone to live there for?"

"Well, it's cheap of course, and warm. The poor old thing always suffered dreadfully from rheumatics."

"And how does he propose passing his days? Rowing sightseers around Grand Harbour?"

I realised that they were talking about Malta. Mortar; Malta. I was more Americanised than I had thought.

My grandmother poured coffee. I watched her and worked out that she must now be in her seventies, but she still looked exactly as I had always remembered her. She was tall, dignified and very good looking, her white hair always immaculate, her eyes, deep set beneath finely arched eyebrows, a bright and piercing blue. (At the moment their effect was charmingly youthful, but I knew that she could register a world of disapproval with a single lift of those eyebrows, accompanied by a chilling blue stare.) Her clothes were ageless too, and entirely becoming. Soft heathery tweed skirts and cashmere sweaters or cardigans. In the day-time she wore constantly her pearls, and a pair of coral earrings, shaped like tear drops. In the evenings a modest diamond or two was likely to spark from her dark velvets, for she was sufficiently old-fashioned to change each evening for dinner, even if it was Sunday and we ate nothing more exciting than scrambled eggs.

And as she sat ensconced at the head of her table, I thought that she had had more than her share of tragedy. Her husband had died, and then she had lost her daughter and now her son, the elusive Aylwyn, who had chosen to live and die in Canada. Sinclair and I were all she had left. And Elvie. But her back remained straight and her manner brisk, and I was thankful that she would never become one of those mournful old ladies, perpetually remembering the old days. She was too interested, too active, too intelligent. Indestructible, I told myself comfortably. That's what she is. Indestructible.

After breakfast Sinclair and I made a ritual tour of the island, missing nothing. We went out through the gate that leads into the graveyard. There we did the rounds of all the old headstones, and peered in through the window-gaps of the ruined church, and then climbed the wall into the field, and went down past the eyes of curious cattle, to the edge of the loch. We disturbed a pair of mallard ducks and had a competition skimming flat stones, seeing who could throw them the farthest. Sinclair won. We walked the length of the jetty to look at the leaky old boat that was such a devil to row, and our footsteps echoed out over the sagging planking.

"One day," I said, "this is going to collapse."

"No point in getting it mended if it's never used."

We went on, around the edge of the water, under the spreading beech where we had built our tree house, and then up through the birch spinney, ringed about by quietly falling leaves, and so back to the house by way of a cluster of outbuildings – abandoned piggeries and henhouses, and stables, and an old coach house which had long since been put to use as a garage.

"Come and see my car," said Sinclair.

We struggled with bolts and the big, old-fashioned door, and it swung creakily back to reveal, alongside my grandmother's large and dignified Daimler, a dark yellow Lotus Elan, black hooded, low to the ground and infinitely lethal.

I said, "How long have you had that?"

"Oh, about six months." He got in behind the driving wheel, and backed it out, the engine purring like an angry tiger, and showed me, like a small boy with a new toy, the car's varied accomplishments: the electrically operated windows; the neat device which worked the hood; the automatic burglar alarm; the headlight covers, which opened and shut like monstrous eyelids.

"How fast does it go?" I inquired nervously.

He shrugged. "Hundred and twenty, hundred and thirty?"

"Not with me in it, you don't."

"Wait until you're invited, my chicken-hearted child."

"You couldn't go sixty on the roads up here without coming off them altogether." He got out of the car. "Aren't you going to put it away?"

"No." He glanced at his watch. "I've got a date to shoot pigeons." I knew I was home. In Scotland men perpetually go and shoot things regardless of any plans their womenfolk may have made for them.

I said, "When'll you be back?"

"Probably for tea." He grinned down at me. "Tell you what, after tea, I'll walk you up to call on the Gibsons. They can't wait to see you and I promised I would."

"All right. Let's do that."

We went back to the house, Sinclair to change and collect all his shooting clobber, and me to go up to my room and unpack.

As I went in through the door the air struck chill and I shivered and realised that already I was missing the Californian sunshine and American central heating. Elvie was thick-walled and south-facing. Open fires burned constantly and there were always gallons of hot water, but the bedrooms were inclined to be decidedly parky. I laid my clothes in the empty drawers and came to the conclusion that although they were Mild-Wash, Drip-Dry and Perma-Pressed, they were not warm. For Scotland I should have to buy some new ones. Perhaps – happy thought – my grandmother would buy them for me.

With this in mind I went downstairs to find her, and met her coming out of the kitchen wearing rubber boots and an ancient raincoat and carrying a basket.

She said, "I was just coming to look for you. Where's Sinclair?"

"Gone pigeon shooting."

"Oh, yes, he said he'd be out for lunch. Come and help me pick sprouts."

Our progress was held up for a moment while I found boots and an old coat and then we set out once more into the quiet morning, only this time we made for the walled garden. Will, the gardener, was there already. He looked up as we came in, stopped digging and came treading cannily over the newly-turned earth to shake me, muddily, by the hand.

"Eh," he said, "itsh a long time since you were lasht at Elvie." He did not always speak very clearly, as he only wore his teeth on Sundays. "And hoo is life in America?"

I told him a little about life in America, and he asked after my father, and I asked after Mrs Will, who appeared to be ailing, as always, and then he went back to his digging and my grandmother and I went off to pick sprouts.

When we had filled the basket, we went back towards the house, but the morning was so fresh and quiet that Grandmother said she didn't want to go back indoors just yet, so we went around and into the garden, and sat on a white-painted, iron seat, looking out over the garden and the water, to the mountains beyond. The herbaceous border was filled with dahlias and zinnias and purple Michaelmas daisies, and the pearly grass was scattered with the dark red leaves of a Canadian maple.

She said, "I always think autumn is a perfect time. Some people think it's sad, but it's really much too beautiful to be sad."

I quoted,

September has come, it is hers,
Whose vitality leaps in the autumn.

"Who wrote that?"

"Louis MacNeice. Does your vitality leap?"

"Well, it might have done twenty years ago." We laughed and she pressed my hand. "Oh, Jane, what a delight to have you back again."

"You wrote so often and I would have come before . . . but it really wasn't possible."

"No, of course not, I quite see that. And it was selfish of me to keep insisting."

"And those . . . letters you wrote to my father. I didn't know anything about them, or I'd have made him reply."

"He was always a very stubborn man." She shot me a glance, very sharp and blue. "He didn't want you to come?"

"I'd made up my mind. He became resigned. Besides, with David Stewart there, waiting to bring me, he could scarcely raise too many objections."

"I was afraid you wouldn't be able to leave him."

"No." I reached down and picked up a maple leaf and started shredding it between my fingers. "No. He has a friend staying with him."

Again that sideways glance. "A friend?"

I looked up ruefully. She had always been high-principled, but never a prude. I said, "Linda Lansing. She's an actress. And his current girlfriend."

After a little, "I see," said my grandmother.

"No, I don't think you probably do. But I like her, and she'll look after him . . . anyway, until I get home again."

"I can't think," said my grandmother, "why he didn't marry again."

"Perhaps because he didn't stay in any one place long enough for the banns to be called?"

"But it's selfish. It hasn't given you a chance to get away, come back and see us all, or even to have some sort of a career."

"A career is one thing I have never wanted."

"But nowadays every girl should be able to support herself."

67

I said that I was very happy being supported by my father, and my grandmother said I was as stubborn as he was and hadn't I ever wanted to do some sort of a job?

I thought hard, but could only remember being eight years old and wanting to join a circus and help wash the camels. I did not think my grandmother would appreciate this, so I said, "Not really."

"Oh, my poor Jane."

I rose like a bird to my father's defence. "Not poor. Not poor anything. I don't feel I've missed a thing." But I added, to soften this, "Except Elvie. I did miss Elvie. And you. And everything." She made no comment on this. I dropped the shredded leaf, and stooped to pick up another. I said, intent on it, "David Stewart told me about Uncle Aylwyn. I didn't say anything to Sinclair . . . but . . . I was sorry . . . I mean, his being so far away and everything."

"Yes." Her voice was expressionless. "But then, that's what he chose . . . to live in Canada, and finally, to die there. You see, Elvie never meant very much to Aylwyn. He was essentially a restless person. He needed, more than anything, the company of a lot of different people. He liked variety in everything he did. And Elvie was never the best place for that."

"It's strange . . . a man being bored in Scotland . . . it's so essentially a man's ambience."

"Yes, but you see he didn't like shooting and he never wanted to fish, he was bored by it. He liked horses and racing. He was a great racing man."

I realised, with some surprise, that this was the first time we had spoken about my Uncle Aylwyn. It was not exactly that the subject had been avoided; just that, before, I had been totally incurious. But now I realised it was unnatural how little I knew about him . . . I did not even know how he had looked, for my grandmother, unlike most women of her generation, was not one for family photographs. Any that she had were neatly filed away in albums, not standing about, silver-framed, on top of the grand piano.

I said, "What sort of a person was he? What did he look like?"

"Look like? He looked like Sinclair does now. And he was very charming . . . he would walk into a room and you could see all the women perk up, and start smiling and being very attractive. It was quite amusing to watch."

I was on the point of asking about Silvia, but she forestalled me by glancing at her watch, and turning businesslike again.

"Now, I must go and give these sprouts to Mrs Lumley or she won't get them in time for lunch. Thank you for helping me pick them. And I've enjoyed our little talk."

Sinclair, true to his word, was home for tea. Afterwards, we put on coats and whistled up the dogs and set off to call on the Gibsons.

They lived in a small keeper's cottage, tucked into a fold of the hill which rose to the north of Elvie, so that we had to walk off the island, and cross the main road, and follow a track which wound up between grass and heather, crossing and re-crossing a tumbling burn which passed under the road by means of a culvert and emptied itself into Elvie Loch. It had travelled from deep and high in the mountains, and the glen down which it ran, and the hills on either side, were all part of my grandmother's estate.

In the old days, there had been shooting parties, with school-children as beaters, and hill ponies to carry elderly gentlemen up to their butts, but now the moor was let off to a syndicate of local businessmen, who enjoyed walking the moor during two or three Saturdays in August but appeared just as well content to bring their families picnicking, or to fish the waters of the burn.

As we approached the cottage, there was a cacophony of barking from the kennels, and, disturbed by the noise, the figure of Mrs Gibson presently appeared through the open door. Sinclair waved and called, "Hello there!" and Mrs Gibson waved back, and then disappeared hastily back inside again.

"Gone to put the kettle on?" I suggested.

"Or warn Gibson to put his teeth in."

"That's not at all kind."

"No. But likely."

There was an old Land-Rover parked by the side of the house with half a dozen white Leghorn hens pecking round its wheels and a line of breeze-stiffened washing. As we came up to the door, Mrs Gibson came out once more, having removed her apron. She wore a blouse with a cameo brooch at the collar and was beaming from ear to ear.

"Oh, Miss Jane, I'd have known you anywhere. I was speaking to Will, and he said you hadna' changed at a'. And Mr Sinclair . . . I didn't know you were up."

"Taken a few days' leave."

"Come away in then, Gibson's just taking his tea."

"I hope we've not come at a bad time . . ." Sinclair stood aside and waited for me to go ahead of him. I ducked my head cannily at the door, and went into the kitchen, where a fire burned redly in the grate and Gibson was heaving himself to his feet from behind a table laden with scones, cakes, butter and jam, tea and milk, and a comb of honey. There was also a strong smell of haddock.

"Oh, Gibson, we *are* disturbing you . . ."

"Not at all, not at all . . ." He put out his hand and I took it, and it felt dry and gnarled as old tree bark. Without his inevitable tweed hat he looked strange and unfamiliar, as vulnerable as a policeman without his helmet, his bald head protected by only a few wisps of white hair. And I realised that, of all my friends at Elvie, he was the only one who had truly aged. His eyes were pale and rimmed with white. He was thinner, more stooped, his voice had lost its manly depth.

"Aye, we haird you were on your way home." He turned as Sinclair followed us into the hot, crowded little room. "An' you, too, Sinclair."

"Hello, Gibson."

Mrs Gibson bustled in behind him, organising us all. "He's just having his tea, Sinclair, but you can just sit down for a wee while, Gibson willna' mind. Now, you sit here, Jane, near the fire where it's nice and warm . . ." I sat, so close to the heat I thought I would roast ". . . would you like a cup of tea?"

"Yes I'd love one."

"And a wee bit to eat." She made for the scullery, laying a hand on her husband's shoulder as she passed behind him, and pressing him back on to his chair. "Sit down, dearie, and finish your haddock, Jane won't mind . . ."

"Yes, please finish it."

But Gibson said that he had had enough, and Mrs Gibson whisked away his plate as though it were indecent, and went off to fill her kettle. Sinclair pulled a chair out from the other side of the table, and sat down, facing Gibson across the electro-plated cake stand. He took out his cigarettes and gave the old keeper one and took one for himself, and then leaned across to light it.

"How've you been?" he asked.

"Oh, no' so bad . . . it's been a braw, dry summer. I hear you were after the pigeons today – how did you get on?"

They talked, and listening to their conversation and seeing them thus, the young strong man, and the old one, it was hard to remember that once Gibson had been the only man the boy Sinclair really respected.

Mrs Gibson bustled back with two clean cups – her best, I realised – and set them on the table, and poured tea, and offered us scones, iced "fancies" and shortbread, all of which we tactfully refused. Then she settled herself down on the opposite side of the fireplace and we gossiped cosily, and once more I was asked for news of my father, and gave it, and then I asked after her sons, and was told that Hamish was in the army, but George had managed to get into Aberdeen University where he was reading Law.

I was very impressed. "But that's wonderful. I never knew he was as clever as that!"

"He was always a very hard-working boy . . . a great one for the books."

"So neither Hamish nor George will follow their father."

"Och, it's not the same for the young ones. They don't want to spend their lives on the hill in all weathers . . . it's too quiet for them. And mind, you can't blame them. It's no life for a young man these days, and while we managed to bring them up all right, there's not the money in it these days. Not when they can earn three times as much with a job in a city, or a factory, or an office."

"Does Gibson mind?"

"No." She looked at him fondly, but he was too involved with Sinclair to notice her glance. "No, he was always anxious that they should do what they wanted, and do well for themselves. He encouraged Geordie all the way . . . and mind," added Mrs Gibson, unconsciously quoting Barrie, "there's nothing like a good education."

"Haven't you got pictures of them? I'd love to see how they look."

She was delighted at being asked. "I have them by my bed. I'll go and fetch them . . ."

She bustled off, and I heard her footsteps, heavy-treaded, up the little staircase, and across the floor of the room above. Behind me, Gibson was saying, "Mind, there's nothing wrong with the old butts . . . when they were built, they were built to last . . . they're just a wee bit overgrown."

"And the birds?"

"Aye, there are ony number of birds. Mind, I got a couple of vixen and their cubs during the spring."

"What about cows?"

"I've kept them awa'. And the heather's great, it was well burnt at the beginning of the season . . ."

"You're not finding it too much for you?"

"Och, I'm fit enough yet."

"My grandmother said you had a week or two in bed last winter."

"That was just a touch of the flu. The doctor gave me a bottle and I was richt as rain . . . you don't need to listen to what the women say . . ."

Mrs Gibson, returning with the photographs, picked this up.

"What's that about women?"

"You're just a lot of auld hens," her husband told her. "Fussing over a wee bit flu . . ."

"Ach, it wisna' so wee . . . and whit a time I had to keep him in bed," she added for Sinclair's benefit. She handed the photographs over for me to study, and warmed to the subject. "And I'm not so sure it was just flu . . . I wanted him to have an X-ray, but he wouldn't hear of it."

"You should, Gibson."

"Ach, I havna' time to be going to Inverness for all that caper . . ." and, as if bored by the subject of his health and wishing to change the subject, he shifted his chair in my direction in order to peer over my shoulder at the photographs of his sons: Hamish, a solid-looking corporal in the Camerons, and George, formally posed in a photographer's salon. "Geordie's at the University, did Mrs Gibson tell you? In his third year now, and he'll end up a lawyer. Do you mind the time he helped you build yon tree house?"

"It's still standing, too. It hasn't blown down yet."

"Onything Geordie did, he always did well. He's a great lad."

We stayed to gossip a little longer, and then Sinclair pushed back his chair and said that it was time to go. The Gibsons came out to see us off, and the dogs, hearing voices again, started up their barking, so we all went over to the kennels to talk to them. There were two, both bitches, one gold and the other black. The one had a soft, creamy coat, and an endearing expression, with dark tip-tilted eyes.

I said, "She looks like Sophia Loren."

"Oh, aye," said Gibson. "She's bonnie. She's on season just now, so I'm taking her over to Braemar tomorrow. There's a man there with a good dog. I thought maybe we'd see if we could get a litter of pups."

Sinclair raised his eyebrows. "You're going tomorrow? What time?"

"I'll be leaving around the back end of nine."

"What's the weather forecast? What sort of a day is it going to be?"

"We should have a bit of a wind tonight, blow all this murk away. It's a good forecast for the weekend."

Sinclair turned to smile at me. "What do you say?"

I had been playing with the dog and scarcely listening to all this. "Uh?"

"Gibson's going to Braemar tomorrow morning. We could get a lift, walk back home through the Lairig Ghru . . ." He turned back to Gibson. "Could you get up to Rothiemurchus in the evening and meet us?"

"Oh aye, I could do that. About what time would that be?"

Sinclair considered. "About six? We should be in by then." He looked at me again. "What do you say, Jane?"

I had never walked the Lairig Ghru. In the old days, every summer, it had been done by someone from Elvie, and I always longed to go, but was never included in the party because my legs were not considered sufficiently long. But now . . .

I looked up at the sky. The cloud of the morning had never cleared and was now turning, as the day died, to a fine mist. "Is it really going to be a good day?"

"Oh, aye, and verra warm."

Gibson's opinion was enough. "I'd like to do it. More than anything."

"Well that's settled. Nine o'clock at the house then?"

"I'll be there," promised Gibson, and we thanked them for the tea and left them, walking down the hill and across the wet road, and so to Elvie. The dank air hung with moisture and beneath the copper beeches it was very dark. I was suddenly depressed. I had wanted nothing to change . . . had wanted Elvie to be exactly as I remembered it, but seeing Gibson, so aged, had brought me up with a jolt. He had been ill, he said. One day he would die. And the thought of death, in that chill, in-between hour, made me shiver.

Sinclair said, "Cold?"

"I'm all right. It's been a long day."

"Are you sure you want to go tomorrow? It's a hell of a walk."

"Yes, of course." I yawned. "We'll have to get Mrs Lumley to give us a picnic."

We came out from under the beeches and the forbidding north aspect of the house reared before us, silhouetted against the lowering sky. A single light burned, shining yellow across the blue dusk. And I decided that before dinner I would have a hot bath, and then I would not feel cold and depressed any longer.

6

I was right. Lapped in silky Scottish water, I dozed. It was still early, so I found a hot-water bottle in the bathroom cupboard and filled it from the tap and went to bed for an hour, lying in the darkness with the curtains undrawn and listening to the endless honking and gabbling of the wild geese.

After this, I dressed again, and with a vague idea of making my first night home something of an occasion, took trouble to pile up my hair and to use every sort of artifice on my eyes. Then I took down my only formal garment, a gold-and-black caftan in heavy silk, all embroidered and frogged in gold, which my father had found in an obscure Chinese shop in a back street of San Francisco and had been unable to resist.

It made me look very regal. I fixed on my earrings, splashed some scent around and went downstairs. I was early, but I wanted to be early. As I lay in bed, I had made a small plan and wanted the place to myself.

My grandmother's drawing-room, made ready for the evening, had an impact as visually charming as a stage set. The velvet curtains had been closed against the darkness, the cushions plumped, magazines straightened, and the fire made up. The room was softly lit by a pair of lamps, and flamelight was reflected in brass fender and coal scuttle, and from lovingly polished wooden surfaces all over the room. There were flowers everywhere, and boxes filled with cigarettes, and the small table which did duty as a bar was neatly lined up with bottles and glasses, an ice-bucket and a small dish of nuts.

Over on the other side of the room, flanking the fireplace, was a highly decorated bombé cabinet, with glass-fronted bookshelves on top, and three deep, heavy drawers beneath. I went over to this, and pushing a small table out of the way, knelt to open the bottom drawer. One of the handles had broken and the drawer was very heavy, and I was struggling with it when I heard the door open again and someone came in. Feeling foiled, I swore to myself, but there wasn't time to get to my feet before a voice said, from just behind me, "Good evening."

It was David Stewart. I looked up over my shoulder, and found him standing over me, looking unexpectedly romantic in a dark blue dinner jacket.

I was too surprised to be polite. "I'd completely forgotten you were coming for dinner."

"I'm afraid I'm a little early. There didn't seem to be anyone around, so I let myself in. What are you doing? Looking for an earring, or playing bears?"

"Neither. I'm trying to get this drawer open."

"What for?"

"It used to be full of photograph albums. Judging from the weight, I should guess it still is."

"Let me have a go."

I moved obediently aside, and watched while he doubled up

78

on his long legs, took hold of the two handles, and gently eased the drawer open.

"It looks so easy," I said, "when someone else does it."

"Are these what you are looking for?"

"That's right." There were three of them, old, bulging albums, weighing a ton.

"Did you intend indulging in a long, nostalgic session? With this lot it should take you the rest of the evening."

"No, of course not. But I want to find a picture of Sinclair's father . . . I thought perhaps there'd be a wedding group."

There was a small silence. Then, "Why this sudden desire to find a photograph of Aylwyn Bailey?"

"Well, it seems ridiculous, but I've never seen one. I mean, Grandmother never had any standing around. I don't think there's even one in her room . . . I don't remember it. It's funny, isn't it?"

"Not necessarily. Not when you know her."

I decided to take him into my confidence. "We were talking about him today. She said that he looked like Sinclair, and that he was very charming. She said that he only had to walk into a room for all the women to start falling about in heaps. I never paid him much heed when I was little . . . he was simply Sinclair's father-in-Canada. But . . . I don't know . . . I suddenly got all curious."

I lifted out the first book, and opened it, but it was dated only ten years ago, so I went down to the bottom of the drawer, and took out the last one. It was a handsome album, bound in leather, and all the photographs – faded now and inclined to be sepia coloured – had been entered with geometrical precision and labelled in white ink.

I leafed through the pages. Shooting parties and picnics, and groups, and studio portraits, complete with painted backdrops and potted palms. A girl in presentation feathers, and a black-stockinged child (my mother) dressed as a gipsy.

And then a wedding group. "This is it." My grandmother, stately in what looked like a velvet turban and a very long dress. My mother, smiling gaily as though determined to look as though she were enjoying herself. My father, young and slim, clean-shaven and wearing his suffering expression. Probably his collar was too tight. An unknown child being a bridesmaid, and finally, the bride and groom: Silvia and Aylwyn, their young faces round and curiously untouched by any sort of experience. Silvia with a little, painted, dark-red mouth and Aylwyn smiling in a private way at the camera, his tip-tilted eyes suggesting that the whole business was the most enchanting joke.

"Well?" said David at last.

"Grandmother was right . . . he's exactly like Sinclair . . . it's just that his hair's shorter and cut differently, and perhaps he's not quite so tall. And Silvia – " I didn't like Silvia " – Silvia left him after they'd only been married about a year. Did you know that?"

"Yes, I knew."

"That's why Sinclair was always at Elvie. What are you doing?"

He was feeling around in the back of the drawer. "Here are some more," he said, and brought out a pile of heavily mounted photographs which had been put away at the back and out of sight.

"What are they?" I laid down the book I had been holding.

He turned them over in his hand. "Yet another wedding. At a guess, I'd say your grandmother's."

Aylwyn was forgotten. "Oh, let me see."

We were back now into the years of the First World War, hobble skirts and enormous hats. The group was posed around on chairs, like Royalty; high collars and cut-away coats, and expressions on faces of enormous solemnity. My grandmother as a young bride was large-bosomed, and draped in lace, her new husband scarcely older than she was, with that same amused, merry expression which even his sombre clothes and considerable moustache could do nothing to quench.

I said, "Here, he looks fun."

"I think he probably was."

"And who's this? The old fellow in whiskers and a kilt?"

David looked over my shoulder. "Probably the bridegroom's father. Isn't he splendid?"

"Who was he?"

"I believe a great character – called himself Bailey of Cairneyhall – they were an old family around here, and legend has it that he used to give himself tremendous airs and graces, despite the fact that he didn't have a ha'penny to bless himself with."

"And my grandmother's father?"

"That impressive-looking gentleman, I imagine. Now, he was a very different kettle of fish. A stockbroker in Edinburgh. He made a lot of money and died a rich man. And your grandmother," he added in lawyer-like tones, "was his only child."

"You mean . . . she was an heiress."

"You could say that."

I looked at the picture again, the solemn, unfamiliar faces who were my ancestors, the people who had made me, with all my faults and my small talents, and had given me my face and my freckles, and my fair Nordic hair.

"I never even heard of Cairneyhall."

"You wouldn't. It became so derelict and ramshackle it eventually had to be pulled down."

"So my grandmother never lived there?"

"I think for a year or two she did, probably in the greatest possible discomfort. But when her husband died, she moved to this part of the world, bought Elvie, and brought her children up here."

"So..." I stopped. I realised that, without ever having thought very much about it, I had always taken it for granted that my grandmother was if not exactly "richly left", then certainly well provided for. But it seemed now that this was not so. Elvie, and everything in it, had come from her own inheritance, belonged solely to her. And it had no connection whatsoever with her marriage to Aylwyn's father.

David was watching me. "So?" he prompted gently.

"Nothing." I was embarrassed. The whole question of money makes me feel uncomfortable, a trait I have inherited from my father, and I hastily changed the subject. "How do you know so much about them all, anyway?"

"Because I look after the family affairs."

"I see."

He closed the photograph album. "Perhaps we'd better put them all away..."

"Yes, of course. And, David... I don't want Grandmother to know I've been asking all these questions."

"I won't say a word."

We put the books and the photographs back where we had found them, and closed the drawer. I moved the table back into its place, then went to take the guard from in front of the fire, and find a cigarette, and light it with a spill. As I straightened, I found David watching me. He said, out of the blue, "You're looking very beautiful. Scotland obviously agrees with you."

I said, "Thank you," which is what nicely raised American girls are taught to say when paid a compliment. (English girls say things like, "Oh, I don't, I look a mess", or "How can you say you like this dress? It's ghastly", which I am assured can be very off-putting.)

And then, because I felt suddenly shy and needed a diversion, I suggested that I should fix him a drink, and he said that in Scotland one didn't fix drinks, one poured them.

"Not martinis," I insisted. "You can't pour a martini until you've fixed it. It stands to reason."

"You have a point. Do you want a martini?"

I was doubtful. "Do you know how to make one?"

"I like to think so."

"My father says only two men in Britain can make a martini, and he's one of them."

"Then I must be the other." He went over to the table and busied himself amongst the bottles and ice and twists of lemon peel. He said, "What have you been doing today?"

I told him, right up to the hot bath and the session on my bed, and then I said, "And tomorrow you couldn't guess what we've planned."

"No, I couldn't. Tell me."

"Sinclair and I are going to walk the Lairig Ghru."

He was gratifyingly impressed. "Are you *really*?"

"Yes, really. Gibson's going to drive us over to Braemar and then meet us at Rothiemurchus in the evening."

"What sort of day is it going to be?"

"Gibson says fine. He says all this murk's going to blow away and it'll be 'verra hot'." I watched him, liking his brown hands, and his dark neat head, and the wide shoulders beneath the soft blue velvet. I said, on an impulse, "You should come too . . ."

He came across the room, carrying the two pale golden, icy drinks. "I'd like to more than anything, but I'm busy all day tomorrow."

I took the glass and said, "Perhaps another time."

"Yes, perhaps."

We smiled, raised glasses, drank. The martini was delicious, cold and heady as fire. I said, "I'll write and tell my father I've met the other martini-fixer," and then I remembered something. "David, I simply have to get some clothes . . ."

He took the abrupt change of subject in his stride. "What sort of clothes?"

"Scottish clothes, sweaters and things. I've got that money my father gave me, but it's all in dollar bills. Do you think you could get them changed for me?"

"Yes, of course, but where do you intend doing your shopping? Caple Bridge isn't exactly the fashion centre of the north."

"I don't want anything fashionable, I just want something warm."

"In that case I suppose it would be all right. When do you want to do this shopping?"

"Saturday?"

"Can you drive your grandmother's car?"

"I can drive it, but I'm not allowed to. I haven't got a British licence . . . but it doesn't matter, I'll catch the bus . . ."

"All right. Then come to the office – I'll tell you how to find it – and I'll give you your money, and then when you've fixed yourself up with woollies, and if you haven't anything better to do, I'll give you lunch."

"Will you?" I had not expected this, and I was delighted. "Where?"

He scratched thoughtfully at the back of his neck. "There's not really much choice. Either the Crimond Arms, or my house, and my housekeeper doesn't come in on a Saturday."

I said, "I can cook. You buy something and I'll cook it. Anyway I'd like to see where you live."

"It's not very exciting."

But I found that I was mildly excited, all the same. I have always thought that you don't know a man until you have seen his home, his books, his pictures, the way he fixes his furniture. David, all that time in California, and while we were travelling home together, had been sweet and kind, but had shown me only the correct and businesslike side of his character. But now he had helped me find the photograph I wanted, and answered, with great patience, all my questions, and finally asked me out to lunch. I realised that there was a great deal more to him than I had first thought, and it was enormously gratifying to imagine that perhaps he felt the same way about me.

By the end of dinner I was overcome once more by fatigue, or jet lag or whatever you like to call it, and using my energetic day tomorrow as an excuse, I said good night to the others, and went to bed where I immediately fell sound asleep.

I awoke, some time later, to the sound of the wind that Gibson had promised us, nudging at the house, whistling under my door, whipping up the waters of the loch into small waves which broke and splashed against the shingle. And, above the sounds of the night, I heard voices.

I reached for my watch, saw that it was not yet midnight, and listened again. The voices became clearer and I realised then that they belonged to my grandmother and Sinclair, and that they were out on the lawn below my room, doubtless taking the dogs for a turn around the garden before locking the house up for the night.

". . . thought he'd aged a lot." That was Sinclair.

"Yes, but what can one do?"

"Pension him off. Get another man."

"But where would they go? It's not as though either of the boys were married, with a home to give them. Besides, he's been here for nearly fifty years . . . as long as I have. I couldn't get rid of him just because he's getting old. Anyway, he'd be dead in two months without a job of work to do."

I realised, uncomfortably, that they were talking about Gibson.

"But he's not able to do this particular job any longer."

"Now, what grounds have you got for saying that?"

"It's obvious. He's past it."

"As far as I'm concerned, he's still perfectly adequate. It's not as though he were expected to run a lot of highly-powered shoots. The syndicate is – "

Sinclair interrupted her. "That's another thing. It's utterly impractical letting off a superb moor like this to one or two local businessmen from Caple Bridge. What they pay you doesn't even begin to cover Gibson's keep."

"The one or two local businessmen, Sinclair, happen to be my friends."

"That's beside the point. As far as I can see, we seem to be running some sort of charitable institution."

There was a pause, and then, coldly, my grandmother corrected him. "I seem to be running some sort of charitable institution."

The iciness of her voice would have silenced me, but Sinclair seemed impervious to it, and I wondered how much of his courage was the Dutch variety, bolstered by post-prandial brandies.

"In that case," he said, "I suggest that you stop. Now. Pension Gibson off and sell the moor, or at least let it to a syndicate that is able to afford to pay a reasonable rent . . ."

"I have told you already . . ."

Their voices faded. They were walking away, still deeply in discussion; they went round the corner of the house, and I could hear them no longer. I found that I was lying rigid in my bed, miserable at having been forced to hear what was obviously not intended for my ears. The thought of them quarrelling made me sick, but worse was what they quarrelled about.

Gibson. I thought of him as he used to be, strong and tireless, and a mine of countryman's lore and wisdom. I remembered him, endlessly patient, teaching Sinclair to shoot and fish, answering questions, letting us tag along at his heels like a pair of puppies. And Mrs Gibson, who had spoiled and petted us, bought us sweets and fed us scones hot from her oven, dripping with the strong yellow butter that she churned herself.

It was impossible to reconcile the past with the present – the Gibson I remembered and the old man I had seen today. And harder still to realise that it was my cousin Sinclair who spoke so glibly of getting rid of Gibson, as if he were a smelly old dog, and the time had come at last to have him painlessly put down.

7

I awoke again, drawn from sleep by some subconscious alarm.
I knew it was daylight. I stirred and opened my eyes, and a man
was standing at the foot of my bed, watching me, cold-eyed. I
let out a gasp of fright, and sat up with my heart pounding, but
it was only Sinclair, come to wake me.

"It's eight o'clock," he said. "We have to leave at nine."

I sat rubbing the sleep out of my eyes, giving myself time
to let the panic run out of my veins. "You gave me the most
dreadful fright."

"Sorry, I didn't mean to . . . I was just going to wake
you up . . ."

I looked up again, and this time saw no menace, simply the
familiar figure of my cousin, arms crossed on the end of my
bed, tip-tilted eyes dancing with amusement. He wore a faded
kilt and a big ribbed pullover, with a scarf knotted at the neck.
He looked clean and brushed, and smelt deliciously of the
after-shave he had slapped on his face.

I scrambled into a kneeling position and hung out of the open
window to inspect the day. It was perfect, bright, clean, cold,
the sky cloudless. I said, in wonder, "Gibson was right."

"Of course he was right. He always is. Did you hear the wind in the night? And there's been a frost, soon all the trees will be turning."

The loch, blue with reflected sky, was flecked with small scuds of white foam, and the mountains opposite were no longer veiled in mist, but clear and sparkling, bruised with great sweeps of purple heather, and in the morning's crystal air, I could trace every rock and crack and corrie that led to their swelling summits.

It was impossible not to be elated by such a day. The uncertainties of the night had gone with the darkness. I had heard what was not intended for my ears. But in the clear light of morning, it seemed perfectly possible that I had been mistaken, had misunderstood. After all, I had not heard the beginning of the discussion, nor the end . . . and it was wrong to make any sort of a judgment when I was in possession of only half the facts.

Relief at having so easily shed my private worries made me suddenly enormously happy. I jumped off the bed, and went, in my nightdress, to find some clothes, and Sinclair, his mission successfully accomplished, went downstairs to start his breakfast.

We ate it in the kitchen, warm and snug by the Aga. Mrs Lumley had fried sausages and I ate four, and drank two enormous cups of coffee, and then I went and found an old rucksack, and we packed it with lunch: sandwiches and chocolate, apples and cheese.

"Do you want a Thermos?" Mrs Lumley wanted to know.

"No," said Sinclair, still filling himself with toast and

marmalade. "Put in a couple of plastic mugs, though, and then we can drink out of the river."

There was the hooting of a car horn from outside, and presently Gibson emerged through the back door. He wore his sagging greenish tweeds, the knickerbockers enormous around his skinny calves. On his head was the old tweed hat.

"Are you ready?" he asked, obviously not expecting that we would be.

But we were. We gathered up waterproof anoraks and the rucksack of rations, bade goodbye to Mrs Lumley, and went out into that glorious morning. The air was icy inside my nose, cut deep into my lungs, made me feel as though I could jump over the house.

"But aren't we lucky?" I crowed. "It's the most perfect day."

And Gibson said, "It's all right," which, being a Scotsman, was the most enthusiastic comment he could muster.

We piled into the Land-Rover. There was room for the three of us in the front, but Gibson's dog looked nervous and in need of company, so I chose to sit in the back with her. To begin with, she whined and was restless and worried, but after a little became used to the lurching of the car and settled down to sleep, with her soft, velvety head across my shoe.

Gibson took the road to Braemar by way of Tomintoul, driving south over the mountains and running down into the gold and sunlit valley of the Dee at about eleven o'clock. The river was in spate, deep and clear as brown glass, winding through fields and farmland and great stands of tall Scots pine. We came to Braemar, and drove through it, and out the other side, and on for another three miles or so until we came to the bridge that crosses the river and leads the way to Mar Lodge.

There we stopped and all got out, the dog was given a little
run, and Gibson went to fetch the key of the forestry gates. Then
we all went into the bar, and Sinclair and Gibson had beer, and
I was given a glass of cider.

"How much farther?" I wanted to know.

"Another four miles or so," Gibson told me. "But the road
is verra rough, maybe you'd be better in the front with us."

So I abandoned the dog, and went and sat in the front between
the two men, and the road was scarcely a road at all, simply
a bulldozed track, deeply rutted, and used by the Forestry
Commission. Every now and then we would pass a team of
foresters, working with huge chain saws and tractors. We waved,
and they waved back, and sometimes had to back their great
lorries off the track so that we could pass. The air was filled
with the piney smell of trees, and when at last we came to the
little lodge, which is used for climbers and weekend expeditions,
and got out of the Land-Rover, stiff and aching from the ride,
there was the most immense quiet. The forests, the moor and
the mountains were all about us, and only a distant trickle of
water, and the soughing of the pines far above us, broke the
silence.

"I'll meet you at Loch Morlich," said Gibson. "Do you
think you can make it by six o'clock?"

"If we don't, wait for us. And if we're not in by dark, get a
call through to the Mountain Rescue." Sinclair grinned. "We'll
stay on the path, so it should be perfectly easy to find us."

"Don't go turning your ankle over," Gibson warned me.
"And have a good day."

We said that we would. We watched him get back into the
car, and turn and drive off the way we had come. The sound

of his engine died away into the immensity of the morning. I looked up at the sky, and thought, not for the first time, that Scotland seems to have more than its fair ration of sky . . . it sweeps and soars and appears to reach to infinity. A pair of curlews flew over and in the distance I could hear the baa-ing of sheep. Sinclair smiled down at me. He said, "Shall we go?"

We walked, and Sinclair led the way, and I followed him up a path that ran alongside a burn set deep in rushes. We came to a solitary sheep farm, set about with wooden pens, and a dog came out to bark at us, and we passed the farm, and went on, and the dog retired to its kennel, and silence fell again. There were, every now and then, small patches of colour, harebells blowing, and huge purple thistles, and the dark stain of heather, humming with bees. The sun climbed up into the sky, and we peeled off our sweaters and tied them around our waists, and the path leaned upwards against the hill, and we climbed through trees and Sinclair, ahead of me, started to whistle under his breath. I remembered the tune: "Mairi's Wedding"; we had sung it as children, after tea in the drawing-room, with Grandmother playing the accompaniment on the piano.

Step we gaily, on we go,
Heel for heel and toe for toe,
Arm in arm and row on row
All for Mairi's wedding.

We came to a bridge and a waterfall, and the waterfall was not brown, but green, the colour of Chinese jade, plunging twenty feet or more into a cauldron of pale rock. We stood on the bridge and watched it, an arc of water bright as a jewel, translucent and shot with sunlight, curving down to the boiling pool, and ringed by a miniature rainbow. I had never seen anything so lovely. Over the roar of the water I said, "Why is it that colour? Why isn't it brown?" and Sinclair told me that it was because the water here dropped fresh from the limestone peaks, and so had not become stained with peat. And we stayed for a little, until he said that we had no time to waste, and must be on our way.

For encouragement, we sang again, each vying with the other at remembering words. We sang "The Road to the Isles", and "Westering Home", and "Come Along", which is the best marching song of all, and then our path began to climb, leading up and over the shoulder of a great mountain, and we stopped singing because we needed all our breath. The ground was thick with old heather roots and very boggy, and with every step dark mud oozed on either side of my shoes. My legs started to ache, and my back; I found that I was short of breath, and, although I would set myself the goal of this summit, and then the next, it seemed there was always another, waiting beyond. It was very disheartening.

And then, just as I was giving up hope of ever getting anywhere, there appeared, ahead of us, a black tooth of a mountain, jagged tip piercing the blue of the sky, and sheer face dropping a thousand feet or more to the foot of a narrow brown valley.

I stopped and pointed. "Sinclair, what's that?"

"The Devil's Peak." He had a map. We sat, and he opened it and flattened it against the wind and identified the surrounding peaks. Ben Vrottan and Cairn Toul, Ben Macdui, and the long ridge that led to Cairngorm.

"And this valley?"

"Glen Dee."

"And the little burn?"

"The little burn, as you call it, is the mighty Dee itself, in its early stages, of course." And indeed it was ludicrous to identify this modest stream with the majestic river we had seen earlier on in the morning.

We ate some chocolate and started off again, mercifully downhill, and now we had joined the long path that leads to the Lairig Ghru itself. It wound ahead of us, a scribble of white through the brown grass, climbing gently to a distant point on the horizon where the mountains and the sky seemed to meet. We walked, and the Devil's Peak towered ahead of us and over us, and then fell behind. We walked and were alone – really alone. There were no rabbits, no hares, no deer, no grouse. No eagles. Nothing broke the silence. No living creature stirred. There was only the sound of our own footsteps, and Sinclair's whistling.

Plenty herring, plenty meal,
Plenty peat to fill her creel
Plenty bonnie bairns as weel
That's the toast for Mairi.

Presently a house came into view, a stone bothy tucked into the foot of the hill on the opposite shore of the river.

"What's that?" I asked.

"It's a refuge hut, for climbers or walkers to use in bad weather."

"What sort of time are we making?"

"Good time."

After a little, "I'm hungry," I told him.

He grinned back at me over his shoulder.

"When we reach the hut," he promised, "we'll eat."

Later we lay supine, cushioned in blowing grass, Sinclair with his head pillowed on his sweater, me with my head pillowed on his stomach. I stared up at the empty blue sky and thought that to be with a cousin was a strange thing – at times we were as close as brother and sister, but at others there was an unease between us. I told myself that it was to do with no longer being children . . . with the fact that I found Sinclair enormously attractive, and yet this could not wholly explain an instinctive restraint, as though, somewhere in the back of my mind, a bell was warning danger.

A fly, a midge, some sort of a bug landed on my face, and I brushed it away. It landed again. I said, "Darn it."

"Darn what?" came, sleepily, from Sinclair.

"A fly."

"Where?"

"My nose."

His hand came down to brush away the fly. It rested against the curve of my jaw and stayed there, his fingers cupping my chin.

He said, "If we go to sleep we'll wake to find Gibson and the entire mountain rescue team come thundering through the pass to find us."

"We won't go to sleep."

"How can you be so sure?"

I did not reply, I could not speak about my inner tensions, the tightening of my stomach at the touch of his hand . . .

the fact was that I did not know if this tightening was caused by sex or – fear? It seemed an extraordinary word to use in connection with Sinclair, but now the conversation that I had heard last night came surfacing up out of my subconscious, and I worried at it again, like a dog with an old and unsavoury bone. I told myself that I should have made a point of seeing my grandmother before coming out this morning. One look at her face, and I would have known the true lie of the land. But she had not appeared before we left, and if she was sleeping then I did not want to disturb her.

I shifted uncomfortably, and Sinclair said, "What's the matter? You're as tense as a string of wire. You must have a secret worry, some sort of a guilt complex."

"What would I have to be guilty about?"

"You tell me. Leaving Poppa perhaps?"

"Father? You must be joking."

"You mean you were quite happy, shaking the dust of Reef Point, California, off your pretty heels?"

"Not at all. But Father, at the moment, is more than well provided for, and not in the least worthy of a guilt complex."

"Then it must be something else." The ball of his thumb moved lightly over my cheek. "I know, it's the love-lorn lawyer."

"The *what*?" Now, my amazement was genuine.

"The lawyer. You know, old pawky-Rankeillour himself."

"Quoting Robert Louis Stevenson will get you nowhere . . . and I still don't know what you're talking about." But of course I did.

"David Stewart, my love. Do you know, he couldn't keep his eyes off you last night? He watched you all through dinner,

97

with a lusty glint to his eye. I must say, you were a fairly toothsome spectacle. Where did you get that Eastern-looking outfit?"

"In San Francisco, and you're being ridiculous."

"Not ridiculous at all . . . honestly, it stuck out a mile. How do you fancy the idea of being an old man's darling?"

"Sinclair, he's not old."

"I suppose about thirty-five. But so dependable, my dear." His voice took on the honeyed tones of some desiccated dowager. "And such a nice boy."

"You're being bitchy."

"So I am." And, without any change of expression, he went on, "When are you going back to America?"

I was taken off-guard. "Why?"

"Just want to know."

"A month?"

"As soon as that? I'd hoped you'd stay. Abandon Father and put down your roots in your ain countree."

"I like my father too much to abandon him. And, anyway, what would I do?"

"Take a job?"

"You sound like Grandmother. And I couldn't take a job because I'm not qualified to do anything."

"You could be a secretary."

"No, I couldn't. Every time I try to type it always comes out red."

He said, "You could get married."

"I don't know anyone."

"You know me," said Sinclair.

His thumb, stroking my cheek, was suddenly still. After a

little I sat up, and turned to look down at him. His eyes were bluer than the sky, but their clean gaze gave nothing away.

"What did you say?"

"I said 'you know me'." His hand moved, and took hold of my wrist, ringing it easily with his fingers.

"You can't be serious."

"Can't I? All right, then let's pretend I am. What would you say?"

"Well, in the first place, it would be practically incest."

"Rubbish."

"And why me?" I warmed to my subject. "You know perfectly well that you've always thought me as plain as a pikestaff, you were forever telling me so . . ."

"Not now. You're not plain now. You've turned into a gorgeous Viking . . ."

". . . and I haven't a single talent. I can't even arrange flowers."

"Why on earth should I want you to arrange flowers?"

"And anyway, I can't believe you haven't got strings of eager females, scattered all over the country, just pining away for love of you and dreaming of the day when you'll ask them to be Mrs Sinclair Bailey."

"Maybe so," said Sinclair with maddening complacency. "But I don't want them."

I considered the idea, and despite myself, found it intriguing.

"Where would we live?"

"In London of course."

"I don't want to live in London."

"You're mad. It's the only place to live. Everything happens there."

"I like the country."

"We'll go to the country at weekends – that's what I do anyway – go and stay with friends . . ."

"And do what?"

"Potter around. Sail, maybe. Go racing."

I pricked up my ears. "Racing?"

"Haven't you ever been to a race meeting? It's the most exciting thing on earth." He sat up, leaning back on his elbows, so that his eyes were on a level with mine. "Am I persuading you?"

I said, "There is a small consideration that you haven't mentioned yet."

"And what is that?"

"Love."

"Love?" He smiled. "But Janey, surely we love each other. We always have done."

"But that's different."

"How different?"

"I can't explain if you don't already know."

"Try."

I sat in a troubled silence. I knew that in a way he was right. I had always loved him. As a child he had been the most important person in my life. But I was not entirely sure about the man he had become. Anxious that he should not read all this in my face, I looked down and began to tug at the tough grass, pulling out tufts by the roots, and then letting them loose, to be blown away by the wind.

I said at last, "I suppose because we've both changed. You have become a different person. And I am, virtually, an American . . ."

"Oh Janey . . ."

"No, it's true. I've been brought up there, educated there . . . the fact that I have a British passport can't alter any of that. Or the way I feel about things."

"You're talking in circles. You know that, don't you?"

"Perhaps I am. But don't forget that this whole conversation is hypothetical anyway . . . we're arguing around an assumption . . ."

He took a deep breath as if to continue the argument and then seemed to change his mind and let it all out again on a laugh. "We could sit here all day, couldn't we, and 'tire the sun with talking'."

"Shouldn't we go?"

"Yes, we've another ten miles, at least, to cover. But we've come a long way, and for your information, that remark is meant to be ambiguous."

I smiled. He put his hand around my neck and pulled my face towards his and kissed my open, smiling mouth.

I had been half-expecting this, but still not prepared for my own panicky reaction. I had to make myself be still in his arms, wait for him to finish, and when at last he drew away, I stayed for a moment where I was, and then slowly began to gather in our rucksack the paper that had wrapped the sandwiches, the red plastic drinking mugs. All at once our solitude was frightening, and I saw the two of us, tiny as ants, the only living creatures in this vast and deserted landscape, and wondered if Sinclair had brought me today with the intention of starting his extraordinary discussion, or whether the idea of marrying was just a whim, blown up out of nothing by the wind.

I said, "Sinclair, we must go. We really must go."

His eyes were thoughtful. But he only smiled and said, "Yes," and stood up, took the rucksack from me, and turned to lead the way, on up the path towards the distant pass.

We were home by dark. The last few miles I had walked blindly, simply putting one foot in front of the other, not daring to stop, for if I had, I should never have got going again. When at last we came round the final curve of the track, and, through the trees, saw the bridge and the gate, and Gibson and the Land-Rover, waiting on the road beyond, I could scarcely believe we had actually made it. Aching in every muscle, I came up the last few yards, climbed the gate, and fell into the car, but when I tried to light a cigarette, I found that my hands were shaking.

We drove home through the blue dusk. To the east a tiny new moon, pale and fine as an eyelash, hung low in the sky. Our headlights probed the road ahead, a rabbit skittered for cover, the eyes of a roaming dog glittered like twin beads, and were gone. Across me the two men talked, but I slumped, silent in an exhaustion which was not entirely physical.

That night I was awakened by the ringing of the telephone. Its shrilling cut across my dreams and pulled me out of sleep like a hooked fish. I had no idea of the time, but, turning my head, saw that the moon hung over the loch, its reflection touching the black water with small brushstrokes of silver.

The ringing continued. Dazed, I stumbled out of bed, across my room, and out on to the dark landing. The telephone was downstairs, in the library, but there was an extension upstairs as well, along a passage that led to the old nurseries, and it was for this that I made.

Some time during my half-conscious progress the ringing must have stopped, but I was too sleepy to register this, so that when I reached the telephone and picked up the receiver, a voice was already speaking. A female voice, unknown to me, but pleasantly pitched, and attractive. ". . . of course I'm certain. I saw the doctor this afternoon and he says there's no doubt at all. Look, I think we should talk about this . . . I'd like to see you anyway, but I can't get away . . ."

Listening dopily, I supposed that the telephone lines had become crossed. The girl on the Caple Bridge exchange had made a mistake, or gone to sleep, or something. This call was not for us. I was about to speak, when a man's voice interrupted, and all at once I was wide awake, and clearly conscious.

"Is it really so urgent, Tessa? Can't it wait?"

Sinclair. On the other line.

"Of course it's urgent . . . we haven't any time to waste . . ." and then, less calmly, as though hysteria was not very far below the surface, "Sinclair, I'm having a baby . . ."

I put down the receiver gently, quietly. The instrument made a tiny click and the voices were extinguished. I stood in the darkness, shivering, and then turned and made my way back to the landing and hung over the banister to listen. The stairs and the hall yawned below me, black as a well, but, from beyond the closed library door, came the unmistakable murmur of Sinclair's voice.

My feet were icy. Crawling with cold I made my way back to my room, and gently closed the door and got back into bed. Presently I heard the single ring of the telephone and knew that the call was finished, and soon after that, Sinclair came quietly upstairs. He went into his room, and there were soft sounds as he moved about, opened and shut drawers, then he came out again, and went down once more. The front door opened and closed, and moments after I heard the tiger hum of the Lotus as it drove off, down the lane, and on to the main road and away.

I found that I was trembling, as I had not done since I was a child, waking from a nightmare, and convinced there were ghosts hiding in my wardrobe.

8

Next morning, when I went downstairs, I found my grandmother already at the breakfast table. As I bent to kiss her, she said, "Sinclair's gone to London."

"How do you know?"

"He left a letter in the hall . . ." She sorted it out from the rest of her opened mail, and handed it to me. He had used the thick writing paper with *Elvie* engraved at its head, and his writing was strong and black and full of his personality.

Terribly sorry, have to go south for a day or two. Should be home Monday night or Tuesday morning. Take care of yourselves while I'm away, and don't get into any sort of trouble.

Much love
Sinclair.

That was all. I laid down the letter, and my grandmother said, "The telephone rang last night at about half past midnight. Did you hear it?"

I went to pour coffee, thankful for a reason not to meet her eyes.

"Yes, I did."

"I was going to answer it, but I was fairly sure it would be for Sinclair, so I let it ring."

"Yes . . ." I brought the full cup back to the table. "Does . . . does he often do this?"

"Oh, every now and then." She sorted out some bills. It occurred to me that she seemed as anxious as I to keep herself occupied. "He leads such a full life, and then this job he has seems to make tremendous demands on his time . . . not like being in an office from nine till five."

"No, I suppose not." The coffee was hot and strong, and helped to loose the knot of tension at the back of my neck. Encouraged by this, I said, "Perhaps it's a girlfriend."

My grandmother shot me a sharp, blue glance. But she only said, "Yes, perhaps."

I leaned my elbows on the table, and tried to sound casual. "I should think he has about a hundred. He's still the best-looking thing on two legs I've ever seen. Does he ever bring them home? Have you ever met any of them . . . ?"

"Oh, sometimes when I've been in London . . . you know, he brings them for dinner, or we go to the theatre or something."

"Did you ever think he'd marry one of them?"

"You can never be sure, can you?" Her voice was cool, almost disinterested. "His life in London is so different from the one he leads when he comes up here. Elvie's sort of a rest-cure as far as Sinclair's concerned . . . he simply potters. I think he's quite glad to get away from late nights and expense-account lunches."

"So there wasn't ever anyone in particular? One you specially liked?"

My grandmother laid down her letters. "Yes, there was."
She took off her spectacles, and sat, looking out of the window,
across the garden to where the loch sparkled blue in the sunshine
of another perfect autumn day. "He met her in Switzerland,
skiing. I think they saw a lot of each other when she got back
to London."

I said, "Skiing? Did you send me a photograph?"

"Did I? Oh, yes, it was New Year at Zermatt. That was where
they met. I think she was taking part in some championship or
other, you know these international races they have . . ."

"She must be very good."

"Oh, she is. She's quite famous . . ."

"Did you ever meet her?"

"Yes, Sinclair brought her for lunch at the Connaught when
I was in town during the summer. She was a charming girl."

I took a piece of toast and started to butter it. "What's she
called?"

"Tessa Faraday . . . You've probably heard of her."

I had heard of her, but not in the way my grandmother meant.
I looked at the toast I was buttering, and suddenly felt that if I
ate it, I should be sick.

After breakfast, I went back upstairs, took up my double folder
of family photographs, and drew out the one of Sinclair that
my grandmother had sent to me, and that I had arranged in
my montage, so that only Sinclair showed, and his companion
was hidden.

But now, I was interested only in her. I saw a small, slim
girl, dark-eyed, laughing, with hair caught back from her face
by a ribbon, and thick gold rings in her ears. She wore a velvet

trouser-suit, banded with some sort of embroidery, and she stood in the curve of Sinclair's arm, the two of them wound and tangled by yards of festive paper streamers. She looked gay and vital, very happy, and, remembering the careful voice on the telephone last night, I was suddenly frightened for her.

The fact that Sinclair had gone so promptly south – presumably to see her – should have reassured me, but somehow it did not. His departure had been too swift and businesslike, unencumbered by any personal consideration of either my grandmother or myself. Reluctantly I was reminded of his attitude towards Gibson, when he and my grandmother had discussed the old keeper's possible retirement, and I realised that, subconsciously, I had been making excuses for Sinclair.

But now it was different, and I was forced to be honest with myself. The word "ruthless" sprang to mind. Where ordinary people were concerned he could be entirely ruthless, and, torn as I was by anxiety for this unknown girl, I could only hope that he could also be compassionate.

From the hall my grandmother called me. "Jane!"

I hastily pushed the picture back in the frame, set it down on the dressing-table, and went back out on to the landing.

"Yes."

"What are you doing today?"

I went down to the half-landing and sat on the stairs, and talked to her from there. "I'm going shopping. I have to buy some sweaters, otherwise I'll die of cold."

"Where did you plan to go?"

"Caple Bridge."

"Darling, you can't buy anything in Caple Bridge."

"I'm sure I can buy a sweater . . ."

"I have to go to Inverness for a hospital board meeting . . . why don't I take you with me in the car?"

"Because David Stewart has some money for me. He changed the dollars Father gave me. And he said he'd give me lunch."

"Oh, how kind . . . but how will you get to Caple Bridge?"

"I'll jump on a bus. Mrs Lumley says there's one every hour at the end of the road."

"Well, if you're sure," but she still sounded doubtful. Standing there, with one hand on the newel post, she took off her glasses, and looked me over carefully from beneath her finely arched brows. "You look tired, Jane. Yesterday was really too much for you after all that travelling."

"No, it wasn't. I loved it."

"I should have made Sinclair wait a day or two . . ."

"But then we might have missed the lovely weather."

"Yes. Perhaps. But I noticed you didn't eat anything for breakfast."

"I never do. Honestly."

"Well, you must make sure David gives you a proper lunch . . ." She turned away and then thought of something else, and turned back. "Oh, and Jane . . . if you are shopping, why not let me stand you a new raincoat? You should have something really warm to wear."

Despite everything, I grinned. I loved it when she ran so true to form. I said wickedly, "But what's wrong with the one I've got?"

"If you must know, it makes you look like a tinker."

"In all the ten years I've been wearing it, I've never had that said to me before."

She sighed. "You get more like your father every day," she

said, and without smiling at my feeble joke, went off to her desk and wrote me a cheque which would have bought me a fur-lined, floor-length, sable-hooded raincoat, if that was what I happened to be wanting.

I waited, in brilliant sunshine, at the end of the road for the bus that would take me to Caple Bridge. I could not remember a day so bright or fresh or full of colour. It had rained a little during the night, so that everything shone newly-washed, and the damp roads reflected back the blue of the sky. The hedges were full of scarlet hips, bracken was gold, and turning leaves every colour from deep crimson to butter yellow. The air, sweeping down from the north, was cold and sweet as iced wine, with a bite to it suggesting that already, much farther north, the first snow of the winter had already fallen.

The bus came around the corner, stopped for me and I got in. It was packed with country people, heading for Caple Bridge for their weekly shopping session, and the only seat I could find was next to a fat woman with a basket on her knee. She wore a blue felt hat, and was so enormous there was only room for half of me on the seat, and every time the bus turned a corner, I was in deadly danger of being thrown off altogether.

It was five miles to Caple Bridge, and I knew the road as well as I knew Elvie itself. I had walked it, ridden on my bicycle, watched the landmarks fly by from the window of my grandmother's car. I knew the names of the people who lived in the wayside cottages . . . Mrs Dargie and Mrs Thomson, and Mrs Willie McCrae. And here was the house with the bad-tempered dog, and there the field where the flock of white goats grazed.

We came to the river, ran alongside it for half a mile or so and then the road swept into a deep S-bend in order to cross the river by means of a narrow humpbacked bridge. Up to now, nothing had apparently changed in all the years I had been away, but as the bus ground cautiously over the crest of the bridge I saw, ahead of us, a roadworks and traffic lights, and realised that considerable excavations were taking place in order to eliminate a dangerous curve.

There were signs and warnings everywhere. Hedges had been bulldozed away, leaving great scars of raw earth in their wake; men were working with picks and shovels, enormous earth removers growled away like prehistoric monsters, and over it all hung the clear and delicious smell of hot tar.

The lights were against us. We waited, engines running, and then the light went from red to green, and the bus rolled on, down the narrow track between the warning signals, and back on to the road. The woman next to me began to shift about, checking the contents of her basket, looking up at the luggage rack.

I said, "Do you want something?"

"Did I put my umbrella up there?"

I stood up and delved for the umbrella, and gave it to her, also a large cardboard box of eggs, and a bundle of shaggy asters, inexpertly wrapped in newspaper. By the time all this had been collected and delivered, we had reached our destination. The bus made a huge turn around the town hall, rolled into the market square and came to a final halt.

Because I had no baskets or encumbrances, I was one of the first out. My grandmother had told me the whereabouts of the lawyers' office, and from where I stood, I could see the square stone building she had described, directly opposite me, across the cobbled marketplace.

Waiting for the passing traffic, I crossed over and went in through the door, and read the indicator board in the hall and saw that Mr D. Stewart could be found in room No. 3 and that he was IN. I went up a dark staircase, nicely decorated in sludge green and mud brown, passed beneath a stained-glass window that let in no light at all, and finally knocked on a door.

He said, "Come in."

I went in and was delighted to find that his office, at least, was light, bright, and had a carpet. The window looked out over the busy market square, there was a jug of Michaelmas daisies on the marble mantelpiece, and somehow he had managed to create an ambience of cheerful business. He wore, I suppose because it was a Saturday, a sporty-looking checked shirt, and a tweed jacket, and when he looked up and smiled a welcome for me the doom-like weight that had lain in the pit of my stomach all morning was suddenly not so doom-like after all.

He stood up, and I said, "It's a gorgeous morning."

"Isn't it? Too good to be working."

"Do you always work on a Saturday?"

"Sometimes . . . depends how much there is to be done. You can get a surprising amount achieved when other people aren't ringing you up on the telephone all the time." He opened a drawer in his desk. "I changed the money for you at the current exchange rate . . . I made a note . . ."

"Don't bother about that."

"You should bother, Jane; your Scottish blood should make certain that I haven't diddled you out of a single bawbee."

"Well, if you have you can count it as personal commission." I held out my hand and he gave me a bundle of notes and some loose change. "Now you'll really be able to join the big spenders, though what you're going to find to spend it on in Caple Bridge is beyond me."

I stuffed the money in the pocket of my tinker's raincoat.

"That's what my grandmother said. She wanted to take me to Inverness, but I said I was having lunch with you."

"Do you like steaks?"

"I haven't had a steak since Father stood me dinner on my birthday. At Reef Point we lived on cold pizzas."

"How long will you be?"

"Half an hour . . ."

He looked astonished. "Is that all?"

"I loathe shopping at the best of times. Nothing ever fits, and when it does I always hate it . . . I shall come back wearing a lot of unsuitable clothes and probably in the worst of tempers."

"I shall say they're charming, and coax you back into a good mood, then." He glanced at his watch. "Half an hour . . . say, twelve? Here?"

"That's fine."

I went out again with a pocket full of money and searched for somewhere to spend it. There were butchers' shops, and grocers, and game merchants, and a gunsmith's and a garage. Eventually, between the inevitable Italian ice-cream parlour that exists in most small Scottish towns, and the post office, I ran Isabel McKenzie Modes to earth. Or more accurately, Isabel MODES McKenzie. I went in, through a glassed door, modestly draped in net, and found myself in a small room lined with shelves of unhopeful-looking clothes. There was a glass counter filled with underclothes in peach and beige, and here and there were tastefully draped, sad, string-coloured pullovers.

My heart sank, but before I could escape, a curtain opened

at the back of the shop and I was joined by a small, mouse-like woman, wearing a jersey suit two sizes too big for her, and a huge Cairngorm brooch.

"Good morning." I guessed that she had started life in Edinburgh and I wondered if she were Isabel Modes McKenzie in person, and if so, what had brought her to Caple Bridge. Perhaps she had been told that the garment trade was brisker here.

"Oh . . . good morning. I – I wanted a sweater."

As soon as I said the word I knew I had made my first mistake.

"We have some very nice *jairseys*. Did you want it in wool or bouclé?"

I said I wanted it in wool.

"And what size would it be?"

I said I supposed a sort of medium size.

She began to pull out shelves, and soon I was picking my way through sweaters in old rose, moss green and dead-leaf brown.

"H – haven't you any other colours?"

"What other colour did you have in mind?"

"Well, navy-blue?"

"Oh, there's very little navy being worn this year." I wondered where she got her information. Perhaps she had a hot line to Paris.

"Now, this is a charming shade . . ."

It was petrol blue, a colour that I am convinced goes with nothing and nobody.

"I really wanted something plainer . . . you know, warm and thick . . . perhaps a polo neck . . . ?"

"Oh no, we haven't any polo necks . . . polo necks aren't being . . ."

I broke in rudely, but I was getting desperate.

"It doesn't matter then, I'll leave the sweater . . . the jersey . . . Perhaps you've got some skirts?"

It started all over again. "Did you want it in tartan, or a tweed . . . ?"

"A tweed, I suppose . . ."

"And what is your waist measurement?"

Beginning to sound terse, I told her. There was more searching, this time through an unhopeful-looking rack. She brought out two, and laid them, with a grand gesture, before me. One was unspeakable. The other not quite so hideous, in a brown-and-white herringbone. Feebly I agreed to try it on, was squeezed into a space as small as a cupboard, closed in by yet another curtain and left to get on with it. With some difficulty I struggled out of the clothes I was wearing, and pulled on the skirt. The tweed prickled, and caught at my stockings as though it had been woven from thistles. I did up the waist hooks and the zip and looked at myself in the long mirror. The effect was startling. The tweed zig-zagged around me like an op-art picture, my hips had become elephantine, and the waistband dug into my meagre flesh like a wire-cutter.

Isabel Modes McKenzie coughed discreetly and whisked back the curtain, like a conjuror.

"Oh, you're lovely in that," she said. "You suit tweed."

"Don't you think it's . . . well, a little bit long?"

"Skirts are longer this season you know . . ."

"Yes, but this one nearly covers my knees . . ."

"Well, if you wanted, I could take it up a fraction . . . it's very good looking . . . there's nothing so good looking as a nice tweed . . ."

To get away, I might have bought it . . . but I took another look in the mirror, and was strong-minded.

"No. No, I'm afraid it really won't do . . . it's not what I wanted." I undid the zipper and tore it off before she could talk me into buying the dreadful thing, and she took it back, sadly, averting her eyes discreetly from my petticoat.

"Perhaps you'd like to try the tartan, the ancient colours are so soft . . ."

"No . . ." I pulled on my old, American drip-dry, un-warm skirt and it felt like a friend. "No, I think I'll leave it . . . it was just an idea . . . thank you so much."

I pulled on my raincoat, picked up my bag, and together, in sidling fashion, we made for the net-curtained door. She reached it first and opened it for me, reluctantly, as though letting a prized animal out of a trap.

"Perhaps if you were passing another day . . ."

"Yes . . . maybe . . ."

"I shall be getting my new stock next week."

Straight from Dior, no doubt. "Thank you . . . I am sorry . . . good morning."

Out and away, and into the blessed open air, I turned and walked off as fast as I could. I passed the gunsmith's, and then, on an inspiration, turned round and walked back and went in, and bought, in two minutes flat, a large navy-blue sweater originally intended for a young man. Relieved beyond words that my morning had not been a total failure, and clasping the sturdily wrapped parcel, I returned to David.

While he stacked papers and locked up filing cabinets, I sat on his desk and told him the saga of my disastrous shopping expedition. Spiced by his comments (he could do an Edinburgh

accent to perfection) the story grew in its telling, and in the end
I laughed so much that my ribs ached. We collected ourselves
at last; David stuffed a pile of files into a bulging briefcase,
gave a last look round, and then closed the door on his office
and we went down the dingy stairs and out into the sunlit,
crowded street.

He lived only a hundred yards or so from the centre of the
little town, and we walked this short distance together. David's
old briefcase slapped and banged against his long legs and every
now and then we had to separate in order to avoid a parked
perambulator or a pair of gossiping women. His house, when
we came to it, was one of a row – identical, small, two-storey
stone houses, each set in its own plot of ground, fronted by a
modest garden, and with a gravel path leading from gate to front
door. David's differed from his neighbours only in that he had
added a garage, built into the space between his house and the
next, with a concrete driveway connecting it to the street. And
he had painted his front door a bright, sunny yellow.

He opened the gate and I followed him down the path and
waited while he unlocked the door. He stood aside and waited
for me to go in ahead of him. There was a narrow hallway
with a staircase rising out of it, doors to right and left, and a
kitchen visible through the open door at the back. It should have
been very ordinary, and yet he – or somebody – had made it
charming with close carpeting and leafy wallpaper, and groups
of precisely arranged sporting prints.

He took my parcel and my raincoat from me, and dumped
them, and his briefcase, on the chair in the hall, and then led
me into a long sitting-room, with windows at either end. And
it was only then that I appreciated the unique position of the

117

unpretentious little house, for the windows to the south had been enlarged into a deep bay, and this looked out over a long narrow garden, sloping gently down towards the river.

The room itself was full of promise. Shelves of books, a stack of records, magazines on the low table in front of the fireplace. There were cushiony-looking armchairs and a little sofa, an old-fashioned cabinet filled with Meissen china, and over the mantelpiece . . . I went to look . . .

"A Ben Nicholson?" He nodded. "But not an original."

"Yes, it is. My mother gave it to me for my twenty-first."

"This reminds me of your mother's flat in London . . . it's got the same sort of feeling . . ."

"Probably because it was furnished more or less from the same house. And of course she helped me choose the curtains and the wallpaper and stuff."

Secretly glad that it was his mother, and no one else, I went over to the window. "Who would have thought you'd have a garden like this?" There was a little terrace, with a wooden table and chairs, and then a lawn, scattered now with fallen leaves, and flower-beds still filled with late roses, and clumps of purple Michaelmas daisies. There was a birdbath and an old, leaning apple tree. "Do you do the gardening yourself?"

"You could hardly call it gardening . . . as you can see, it's not very big."

"But having the river and everything . . ."

"That's what decided me when I bought the house. I tell all my friends that I have fishing on the Caple, and they're all enormously impressed. I don't tell them that it's only ten yards . . ."

There was a clutter of photographs and snapshots arranged on the top of the bookcase, and I was irresistibly drawn to them. "Is this your mother? And your father? And you?" About twelve years old with an engaging grin. "Is this you?"

"Yes, it is."

"You didn't wear glasses then."

"I didn't wear glasses till I was sixteen."

"What happened?"

"I had an accident. It was a paper chase, at school, and the boy in front of me let a branch of a tree snap back into my eye. It wasn't his fault, it could have happened to anyone. But I partly lost the sight of the eye, and I've worn glasses ever since."

"Oh, what bad luck!"

"Not really. I can do most things I want . . . except play tennis."

"Why can't you play tennis?"

"I don't quite know. But if I can see the ball I can't hit it, and if I can hit it, I can't see it. It doesn't make for much of a game."

We went through to the kitchen, which was as small as a galley in a yacht and so tidy that I felt ashamed at the memory of my own inadequacies. He peered into the oven where he had left some potatoes baking, and then found a frying-pan, and butter, and took a bloodstained parcel from the fridge and unfolded it to reveal a couple of inch-thick Aberdeen Angus steaks.

"Will you cook them, or shall I?" he asked.

"You cook them . . . I'll lay the table or something." I opened the door that led on to the terrace, baking in the unseasonable heat. "Can't we have lunch here? It's like being in the Mediterranean."

"If you want."

"It's blissful . . . shall we use this table?"

Talking, getting in his way, having to ask where everything was, I eventually got the table laid. While I did this, he had tossed a salad, unwrapped a crisp French loaf and taken small dishes of frosty cold butter from the refrigerator. With all this completed and the steaks gently sizzling in the pan, he poured two glasses of sherry and we went out to sit in the sunshine.

He shucked off his jacket, and leaned back, long legs stretched before him, and turned up his face to the heat.

"Tell me about yesterday," he said suddenly.

"Yesterday?"

"You walked the Lairig Ghru – " he cocked an eye at me " – or didn't you?"

"Oh. Yes, we did."

"What was it like?"

I tried to think what it had been like, and found I could remember nothing save the extraordinary discussion I had had with Sinclair after lunch.

"It was . . . all right. Marvellous, really."

"You don't sound very enthusiastic."

"Well, it was . . . marvellous." I couldn't think of any other word.

"But exhausting, perhaps."

"Yes. I was tired."

"How long did it take?"

Again, I could hardly remember. "Well, we were back by dark. Gibson met us at Loch Morlich . . ."

"Umm." He seemed to consider this. "And what's cousin Sinclair doing today?"

I stooped and picked up a piece of gravel and began to toss it, catching it on the back of my hand as though I were playing jacks. "He's gone to London."

"To London? I thought he was on leave."

"Yes, he is." I dropped the stone, bent to pick up another. "But he had a phone call last night . . . I don't know what about . . . we found a note when we came down for breakfast this morning."

"Did he drive?"

I remembered the tiger roar of the Lotus, splitting the still darkness. "Yes, he took the car." I dropped the second stone. "He'll be back in a day or so. Monday evening, perhaps, he said." I did not want to talk about Sinclair. I was afraid of David asking questions, and, clumsily, tried to change the subject. "Do you really fish from the bottom of your garden? I shouldn't think there'd be room to cast . . . and you'd get all tied up in your apple tree . . ."

And so the conversation veered to fishing, and we talked about this, and I told him about the Clearwater river in Idaho where my father once took me for a holiday.

". . . it runs with salmon . . . you can practically lift them out with a bent pin . . ."

"You like America, don't you?"

"Yes. Yes, I do." He was silent, supine in the sunshine, and encouraged by his silence, I warmed to the subject, and the dilemma in which, inevitably, I found myself. "It's funny belonging to two countries, you never seem to quite fit into either. When I was in California I used to wish I were at Elvie. But now I'm at Elvie . . ."

"You wish you were back in California."

"Not exactly. But there are things I miss."

"Such as?"

"Well, specific things. My father, of course. And Rusty. And the sound of the Pacific, late at night, when the rollers come pouring up on to the beach."

"And what about the unspecific things?"

"That's more complicated." I tried to decide what I really missed. "Ice water. And the Bell Telephone Company. And San Francisco. And central heating. And the garden centres where you can go and buy plants and stuff and everything smells of orange blossom." I turned towards David, and found that he was watching me. Our eyes met, and he smiled. I said, "But there are good things over here too."

"Tell me about them."

"Post offices. You can buy anything in a country post office – even stamps. And the way the weather is never the same, two days running. It's so much more exciting. And afternoon tea, with scones and biscuits and soggy gingerbread . . ."

"Are you reminding me in your subtle way that it's time to eat those steaks?"

"Not consciously I wasn't."

"Well, if we don't eat them now, they're not going to be eatable. Come along."

It was a perfect meal, eaten under perfect circumstances. He even opened a bottle of wine, rough and red, the exact complement to steaks and French bread, and we finished with cheese and biscuits and a bowl of fresh fruit, topped with a cluster of white grapes. I found that I was ravenous and ate enormously, wiping my plate clean with a thick white crust, and going on to peel an orange so juicy that it dripped from the ends of my fingers. When he had completely finished, David went inside to make coffee.

"Shall we have it outside?" he asked through the open door.

"Yes, let's, down by the river." I went in to join him, to run my sticky hands under a tap.

He said, "You'll find a rug in the chest in the hall. You take it down and settle yourself and I'll bring the coffee."

"What about the dishes?"

"Leave them . . . it's too good a day to waste slaving over a hot sink."

It was comfortably like the sort of remark my father would make. I went and found the rug, and took it back outside, and went down to the sloping lawn and spread the rug on the sunlit grass, only a few yards from the edge of the river. After the long dry summer, the Caple was running low, and there was a bank of pebbles, like a miniature beach, between the grass and the deep brown water.

The apple tree was loaded with fruit, windfalls lay at its feet. I went to shake it, and a few more tumbled to the grass, making soft plopping noises. Beneath the tree it was shady and cool and smelled pleasantly musty, like old lofts. I leaned against its trunk, and watched the sunlit river through a lace-work of branches. It was very peaceful.

Soothed by this, comforted by good food and easy company, I felt my spirits rise, and told myself briskly that this was a suitable moment to start being sensible about all my half-acknowledged fears. What was the point of letting them churn around at the back of my mind, nagging like a bad tooth, and giving me a perpetual stomach ache?

I would be realistic about Sinclair. There was no reason to

suppose that he wouldn't accept responsibility for the baby that Tessa Faraday was going to have. When he returned to Elvie on Monday, he would probably tell us that he was going to be married, and Grandmother would be delighted (hadn't she thought the girl was charming?) and I would be delighted too, and need never say a word about the telephone call I had overheard.

And as for Gibson, he *was* getting old, there was no denying it, and perhaps it would be better for all concerned if he were to be retired. But if he did have to go, then Grandmother and Sinclair between them could surely find him a little cottage, perhaps with a garden, where he could grow vegetables, and have a few hens, and so keep himself happy and occupied.

And as for myself . . . This was not so easy to shrug off. I wished I knew why, yesterday, he had brought up the question of our getting married. Perhaps it had been simply an amusing idea to pass the half-hour after our picnic lunch. As such, I would have been prepared to accept it, but his kiss had been neither cousinly, nor light-hearted . . . just to remember it made me uncomfortable, and it was because of this that I felt so utterly confused. Perhaps he had done it deliberately, to upset me. He had always been a wicked tease. Perhaps he simply wanted to gauge my reactions . . .

"Jane."

"Um?" I turned and saw David Stewart watching me from the sunlight beyond the broken shadow of the tree. Behind him, I saw the coffee tray, set down by the rug, and I realised that he had spoken my name before, but that I had not heard. He dipped his head under the low branches and came to stand in front of me, putting up a hand to prop himself against the tree.

124

He said, "Is anything wrong?"

"Why do you ask that?"

"You look a little worried. You also look very pale."

"I'm always pale."

"And always worried?"

"I didn't say I was worried."

"Did . . . anything happen yesterday?"

"What do you mean?"

"Just that I noticed you weren't very anxious to talk about it."

"Nothing happened . . ." I wished I could walk off and leave him, but his arm was over my shoulder, and I couldn't get away without deliberately ducking beneath it. He turned his head to watch me from the corner of his eye, and beneath this familiar, disconcerting regard, I felt my face and neck grow warm.

"You once told me," he said pleasantly, "that when you lie, you blush. Something is wrong . . ."

"No, it isn't. And anyway, it's nothing . . ."

"If you wanted to tell me, you would, wouldn't you? Perhaps I could help."

I thought of the girl in London, and Gibson . . . and myself, and all my fears came flooding up again. "Nobody can help," I told him. "Nobody can do anything."

He left it at that. We went back into the sunlight, and I found that I was cold, my skin crawled with goose-flesh. I sat on the warm rug and drank coffee, and David gave me a cigarette to keep the midges away. After a little, I lay down, my head on a cushion, my body spread to the sun. I was tired and the wine had made me drowsy. I closed my eyes, and the river noises took over, and presently I was asleep.

I awoke about an hour later. David lay a yard or so from me, propped on one elbow and reading the paper. I stretched and yawned, and he looked up, and I said, "This is the second time this has happened."

"What has happened?"

"I've woken, and found you there."

"I was going to wake you in a moment anyway. Wake you up and take you home."

"What time is it?"

"Half past three."

I eyed him drowsily. "Will you come back for tea at Elvie? Grandmother would love to see you."

"I would, but I have to go and see an old boy who lives out in the back of beyond. Every now and then he starts fretting about his will, and I have to go and reassure him."

"It's rather like Scottish weather, isn't it?"

"What do you mean by that?"

"One week you're in New York, doing goodness-knows-what. The next you're trailing up some remote glen to set an old man's mind at rest. Do you like being a country lawyer?"

"Yes, as a matter of fact, I do."

"You fit in so well. I mean . . . as though you'd been here all your life. And your house and everything . . . and the garden. It all goes together as though someone had matched you up."

"You match too," said David.

I longed for him to enlarge on this, and for a moment thought he was going to, but he seemed to change his mind, and instead got up, collected the coffee things and his paper and carried them back up to the house. When he returned I was still lying there, watching the river, and he stood over me, put his hands under my shoulders and pulled me to my feet. I turned and found myself in the circle of his arms, and I said, "I've done this before, too."

"Only then," said David, "your face was all swollen and blotched with crying, and today . . ."

"What about today . . ."

He laughed then. "Today you've collected about six dozen more freckles. And a lot of old apple leaves and grass in your hair."

He drove me home. The hood of his car was down, and my hair blew all over my face, and David found an old silk scarf in the cupboard on the dashboard and gave it to me, and I tied it over my head.

When we came to the roadworks, the lights were red, so we waited, the engine of the car idling, and watched the approaching traffic filing towards us down the single-line track.

"I can't help feeling," said David, "that instead of straightening out this bit of road, it would have been better to demolish the bridge and build a new one . . . or even to do something about that hellish corner on the other side."

"But the bridge is so pretty . . ."

"It's dangerous, Jane."

"But everyone knows about it, and takes it about one mile an hour."

"Not everyone knows about it," he corrected me drily. "In summer every other driver is a visitor."

The lights turned green and we moved forward, past a huge sign saying RAMP. A funny thought occurred to me. "David, you've broken the law."

"Why?"

"The notice said Ramp. And you didn't."

127

There was a long silence, and I thought, Oh, God, which is what I think when I've said something funny and the other person doesn't think it is.

"I don't know how to," he said at last.

"You mean you've never been taught?"

"My mother was a poor widow. She couldn't afford lessons."

"But everyone ought to be able to ramp, it's one of the social graces."

"Well," said David, easing his car over the humpbacked bridge, "for your sake, I'll make a point of learning," and with that he put down his foot, and with the wind roaring about my ears, he drove me back to Elvie.

Later, I showed my grandmother my single purchase, the navy-blue sweater I had bought in the gunsmith's.

"I think," she said, "you were very clever to find anything at all in Caple Bridge. And it certainly looks very warm," she added kindly, eyeing the shapeless garment. "What will you wear it with?"

"Pants . . . anything. I really wanted a skirt, but I couldn't find anything."

"What sort of a skirt?"

"Something warm . . . perhaps next time you go to Inverness . . ."

"What about a kilt?" said my grandmother.

I had not thought of this. It seemed a splendid idea. Kilts are the cosiest things in the world, and the colours are always mouth-melting. "Where could I buy a kilt?"

"Oh, my dear, you don't need to buy one, the house is full of them. Sinclair's worn kilts since he could walk and not one has ever been thrown away."

I had forgotten the happy fact that a kilt, unlike a bicycle, is sexless. "But that's a marvellous idea! Why didn't we think of it before? I'll go and look right away. Where are they? In the attic?"

"Not at all. They're in Sinclair's room, in the cupboard on top of his wardrobe. I packed them all away in mothballs, but if you do want one, we can hang it out to air, and get rid of the smell, and it'll be as good as new."

Not wanting to waste a moment, I went in search of a kilt. Sinclair's room, for the moment vacant of its owner, had been cleaned and swept, and was immaculately tidy. I remembered this inherent neatness had always been strong in his character. As a boy he could not stand disorder, and never had to have his clothes folded, or his toys put away.

I took up a chair and went across to his cupboard. This had been built into the alcove at the side of the fireplace, and the space above the top of the wardrobe was put to use as extra cupboard space for suitcases and out-of-season clothes. I stood on the chair and opened the doors, and saw a neat stack of books, some motoring magazines, a squash racket, a pair of swimming flippers. There was a strong smell of camphor coming from a huge dress box, all laced up with string, and I reached up to lift this down. It was heavy and awkward, and as I struggled with it, my elbow caught the pile of books, and dislodged them. Encumbered as I was, there was nothing I could do to stop them falling, and I simply stood on the chair and listened to them crashing, in terrible disorder, to the floor.

I swore, took a firmer grip of my burden, lifted it down, laid it on the bed, and stooped to retrieve the books. They were mostly textbooks, a Thesaurus, *Le Petit Larousse*, a life of Michelangelo, and, at the bottom . . .

It was thick and heavy, bound in scarlet leather, the cover emblazoned with a private coat-of-arms, the title tooled in gold letters on the crimson spine, *A History of the Earth and Animated Nature*, Volumes I and II.

I knew that book. I was six years old again, and my father had brought it back to Elvie after one of his spasmodic forays into Mr McFee's second-hand book-shop in Caple Bridge. Mr McFee had died a long time ago, and the shop was now a tobacconist's, but in those days my father had spent many happy hours discoursing with Mr McFee, a cheerful eccentric with no tiresome prejudices about dirt or dust, and browsing through endless shelves of musty volumes.

He had found Goldsmith's *Animated Nature* by chance, and brought it home in triumph, for not only was it a rare volume, but it had been privately bound by some previous noble owner, and was, in itself, a thing of beauty. Delighted with it, wanting to share his pleasure, the first thing my father did was to bring it up to the nursery to show to Sinclair and myself. My reaction was probably disappointing. I stroked the pretty leather, looked at one or two pictures of Asian elephants, and then returned to my jigsaw puzzle.

But with Sinclair it was different. Sinclair loved everything about it, the old printing, the thick pages, the aquatints, the detail of the tiny drawings. He loved the smell, and the marbled endpapers, and the very weight of the big old book.

The addition of such a prize to my father's collection seemed to merit some sort of ceremony. Accordingly, he went off to fetch one of his own Ex Libris labels, a woodcut, with his initial wound about with much decorative plant life, and solemnly affixed it to the marbled endpaper of Goldsmith's *Animated*

Nature. Sinclair and I watched this operation in total silence, and when it was done I heaved a sigh of satisfaction, because it had been accomplished so neatly, and because it proved, beyond any shadow of doubt, that the book now belonged to my father.

It was then taken downstairs and left on a table in the drawing-room, along with some magazines and daily newspapers, where it could be admired, and handled, and perused in passing. It was not spoken of again until two or three days later when my father realised that it had disappeared.

No one was particularly concerned, Goldsmith's *Animated Nature* had simply been moved. Someone had borrowed it, perhaps, forgotten to put it back. But no one had. My father began to ask questions, and drew nothing but blanks. My grandmother searched diligently, but the book did not come to light.

Sinclair and I were then involved. Had we seen the book? But of course we hadn't, and said so, and our innocence was never questioned. My mother started to say, "Perhaps a burglar . . ." but my grandmother pooh-poohed this. What burglar would turn a blind eye to the Georgian silver and make off with only an old book? She insisted that Goldsmith's *Animated Nature* was simply mislaid. It would turn up. Like any nine-day wonder the mysterious affair died a natural death, but the book was never found.

Until now. In Sinclair's cupboard, neatly filed away with some other possessions for which he did not have a regular use. And it was as beautiful as ever, the red leather smooth and soft to touch, the lettering bright and gold. Standing with it, heavy as lead in my hands, I remembered Father's Ex Libris, and I lifted the front cover of the book, and saw that the marble endpaper and the Ex Libris had been removed altogether, delicately and finely, close to the spine, probably with a razor blade. And on the white fly-leaf which lay below was written in Sinclair's firm, black, twelve-year-old writing:

Sinclair Bailey,
Elvie.
THIS IS HIS BOOK.

9

The beautiful, fine weather went on. On the Monday afternoon, my grandmother, armed with a spade and a pair of gardening gloves, went out to plant bulbs. I offered to help her, but she declined. If I was there, we would only talk, she said, and nothing would get done. She would be quicker on her own. Thus rejected, I whistled up the dogs and set off for a walk. I don't much like gardening anyway.

I went for miles and was out for two hours or more. By the time I returned, the brightness of the day was beginning to fade, and it was turning cold. A few clouds had appeared over the tops of the mountains, blown from the north, and a drift of mist lay over the loch. From the walled garden, where Will was stoking a bonfire, plumed a long feather of blue smoke, and the air was filled with the smell of burning rubbish. With my hands deep in my pockets, and my head full of thoughts of tea by the fire, I crossed the causeway and came up the road beneath the copper beeches. One of the dogs began to bark, and I looked up, and saw, parked in front of the house, the dark yellow Lotus Elan.

Sinclair was back. I looked at my watch. Five o'clock. He was early. I went on, across the grass, ankle-deep in fallen leaves, on to the gravel. As I passed the car, I trailed my hand across one glossy bumper, as if to reassure myself that it was really there. I went into the warm, peat-smelling hall, waited for the dogs, and then shut the door behind me.

I heard the murmur of voices from the drawing-room. The dogs went to drink from their bowl and then collapsed in front of the hall fire. I unbuckled the belt of my raincoat, and pulled it off, toed off my muddied shoes, smoothed my hair down with my hands. I crossed the hall and opened the door. I said, "Hello Sinclair."

They had been sitting on either side of the fire, with a low tea-table between them. But now Sinclair got up and came across the room to greet me.

"Janey . . . where have you been?" He kissed me.

"For a walk."

"It's nearly dark, we thought you'd got lost."

I looked up at him. I had thought that he would be noticeably different. Quieter; tired, perhaps, from his long drive. More thoughtful, weighed down with new responsibilities. But it was obvious that I had thought wrong. If anything, he looked happier, younger and more light-hearted than ever. There was a glitter to him that evening – a shine of excitement, like a child on Christmas Eve.

He took my hands. "And you're as cold as ice. Come on over by the fire and get warm. I've kindly left you one piece of toast, but I'm sure if you want some more Mrs Lumley will make it."

"No, that's fine." I pulled up a low leather stool and sat between them, and my grandmother poured my tea. "Where did you go?" she asked, and I told her. "Have the dogs had a drink? Were they wet and muddy? Did you dry them?" I assured her that they had, they weren't, and I hadn't needed to. "We didn't go anywhere wet, and I picked up all the heather off their coats before we got home." She handed me the cup and I folded my cold hands round it, and looked at Sinclair.

"How was London?"

"Hot and stuffy." He grinned, his eyes glinting with amusement. "Full of exhausted businessmen in winter suits."

"Did you . . . achieve what you went to do?"

"That sounds very pompous. Achieve. Where did you learn a long word like that?"

"Well, did you?"

"Yes, of course I did, I wouldn't be here otherwise."

"When – when did you leave London?"

"Early this morning . . . about six o'clock . . . Grandmother, is there any more tea in that pot?"

She lifted the teapot, took off the lid to look. "Not really. I'll go and make some more."

"Get Mrs Lumley . . ."

"No, her feet are hurting, I'll make it. I want to talk to her about dinner anyway, we'll need to put another pheasant in the casserole."

When she had gone, "Delicious, pheasant casserole," said Sinclair, and he took my wrist in his fingers, ringing it, like a bracelet, with his fingers. His touch was cool and light. He said, "I want to talk to you."

This was it. "What about?"

"Not here, I want you all to myself. I thought after tea we'd go out in the car. Up to the top of Bengairn and watch the moon rise. Will you come?"

If he wanted to tell me privately about Tessa, I supposed that

135

the inside of the Lotus Elan was as good a place as any. I said, "All right."

Driving in the Lotus was, for me, a new experience. Lashed low into the seat by the band of my seat belt, I felt as if I was on my way to the moon, and the speed with which Sinclair took off did nothing to dispel this impression. We roared up the lane, paused for a moment at the main road, and then streamed out and on to it, the needle of the speedometer climbing to seventy in a matter of seconds, and fields and hedges and familiar landmarks flying up and falling away in dizzying succession.

I said, "Do you always drive so fast?"

"Darling, this isn't fast."

I left it at that. In no time it seemed, we were at the humpbacked bridge, slowed slightly, and then swept over it – leaving my stomach suspended somewhere two feet over my head – and poured down towards the roadworks. The lights were green, and Sinclair accelerated, so that we were through the obstruction and well beyond before they changed back to red.

We came to Caple Bridge and the thirty-mile limit. In deference to the local police constable, and much to my relief, he changed down, and idled the Lotus through the town at the regulation speed, but once the last house had dropped behind, we were off again. Now, there was no traffic. The road, smoothly cambered, curved ahead of us, and the car leapt forward, like a horse given its head.

We came to our turning, the small side road that led to the south, climbing in a succession of steep bends, up to and over the summit of Bengairn. Fields and the farmland dropped below us; with a roar of tyres we crossed the cattle grid, and were now on the moor, the blown grass patched with heather, and populated only by mildly interested flocks of black-faced sheep. The cold air, blown through the open window, smelled of peat, and there was mist ahead of us, but before we had driven into this, Sinclair turned the Lotus into a lay-by, and switched off the engine.

The view spread before us, the valley quiet beneath a sky of pale turquoise, more green than blue, and washed, in the east, with the pink of sunset. Far below, Elvie Loch lay still and bright as a jewel, and the Caple was a winding silver ribbon. It was very quiet; only the wind nudging at the car, and the cry of curlews.

Beside me, Sinclair undid his seat belt, and then, when I did not move to follow his example, leaned over to undo mine. I turned then, to look at him, and without saying anything, he took my face between his gloved hands and kissed me. After a little, I pushed him gently away. I said, "You wanted to talk to me, remember?"

He smiled, not in the least put out, and heaved himself around in order to reach a pocket. "I've got something for you . . ." He took out a small box and opened it, and it seemed that all the sky was reflected in the star-sparkle of diamonds.

I felt as though I was rolling, somersaulting, topsy-turvy down a long, steep bank. I came out of it reeling and stupid. When I could speak, I could only say, "But Sinclair, that's not for *me*."

"Of course it is. Here . . ." He took out the ring, tossed the little box casually on to the shelf on the dashboard, and before I could stop him had taken my left hand and thrust the ring deep on to my finger. I tried to pull away, but he held on to my hand, and closed it, clenched round the ring, so that the diamonds bit into my flesh and hurt.

"But it *can't* be for me . . ."

"Just for you. Only for you."

137

"Sinclair, we have to talk."

"That's why I brought you here."

"No, not about this. About Tessa Faraday."

If I had thought this would shock him, I was mistaken. "What do you know about Tessa Faraday?" He sounded indulgent, not in the least upset.

"I know that she's going to have a baby. Your baby."

"And how did you find that out?"

"Because the night she rang up, I heard the telephone and I went to answer it, on the upstairs extension. But you'd answered it already, and I heard her . . . telling you . . ."

"So it was you?" He sounded quite relieved as though some small dilemma had been solved. "I thought I heard the other line cut off. How very tactful of you not to listen to the end of the conversation."

"But what are you going to do about it?"

"Do? Nothing."

"But that girl is having your baby."

"Darling Janey, we don't know that it is my baby."

"But it *could* be yours."

"Oh, yes, it could be. But that doesn't mean that it is. And I am not taking the responsibility for another man's carelessness."

I thought of Tessa Faraday and the image I had built up of her. The gay and pretty girl, held, laughing, in the curve of Sinclair's arm. The successful, dedicated skier, with her own chosen world at her feet. The young woman, approved and admired, lunching at the Connaught with my grandmother. "Such a charming girl," my grandmother had said, and she was seldom mistaken about people. None of this had anything to do with the impression that Sinclair was trying to give me.

138

I said, carefully, "Did you tell her that?"

"In so many words, yes."

"What did she say?"

He shrugged slightly. "She said if that was how I felt, she would make other arrangements."

"And you left it at that?"

"Yes. We left it at that. Don't be too naive, Jane, she's been around, she's a sensible girl." All this time, he had not loosened his grip on my arm, but now he let it go, and I was able to unfold and stretch my cramped fingers, and he took hold of the ring between his forefinger and thumb, and turned it a little, to and fro, as though he were screwing it on. "Anyway," he said, "I told her that I was going to marry you."

"You told her *what*?"

"Oh, darling, do listen. I told her I was going to marry you ...."

"But you had no right to do that . . . you haven't even asked me."

"Of course I've asked you. What did you think we were discussing the other day? What did you think I was doing?"

"Play-acting."

"Well – I wasn't. And, what's more, you know I wasn't."

"You're not in love with me."

"But I love you." He made it sound entirely reasonable. "And being with you, and having you back at Elvie, is the best thing that's ever happened to me. There's such a freshness about you, Janey. One moment you're as naive as a child, and the next, you come out with something so astonishingly wise. And you make me laugh; and I find you deliciously attractive. And you know me almost better than I know myself. Isn't all that better than simply being in love?"

I said, "But if you marry someone, it's for ever."

"Well?"

"You must have been in love with Tessa Faraday, and now you don't want anything more to do with her . . ."

"Janey, that was entirely different."

"How different? I don't see how it's so different."

"Tessa's attractive and gay and very easy to be with, and I enjoyed her company enormously . . . but for a lifetime . . . no."

"She's going to have that child for the rest of her life."

"I've already told you, it almost certainly isn't mine."

It was obvious that from that angle he considered himself invulnerable. I tried another tack. "Supposing, Sinclair, just supposing, that I didn't want to marry you. Like I said the other day, we're first cousins . . ."

"It's happened before . . ."

"We're too close . . . I wouldn't want to risk it."

"I love you," said Sinclair. It was the first time anyone had ever said that to me. I had often imagined it happening in secret teenage daydreams. But never like this.

"But . . . but I don't love you . . ."

He smiled. "You don't sound very sure."

"But I am. Quite sure."

"Not even enough to . . . help me?"

"Oh, Sinclair, you don't need help."

"But that's where you're wrong. I do. If you don't marry me, then my world will come crashing in little pieces around my ears."

It was a lover-like statement, and yet I did not believe it was said with love.

"You mean that literally, don't you?"

"How perceptive you can be, Janey. Yes, I do."

"Why?"

He was suddenly impatient, dropping my hand as though he were bored with it, turning for diversion to search for a cigarette. There were some in his coat pocket. He took one, and lit it from the lighter on the dashboard. "Oh, because," he said at last.

After a little, "Because?" I prompted him.

He took a deep breath. "Because I'm over my ears in debt. Because I have either to find the money to pay it, or the security to borrow, and I haven't got either. And if it all comes out, which it's in deadly danger of doing, then I have every certainty that my managing director will send for me and reluctantly inform me that he can do very nicely without my services, thank you."

"You mean, you'll lose your job?"

"Not only perceptive, but also quick on the uptake."

"But . . . how did you get into debt?"

"How do you think? Backing horses, playing blackjack . . ."

It sounded very harmless. "But how much for?"

He told me. I couldn't believe anyone could have so much money, let alone owe it. "You must be out of your mind. You mean, just playing cards . . ."

"Oh, for heaven's sake, Jane, you can lose that much in some gambling clubs in London in a single evening. And it's taken me the best part of two years."

It took me a moment or two to accept the fact that any man could be such a fool. I had always thought my father was completely unrealistic about money, but this . . .

"Couldn't Grandmother help you? Lend you the money?"

"She's helped me before . . . without obvious enthusiasm, I may add."

"You mean, this isn't the first time."

"No, it isn't the first time, and you can take off that shocked, pie-faced expression. Besides, our grandmother doesn't have that much money lying around. She belongs to a generation that believes in tying up her capital, and hers is all in trusts and investments and land."

Land. I said, casually, "How about selling some land, then? The . . . moor, for instance?"

Sinclair sent me a sideways glance, full of reluctant respect. "I'd already thought of that. I'd even lined up a group of Americans more than anxious to buy the moor, or if they couldn't do that, then to take it yearly at a substantial rent. To be honest, Janey, that's why I took this bit of leave, to come north and put the idea to her. But of course, she won't think of it . . . though what possible good it can be to her as it is, is more than I can imagine."

"It's rented out already . . ."

"For peanuts. The rent that little syndicate pays her scarcely covers the cost of Gibson's cartridges."

"And Gibson?"

"Oh, to hell with Gibson. He's past it anyway, it's time he was pensioned off."

We fell silent once more. Sinclair sat smoking, and I, beside him, tried frantically to sort out a confusion of thoughts. I found that what astonished me was not his soulless attitude – I had already suspected this – nor the fact that he had got himself into such a mess; but simply that he had been so frank with me. Either he had given up all idea of our getting married, and so had nothing to lose, or else his conceit of himself was without bounds.

I was beginning to be angry. I lose my temper slowly and seldom, but once I do I become quite incoherent. Knowing this, and anxious for it not to happen, I deliberately battened down my finer feelings, and concentrated on staying cool and practical.

"I don't really see why it should be my grandmother's decision any more than yours. After all, Elvie will belong to you one day. If you want to sell off great chunks of it now, I should think that that would be your concern."

"What makes you say that Elvie will belong to me?"

"Of course it will. You're her grandson. There isn't anyone else."

"You talk as though it were entailed, as though it had come down through generations, from father to son. But it isn't. It hasn't. It belongs to our grandmother, and if she chooses, she can leave it to a cats' home."

"But why not you?"

"Because, my darling, I am my father's son."

"And what is that meant to mean?"

"It means that I am a no-good, a ne'er-do-well, a black sheep. A true Bailey, if you like." I stared at him blankly, and suddenly he laughed and it was not a pleasant sound. "Didn't anyone ever tell you, little innocent Jane, about your Uncle Aylwyn? Didn't your father tell you?"

I shook my head.

"I was told when I was eighteen . . . as a sort of unwanted birthday present. You see, Aylwyn Bailey was not merely dishonest, but incompetent as well. Five of those years he spent in Canada, he spent in jail. For fraud and embezzlement and God knows what else. Didn't it ever occur to you that the whole set-up was a little unnatural? No visits. Very few letters. And not a single photograph in the whole of the house?''

It was suddenly so obvious that I wondered why I had never realised the truth for myself. And I thought of the conversation I had had with my grandmother, only days ago, and the tiny glimpses she had let me have of her only son. *He chose to live in Canada, and finally to die there. Elvie never meant very much to Aylwyn . . . He looked like Sinclair. And he was very charming.*

I said, stupidly, ''But why did he never come back?''

''I suppose he was a sort of remittance man . . . probably our grandmother imagined that I would be better off without his influence.'' He pressed the button that lowered his window, and tossed away the half-smoked cigarette. ''But the way things turned out, I don't suppose it made any difference, one way or the other. I've simply inherited the family disease.'' He smiled at me. ''And what can't be cured must be endured.''

''You mean everyone else has to do the enduring.''

''Oh, come, it's not easy for me either. You know, Janey, it's odd that you should bring that up – about Elvie eventually coming to me – because the other night, when we were discussing selling the moor and what to do about Gibson, that was my final ace, the one I'd kept tucked up my sleeve. 'Elvie will be mine one day. Sooner or later it will be mine. So why shouldn't I decide now what is to be done with it?' '' He turned to me and smiled . . . his charming, disarming smile. ''And do you know what our grandmother said?''

''No.''

''She said, 'But Sinclair, that's where you are mistaken. Elvie means nothing to you except as a source of income. You've

144

made a life for yourself in London and you would never want to live here. Elvie will go to Jane.' "

And so this was how I came into it. This was the final piece of the jigsaw and now the picture was complete.

"So that's why you want to marry me. To get your hands on Elvie."

"It sounds a little bald put that way . . ."

"*Bald!*"

". . . but I suppose you could say that that was the rough idea. On top of all the other reasons I have already given you. Which are real and true and entirely sincere."

It was his use of those words which finally tipped my temper over the bounds of control, like a boulder sent rolling down a hill.

"Real and true and sincere. Sinclair, you don't even know the meaning of those words, and how you can use them, in the same breath . . . as telling me all this . . ."

"You mean about my father?"

"No, I don't mean about your father. I don't give a damn about your father and neither should you. And I don't give a damn about Elvie. I don't even want Elvie, and if Grandmother leaves it to me, I shall refuse it, burn it down, give it away, rather than let you get your greedy hands on it."

"That's not very charitable."

"I don't mean it to be charitable. You don't merit charity. You're obsessed by possessions, you always have been. You always had to *have* things . . . and if you didn't have them, you simply took them. Electric trains, and boats, and cricket bats and guns when you were small. And now fancy cars, and flats in London and money and money and more money. You'd never be satisfied. Even if I did everything you wanted me to, married you and handed Elvie over, lock, stock and barrel, that wouldn't be enough . . ."

"You're being unrealistic."

"I don't call it that. That's not what it's called. It's simply a question of getting your priorities right and knowing that people matter more than things."

"People?"

"Yes, people. You know, human beings, with feelings and emotions and all the things you seem to have forgotten about, if you ever knew they existed. People like our grandmother, and Gibson, and that girl Tessa, having your baby . . . and don't start telling me that it isn't your child, because I know, and what is more, you know damn well that it is. They've served their purpose and they're expendable, and so you simply push them overboard."

"Not you," said Sinclair. "I'm not pushing you. I'm taking you with me."

"Oh, no you're not." The ring was too tight. I dragged it off, bruising my knuckle, and just managed to resist throwing it in his face. I reached for the little jeweller's box, jammed the ring back into the velvet, snapped the box shut, and tossed it back on to the shelf. "You were right when you said we loved each other. We did, and I always thought you were the most wonderful person in the world. But you've turned out to be not only despicable, but stupid as well. You must be out of your mind to imagine that I would simply play along with you as though nothing had happened. You must think that I am the most terrible fool."

To my horror I heard my voice start to shake. I flung myself away from him, and sat trembling, longing to be out in the open, or in some enormous room where I could scream and throw things around and generally indulge in a fit of hysterics. But I wasn't. I was pinned into the tiny space of Sinclair's car, and there was scarcely room in it for our seething emotions, let alone us.

Beside me, I heard him sigh. He said, "Who would have thought you'd return from America with such a set of lofty principles."

"It has nothing to do with America. It's just the way I am and the way I'll always be." I could feel my mouth go down, my eyes fill with tears. "And now I want to go home."

It wasn't any good. Despite my efforts, I started to cry in earnest. I searched for a handkerchief, but of course couldn't find one, and eventually had to accept Sinclair's which, silently, he handed me.

I wiped my eyes and blew my nose, and for some ridiculous reason this mundane action broke the tension between us. He took a couple of cigarettes from his pocket and lit them both and gave me one. Life went on. I noticed that while we talked the light had faded. The moon, not new any more, but still curved and delicate, was rising in the east, but its clarity was blurred by the mist which had dropped from the top of the mountain, and now enveloped us.

I blew my nose again. I said, "What will you do?"

"God knows."

"Perhaps if we spoke to David Stewart."

"No."

"Or my father. He may not be very practical, but he's very wise. We could call him . . ."

"No."

147

"But, Sinclair . . ."

"You were right," he said. "It's time to go home." He put out a hand to switch on the ignition. The engine purred into life, drowning all other sounds. "But we'll stop off for a drink in Caple Bridge on the way. I think we both need one – I certainly do, and it'll give your face time to recover before Grandmother sees it."

"What's wrong with my face?"

"It's all puffy and swollen. Just like when you had the measles. It makes you look like a little girl again."

10

The serious business of drinking in Scotland is, like going to funerals, a purely male prerogative. Females of any sort are not welcomed in the public bars, and if a man should make the mistake of taking his wife or girlfriend into a pub, he is expected to do his entertaining in some dim parlour, well out of sight and sound of the rest of his roistering cronies.

The Crimond Arms in Caple Bridge was no exception to this rule. We were shown that evening into a chill and unwelcoming room, papered in orange, furnished with cane chairs and tables, and decorated with flights of plaster ducks and the occasional vase of dusty plastic flowers. There was a gas fire, unlit, some large brewery ashtrays, and an upright piano which, on inspection, proved to be firmly locked. We were defied to enjoy ourselves.

Depressed and chilled by the room, by nameless fears for Sinclair, by everything that had happened, I sat alone, waiting for him. He came at last, bearing a small pale sherry for me, and a large dark whisky for himself. He said at once, "Why haven't you lit the fire?"

Thinking of the locked piano and the general air of

disapproving unwelcome, I said, "I didn't think I'd be allowed to."

"You're ridiculous," said Sinclair, and took a match and knelt to light the gas fire. There was a small explosion, a strong smell, and a blaze of little flames, and a ray of heat impinged upon a minute area around my knees.

"Is that better?"

It wasn't, for my chill seeped from deep inside me, and couldn't be warmed away, but I said that it was. Satisfied, he sat himself in a little cane chair which stood across the fancy hearthrug, found a cigarette and lit it, and raised his whisky glass in my general direction.

"I looks towards you," he said.

It was an old joke, and as such, recognisable as a flag of truce. I was meant to say, "And I raises my glass," but I didn't because I was not sure if I could ever be friends with him again.

After that, he did not speak again. I finished my sherry, put down my empty glass, and seeing that he was only halfway through his, said that I would go and find a Ladies', with the idea of checking on my general appearance before facing up to my grandmother. Sinclair said that he would wait, so I went out and stumbled down a passage and up a flight of stairs and found the Ladies', which was no more welcoming or prepossessing than the dismal room downstairs. I looked in the mirror and was met by a dejected reflection, my face blotchy and swollen, and my mascara smudged. I washed my hands and face in cold water, and found a comb in my pocket and smoothed the tangles out of my hair, and all the time felt as though I were dressing a dead body, like those macabre stories about American morticians.

All this took some time, and when I went back downstairs

again, I found the cheerless room empty, but heard, from behind the door which led into the bar proper, the sound of Sinclair's voice, talking to the barman, and guessed that he had grabbed the opportunity of buying himself the other half and drinking it under more congenial circumstances.

Not wanting to hang around, I went out to the car to wait for him. It had begun to rain, and the market-place was wet and black as a lake, shimmering with the orange reflections of the street lights. I sat huddled and cold, lacking even the energy to find and light a cigarette, and presently I saw the door of the Crimond Arms open. Sinclair's silhouette showed black for a moment, and then the door fell shut, and he came across the wetness towards me.

He was carrying a newspaper.

He got into the Lotus, behind the wheel, slammed the door, and simply sat there, breathing. There was a smell of whisky, and I found myself wondering just how many whiskies he had found time to drink while I was upstairs washing my face. After a little, when he still made no move to start the car, I said, "Is anything wrong?"

He did not reply. He simply sat, looking down, his profile pale, his lashes lying dark and thick against the bones of his cheek.

I was suddenly concerned. "Sinclair."

He handed me the paper. I saw that it was the local evening news, which he had, presumably, picked up off the bar. By the light of the street lamps, I read the headlines which told of a bus accident; there was a photograph of a newly-elected town councillor, a column on some Thrumbo girl who had made good in New Zealand . . .

And then I found it, an inch of type, down in the bottom corner.

DEATH OF WELL-KNOWN SKIER

The body of Miss Tessa Faraday was found yesterday morning in her home at Crawley Court, London, S.W.1. Miss Faraday, who was 22, was the winner of the Ladies' Ski Championship held last winter . . .

The print danced and swam and was lost. I closed my eyes, as though to shut the horror away, but the darkness only made it worse and I knew that there could be no escape from the inside of my own head. *She said she would make other arrangements*, Sinclair had told me. *She's been around. She's a sensible girl.*

I said, stupidly, "But she's killed herself . . ."

I opened my eyes. He had not moved. I heard my own voice, saying, "Did you know what the other arrangements were going to be?"

He said, dully, "I thought she meant she'd get rid of it."

I was suddenly very wise. I knew. I said, "She wouldn't have been afraid of having the baby. She wasn't that sort of a girl. She killed herself because she knew you didn't love her any longer. You were going to marry someone else."

He suddenly rounded on me savagely in a storm of rage. "Shut up, and don't say anything about her, do you hear? Don't speak about her, talk about her, say one single, solitary word. You don't know anything about her, so don't pretend to. You don't understand, and you could never be expected to."

And with that, he switched on the ignition, let off the brake, and with a great swish of wet tyres on wet cobbles, swung the Lotus round, across the square, and in the direction of the street that led out into the country, and so to Elvie.

He was drunk, or frightened, or heartbroken, or shocked. Or perhaps all of these things. There was no thought now of rules or regulations or even simple native caution. Sinclair was escaping, hounded by a thousand devils, and speed was his only defence.

We roared through the narrow streets of the little town, and rocketed out into the dark country beyond. Reality became nothing but the road ahead, the white lines and cat's-eyes at its centre pouring headlong towards us so that they were all blurred into a single entity. I had never before been really physically frightened, but now I found my teeth were clenched until they ached, and my foot pressed down so hard upon an imaginary brake that I was in real danger of dislocating my spine. We came around the last corner, and the way lay clear to the roadworks. The light was green, and in order to get through before it changed colour, he gave the Lotus more power, and we surged forward, faster than ever. I found myself praying, *Let the light go red. Now. Please let the light go red.*

And then, with only fifty yards or so to go, the miracle happened, and the light did go red. Sinclair started to brake, and I knew in that moment what I should do. To the tearing of tyres the Lotus finally jarred to a stop, and, shaking all over, I opened the door on my side, and got out.

He said, "What are you doing?"

I stood in the rain and the darkness, caught like a moth in the beam of slowly approaching headlights, as the traffic from the other direction moved towards us.

"I'm frightened," I told him.

He said, quite kindly, "Get back in. You'll get wet."

"I'll walk."

"But it's four miles . . ."

"I want to walk."

"Janey . . ." He leaned across as though to pull me back into the car, but I stepped back out of his reach.

"Why?" he asked.

"I told you, I'm frightened. And the light's gone green again . . . you must go or you'll hold everybody up."

To add conviction to my words, a small van, drawn in behind Sinclair, blew its horn. It made a rude and impudent noise, the sort of noise which, in other times, and other places, would have made us laugh.

He said at last, "All right." He took hold of the door-handle to pull it shut, and then hesitated.

"You were right about one thing, Janey," he said.

"What was that?"

"That baby of Tessa's. It *was* mine."

I began to cry. Tears mingled with the rain on my face and I could do nothing to stop them, could think of nothing to say, no way of helping him. Then the door slammed shut between us, and the next moment he was gone, the car moving away from me through the obstructions and the flashing lights, faster and faster towards the bridge.

Like a nightmare, for no reason, I found that my head was full of music jangling like a barrel organ, and it was Sinclair's tune, and now that it was too late, I wished that I had gone with him.

Step we gaily, on we go,
Heel for heel and toe for toe,
Arm in arm and row on row . . .

He had reached the bridge now, and the Lotus took its soaring humpback like a steeplechaser. The tail-light disappeared over the edge of the curve and the next moment the still night was torn with the scream of brakes, of tyres skidding on wet tarmac. And then the crunch of shattered metal, a spatter of broken glass. I began to run, as useless as a person in a dream, stumbling and splashing through the puddles, surrounded by flashing lights and great red cat's-eyes spelling out DANGER, but before I had got within a hundred yards of the bridge, there came the soft thud of an explosion, and, before my eyes, the whole night flowered into the rosy glow of flamelight.

It was not until after Sinclair's funeral that I had the chance to talk to my grandmother. Before that, any sort of conversation had been impossible. We were both shocked and instinctively shied away from the mention of his name, as though even to talk about him would open the flood-gates of our carefully controlled grief. To add to this, there was so much to do, so much to arrange and so many people to see. Especially so many people to see. Old friends, like the Gibsons, and Will the gardener, the minister, and Jamie Drysdale, the Thrumbo joiner, transformed by sober clothes and a suitable expression of pious gloom, into an undertaker. There were interviews with the police, and telephone calls from the press. There were flowers, and letters, dozens of letters. We started to reply to them, but finally gave up, leaving them to pile up on the brass tray in the hall.

My grandmother, belonging to a generation that is not afraid of the idea of death, and so is undistressed by its trappings, had insisted on a proper, old-fashioned funeral, and had come

155

through it without visible tremor, even when Hamish Gibson, on leave from his regiment, played "The Flowers of the Forest" on his pipes. She had sung the hymns in church, stood, for half an hour or more, shaking hands; remembered to thank even those who had performed the most humble tasks.

But now she was tired. Mrs Lumley, exhausted with emotion and standing, had returned to her room to put up her swollen feet, so after I had lit the drawing-room fire, I settled my grandmother beside it, and went into the kitchen to make a cup of tea.

Standing against the warmth of the Aga, waiting for the kettle to boil, I stared absently out of the window at the grey world beyond. It was October now, the afternoon cold and quite motionless. Not a breath of wind stirred the last few remaining leaves from the trees. The loch, reflecting the grey sky, was still as a sheet of silver, the hills beyond bloomed softly, like plums. Tomorrow, perhaps, or the day after, they would be frosted with the first snows – it was cold enough for that – and we would be into winter.

The kettle boiled, so I made the tea, and carried it back to the drawing-room, and the chink of teacups and the crackle of the fire were comforting, as small things always are in the face of tragedy.

My grandmother was knitting a child's woollen hat in scarlet and white, destined, I knew, for the church Christmas bazaar. Thinking that she wanted to be quiet, I had set down my empty teacup, lit a cigarette and was reading the paper, half-lost in a review of a new play, when she suddenly spoke.

"I've been feeling very guilty, Jane. I should have told you about Aylwyn, that day when we were sitting out in the garden, and you started to ask me about him. I was on the verge of doing so, and then something made me change my mind. It was very stupid of me."

I had lowered the paper, and now folded it. Her needles clicked gently on, she had not looked up from her knitting.

I said, "Sinclair told me . . ."

"Did he? I thought perhaps he would. It mattered very much to Sinclair. It would be important to him that you should know. Were you very shocked?"

"Why should I be shocked?"

"For a number of reasons. Because he was dishonest. Because he went to prison. Because I tried to hide it from you all."

"It was probably better hidden. It would have done us no good to know. Nor him."

"I always thought perhaps your father would have told you."

"No."

"That was good of him . . . he knew how fond you were of Sinclair."

I put the newspaper down and lowered myself on to the hearthrug – a good place for confidences. "But why was Aylwyn *like* that? Why wasn't he like you?"

"He was a Bailey," said my grandmother simply. "And a feckless lot they've always been, but with all the charm in the world. Not a penny to bless themselves with, and less idea of earning money or holding on to it than the man in the moon."

"Was your husband like that?"

"Oh, yes." She smiled to herself as though remembering a long-ago joke. "Do you know the first thing that happened after we were married? My father paid off all his debts. But it didn't take him long to acquire some new ones."

"Did you love him?"

157

"Madly. But I very soon learned that I'd married an irresponsible boy without the slightest intention of reforming."

"But you were happy."

"He died so soon after we were married, I didn't have time to be anything else. But I realised then that I was on my own, and I decided that it would be better for my children if I made an entirely new start, away from the Baileys. So I bought Elvie, and I brought my children here. I thought everything would be different. But you know, environment doesn't entirely cancel out heredity, whatever child psychologists may say. I told you about Aylwyn. I watched him grow up, and turn into his father all over again, and there wasn't a thing I could do to stop him. He grew up and he went to London and he got a job, but in no time at all he was in a financial mess. I helped him, of course, over and over again, but the day inevitably came when I couldn't help. He'd manipulated some shares, or taken some sort of fraudulent action, and the head of his firm said, quite rightly, that it was a matter for the police. But in the end I persuaded him otherwise, and he agreed to say nothing, provided Aylwyn gave his word never to practise in the City of London again. So that's why he went to Canada. But of course, the whole business simply repeated itself, and that time poor Aylwyn wasn't so lucky. It would have been different, you know, Jane, if he'd married a sensible girl with her feet on the ground, and strength of character that would have kept Aylwyn's feet there, too. But Silvia was as feather-headed as he was, they were just a pair of children. Heaven knows why she decided to marry him in the first place, perhaps she thought he had money; one can hardly believe that she was in love, leaving Aylwyn and the baby the way she did."

"Why didn't Aylwyn ever come back from Canada?"

"Because of Sinclair. Sometimes, the image of a father can be better than . . . the father himself. Sinclair is . . ." she corrected herself, with scarcely a tremor to her voice, "Sinclair was another Bailey. It's astonishing how a single bad trait will go right down through generations of the same family."

"You mean, all that gambling and stuff."

"Sinclair did talk to you, didn't he?"

"A little."

"There was no need for it, you know. He had a good job and a good salary, but he simply couldn't resist the thrill. And the fact that we don't understand it should never make us unsympathetic, although I sometimes think it was all Sinclair lived for."

"But he loved coming to Elvie."

"Only now and again. He didn't feel about it as your mother did . . . or you. In fact – " she turned her needles and started in on another row " – I decided some time ago, that it would be a good idea if Elvie should belong to you one day. Would you welcome that?"

"I . . . I don't know . . ."

"That was the real reason I was so anxious for your father to let you come home, and bombarded him with letters which the wretch refused to answer. I wanted to talk to you about Elvie."

I said, "It's a wonderful idea, but I'm scared of owning things . . . I don't think I'd want to be tied down by all the responsibilities of a place like Elvie. And I wouldn't be free to get up and go the way I'd want to."

"That sounds very chicken-hearted, and also a little like your father talking. If he'd been more realistic about possessions, he might have put down a few roots by now, and a good thing too.

Don't you want roots, Jane? Don't you want to get married and have a family?''

I looked into the fire and thought of many things. Of Sinclair and my father . . . and David. And I thought of all the world I had seen, and the vast tracts of it which I hoped very much that one day I would see. And I thought of children at Elvie, my children, being brought up in this perfect place, and doing all the things that Sinclair and I had done . . .

I said at last, ''I don't know what I want. And that's the truth.''

''I didn't think you did. And today, when neither of us is in a frame of mind to be sensible about anything, is not the best time to discuss it. But you should think about it, Jane. Weigh up the pros and cons. There's all the time in the world to discuss it together.''

A log broke, and fell into the smouldering embers of the fire. I got up to put on another, and while I was on my feet, stooped to pick up the tea tray, and carry it out to the kitchen, but as I reached the door, and stood, juggling with the tray and the door-handle, my grandmother spoke again.

''Jane.''

''Yes.''

Still holding the tray, I turned to face her. She had stopped knitting and now she took off her glasses, and I saw the blueness of her eyes, set deep in the pallor of her face. I had never seen her look so pale. I had never seen her look so old.

''Jane . . . do you remember, we were talking the other day, about Sinclair's friend, Tessa Faraday?''

My fingers closed over the handles of the tray and my knuckles showed white. I knew what was coming and prayed that it wouldn't.

"Yes."

"I saw in the paper that she had died. Something about an overdose of barbiturates. Did you see that?"

"Yes, I did."

"You never said anything."

"No, I know."

"Was it . . . had it anything to do with Sinclair?"

Across the room, our eyes met and held. I would have given my soul at that moment to be able, convincingly, to lie. But I was incompetent, and my grandmother knew me very well. I hadn't a hope in hell of getting away with it.

I said, "Yes, it had." And then, "She was going to have his baby."

My grandmother's eyes filled with tears, and it was the only time I ever saw her cry.

11

David came the next afternoon. My grandmother was writing letters, and I had retreated to the garden and was sweeping up leaves, having once been told that physical toil is the best form of therapy for mental distress. I had made a small pile, and was about to transfer it to a handy wheelbarrow, when the french windows opened, and David came out to join me. I straightened to watch him cross the grass, all tall lankiness and wind-ruffled hair, and wondered in that moment how we would have got through the last few days without him. He had done everything, seen to everything, arranged everything, even finding time to put through a person-to-person call to my father, and tell him personally of Sinclair's death. And I knew that, whatever happened to the two of us, I should never cease being grateful to him.

He took the last bit of the bank in a single stride and was at my side. "Jane, what are you going to do with that little handful of leaves?"

"Put them into the barrow," I said, and did. They fluttered around, and most of them blew out again.

He said, "If you can lay your hands on a couple of bits of

wood, you'll speed the process up considerably. I've brought you a letter . . .''

He took it out of his capacious pocket and I saw that it was from my father.

"How did you get this?"

"It was enclosed in one he wrote to me. He asked me to give it to you."

We abandoned the wheelbarrow and the broom, went down the garden, jumping the ha-ha into the field, and so on to the old jetty, where we settled ourselves, in some danger, side by side on the rotting boards, and I opened the letter and read it aloud to David.

My darling Jane,

I was so very sorry to hear about Sinclair and your involvement in his death, but glad that you were able to be with your grandmother, and no doubt of the greatest possible comfort to her.

I feel guilty – and have been, ever since you went away – that I let you return to Elvie without putting you in the picture as regards your Uncle Aylwyn. But somehow, with one thing and another and the dramatic fashion in which you departed, the opportunity never presented itself. I did, however, mention it to David Stewart, and he promised to keep an eye on you and the general situation . . .

I said, "But you never told me."

"It wasn't my business."

"But you knew."

"Of course I knew."

"And you knew about Sinclair as well?"

"I knew that he was getting through a hell of a lot of your grandmother's money."

"There's worse to come, David."

"What do you mean by that?"

"Sinclair died owing the most terrible amount."

"I was afraid that would happen. How did you know about this?"

"Because he told me. He told me lots of things." I went back to the letter.

The reason that I was never over-anxious for you to return to Elvie was not so much what your Uncle had been, but what I was pretty sure your cousin Sinclair had become. After your mother died, your grandmother suggested that I should leave you with her, and indeed, this would have seemed to be the obvious answer. But there was the question of Sinclair. I knew how fond you were of him and how much he meant to you, and I was pretty sure that if you continued to see so much of him, the day would come when you would either have your heart broken, or your illusions shattered. Either process was bound to be painful, if not disastrous, and so instead, I kept you with me and brought you to America.

David interrupted. "I wonder what made him so sure about Sinclair."

I thought of the book, of Goldsmith's *Animated Nature*, and for a moment considered telling David the whole story. And then I decided against it. The book was no more. The day after Sinclair was killed, I retrieved it from his cupboard, took it downstairs and shovelled it into the boiler, where I watched it burn. Now, there was no trace left of it. Out of loyalty to Sinclair, it was best forgotten.

"I don't know . . . I suppose, instinct. He was always a very perceptive person, and impossible to fool." I went on reading:

This was also the reason I was so tardy in replying to your grandmother's requests that you should return to Elvie. It would have been different if Sinclair were married, but I knew he wasn't and was devilled with apprehensions.

I expect you will want to stay at Elvie for a bit, but business here has been fairly brisk. Sam Carter is doing great stuff for me, so I am in the money as the saying goes, and could even afford to buy you a ticket back to sunny California whenever you say the word. I miss you very much, and so does Rusty. Mitzi the poodle is small compensation for your absence, though Linda is determined that when the time is ripe and the moon in the right quarter, Mitzi and Rusty will fall madly in love and get themselves a family, but it is my considered opinion that the issue of such a union simply does not bear thinking about.

Linda is well, adores Reef Point and what she calls the simple life, and has started, surprisingly, to paint. I don't know if my instincts are right or not, but I have a feeling that she may be very good. Who knows, she may yet be able to support me in the style to which I would like to be accustomed. Which is more than I could ever say for you.

My love, darling child,
from your father.

In silence I folded the letter, and put it back into its envelope, and so into the pocket of my coat. After a little, I said, slowly, "It sounds to me as though he's trying to talk her into marrying him. Or maybe she's trying to talk him into marrying her. I'm not sure which."

"Perhaps they're trying to talk each other. Would you like that to happen?"

"Yes, I think I would. Then I wouldn't feel responsible for him any longer. I'd be free."

The word had a disappointingly empty ring to it. It was very cold out on the jetty and suddenly I shivered, and David put an arm around me and drew me close into the warm circle of his arm, so that I was warmed by his warmth, my head supported by his solid tweed-clad shoulder.

"In that case," he said, "perhaps this is as good a time as any to start talking you into marrying a half-blind country lawyer who's adored you since the first moment he set eyes on you."

I said, "You wouldn't need to talk very hard."

His arm tightened and I felt his lips brush against the top of my head. "You wouldn't mind living in Scotland?"

"No. Provided you acquire yourself plenty of clients in New York, and California, and perhaps even farther afield, and promise faithfully to take me with you whenever you go to see them."

"That shouldn't be too difficult."

"And it would be nice if I could have a dog."

"Of course you shall . . . not another Rusty, of course, he has to be unique. But perhaps one with the same interesting ancestry and equal intelligence and charm."

I turned in his arms, and buried my face in his chest. I thought for a dreadful moment that I was going to cry, but that was ridiculous, people didn't cry when they were happy, only in books. I said, "I love you," and David held me very close, and I did cry after all, but it didn't matter.

We sat there, wrapped around in David's coat, making unrealistic plans, like being married in the Reef Point Mission, and having Isabel Modes McKenzie knit me a wedding dress – which inevitably dissolved into laughter. So we abandoned them and made others, and so preoccupied were we that we did not notice the light fade, and the evening air grow chill. We were finally disturbed by my grandmother, opening the window and calling out to tell us that tea was ready, so we stood up, cramped and cold, and started back to the house.

The garden was bloomed with dusk and thick with shadows. We had not spoken again of Sinclair but all at once I felt him everywhere, not the man, but the boy I remembered. He ran, soft-footed, across the grass, and from the shadows beneath the trees came the soft scuffle of fallen leaves. And I wondered if Elvie would ever be free of him, and this made me sad, for whatever happened, and whoever lived there, I did not want it to be a haunted place.

David, going ahead of me, had stopped to collect my broom and the wheelbarrow and stow them, out of harm's way, under the maple. Now, he waited, his tall figure silhouetted against the lights of the house.

"What is it, Jane?"

I told him. "Ghosts."

"There aren't any," he said, and I looked again, and saw that he was right. Only sky and water, and the wind stirring the leaves. No ghosts. I went on and he took my hand in his, and together we went in to tea.

ROSAMUNDE PILCHER

SEPTEMBER

As spring comes to Scotland and the hills burst into life, a dance is planned for September. The invitations summon home the group of people Violet Aird has cared for most in her long life.

The oldest, strongest and wisest of them all, she sees Alexa, her vulnerable granddaughter, find love for the first time, while the decision to send her little grandson away to school is driving parents Edmund and Virginia ever further apart. Far from them all is Pandora, the glamorous, exciting girl who ran away twenty years before. All will converge in Scotland this September.

'Wonderful, evocative and inviting'
Woman and Home

'Very special indeed'
Books

'Beautifully captures the magic of
north-of-the-border country'
Sunday Telegraph

HODDER AND STOUGHTON PAPERBACKS

ROSAMUNDE PILCHER

THE SHELL SEEKERS

Artist's daughter Penelope Keeling can look back on a full and varied life: a Bohemian childhood in London and Cornwall, an unhappy wartime marriage, and the one man she truly loved. She has brought up three children – and learned to accept each of them as they are.

Yet she is far too energetic and independent to settle sweetly into pensioned-off old-age. And when she discovers that her most treasured possession, her father's painting, *The Shell Seekers,* is now worth a small fortune, it is Penelope who must make the decisions that will determine whether her family can continue to survive as a family, or be split apart.

'A deeply satisfying story written with love and confidence'
Maeve Binchy, in the New York Times Book Review

'A beautiful, haunting story . . . that will tug at your
heart strings'
Prima

'Her genius is to create characters you really care about'
Daily Express

'A long, beguiling saga, typically English . . . splendid'
The Mail on Sunday

HODDER AND STOUGHTON PAPERBACKS

ROSAMUNDE PILCHER

WILD MOUNTAIN THYME

Victoria Bradshaw fell in love with London playwright Oliver Dobbs when she was just eighteen. But he had left her and disappeared from her life. Now, years later, he was a widower standing on her doorstep with his two-year-old son in his arms. And Victoria was foolish enough to want to take him back. Their early spring journey to a castle in Scotland would become an odyssey of emotional discovery . . . in a novel about relationships as real as those you've experienced and a love as rich and unpredictable as dreams can be.

HODDER AND STOUGHTON PAPERBACKS

ROSAMUNDE PILCHER

THE BLUE BEDROOM

The big bedroom was lovely: all pale blue and white, satin and muslin, cool and airy, the windows looking out over the garden to the creek.

But to fourteen-year-old Emily, beautiful though it was, it was all wrong. Her stepmother's bedroom now: everything changed since her own mother had died.

And stretched out on the bed: Stephanie, very white and pained. The new baby on its way, a month early. All of a sudden, with her father away on business, Emily had to take charge, keep calm, ring for the doctor and the ambulance. The time for looking back had gone.

The Blue Bedroom is just one of Rosamunde Pilcher's magical collection of stories. Stories that will enchant everyone who has read and loved *The Shell Seekers.*

'It's never too soon to discover Rosamunde Pilcher. To all who do so with this fine collection: be alert. Her work may bestow unforeseen blessings.' *Good Housekeeping*

HODDER AND STOUGHTON PAPERBACKS